Charles James Lever

Gerald Fitzgerald, the Chevalier

A Novel

Charles James Lever

Gerald Fitzgerald, the Chevalier
A Novel

ISBN/EAN: 9783337032876

Printed in Europe, USA, Canada, Australia, Japan

Cover: Foto ©Andreas Hilbeck / pixelio.de

More available books at **www.hansebooks.com**

GERALD FITZGERALD

THE CHEVALIER

A Novel

By CHARLES LEVER

AUTHOR OF
'HARRY LORREQUER'
ETC.

WITH A FRONTISPIECE BY A. D. M'CORMICK

LONDON

DOWNEY AND CO., LIMITED

12 YORK STREET, COVENT GARDEN

1899

PUBLISHERS' NOTE

THE Publishers feel that some explanation is necessary concerning the tardy publication in book form of this story. *Gerald Fitzgerald* appeared as a serial in the *Dublin University Magazine*. The Magazine at the time was changing hands, Lever's old friend and publisher, James M'Glashan, having just died. Lever was always eager to avoid trouble, and ever readier to undertake new work than to concern himself about work already done; and possibly—for there is not sufficient evidence to speak with certainty—owing to some trouble with the new proprietors of the *Dublin University Magazine*, he decided to put aside *Gerald Fitzgerald*. When he was rearranging his novels for a fresh issue, shortly before his death, he omitted a few of his stories from the collection, but for no adequate reason which can be discovered. He was assisted in the preparation of this collected edition by his daughter, Mrs. Nevill, who died last year. Mrs. Nevill could not account for the omission of *Gerald Fitzgerald*, and left it to the judgment of the present publishers whether the work should be issued or not. After very careful considera-

v

tion, and with full respect for Lever's memory and reputation, they have decided that the novel should be issued as a substantive work. It is evident that Lever spent much pains upon the story ; and though it is not to be expected that it will rival in popularity his earlier and more boisterous performances, yet the publishers believe it will not in any way damage his reputation as a story-teller.

LONDON, *March* 1899.

CONTENTS

BOOK THE FIRST

BOOK THE SECOND

BOOK THE THIRD

GERALD FITZGERALD

BOOK THE FIRST

CHAPTER I

THE THIEVES' CORNER

AT the foot of the hill on which stands the Campidoglio at Rome, and close beneath the ruins that now encumber the Tarpeian rock, runs a mean-looking alley, called the Viccolo D'Orsi, but better known to the police as the 'Viccolo dei Ladri,' or 'Thieves' Corner'—the epithet being, it is said, conferred in a spirit the very reverse of calumnious.

Long and straggling, and too narrow to admit of any but foot-passengers, its dwellings are marked by a degree of poverty and destitution even greater than such quarters usually exhibit. Rudely constructed of fragments taken from ancient temples and monuments, richly carved architraves and finely cut friezes are to be seen embedded amid masses of crumbling masonry, and all the evidences of a cultivated and enlightened age mingled up with the squalor and misery of present want.

Not less suggestive than the homes themselves are the population of this dreary district; and despite rags, and dirt, and debasement, there they are—the true descendants of those who once, with such terrible truth, called themselves 'Masters of the World.' Well set-on heads of massive mould, bold and prominent features, finely fashioned jaws, and lips full of vigour and sensual meaning, are but the base counterfeits of the traits that meet the eye in the Vatican. No

A

effort of imagination is needed to trace the kindred. In every gesture, in their gait, even in the careless ease of their ragged drapery, you can mark the traditionary signs of the once haughty citizen.

With a remnant of their ancient pride, these people reject all hired occupation, and would scorn, as an act of slavery, the idea of labour; and, as neither trade nor calling prevails among them, their existence would seem an inscrutable problem, save on the hypothesis which dictated the popular title of this district. But without calling to our aid this explanation, it must be remembered how easily life is supported by those satisfied with its meanest requirements, and especially in a land so teeming with abundance. A few roots, a handful of chestnuts, a piece of black bread, a cup of wine, scarcely more costly than so much water, these are enough to maintain existence; and in their gaunt and famished faces you can see that little beyond this is accomplished.

About the middle of the alley, and over a doorway of sculptured marble, stands a small statue of Vesta, which, by the aid of a little paint, a crown of gilt paper, and a candle, some pious hands had transformed into a Madonna. A little beneath this, and on a black board, scrawled with letters of unequal size, is the word 'Trattoria' or eating-house.

Nothing, indeed, can be well further from the ordinary aspect of a tavern than the huge vaulted chamber, almost destitute of furniture, and dimly lighted by the flame of a single lamp; a few loaves of coarse black bread, some wicker-bound flasks of common wine, and a wooden bowl containing salad, laid out upon a table, constituting all that the place affords for entertainment. Some benches are ranged on either side of the table, and two or three more are gathered around a little iron tripod, supporting a pan of lighted charcoal, over which now two figures are to be seen cowering down to the weak flame, while they converse in low whispers together.

It is a cold and dreary night in December; the snow has fallen not only on the higher Apennines, but lies thickly over

Albano, and is even seen in drifts along the Campagna. The wailing wind sighs mournfully through the arches of the Colosseum and among the columns of the old Forum, while at intervals, with stronger gusts, it sweeps along the narrow alley, wafting on high the heavy curtain that closes the doorway of the Trattoria, and leaving its occupants for the time in total darkness.

Twice had this mischance occurred; and now the massive table is drawn over to the door, to aid in forming a barricade against the storm.

' 'Tis better not to do it, Fra Luke,' said a woman's voice, as the stout friar arranged his breastwork. ' You know what happened the last time there was a door in the same place.'

' Never mind, Mrs. Mary,' replied the other; 'they 're not so ready with their knives as they used to be, and, moreover, there 's few of them will be out to-night.'

Both spoke in English, and with an accent which told of an Irish origin; and now, as they reseated themselves beside the brazier, we have time to observe them. The woman is scarcely above forty years of age, but she looks older from the effects of sorrow: her regular features and deeply-set eyes bear traces of former beauty. Two braids of rich brown hair have escaped beneath her humble widow's cap and fallen partly over her cheeks, and, as she tries to arrange them, her taper and delicately formed fingers proclaim her of gentle blood: her dress is of the coarsest woollen stuff worn by the peasantry, but little cuffs of crape show how, in all her poverty, she had endeavoured to maintain some semblance to a garb of mourning. The man, whose age might be fifty-seven or eight, is tall, powerfully built, and although encumbered by the long dress of a friar, shows in every motion that he is still possessed of considerable strength and activity. The closely cut hair over his forehead and temples gives something of coarseness to the character of his round full head; but his eyes are mild and gentle-looking, and there is an unmistakable good-nature in his large and thick-lipped mouth.

If there is an air of deference to his companion in the way he seats himself a little distance from the 'brazier,' there is, more markedly still, a degree of tender pity in the look that he bestows on her.

'I want to read you the petition, Mrs. Mary,' said he, drawing a small scroll of paper from his pocket, and unfolding it before the light. ''Tis right you'd hear it, and see if there's anything you'd like different—anything mispleasing you, or that you'd wish left out.' She sighed heavily, but made no answer. He waited for a second or two, and then resumed : ''Tisn't the like of me—a poor friar, ignorant as I am—knows well how to write a thing of the kind, and, moreover, to one like *him*; but maybe the time's coming when you'll have grander and better friends.'

'Oh, no! no!' cried she passionately; 'not better, Fra Luke—not better; that they can never be.'

'Well, well, better able to serve you,' said he, as though ashamed that any question of himself should have intruded into the discussion; 'and that they may easily be. But here's the writing; and listen to it now, for it must be all copied out to-night, and ready for to-morrow morning. The cardinal goes to him at eleven. There's to be some grandees from Spain, and maybe Portugal, at twelve. The Scottish lords come after that; and then Kelly tells me he'll see any that likes, and that has letters or petitions to give him. That's the time for us, then; for ye see, Kelly doesn't like to give it himself: he doesn't know what the Prince would say, and how he'd take it; and, natural enough, he'd not wish to lose the favour he's in by any mistake. That's the word he said, and sure enough it sounded a strange one for helping a friend and a countrywoman; so that I must contrive to go myself, and God's my judge, if I wouldn't rather face a drove of the wild cattle out there on the Campagna, than stand up before all them grand people!' The very thought of such an ordeal seemed too much for the poor friar, for he wiped his forehead with the loose cuff of his robe, and for some minutes appeared to be totally lost in reflection.

With a low sigh he at last resumed : 'Here it is, now; and I made it short, for Kelly said, "if it 's more than one side of a sheet he 'll never look at it, but just say 'Another time, my good friend, another time. This is an affair that requires consideration ; I 'll direct Monsignore to attend to it.' When he says that, it 's all over with you," says Kelly. Monsignore Bargalli hates every one of us—Scotch, English, and Irish alike, and is always belying and calumniating us; but if he reads it himself, there 's always a chance that he may do something, and that 's the reason I made it as short as I could.'

With this preface, he flattened out the somewhat crumpled piece of paper, and read aloud :

'"To His Royal Highness the Prince of Wales, the trueborn descendant of the House of Stuart, and rightful heir to the Crown of England, the humble and dutiful petition of Mary Fitzgerald, of Cappa-Glyn, in the County Kildare, Ireland——'

'Eh, what ?' cried he suddenly ; for a scarcely audible murmur proclaimed something like dissent or correction.

'I was thinking, Fra Luke,' said she mildly, 'if it wouldn't be better not to say "of Cappa-Glyn." 'Tis gone away from us now for ever, and—and——'

'What matter—it was yours once. Your ancestors owned it for hundreds and hundreds of years; and if you're not there now, neither is he himself where he ought to be.'

The explanation seemed conclusive, and he went on :

'"County Kildare, Ireland. Ay ! May it please your illustrious Royal Highness—The only sister of Grace Geraldine, now in glory with the saints, implores your royal favour for the orphan boy that survives her. Come from a long way off, in great distress of mind and body, she has no friend but your highness and the Virgin Mary—that was well known never deserted nor forsook them that stood true to your royal cause—and being in want, and having no shelter or refuge, and seeing that Gerald himself, with the blood in his veins that he has, and worthy of being what your Royal Highness knows he is—"

'That's mighty delicately expressed, ye see, not to give offence,' said the friar, with a most complacent smile at his dexterity—

'"—— hasn't as much as a rag of clothes under his student's gown, nor a pair of shoes, barring the boots that the sub-rector lent him ; without a shirt to his back, or a cross in his pocket ; may at a minute's warning be sent away from the college by reason of his great distress—having no home to go to, nor any way to live, but to starve and die in naked-ness, bringing everlasting disgrace on your royal house, and more misery to her who subscribes herself in every humility and contrite submission, your Royal Highness's most dutiful, devoted, and till death release her from sorrows, ever attached servant,   MARY FITZGERALD."

'I didn't put any address,' said the Fra, 'for, you see, this isn't one of the genteelest quarters of the town. Here they are, Mrs. Mary—here they are!' cried he suddenly, and while he spoke, the hasty tramp of many feet and the discordant voices of many people talking noisily was heard from without.

'Sangue dei Santi!' shouted a rude voice, 'is this a fortress we have here, or a public tavern?' and at the same instant a strong hand seized the table in the doorway and flung it on the floor.

The fellow who thus made good his entrance was tall and muscular, his stature seeming even greater from the uncouth covering of goat-skins, which in every conceivable fashion he wore around him, while in his hand he carried a long lance, terminating with a goad, such as are used by the cattle-drivers of the Campagna.

'A hearty reception, truly, Signora Maria, you give your customers,' cried he, as he strode into the middle of the chamber.

'It was a barrier against the storm, not against our friends——'

'Ha! you there, Fra Luke!' shouted the other, interrupt-ing him, while he burst out into a fit of coarse laughter.

'Who could doubt it, though ?—wherever there's a brazier, a wine-shop, and a pretty woman, there you will find a Frate ! But come in, lads,' added he, turning once more toward the doorway; 'here are only friends—neither spies nor Swiss among them.'

A ragged group of half-starved wretches now came forward, from one of whom the first speaker took a small leathern portmanteau that he carried, and threw it on the table.

'A poor night's work, lads,' said he, unstrapping the leather fastenings around it; 'but these travellers have grown so wary nowadays, it's rare to pick up anything on the Campagna; and what with chains, bolts, and padlocks around their luggage, you might as well strive to burst open the door of the old Mamertine Prison yonder. There's no money here, boys—not a baiocco—nor even clothes, nothing but papers. Cursed be those who ever taught the art of writing !—it serves for nothing but to send brave men to the galleys.'

'I knew he was a courier,' said a small decrepit-looking man, with a long stiletto stuck in his garter, 'and that he could have nothing of any use to us.'

'Away with the trunk, then ! throw it over the parapet into the ditch, and make a jolly blaze with the papers. Ah, Signora Maria, time was when a guidatore of the Campagna seldom came back at night without his purse filled with sequins. Many a gay silk kerchief have I given a sweetheart, ay, and many a gold trinket too, in those days. Cattle-driving would be but a poor trade if the Appian Way didn't traverse the plain.' While he spoke he continued to feed the flame with the papers, which he tore and threw on the burning charcoal. 'Heap them on the fire, Fra, and don't lose time spelling out their meaning. You get such a taste for learning people's secrets at the confessional, you can't restrain the passion.'

'If I mistake not,' said Fra Luke, ' these papers are worth more than double their weight in gold. They treat of very great matters, and are in the writing of great people.'

'Per Bacco! they shall never bring me to the galleys, that I'll swear,' cried the herdsman. 'Popes and princes would fret little about me when they gained their ends. There, on with them, Fra. If I see you steal one of them inside those loose robes of yours, by the blood of the martyrs, I'll pin it to your side with my poniard.'

'You mangy, starved hound of a goatherd!' cried Fra Luke, seizing the massive iron tongs beside him; 'do you think it's one of yourselves I am, or that I have the same cowardly heart that can be frightened because you wear a knife in your sleeve? May I never see glory, if I wouldn't clear the place of you all with these ould tongs, ay, and hunt every mother's son of you down the alley.' The sudden spring forward as he said this, seeming to denote an intention of action, so appalled his hearers that they rushed simultaneously to the door, and, in all the confusion of terror, fled into the street, the herdsman making use of all his strength to cleave his way through the rest.

'Think of the Vendetta, Fra Luke! They never forgive!' cried the woman, in a voice of anguish.

'Faix, it's more of the police I'm thinking, Mrs. Mary,' said the friar. 'You'll see, them fellows will be off now to bring the Swiss guard. Burn the papers as fast as you can; God knows what mischief we're doing, but we can't help it. Oh dear! isn't it a sin and a shame? Here's a letter, signed Alberoni, the great Cardinal in Spain. Here's two in English, and what's the name—Watson, is it? No; Wharton, the Duke of Wharton, as I live! There, fan the coals; quick, there's no time to lose. Oh dear, what's this about Ireland! I must read this, Mrs. Mary, come what may. "Cromarty says that the P—— regrets he didn't try Ireland in the place of Scotland. Kelly persuades him that the Irish would never have abandoned his cause for any consideration for themselves or their estates." That's true, anyhow,' cried the Fra. '"And that as long as he only wanted rebellion, and did not care to make them loyal subjects, the Irish would stand to him to the last." Faix,

Kelly's right!' murmured the Fra. ' "The Scotch, besides, grow weary of civil war, and desire to have peace and order; while the others think fighting a government the best diversion of all, and would ask for nothing better than its continuance. For these reasons, and another that is more of a secret, the Prince is sorry for the choice he made. As to the secret one: there was a certain lady of good family, one of the best in the Island, they say, called Grace Fitz-gerald——" '

A shriek from the woman arrested the Fra at this instant, and with a spring forward she tore the paper from his hand to read the name.

'What of her—what of Grace?' cried she, in a voice of heartrending anxiety.

'Be calm, and I 'll read it all, Mrs. Mary. It was God's will, may be, put this into our hands to-night. There, now, don't sob and agitate yourself, but listen. "She followed him to France," ' continued he, reading.

'She did—she did!' burst out the other, in a passion of tears.

—' "To France, where they lived in retirement at the Château de Marne, in Brittany. Kelly says they were married, and that the priest who solemnised the marriage was a nephew of Cardinal Tencin, called Danneton, or Banneton, but well known as Father Ignatius, at the Seminary of Soissons. To his own dishonour and disgrace, and perhaps to his ruin also, this happy union did not long continue. He was jealous at first; at last he neglected her. Be this as it may, Godfrey Moore and O'Sullivan broke with him for ever on her account; and Ruttledge tore his patent of Baron to pieces, and swore, to his face, that one who could be so false to his love could be little relied on in his friendship." '

'Who writes this, Fra Luke? Who knew these things so well?' cried the woman.

'It is signed "R. W.," and dated from Ancona, something more than ten years back. The remainder treats of money matters, and of names that are new to us. Here is the postscript: "You are right in your estimate of him—too right; still I am inclined to think that Kelly's influence has worked more ill than all his misfortunes. They drink together all day, and even his brother cannot see him without permission; and if you but saw the man—coarse, low-minded, and ill-educated as he is—so unlikely in every way to have gained this ascendency over one of cultivated taste and refinement; but Kinloch said truly, 'What have your Royal Highness's ancestors done, that God should have cursed you with such companionship!' To what end, then, this new plan—this last attempt to avert failure? I'll go, if I must, but it will be only to expose myself to the same impertinences as before."

'I wish I could make out his name, or even to whom it was addressed; but it is only inscribed "G. H., care of Thomas Foster." Is that any one coming, Mrs. Mary?'

'No, it's only the wind; it often sounds like voices moaning through those old corridors,' said the woman sorrowfully. 'You'll keep that letter safe, Fra Luke?'

'That I will, Mrs. Mary. I'll put it now with the rest, in that old iron box in the wall behind the chimney.'

'But if we should have to leave this?'

'Never fear, I'll take care to have it where we can come at it.' He paused for a second or so, and then said, 'Yes, you can't stay here any longer; you must go at once too.'

'Let it be, then, to some spot where I can see him,' cried she eagerly. 'I've borne the misery of this gloomy spot for years back, just because that each day he passes near my door. Down the Capitoline, to the old Forum, is their walk; and how my heart beats as I see the dark procession winding slowly down the hill, till my eyes rest on him— my own dear Gerald. How proudly he steps in all his poverty!—how sorrowful in his youth! What would I not suffer to speak to him—to tell him that I am the sister of his mother—that he is not all forgotten or forsaken, but that through long days and nights I sit to think on him!'

'But you know this cannot be, as yet.'

'I know it—I know it!' cried she bitterly. 'It is not to a home of crime and infamy—to such pollution as this—I would bring him. Nor need this any longer be endured. The slavery is now unrecompensed. I can earn nothing. It is four months since I last sent him a few pauls.'

'Come, come, do not give way thus; to-morrow may be the turn to better fortune. Ask of the Virgin to aid us—pray fervently to those who see our need, and hope—ay, . hope, Mrs. Mary, for hope is faith.'

'My heart grows too cold for hope,' said she with a faint shudder; and then, with a low 'good-night,' she lighted the little lamp that stood beside her, and ascended the narrow stairs to her room, while the Fra proceeded to gather up the papers that lay scattered about: having accomplished this task, he listened for a while, to ascertain that all was quiet without, and then, drawing his cowl over his head, set out for his humble home—a small convent behind the Quirinal.

CHAPTER II

THE LEVEE

For many a year after the failure of the Jacobite expedition —long after all apprehension from that quarter had ceased to disturb the mind of England—the adherents of Charles Edward abroad continued to plot, and scheme, and plan, carrying on intrigues with nearly every court of Europe, and maintaining secret intercourse with all the disaffected at home. It would, at first sight, seem strange that partisans should maintain a cause which its chief had virtually abandoned as hopeless; but a little consideration will show us that the sympathy felt by foreign Governments for the Stuarts was less based on attachment to their house, than a devotion to the religious principles of which they were the assertors. To Catholicise England was the great object at

heart—to crush that heresy, whose right of private judgment
was as dangerous to despotism as to bigotry—-this was a cause
far too portentous and important to be forsaken for any
casual check or momentary discouragement. Hence, for
years after the hopes of the 'Pretender's' friends had died
out in Scotland, his foreign followers traversed the Continent
on secret missions in every direction, exerting at times no
slight influence even in the cabinets which England believed
to be best affected toward her.

There was, it is true, nothing in the state of Europe
generally, nor of England itself, to revive the hopes of that
party. Of the adherents to the Stuart cause, the staunchest
and the best had paid the penalty of their devotion : some
were exiles, and some, like Lord Lovatt, had purchased safety
by dishonour, but scarcely one was to be found ready to peril
life and fortune once more in so barren an enterprise. None,
indeed, expected that 'the king should have his own again,'
but many thought that the claim of a disputed succession
might be used as a terrible agency for disturbance, and the
cause of a dethroned monarch be made an admirable rallying-
point for Catholic Europe. These intrigues were carried on
in every court of the Continent, but more especially at Rome
and Madrid, between which two capitals the emissaries of the
Prince maintained a close and frequent intercourse.

With all the subtlety of such crafty counsellors, every
question of real moment was transacted in the strictest
secrecy, but all trivial and unimportant affairs were blazoned
forth to the world with a degree of display that seemed to
court publicity. In this way, for instance, every eventful era
of the Stuart family was singled out for observance, and the
ceremonies of the Church were employed to give the epochs
a due solemnity. It is to an occasion of this kind we would
now invite our reader's presence—no less a one than the
birthday of Charles Edward.

From an early hour on the morning of the 20th December
178—, the courtyard of the Altieri Palace was a scene of
unusual stir and movement. Country carts, loaded with

orange-trees and rare plants from the conservatories of the princely villas around Rome, great baskets of flowers— bouquets which had cost a twelvemonth's care to bring to perfection—were unpacking on every side, while delicious fruits and wines of extreme rarity were among the offerings of the auspicious day. Servants in the well-known livery of every noble house passed and repassed, and the lodge of the porter was besieged by crowds who were desirous of testifying their respect for the exiled majesty of England, even though their rank did not entitle them to be presented. The street front of the palace was decorated with gorgeous hangings from all the windows, some emblazoned with the armorial insignia of royalty, some with the emblems of different orders of knighthood, and some simply with the fleur-de-lis or the cross of St. Andrew. A guard of honour of the Pope's Swiss stood at the gate, and two trumpeters, with two heralds in full costume, were mounted on white chargers within the arched entrance, ready, when the clock struck eleven, to proclaim the birthday of the king of England.

For years back the occasion had been merely marked by a levee, at which the Prince's personal friends and followers were joined by a few cardinals and one or two of the elders among the noble families; but now, for some unexplained reason, a greater display was made, and an unusual degree of splendour and preparation betokened that the event was intended to be singled out for peculiar honour. Pickets of dragoons, stationed at intervals through the neighbouring streets, also showed that measures were taken to secure public tranquillity, and prevent the inconvenience which might arise from overcrowded thoroughfares. That such precautions were not unneeded, the dense mass of people that now crowded the streets already showed.

Few, indeed, of the assembled multitude knew the meaning of the ceremonial before them. To most, the name of England was like that of some fabulous dream-land. Others clearly saw some vassalage to the Pope in this temporary display of royalty; a yet smaller number looked on with compassionate sorrow at this solemn mockery of a state so unreal and un-substantial. Meanwhile, a certain cautious reserve, a degree of respectful quiet, pervaded all the arrangements within the palace. The windows of the apartments occupied by the Prince were still closed, and the noiseless tread of the servants, as they passed in that direction, showed the fear of disturbing him. For above a year back Charles Edward had been suffering severely from ill health. Two attacks of apoplexy, one following quickly on the other, had left him weak and debilitated, while from the abandonment of his habits of dissipation, enforced by his physician, there ensued that low and nervous condition, the invariable penalty exacted from debauchery.

He had lived of late years much secluded from society, passing his time in the company of a few intimates whose character and station were, indeed, but ill-adapted to his rank. Of these the chief was a certain Kelly, an Irishman, and a friar of the order of Cordeliers, with whom the Prince had become acquainted in his wanderings in Spain, and by whose influence he first grew attached to habits of low dissipation. Kelly's recommendations to favour were great personal courage, high animal spirits, and a certain dashing reckless-ness, that even to his latest hour had a fascination for the mind of Charles Edward. Perhaps, however, there was nothing in Kelly's character which so much disposed the Prince toward him as the confidence—real or pretended—with which he looked forward to the restoration of the exiled family, and the return of the Stuarts to the throne of England. The pro-phecies of Nostradamus and the predictions of Kelly fostered hopes that survived every discomfiture, and survived when there was really not even a chance for their accomplishment. This friar had become, in fact, though not formally, the head of the Prince's household, of which he affected to regulate the expenditure and watch over the conduct. The reckless waste, however, that prevailed; the insubordination of the servants; and the utter disorganisation of everything, were far from being complimentary to his administrative powers.

The income of the Prince was small and precarious. The sums contributed by Spain came irregularly. The French contingent was scarcely better paid. The Roman portion alone could be relied upon to maintain the cost of a household which, for its ill-management and profusion, was the scandal of the city. There were many rumours current of Kelly's financial resources—traits of pecuniary strategy which might have shamed a Chancellor of the Exchequer; but these, of course, were difficult to prove, and only natural to prevail on such a subject. Although there is abundant evidence of the man's debasement and immorality, it is equally well known that he amassed no wealth in the service of the Prince. We have been somewhat prolix in this reference to one who is not a chief figure in our picture, but without whom any sketch of the Stuart household would be defective. The Fra Laurentio, as he was called, was indeed a person of importance, nor was any name so often uttered as his on the eventful morning we have referred to.

Soon after ten o'clock, a certain movement in the streets, and the appearance of the dragoons waving back the populace, showed that the visitors were about to arrive; and at last a stately old coach, containing some officials of the Pope's household, drove into the courtyard. This was quickly followed by the judges of the superior courts and the secretaries of the tribunals, to whom succeeded a long line of Roman nobles, their sombre equipages broken occasionally to the eye by the scarlet panels of a cardinal or the emblazoned hammercloth of a foreign ambassador. Despite the crowd, the movement, the glitter of uniform and the gorgeous glare of costume, there was an air of indescribable gloom in the whole procession. There was none of that gorgeous courtesy, that look of pleasure, so associated with the trace of a royal birthday; on the contrary, there was an appearance of depression—almost of shame—in the faces of the principal persons, many seeming to shrink from the public gaze and to feel abashed at the chance mention of their names by the people in the street, as they passed.

Among those who watched the proceedings with a more than common interest was a large burly man, in the brown robe of a Carthusian, whose bald, bare head overtopped the surrounders. Closely stationed near the gate, he had formed an acquaintance with a stranger who seemed familiar with almost every face that came by. The friar was our friend Fra Luke; and truly his bluff, honest features, his clear blue eye, and frank brow, were no unpleasing contrast to the treacherous expressions and gaunt, sallow cheeks on either side of him. Few of the names were familiar to the honest Carthusian; and it is but truth to say that he heard of the great Spanish diplomatist, Guadalaraxa, the wily Cardinal Acquavesia, and the intriguing envoy, Count Boyer, without a particle of interest in them; but when his informant whispered, 'There goes the Earl of Dunbar, that sallow-faced man in deep mourning; that yonder is the Irish chieftain, O'Sullivan,' then the friar's eyes brightened, and his whole countenance gleamed with animation and excitement. This faithful adherent to the Stuart cause was now in his eighty-seventh year, but still carried himself erect, and walked with the measured step of an old soldier; his three-cornered hat, trimmed with ostrich feathers, and wide-skirted blue coat, turned up with red, recalling the time of Louis XIV., of whose court he had once been a distinguished ornament. Soon after him came MacNiel of Barra, a tall, hard-visaged man, but whose muscular figure and well-knit limbs were seen to great advantage in the full dress of a Highland chieftain. He was preceded by the piper of his clan, and a henchman, with a pistol on full cock in his hand, walked after him. A few of lesser note, many of whom exhibited unmistakable signs of narrow fortune, came after these. It was a group which had gone on diminishing each year, and now, by the casualties of death, sickness, and exile, had dwindled down at last to scarcely a dozen; and even of these few, it was plain to see, some were offering the last homage they were ever like to render on earth.

Equipage after equipage rolled into the court; and although

a vast number had now arrived, the rumour ran that the windows of the Prince's apartment were still closed, nor was there any sign of preparation in that part of the palace. The vague doubts and surmises which prevailed among the crowd without were shared in by the guests assembled within doors. Gathered in knots, or walking slowly along through the vast salons, they conversed in low whispers together—now stopping to listen for anything that might indicate the approach of the Prince, and then relapsing into the same muttered conversation as before. So estranged had Charles Edward lived latterly from all his former associates, that it was in vain to ask for any explanation from those whose titles implied the duties of his household; and Keith, Murray, MacNiel, and Upton frankly avowed that they were as great strangers within those walls as any of those who now came to offer their formal compliments. Kelly alone, it would seem, by the frequent mention of his name, could account for the Prince's absence; and yet Kelly was not to be found.

Ill-regulated and ill-ordered as were all the arrangements of that household, there seemed something beyond all bounds in this neglect of fitting courtesy; and many did not scruple to say aloud how deeply they felt the insult. At one moment they half resolved on deputing a message to the chamber of the Prince; at another they discussed the propriety of departing in a body. Various opinions were given as to the most fitting course to follow; in the midst of which their debate was interrupted by the hoarse flourish of trumpets without, and the loud-voiced proclamation by the heralds, 'That his Majesty of England had entered into his fifty-second year.' A faint cheer—the tribute of the careless crowd in the street—and a salvo of cannon from the Quirinal, closed the ceremony, and all was still—so still that for some seconds not a word was heard in those thronged and crowded salons.

'Ma foi!' cried Count Boyer at last, 'I suppose we may go home again. Not ours the fault if our duty has not been offered with sufficient respect.'

B

'My master,' said the Spanish envoy haughtily, 'will probably think my patience but little deserving of his praise.'

'And I,' said a German baron, all covered with decorations, 'have brought this letter of gratulation from the Margrave of Baden, and, for aught I see, am like to carry it back to his Serene Highness.'

'As for me,' said Count Bjosterna, the Swedish minister, 'I serve a master who never brooked an insult; and lest this should become such, I'll take my leave.'

'Not so, messieurs,' cried O'Sullivan, stepping forward, and placing himself in front of the door. 'You have come here to pay my master, the king of England, certain marks of your respect. It is for him to choose the time he will accept of them. By heaven! not a man of you shall leave this till his good pleasure in that matter be known.'

'Well said, O'Sullivan!' said General Upton, grasping the old man's hand; while MacNiel and some other chieftains pushed forward and ranged themselves before the door in solemn silence.

'Nay, nay, gentlemen,' interposed the cardinal-secretary, Gualtieri—a man whose venerable appearance commanded universal respect; 'this would be most unseemly on every hand. We are all here animated by one feeling of sincere deference and attachment to a great prince. There may be good and sufficient reasons why he has not received our homage. It would ill become us to inquire into these. Not enough for us that our intentions are those of respectful duty; we must mark, by our conduct, that we appreciate the rank of him to whom we offer them.' To these words, uttered aloud, he added something in a whisper to the principal persons at either side; and, seeming to yield to his instances, they fell back, while O'Sullivan, bowing respectfully to the cardinal, in token of acquiescence, moved slowly away, followed by the chieftains.

This little incident, as may be supposed, contributed nothing to remove the constraint of the scene; and an almost unbroken stillness now prevailed, when at length a carriage was seen to drive from the courtyard.

'There goes Monsignore Alberti,' said Count Boyer. 'Where the secretary of the Pope gives the initiative, it is surely safe to follow. My duty is paid.' And so saying, and with a deep obeisance to all at either side of him, he passed out. The Spanish minister followed; and now the whole assemblage gradually moved away, so that in less than an hour the salons were deserted, and none remained of all that crowded mass which so late had filled them, except O'Sullivan, MacNiel, and a few Highland chieftains of lesser note.

'One might be tempted to say that there was a curse upon this cause,' said MacNiel sternly, as he threw himself down into a seat. 'Who ever saw a morning break with brighter hopes; and see already, scarcely an hour past the noon, and they are all gone—wafted to the winds.'

'No, no, MacNiel,' said O'Sullivan gravely; 'you are wrong, believe me. These butterflies knew well that it was only a gleam of sunshine, not a summer. The hopes of the Stuarts are gone for ever.'

'Why are you here, then, if you think so?' cried the other impetuously.

'For that very reason, sir. I feel, as you and all these gentlemen here do, that fidelity is a contract made for life.'

'They were the luckiest that closed that account first,' muttered one of the lairds, half aloud. 'By my saul, Culloden wasn't colder lying than the Campagna.'

'Come along, we may as well follow the rest,' said Mac-Niel, rising. 'Will you dine with us, O'Sullivan? Mac-Allister and Brane are coming.'

'No, MacNiel. I have made this anniversary a day of fasting for many a year back. I took a vow never to taste meat or wine on this festival, till I should do so beneath the king's roof, in his own land.'

'Ye're like to keep a black Lent o' it, then,' muttered the

old laird, with a dry laugh, and shuffled along after his chieftain, as he led the way toward the door.

O'Sullivan waited till they had gone; and then, with a sad glance around him, as if like a leave-taking, left the palace and turned homeward.

CHAPTER III

THE ALTIERI PALACE

In a large and splendid chamber, whose only light was a small lamp within a globe of alabaster, Charles Edward lay, full-dressed, upon his bed. His eyes were closed, but his features did not betoken sleep: on the contrary, his flushed cheek told of intemperance, and the table, covered with wine-decanters and glasses, beside him, confirmed the impression. His breathing was thick and laboured, and occasionally broken by a dry, short cough. There was, indeed, little to remind one of the handsome chevalier in the bloated face, the heavy, hanging jaws, and the ungainly figure of him who, looking far older than his real age, now lay there. Though dressed with peculiar care, and covered with the insignia of several orders, his embroidered vest was unbuttoned, and showed the rich lace of his jabot, stained and discoloured by wine. A splendidly ornamented sword lay beside him, on which one hand rested, the fingers tremulously touching the richly embossed hilt. Near the foot of the bed, on a low, well-cushioned chair, sat another figure, whose easy air of jocularity and good-humoured, sensual countenance presented a strong contrast to the careworn expression of the Prince's face. Dressed in a long loose robe of white cloth, which he wore not ungracefully, his well-rounded legs crossed negligently in front of him, and his hands clasped with an air of quiet and happy composure, the man was a perfect picture of a jolly friar, well-to-do and contented. This was George Kelly, the very type of happy, self-satisfied sensuality. If a phrenologist would have augured favourably from the noble development of forehead and temples, the massive back-head and widely spreading occiput would have quickly shown that nature had alloyed every good gift with a counterpoise of low tastes and bad passions, more than enough to destroy the balance of character.

'Who's there? Who's in waiting?' muttered the Prince, half aloud, as if suddenly arousing himself.

'Kelly—only Kelly,' answered the friar.

'Then the wine is not finished, George, eh? that's certain; the decanters are not empty. What hour is it?'

'As well as I can see, it wants a few minutes of five.'

'Of five! of five! Night or morning, which?'

'Five in the evening. I believe one might venture to call it night, for they're lighting the lamps in the streets already.'

'What's this here for, George?' said the Prince, lifting up the sword. 'We're not going to Bannockburn, are we? Egad! if we be, I trust they'll give me a better weapon. What nonsense of yours is all this?'

'Don't you remember it was your Majesty's birthday, and that you dressed to receive the ministers?'

'To be sure I do; and we did receive them, George, didn't we? Have I not been drinking loyal toasts to every monarchy of Europe, and wishing well to those who need it not? Fifty-one, or fifty-two, which are we, George?'

'Faith, I forget,' said Kelly carelessly; 'but, like this Burgundy, quite old enough to be better.'

'The reproach comes well from you, you old reprobate! Whose counsels have made me what I am? Bolingbroke warned me against you many a long year back. Atterbury knew you too, and told me what you were. By Heaven!' cried he, with a wilder energy, 'it was that very spirit of dictation, that habit of prescribing to me whom to know, where to lean, what to say, and what to leave unsaid, has made me so rash and headstrong through life. A fellow of your caste had otherwise obtained no hold upon me; a low-bred, illiterate drunkard——'

A hearty burst of laughter from Kelly here stopped the speaker, who seemed actually overwhelmed by the cool insolence of the friar.

'Leave me, sir; leave the room!' cried Charles Edward haughtily. 'Let Lord Nairn—no, not him; let Murray of Blair, or Kinloch, attend me.'

Kelly never stirred nor uttered a word, but sat calm and motionless, while Charles, breathing heavily from his recent outburst of passion, lay back, half-exhausted, on the bed. After a few minutes he stretched out his hand and caught his wine-glass; it was empty, and Kelly filled it.

'I say, George,' cried he, after a pause, 'it must be growing late. Shall we not have these people coming to our levee soon?'

'They've come and gone, sire, six hours ago. I would not permit your Majesty to be disturbed for such a pack of false-hearted sycophants; the more that they sent such insolent messages, demanding as a right to be received, and asking how long they were to wait your royal pleasure.'

'Did they so, George? Is this true?'

'True as Gospel. That Spaniard, with the red-brown beard, came even to your Majesty's antechamber, and spoke so loud I thought he'd have awoke you; nor was Count Boyer much better-mannered——'

'Come and gone!' broke in Charles. 'What falsehoods will grow out of this! You should have told me, Kelly. Health, ease, happiness—I'd have sacrificed all to duty. Ay, George, kings have duties like other men. Were there many here?'

'I never saw one-half the number. The carriages filled the Corso to the Piazza del Popolo. There was not a minister absent.'

'And of our own people?'

'They were all here. O'Sullivan, Barra, Clangavin——'

'Where was Tullybardine?—Ah! I forgot,' broke in

Charles, with a deep sigh. ' "Here's to them that are gone," George, as the old song says. Did they seem dissatisfied at my absence ?—how did you explain it ?'

' I said your Majesty was indisposed ; that State affairs had occupied you all the preceding night, and that you had at last fallen into a slumber.'

' Was Glengariff among them ?'

' You forget, sire. We buried him six weeks ago.'

'To be sure we did. Show me that glass, George—no, the looking-glass, man—and light those tapers yonder.'

Kelly obeyed, but with an evident reluctance, occupying time, so as to withdraw the other's attention from his project. This stratagem did not succeed, and Charles waited patiently till his orders were fulfilled, when, taking the mirror in his hand, he stared long and steadfastly at the reflection of his features. It was several minutes before he spoke, and when he did, the voice was tremulous and full of deep feeling.

'George, I am sadly changed ; there is but little of the handsome Chevalier here. I didn't think to look like this these fifteen years to come.'

' Faith ! for one who has gone through all that you have, I see no such signs of wear and tear,' said Kelly. ' Had you been a Pope or a Cardinal—had you lived like an Elector of Hanover, with no other perils than a bare head in a procession, or the gouty twinges of forty years' "sauer kraut ——" '

' Keep your coarse ribaldry for your equals, sirrah. Let there be some, at least, above the mark of your foul slander,' cried Charles angrily ; and then, throwing the looking-glass from him, he fell back upon his bed like one utterly exhausted. Kelly (who knew him too well to continue an irritating topic, his habit being to leave quietly alone the spirit that forgot more rapidly than it resented) sipped his wine in silence for some minutes. ' This day, sixteen years ago, I breakfasted in Carlisle, at the house of a certain Widow Branards. It's strange how I remember a name I have never heard since,' said Charles, in a voice totally altered from its late tone of excitement. ' Do you know, Kelly, that it was on the turn of a straw the fate of England hung that morning? Keppoch had cut his hand with the hilt of his claymore, and instead of counselling—as he ever did—a forward movement, he joined those who advised retreat. Had we gone on, George, the game was our own. There is now no doubt on the matter.'

'I have always heard the same,' said Kelly; 'and that your Majesty yielded with a profound conviction that the counsel was ruinous. Is it true, sire, that O'Sullivan agreed with your Majesty?'

'Quite true, George; and the poor fellow shed tears—perhaps for the only time in his life—when he heard that the decision was given against us. Stuart of Appin and Kerr were of the same mind; but *Diis aliter visum*, George. We turned our back on Fortune that morning, and she never showed us her face after.'

'You are not forgetting Falkirk, surely?' said Kelly, who never lost an opportunity of any flattering allusion to the Prince's campaigns.

'Falkirk was but half what it ought to have been. The chieftains got to quarrel among themselves, and left Hawley to pursue his retreat unmolested; as the old song says,

'"The turnkey spat in the jailer's face,
While the prisoner ran away!"

And now they are all gone, George—gone where you and I must meet them some day—not a far-off one, maybe.'

'O'Sullivan was here to-day, sire, to wish your Majesty long life and happiness; and the old fellow looked as hearty and high-spirited as ever. I saw him as he passed out of the courtyard, and you'd have guessed, by his air and step, that he was a man of forty.'

'He's nigh to eighty-five, then, or I mistake me.'

'Life's strong in an Irishman—there's no doubt of it,' cried Kelly enthusiastically; 'there's no man takes more out of prosperity, nor gives way less to bad fortune.'

'What's that song of yours, George, about Paddy O'Flynn

—isn't that the name?' said the Prince, laughing. 'Let's have it, man.'

'You mean Terry O'Flynn, sire,' said Kelly; 'and, faith, 'twould puzzle me to call to mind one verse of the same song.'

'Do you even remember the night you made it, George, in the little wayside shrine, eight miles from Avignon? I'll never forget the astonished faces of the two friars that peeped in and saw you, glass in hand, before the fire, chanting that pleasant melody.'

'The Lord forgive you! 'tis many a bad thing you led me into,' said Kelly with affected sorrow, as he arose and walked to the window. Meanwhile the Prince, in a low kind of murmuring voice, tried to recall some words of the song. 'Talking of friars,' said Kelly, 'there's a thumping big one outside, with his great face shining like the dial of a clock. I'm much mistaken if he's not a countryman of my own!'

'Can he sing, George? Has he the gift of minstrelsy, man?'

'If your Royal Highness would like to hear the canticles, I'm sure he'd oblige you. Faith, I was right; it's poor Luke MacManus—a simple, kind-hearted creature as ever lived. I remember now that he asked me when it was possible to see your Royal Highness; and I told him that he must put down into writing whatever he wanted to say, and come here with it on the 20th; and sure enough, there he is now.'

'And why did you tell him any such thing, sir?' said the Prince angrily. 'What are these petitions but demands for aid that we have not to bestow—entreaties we cannot satisfy? Are we not pensioners ourselves? ay, by the Lord Harry, are we, and beggarly enough in our treatment too. None knows this better than yourself, Master Kelly. It is not ten days since you pawned my George. Ay, and, by the way, you never brought me the money. What do you say to that?'

'I received twenty-four thousand francs, sire,' said Kelly

calmly; 'eighteen of which I paid, by your Royal Highness's order, to the Countess.'

'I never gave such an order—where is it?'

'Spoken, sire, in the words of a prince; and heard by one who never betrayed him,' said the friar quickly—'the Countess herself——'

'No more of this, sir. We are not before a court of justice. And now let me tell you, Kelly, that the town is full of the malversation of this household; and that however proverbial Irish economy and good management be in its own country, climate and change of air would seem to have impaired its excellence. My brother tells me that our waste and extravagance are public town talk.'

'So much the better, sire—so much the better!'

'What do you mean by that, sirrah?' cried the Prince angrily.

'Your Royal Highness has heard of Alcibiades, and why he cut the tail off his dog! Well, isn't it a comfort to think that they never say worse of us here than that we spend freely what's given grudgingly; and that the penury of others never contaminated the spirit of your Royal Highness?'

'Have a care, sir,' said the Prince, with more dignity than he had shown before: 'there will come a day, perhaps, when we may grow weary of this buffoonery.'

'I'm sorry for it, then,' replied Kelly unabashed; 'for when it does, your Royal Highness will just be as little pleased with wisdom.'

It was thus alternately flattering and outraging Charles Edward—now insinuating the existence of qualities that he had not—now disparaging gifts which he really possessed—that this man maintained an influence which others in vain tried to obtain over the Prince. It was a relief, too, to find one whose pliancy suited all his humours, and whose character had none of that high-souled independence which animated his Scottish followers. Lastly, Kelly never asked favours for himself or for others. Enough for him the

privilege of the intimacy he enjoyed. He neither sought
nor cared for more. Perhaps, of all his traits, none weighed
more heavily in his favour than this one. It was, then, in
a kind of acknowledgment of this single-mindedness that
the Prince, after a pause, said:

'Let your countryman come up here, George. I see he's
the only courtier that remains to us.'

Kelly rose without a word, and left the room to obey the
command.

Little as those in waiting on the Prince were ever disposed
to resist Kelly in any proceeding, they were carried very
nearly to insubordination, as they saw him conducting
through the long line of salons the humbly-clad, barefooted
friar, who, with his arms reverently crossed on his breast,
threw stealthy glances, as he passed, at the unwonted
splendour around him.

'I hope, sir,' said Fra Luke respectfully, 'that your kindness to a poor countryman won't harm yourself; but if ever
you were to run the risk, 'tis an occasion like this might
excuse it.'

'What do you mean?' said Kelly hastily, and staring
him full in the face.

'Why, that the petition I hold here is about one that has
the best blood of Ireland in his veins; but maybe, for all
that, if you knew what was in it, you mightn't like to give
it.'

Kelly paused for a few seconds, and then, as if having
formed his resolution, said:

'If that be the case, Luke, it is better that I should not
see it. There's no knowing when my favour here may
come to an end. There's not a morning breaks, nor an
evening closes, that I don't expect to hear I'm discarded,
thrown off, abandoned. Maybe it would bring me luck if
I was to do one, just one, good action, by way of a change,
before I go.'

'I hope you've done many such afore now,' said Luke
piously.

Kelly did not reply, but a sudden change in his features told how acutely the words sank into his heart.

'Wait for me here a minute,' said he; and motioning to Luke to be seated, he passed noiselessly into the chamber of the Prince.

CHAPTER IV

THE PRINCE'S CHAMBER

BRIEF as Kelly's absence had been, it was enough to have obliterated from the Prince's mind all the reasons for his going. No sooner was he alone than he drank away, muttering to himself, as he filled his glass, snatches of old Jacobite songs—words of hope and encouragement; or at times, with sad and broken utterance, phrases of the very deepest despondency.

It was in this half-dreamy state that Kelly found him as he entered. Scotland—Rome—the court of France—the château at St. Germains—the sheiling where he sought refuge in Skye—the deck of the French privateer that landed him at Brest—were, by turns, the scenes of his imagination; and it was easy to mark how, through all the windings of his fancy, an overweening sense of his own adventurous character upheld and sustained him. If he called up at times traits of generous devotion and loyalty— glorious instances wherein his followers rose to the height of heroes—by some artful self-complacency he was ever sure to ascribe these to the great cause they fought for; or, oftener still, to his own commanding influence and the fascination of his presence. In the midst of all, however, would break forth some traits that bespoke a nobler nature. In one of these was it that he alluded to the proposition of Cardinal Tencin, to make the cession of Ireland the price of the French adhesion to his cause. 'No, no, Monsieur le Cardinal,' cried he several times energetically; '*tout ou rien!*

tout au rien! . . . Must not my cause have been a poor one,
when he dared to make me such an offer? Ay, Kelly, and
I swear to you he did so!'

These last words were the first that showed a consciousness of the other's presence.

'The Dutchman was better than that, George, eh?—a
partition of the kingdom!—never, never. Ireland, too! The
very men who stood truest to me—the very men who never
counselled retreat. Think of Lovatt, George. If you had
but seen him that day! He could not bide the time I took
to eat a morsel of breakfast, so eager was he to be rid of me.
I laughed outright at his impatience, and said that he remembered but the worst half of the old Highland adage which
tells you "to speed the parting guest." He never offered me
a change of linen, George, and I had worn the same clothes
from the day before Culloden. "Wae's me for Prince
Charlie!"'

'It's a proud thing for me to hear how you speak of my
countrymen, sire,' said Kelly.

'Glorious fellows they were, every man of them!' cried
the Prince with enthusiasm. 'Light-hearted and buoyant,
when all others looked sad and downcast; always counselling
the bold course, and readier to do than say it! I never met
—if I ever heard of—but one Irishman who was not a man
of honour. *He* was enough, perhaps, to leaven a whole nation
—a low, mean sycophant, cowardly, false, and foul-tongued:
a fellow to belie you and betray you—to track you into
evil that others might stare at you there. I never thought
ill of mankind till I knew him. Do you know whom I mean
—eh, George?'

'Faith, if the portrait be not intended for myself, I am at
a loss to guess,' said Kelly good-humouredly.

'So it is, you arch-scoundrel; and, shameless though you
be, does it never occur to you how you will go down to
posterity? The corrupter of a Prince; the fellow who de-
bauched and degraded him!'

'Isn't it something that posterity will ever hear of me at

all ?' said Kelly. 'Is it not fame, at any rate ? If there
should be any records of our life together, who knows but
a clever commentator will find out that but for me and my
influence the Prince of Wales would have been a downright
beast ?—"that Kelly humanised your Royal Highness, kept
you from all the contamination of cardinals and scheming
Monsignori, rallied your low spirits, comforted your dark
hours, and enjoyed your bright ones."'

'For what—for what ? what was his price ?' cried Charles
eagerly.

'Because he felt in his heart that, sooner or later, you'd
be back, King of England and Ireland, and George Kelly
wouldn't be forgotten. No, faith; Archbishop of Westminster; and devil a less I'd be—that's the price, if you
wish to hear it !'

The Prince laughed heartily, as he ever did when the friar
gave way to his impertinent humour, and then, sitting up in
his bed, told Kelly to order coffee. To his last hour, coffee
seemed to exercise the most powerful effect on him, clearing
his faculties after hours of debauch, and enabling him to
apply himself to business when he appeared to be utterly
exhausted. Kelly, who well knew how to adapt himself to
each passing shade of temperament, followed the Prince into
a small dressing-room in silence, and remained standing at a
short distance behind his chair.

'Tell Conway,' said he, pointing to a mass of papers on the
table, 'that these must wait. I'll go down to Albano to-
morrow or next day for a change of air. I'll not hear of
anything till I return. Cardinal Altieri knows better than
I do what Sir Horace Mann writes home to England. This
court is in perfect understanding with St. James's. As to
the Countess, Kelly, let it not be spoken of again; you hear
me ? What paper is that in your hand ?'

'A petition, I believe, sire; at least, the quarter it comes
from would so bespeak it.'

'Throw it on the fire, then. Is it not enough to live thus,
but that I must be reminded thirty, forty times a day of my

poverty and incapacity? Am I to be flouted with my fallen fortune? On the fire with it, at once!'

'Poor Luke's prayers were offered at an untimely moment,' said Kelly, untying the scroll, as if preparing to obey. 'Maybe, after all, he is asking for a new rosary, or a pair of sandals. Shall I read it, sire?'

The Prince made no reply, and Kelly, who thoroughly understood his humour, made no further effort to obtain a hearing for his friend; but, tearing the long scroll in two, he muttered the first line that caught his eye:

'"Petition of Mary Fitzgerald."'

'What—of whom? Fitzgerald! what Fitzgerald?' cried Charles, catching the other's wrist with a sudden grasp.

'"Sister of Grace Geraldine."'

The words were not well uttered when Charles snatched the paper from Kelly's hand, and drew near to the lamp.

'Leave me; wait in the room without, Kelly!' said he; and the tone of his voice implied a command not to be gainsaid. The Prince now flattened out the crumpled document before him, holding the fragments close together; but, although he bent over them attentively for several minutes, he made little progress in their contents, for drop by drop the hot tears rose to his eyes, and fell heavily on the paper. Gradually, too, his head declined, till at last it fell forward on the table, where he lay, sobbing deeply. It was a long time before he arose from this attitude; and then his furrowed cheeks and glazed eyes told of intense sorrow. 'What ruin have I brought everywhere!' was the exclamation that broke from him, in a voice tremulous with agony. 'Kinloch said truly: "We must have sinned heavily, to be so heavily cursed!"' Again and again did he bend over the paper, and, few as were the lines, it was long before he could read them through, such was the gush of emotion they excited. 'Was there ever a cause so hallowed by misfortune?' cried he, in an accent of anguish. 'Oh! Grace, had you been spared to me, I might have been other than this. But, if it were to be—if it were indeed fated that I should become the thing I am, thank God you have not lived to see it! George,' cried he suddenly, 'who brought this paper?'

Kelly came at once at his call, and replied that the bearer was a poor friar, by name MacManus.

'Let me see him alone,' said the Prince; and the next moment Fra Luke entered the chamber, and, with a low and deferential gesture, stooped down to kiss his hand. 'You are an Irishman,' said Charles, speaking with a thick but rapid utterance; 'from none of your countrymen have I met with anything but loyalty and affection. Tell me, then, frankly, what you know of this paper—who wrote it?'

'I did, myself, your Royal Highness,' said Luke, trembling all over with fear.

'Its contents are all true—strictly true?'

'As the words of this holy Book,' said Luke, placing his hand on his breviary.

'Why were they not made known to me before—answer me that?' cried Charles angrily.

'I'll tell your Royal Highness why,' replied Luke, who gained courage as he was put upon the defensive. 'She that's gone—the Heavens be her bed!—made her sister promise, in her last hour, never to ask nor look for favour or benefit from your Royal Highness.'

'I will not believe this,' broke in Charles indignantly; 'you are more than bold, sir, to dare to tell me so.'

''Tis true as Gospel,' replied the friar. 'Her words were: "Let there be one that went down to the grave with the thought that loving him was its best reward! and leave me to think that I live in his memory as I used in his heart."'

The Prince turned away, and drew his hand across his eyes.

'How came she here—since when?' asked he suddenly.

'Four years back; we came together. I bore her company all the way from Ireland, and on foot too, just to put the child into the college here.'

'And she has been in poverty all this while?'

'Poverty! faith, you might call it distress!—keeping a

little trattoria in the Viccolo d'Orso, taking sewing, washing —whatever she could; slaving and starving, just to get shoes and the like for the boy.'

'How comes it, then, that she has yielded at last to write me this?' said Charles, who, in proportion as his self-accusings grew more poignant, sought to turn reproach on any other quarter.

'She didn't, nor wouldn't,' said the Fra; ''twas I did it myself. I told her that she might ease her conscience, by never accepting anything; that I'd write the petition and go up with it, and that all I'd ask was a trifle for the child.'

'She loves him, then,' said Charles tenderly.

The friar nodded his head slowly twice, and muttered, 'God knows she does.'

'And does he repay her affection?'

'How can he? Sure he doesn't know her; he never sees her. When we were on the way here, he always thought it was his nurse she was; and from that hour to this he never set eyes on her.'

'What motive was there for all this?'

'Just to save him the shame among the rest, that they couldn't say his mother's sister was in rags and wretchedness, without a meal to eat.'

'She never sees him, then?'

'Only when he walks out with the class, every Friday; they come down the hill from the Capitol, and then she's there, watching to get a look at him.'

'And he—what is he like?'

The friar stepped back, and gazed at the Prince from head to foot in silence, and then at length said: 'He's like a Prince, sorrow less! The black serge gown, the coarse shoes, the square cap, ugly as they are, can't disfigure him; and though they cut off his beautiful hair, that curled half-way down his back, they couldn't spoil him. He has the great dark blue eyes of his mother, and the long lashes, almost girlish to look at.'

'He's mild and gentle, then?' said Charles pensively.

C

'Indeed and I won't tell you a lie,' said Luke, half mournfully, 'but that's just what I believe he isn't. The sub-rector says there's nothing he couldn't learn, either in the sciences or the humanities. He can write some of the ancient and three of the modern tongues. His disputations got him the medal; but somehow——'

'Well—go on. Somehow——'

'He's wild—wild,' said the friar, and as if he was glad to have found the exact word he wanted; 'he'd rather go out on the Campagna there and ride one of the driver's ponies all day, than he'd walk in full procession with all the cardinals. He'd like to be fighting the shepherds' dogs, wicked as they are, or goading their mad cattle till they turn on him. Many a day they've caught him at that sport; and, if I'm not mistaken, he's in punishment now, though Mrs. Mary doesn't know it, for putting a ram inside the railings of a fountain, so that the neighbours durstn't go near to draw water. 'Tis diversions like these has made him as ragged and tattered as he is.'

'Bad stuff for the cloister,' said Charles, with a faint smile.

'Who knows? Sure Cardinal Guidotti was at every mischief when a boy; and there's Gardoni, the secretary of the Quirinal, wasn't he the terror of the city with his pranks?'

'Can I see this boy—I mean, could he be brought here without his knowing or suspecting to whom he was presented?'

'Sure, if Kelly was to——'

'Ay, ay, I know as well as you do,' broke in the Prince, 'George Kelly has craft and cunning enough for more than that; but supposing, my worthy Fra, that I did not care to intrust Kelly with this office: supposing that, for reasons known to myself, I wished this matter a secret, can you hit upon the means of bringing the lad here, that I might see and speak with him?'

'It should be after dark, your Royal Highness, or he would know the palace again, and then find out who lived in it.'

'Well, be it so.'

'Then there's the rules of the college; without a special leave a student cannot leave the house, and even then he must have a professor with him.'

'A cardinal's order would, of course, be sufficient,' said the Prince.

'To be sure it would, sir,' said the friar, with a gesture that showed how implicitly his confidence was given to such a conjuncture.

'The matter shall be done then, and thus: on Tuesday next Kelly goes to Albano, and will not return till Wednesday or Thursday evening. At seven o'clock on Tuesday evening you will present yourself at the college, and ask for the president: you will only have to say that you are come for the youth Fitzgerald. He will be at once given into your charge; drive then at once to the Corso, where you can leave the carriage, and proceed hither on foot. When you arrive here, you shall be admitted at once. One only caution I have to give you, friar, and it is this: upon your reserve and discretion it depends whether I ever befriend this boy, or cast him off for ever. Should one syllable of this interview transpire—should I ever discover that, under any pretence or from any accident, you have divulged what has passed between us here—and discover it I must, if it be so—from that instant I cease to take interest in him. I know your cloth well; you can be secret if you will: let this be an occasion for the virtue. I need not tell you more; nor will I add one threat to enforce my caution. The boy's own fortune in life is on the issue; that will be enough.'

'Is Mrs. Mary to be intrusted with the secret?' said the Fra timidly.

'No; not now at least.' The Prince sat down, and leaned his forehead on his hand in thought. At length he said: 'The boy will ask you, in all likelihood, whither you are leading him. You must say that a countryman of his own, a man of some influence, and who knew his friends, desires to see and speak with him. That he is one with whom he may be frank and open-hearted; free to tell whatever he feels; whether he likes his present life or seeks to change it. He is to address me as the Count, and be careful yourself to give me no higher title. I believe I have said all.'

'If Kelly asks me what was my business with your Royal Highness?'

'Ay; well thought of. Say it was a matter of charity; and take these few crowns, that you may show him as you pass out.'

'Well, did you succeed?' asked Kelly, as the poor friar, flushed and excited from the emotion of his interview, entered the antechamber.

'I did indeed; and may the saints in heaven stand to *you* for the same! It's a good work you done, and you'll have your reward!'

'Egad,' cried Kelly, in a tone of levity, 'if I had any friends among the saints, I must have tried their patience pretty hard these last eight or nine years; but who is this Mary Fitzgerald—I just caught the name on the paper?'

'She's—she's—she's—a countrywoman of our own,' stammered out Fra Luke, while he moved uneasily from foot to foot, and fumbled with his hands up the sleeves of his robe.

'It was lucky for you, then, we were just talking about Ireland before you went in. He was saying how true and staunch the Irish always showed themselves.'

'And does he talk of them times?' asked the Fra in astonishment.

'Ay, by the hour. Sometimes it's breaking day before I go to bed, he telling me about all his escapes and adventures. I could fill a book with stories of his.'

'Musha! but I'd like to hear them,' cried Luke with honest enthusiasm.

'Come up here, then—let me see what evening—it mustn't be Tuesday—nor Wednesday—maybe, indeed, I won't be back before Friday. Oh, there's the bell now; that's for *me*,' cried he; and before he could fix the time he hurried off to the Prince's chamber.

CHAPTER V

AFTER DARK

It was a long and weary day to the poor friar, watching for that Tuesday evening when he should appear at the gate of the Jesuits' College and ask for the young Fitzgerald. He felt, too, as though some amount of responsibility had been imposed on him to which he was unequal. It seemed to his simple intelligence as if it were a case that required skill and dexterity. The rector might possibly ask this, or wish to know that; and then, how was he to respect the secrecy he had pledged to the Prince? or was he to dare to deceive the great president of the college? Supposing, too, all these difficulties over, what of the youth himself? How should he answer the inquiries he was certain to make—whither he was going—with what object—and to whom? Greater than all these personal cares was his anxiety that the boy should please his Royal Highness; that the impression he made should be favourable; that his look and bearing might interest the Prince and ensure his future advancement. Let us own that Fra Luke had his grave misgivings on this score. From all he could pick up through the servitors of the convent, Gerald was a wild, headstrong youth, constantly 'in punishment,' and regarded by the superiors as the great instigator of every infraction to the discipline of the college. 'What will a prince think of such an unruly subject?' was the sad question the simple-hearted friar ever posed to himself. 'And if the rector only send a report of him, he'll have no chance at all.' With this sorrowful thought he brought his reflections to a close; and, taking out his beads, set himself vigorously to implore the intercession of the saints in a cause intrusted to hands so weak and unskilful as his own.

The grim old gate of the college, flanked with its two low towers, looked gloomy enough as the evening closed in. The little aperture, too, through which questions were asked or answered, was now shut up for the night, and all intercourse with the world without suspended. The Fra had yet a full hour to wait, and he was fain to walk briskly to and fro, to warm his blood, chilled by the cold wind that came over the Campagna. For a while the twinkling of a stray light, high up in the building, set him a-thinking where the cell of the boy might be; gradually these lights disappeared, and all was wrapped in gloom and darkness, when suddenly the chapel became illuminated, and the rich, full swell of an organ toned out its solemn sounds on the still night. The brief prelude over, there followed one of those glorious old chants of the church which combine a strain of intense devotion with a highly exalted poetic feeling. In a perfect flood of harmony the sounds blended, until the very air seemed to hold them suspended. They ceased; and then, like the softest melody of a flute, a young voice arose alone, and, soaring upward, uttered a passage of seraphic sweetness. It was as though the song of some angelic spirit, telling of hope and peace; and, as a long, thrilling shake concluded the strain, the loud thunder of the organ and the full swell of the choir closed the service. The moment after, all was silent and in darkness.

Bell after bell, from the great city beneath, tolled out seven o'clock; and Fra Luke knocked modestly at the gate of the college. His visit appeared to have been expected, for he was admitted at once and conducted to the large hall, which formed the waiting-room of the college. The friar had not long to wait; for scarcely had he taken his seat when the door opened, and young Fitzgerald appeared. Advancing with an easy air, and a degree of gracefulness that contrasted strangely with his poverty-struck dress, the boy said, 'I am told you wish to speak to me, father.'

'Are you Gerald Fitzgerald, my son?' asked Fra Luke softly.

'Yes; that's my name.'

The Fra looked at the beaming face and the bright blue

eyes, soft in their expression as a girl's, and the dimpled cheek, over which a slight flush was mantling, and wondered to himself could this be the wild, reckless youth they called him?—had they not been calumniating that fine and simple nature? So deeply was the Fra impressed with this senti- ment that he forgot to continue the interrogatory, and stood gazing with admiration on him.

'Well,' said the boy, smiling good-humouredly, 'what is your business with me, for it is nigh bed-time, and I must be going?'

'It was *your* voice I heard in the solo a few minutes ago,' cried the Fra eagerly; 'I know it was. It was *you* who sang the

> 'Virgo virginum præclara,
> Mihi jam non sis amara?'

'Yes, yes,' said the youth, reddening. 'But what of that? You never came here to-night to ask me this question.'

'True enough,' said the Fra, sighing painfully—less, indeed at the rebuke than the hot-tempered tone of the boy as he spoke it. 'I came here to-night to fetch you along with me, to see one who was a friend of your family long, long ago; he has heard of you here, and wishes to see and speak with you. He is a person of great rank and high station, so that you will show him every deference, and demean yourself toward him respectfully and modestly; for he means you well, Gerald; he will befriend you.'

'But what need have I of his friendship or his good offices?' said the youth, growing deadly pale as he spoke. 'Look at this serge gown—see this cap—they can tell you what I am destined for. I shall be a priest one of these days, Fra; and what has a priest to do with ties of affection or friendship?'

'Oh! for the blessed Joseph's sake,' whispered the Fra, 'be careful what you say. These are terrible words to speak —and to speak them here, too,' added he, as he threw his eyes over the walls of the room.

'Is this man a cardinal?'

'No,' said the Fra; 'he is a layman, and a count.'

'Better that; had he been a cardinal, I'd not have gone. Whenever the old cardinal, Caraffa, comes here, I'm sure to have a week's punishment; and I hate the whole red-stockinged race——'

'There, there—let us away at once,' whispered the Fra. 'Such discourse as this will bring misfortune upon us both.'

'Have you the superior's permission for my going out with you?' asked Gerald.

'Yes; I have his leave till eleven o'clock—we shall be back here before that time.'

'I'm sorry for it,' said the boy sternly. 'I'd like to think I was crossing that old courtyard there for the last time.'

'You will be cold, my poor boy,' said the friar, 'with no other covering but that light frock; but we shall find a carriage as we go along.'

'No, no, no,' cried the boy eagerly. 'Let us walk, Fra; let us walk, and see everything. It's like one of the old fairy tales nurse used to tell me long ago—to see the city all alight thus, and the troops of people moving on, and all these bright shops with the rich wares so temptingly displayed. Ah! how happy must they be who can wander at will among all these—exchanging words and greetings, and making brotherhood with their fellows! See, Fra—see!' cried he, 'what is it comes yonder, with all the torches, and the men in white?'

'It is some great man's funeral, my child. Let us say a *Pax eterna*,' and he fumbled for his beads as he spoke.

'Let us follow them,' said the boy; 'they are bearing the catafalque into that small church—how grand and solemn it all is!' and now, attaching himself to the long line of acolytes, the boy walked step for step with the procession, mingling his clear and liquid notes in the litany they were chanting. While he sang with all the force of intense expression, it was strange to mark how freely his gaze wandered over all the details of the scene—his keen eyes

scrutinised everything—the costumes, the looks, the gestures
of all; the half tawdry splendour below—the dim and solemn
grandeur of the Gothic roof overhead. If there was nothing of levity, as little was there anything of reverence
in his features. The sad scene, with all its trappings
of woe, was a spectacle, and no more, to him; and, as
he turned away to leave the spot, his face betrayed the
desire he felt for some new object of interest. Nor had
he long to search for such; for, just as they entered the
Piazza di Spagna, they found a dense crowd gathered around.
a group of those humble musicians from Calabria — the
Pifferari, they call them—stunted in form, and miserably
clad: these poor creatures, whose rude figures recall old
pictures of the ancient Pan, have a wonderful attraction
for the populace. They were singing some wild, rude air
of their native mountains, accompanying the refrain with
a sort of dance, while their uncouth gestures shook the crowd
with laughter.

'Oh! I love these fellows, but I never have a chance of
seeing them,' cried the boy; so bursting away, he dashed
into the thick of the assembled throng. It was not without
a heartfelt sense of shame that the poor friar found himself
obliged to follow his charge, whom he now began to fear
might be lost to him.

'Per Bacco! cried one of the crowd, 'here's a Frate can't
resist the charms of profane melody, and is elbowing his
way, like any sinner, among us.'

'It's the cachuca he wants to see,' exclaimed another;
'come, Marietta, here's a connoisseur worth showing your
pretty ankles to.'

'By the holy rosary!' cried a third, 'she is determined on
the conquest.'

This outburst was caused by the sudden appearance of
a young girl, who, though scarcely more than a child, bore
in her assured look and flashing eyes all the appearances
of more advanced years. She was a deep brunette in
complexion, to which the scarlet cloth that hung from her

black hair gave additional brilliancy. Her jupe, of the same colour, recrossed and interlaced with tawdry gold tinsel, came only to the knee, below which appeared limbs that many a Roman statuary had modelled, so perfect were they in every detail of symmetry and beauty. Her whole air was redolent of that *beauté du diable*, as the French happily express it, which seems never to appeal in vain to the sympathies of the populace. It was girlhood, almost child-like girlhood, but dashed with a conscious effrontery that had braved many a libertine stare—many a look significant in coarseness.

With one wild spring she bounded into the open space, and there she stood now on tiptoe, her arms extended straight above her head, while with clasped hands she remained motionless, so that every line and lineament of her faultless figure might be surveyed in unbroken symmetry.

'Ah carina—che bellezza! come e graziosa!' broke from those who, corrupt, debased, and degraded in a hundred ways as they were, yet inherited that ancient love of symmetry in form which the games and the statues of antique Rome had fostered. With a graceful ease no ballarina of the grand opera could have surpassed, she glided into those slow and sliding movements which precede the dance—movements meant to display the graces of form, without the intervention of action. Gradually, however, the time of the music grew quicker, and now her heightened colour and more flashing eye bespoke how her mind lent itself to the measure. The dance was intended to represent the coy retirings of a rustic beauty from the advances of an imaginary lover; and, though she was alone, so perfectly did she convey the storied interest of the scene, that the enraptured audience could trace every sentiment of the action. At one moment her gestures depicted the proudest insolence and disdain; at the next a half-yielding tender-ness—now, it was passion to the very verge of madness—now, it was a soul-subduing softness, that thrilled through every heart around her. Incapable, as it seemed, of longer resisting the solicitations of love, her wearied steps grew heavier, her languid head drooped, and a look of voluptuous waywardness appeared to steal over her. Wherever her eye turned a murmured sigh acknowledged how thoroughly the captivation held enthralled every bosom around, when suddenly, with a gesture that seemed like a cry—so full of piercing agony it seemed—she dashed her hands across her forehead and stared with aching eye-balls into vacancy,—it was jealousy: the terrible pang had shot through her heart, and she was wild. The horrible transitions from doubt to doubt, until full conviction forced itself upon her, were given with extraordinary power. Over her features, in turn, passed every expression of passion. The heartrending tenderness of love—the clinging to a lost affection—the straining effort to recall him who had deserted her — the black bitterness of despair—and then, with a wild spring, like the bound of a tiger, she counterfeited a leap over a precipice to death!

She fell upon the ground, and as the mingled sobs and cries rose through the troubled crowd, a boy tore his way through the dense mass, and fighting with all the energy of infuriated strength, gained the open space where she lay. Dropping on his knees, he bent over, and clasping her hand kissed it wildly over and over, crying out in a voice of broken agony, 'Oh! Marietta, Marietta mia, come back to us—come back, we will love you and cherish you.'

A great roar of laughter—the revulsion to that intensity of feeling so lately diffused among them—now shook the mob. Revenging, as it were, the illusion that had so enthralled themselves, they now turned all their ridicule upon the poor boy.

'Santissima Virgina! if he isn't a scholar of the Holy Order!' shouted one.

'Ecco! a real Jesuit!' said another; 'had he been a little older, though, he'd have done it more secretly.'

'The little priest is offering the consolation of his order,' cried a third; and there rained upon him, from every side, words of mockery and sarcasm.

'Don't you see that he is a mere boy—have you no shame that you can mock a simple-hearted child like this?' said the burly Fra, as he pushed the crowd right and left, and forced a passage through the mob. 'Come along, Gerald, come along. They are a cowardly pack, and if they were not fifty to one, they'd think twice ere they'd insult us.' This speech he delivered in Italian, with a daring emphasis of look and gesture that made the craven listeners tremble. They opened a little path for the friar and his charge to retire; nor was it until they had nearly gained the corner of the Piazza that they dared to yell forth a cry of insult and derision.

The boy grasped the Fra's hand as he heard it, and looked up in his face with an expression there was no mistaking, so full was it of wild and daring courage.

'No, no, Gerald,' said he, 'there are too many of them, and what should we get by it after all? See, too, how they have torn your soutane all to pieces. I almost suspect we ought to go back again to the college, my boy. I scarcely like to present you in such a state as this.'

Well indeed might the Fra have come to this doubtful issue, for the youth's gown hung in ribbons around him, and his cap was flattened to his head.

'I wish I knew what was best to be done, Gerald,' said he, wiping the sweat from his brawny face. 'What do you advise yourself?'

'I'd say, go on,' cried the youth. 'Will a great signor think whether my poor and threadbare frock be torn or whole? —he'll not know if I be in rags or in purple. Tell him, if you like, that we met with rough usage in the streets. Tell him, that in passing through the crowd they left me thus. Say nothing about Marietta, Fra; you need not speak of her.'

The boy's voice, as he uttered the last words, became little louder than a mere whisper.

'Come along then; and, with the help of the saints, we'll go through with what we've begun.'

And with this vigorous resolve the stout friar strode along down the Corso.

CHAPTER VI

THE INTERVIEW

IT was full an hour after the time appointed when the friar, accompanied by young Gerald, entered the arched gate of the Altieri Palace.

'You have been asked for twice, Frate,' said the porter; 'and I doubt if you will be admitted now. It is the time his Royal Highness takes his siesta.'

'I must only hope for the best,' sighed out the Fra, as he ascended the wide stairs of white marble, with a sinking heart.

'Let us go a little slower, Fra Luke,' whispered the boy; 'I'd like to have a look at these statues. See what a fine fellow that is strangling the serpent; and, oh! is she not beautiful, crouching in that large shell?'

'Heathen vanities, all of them,' muttered the Fra; 'what are they compared to the pure face of our blessed Lady?'

The youth felt rebuked, and was silent. While the friar, however, was communicating with the servant in waiting, the boy had time to stroll down the long gallery, admiring as he went the various works of art it contained. Stands of weapons, too, and spoils of the chase abounded, and these he examined with a wistful curiosity, reading from short inscriptions attached to the cases, which told him how this wolf had been killed by his Royal Highness on such a day of such a year, and how that boar had received his death-wound from the Prince's hand at such another time.

It almost required force from the friar to tear him away from objects so full of interest, nor did he succeed without a promise that he should see them all some other day. Passing through a long suite of rooms, magnificently furnished, but whose splendour was dimmed and faded by years, they reached an octagonal chamber of small but beautiful proportions; and here the friar was told the youth was to wait, while he himself was admitted to the Prince.

Charles Edward had just dined—and, as was his wont, dined freely—when the Fra was announced. 'You can retire,' said the Prince to the servants in waiting, but never turning his head toward where the friar was standing. The servants retreated noiselessly, aud all was now still in the chamber. The Prince had drawn his chair toward the fire, and sat gazing at the burning logs in deep reverie. Apparently he followed his thoughts so far as to forget that the poor friar was yet in waiting; for it was only as a low, faint sigh escaped him that the Prince suddenly turning his head, cried out, 'Ah! our Frate. I had half forgotten you. You are somewhat late, are you not?'

In a voice tremulous with fear and deference Fra Luke narrated how they had been delayed by a misadventure in the Piazza, contriving to interweave in his story an apology for the torn dress and ragged habiliments the boy was to appear in. 'He is not in a state to be seen by your Royal Highness at all. If it wasn't that your Royal Highness will think little of the shell where the kernel is sound——'

'And who is to warrant me that, sir?' said the Prince angrily. 'Is it your guarantee I'm to take for it?'

The poor friar almost felt as if he were about to faint at the stern speech, nor did he dare to utter a word of reply. So far, this was in his favour, since, when unprovoked by anything like rejoinder, Charles Edward was usually disposed to turn from any unpleasant theme, and address his thoughts elsewhere.

'I'm half relenting, my good friar,' said he, in a calmer tone, 'that I should have brought you here on this errand. How am I to burden myself with the care of this boy? I am but a pensioner myself, weighed down already with a mass of followers. So long as hope remained to us we struggled on manfully enough. Present privation was to have had its recompense—at least we thought so.' He stopped suddenly, and then, as if ashamed of speaking thus confidentially to one he had seen only once before, his voice assumed a harsher, sterner accent as he said : ' These are not your concerns. What is it you propose I should do ? Have you a plan ? What is it ? '

Had Fra Luke been required to project another scheme of invasion, he could not have been more dumbfounded and confused, and he stood the very picture of hopeless incapacity.

Charles Edward's temper was in that state when he invariably sought to turn upon others the reproaches his own conscience addressed to him, and he angrily said : ' It is by this same train of beggarly followers that my fortunes are rendered irretrievable. I am worried and harassed by their importunities ; they attach the plague-spot of their poverty to me wherever I go. I should have freed myself from this thraldom many a year ago ; and if I had, where and what might I not have been to-day ? You, and others of your stamp, look upon me as an almoner, not more nor less.' His passion had now spent itself, and he sat moodily gazing at the fire.

' Is the lad here ? ' asked he, after a long pause.

' Yes, your Royal Highness,' said the friar, while he made a motion toward the door.

Charles Edward stopped him quickly as he said, ' No matter, there is not any need that I should see him. He and his aunt—she is his aunt, you said—must return to Ireland ; this is no place for them. I will see Kelly about it to-morrow, and they shall have something to pay their journey. This arrangement does not please you, Frate, eh ? Speak out, man. You think it cold, unnatural, and unkind —is it not so ? '

' If your gracious Highness would just condescend to say a word to him—one word, that he might carry away in his heart for the rest of his days.'

' Better have no memory of me,' sighed the Prince drearily.

' Oh, don't say so, your Royal Highness ; think what pride

it will be to him yet, God knows in what far-away country, to remember that he saw you once, that he stood in your presence, and heard you speak to him.'

'It shall be as you wish, Frate; but I charge you once more to be sure that he may not know with whom he is speaking.'

'By this holy Book,' said the Fra, with a gesture implying a vow of secrecy.

'Go now; send him hither, and wait without till I send for you.'

The door had scarcely closed behind the friar when it opened again to admit the entrance of the youth. The Prince turned his head, and, whether it was the extreme poverty of the lad's appearance, more striking from the ragged and torn condition of his dress, or that something in Gerald's air and look impressed him painfully, he passed his hand across his eyes and averted his glance from him.

'Come forward, my boy,' said he at last. 'How are you called?'

'Gerald Fitzgerald, Signor Conte,' said he, firmly but respectfully.

'You are Irish by birth?' said the Prince, in a voice slightly tremulous.

'Yes, Signor Conte,' replied he, while he drew himself up with an air that almost savoured of haughtiness.

'And your friends have destined you for the priesthood, it seems.'

'I never knew I had friends,' said the boy; 'I thought myself a sort of castaway.'

'Why, you have just told me of your Irish blood—how knew you of that?'

'So long as I can remember I have heard that I was a Geraldine, and they call me Irish in the college.'

There was a frank boldness in his manner, totally removed from the slightest trace of rudeness or presumption, that already interested the Prince, who now gazed long and steadily on him.

'Do I remind you of any one you ever saw or cared for, Signor Conte?' asked the boy, with an accent of touching gentleness.

'That you do, child,' said he, laying his hand on the youth's shoulder, while he passed the other across his eyes.

'I hope it was of none who ever gave you sorrow,' said the boy, who saw the quivering motion of the lip that indicates deep grief.

Charles Edward now removed his hand, and turned away his head for some seconds.

At last he arose suddenly from his chair, and with an effort that seemed to show he was struggling for the mastery over his own emotions, said, 'Is it your own choice to be a priest, Gerald?'

'No; far from it. I'd rather be a herd on the Campagna! You surely know little of the life of the convent, Signor Conte, or you had not asked me that question.'

Far from taking offence at the boy's boldness, the Prince smiled good-naturedly at the energy of his reply.

'Is it the stillness, the seclusion that you dislike?' asked he, evidently wanting the youth to speak of himself and of his temperament.

'No, it is not that,' said Gerald thoughtfully. 'The quiet, peaceful hours, when we are left to what they call meditation, are the best of it. Then one is free to range where he will, in fancy. I've had as many adventures, thus, as any fortune-seeker of the Arabian Nights. What lands have I not visited! what bold things have I not achieved! ay, and day after day, taken up the same dream where I had left it last, carrying on its fortunes, till the actual work of life seemed the illusion, and this, the dream-world, the true one.'

'So that, after all, this same existence has its pleasures, Gerald?'

'The pleasures are in forgetting it! ignoring that your whole life is a falsehood! They make me kneel at confession to tell my thoughts, while well I know that, for the

D

least blamable of them, I shall be scourged. They oblige me to say that I hate everything that gives a charm to life, and cherish as blessings all that can darken and sadden it. Well, I swear the lie, and they are satisfied! And why are they satisfied?—because out of this corrupt heart, debased by years of treachery and falsehood, they have created the being that they want to serve them.'

'What has led you to think thus hardly of the priesthood?'

'One of themselves, Signor Conte. He told me all that I have repeated to you now, and he counselled me, if I had a friend—one friend on earth—to beseech him to rescue me ere it was too late, ere I was like him.'

'And he—what became of him?'

'He died, as all die who offend the Order, of a wasting fever. His hair was white as snow, though he was under thirty, and his coffin was light as a child's. Look here, Signor Conte,' cried he, as a smile of half incredulity, half pity, curled the Prince's lip, 'look here. You are a great man and a rich: you never knew what it was in life to suffer any, the commonest of those privations poor men pass their days in——'

'Who can dare to say that of me?' cried Charles Edward passionately. 'There's not a toil I have not tasted, there's not a peril I have not braved, there's not a sorrow nor a suffering that have not been my portion; ay, and, God wot, with a heavier stake upon the board than ever man played for!'

'Forgive me, Signor Conte,' stammered out the boy, as his eyes filled up at the sight of the emotion he had caused, 'I knew not what I was saying.'

The Prince took little heed of the words, for his aroused thoughts bore him sadly to the mist-clad mountain and the heathery gorges far away; and he strode the room in deep emotion. At last his glance fell upon the youth as, pale and terror-stricken, he stood watching him, and he quickly said: 'I'm not angry with you, Gerald; do not grieve, my poor boy. You will learn, one of these days, that sorrow has its place at fine tables, just as at humbler boards. It helps the rich man to don his robe of purple, just as it aids the beggar to put on his rags. It's a stern conscription that calls on all to serve. But to yourself: you will not be a priest, you say? What, then, would you like—what say you to the life of a soldier?'

'But in what service, Signor Conte?'

''That of your own country, I suppose.'

'They tell me that the king is a usurper, who has no right to be king; and shall I swear faith and loyalty to him?'

'Others have done so, and are doing it every day, boy. It was but yesterday, Lord Blantyre made what they call his submission; and he was the bosom friend of—the Pretender'; and the last words were uttered in a half-scornful laugh.

'I will not hear him called by that name, Signor Conte. So long as I remember anything, I was taught not to endure it.'

'Was that your mother's teaching, Gerald?' said the Prince tenderly.

'It was, sir. I was a very little child; but I can never forget the last prayer I made each night before bed: it was for God's protection to the true Prince; and when I arose I was to say, "Confusion to all who call him the Pretender!"'

'He is not even *that* now,' muttered Charles Edward, as he leaned his head on the mantelpiece.

'I hope, Signor Conte,' said the boy timidly, 'that you never were for the Elector.'

'I have done little for the cause of the Stuarts,' said Charles, with a deep sigh.

'I wish I may live to serve them,' cried the youth, with energy.

The Prince looked long and steadfastly at the boy, and, in a tone that bespoke deep thought, said:

'I want to befriend you, Gerald, if I but knew how. It is clear you have no vocation for the church, and we are here in a land where there is little other career. Were we in

France something might be done. I have some friends, however, in that country, and I will see about communicating with them. Send the Frate hither.'

The boy left the room, and speedily returned with Fra Luke, whose anxious glances were turned from the Prince to the youth, in eager curiosity to learn how their interview had gone off.

'Gerald has no ambition to be a monsignore, Frate,' said the Prince laughingly, 'and we mustn't constrain him. They who serve the church should have their hearts in the calling. Do you know of any honest family with whom he might be domesticated for a short time—not in Rome, of course, but in the country; it will only be for a month or two at farthest?'

'There is a worthy family at Orvieto, if it were not too far——'

'Nothing of the kind; Orvieto will suit admirably. Who are these people?'

'The father is the steward of Cardinal Caraffa; but it is a villa that his eminence never visits, and so they live there as in their own palace; and the mountain air is so wholesome there, sick people used to seek the place; and so Tonino, as they call him, takes a boarder, or even two——'

'That is everything we want,' said the Prince, cutting short what he feared might be a long history. 'Let the boy go back now to the college, and do you yourself come here on Saturday morning, and Kelly will arrange all with you.'

'I wish I knew why you are so good to me, Signor Conte,' said the boy, as his eyes filled up with tears.

'I was a friend of your family, Gerald,' said Charles, as he fixed his eyes on the friar, to enforce his former caution.

'And am I never to see you again, signor?' cried he eagerly.

'Yes, to be sure, you shall come here; but I will settle all that another time—on Saturday, Fra; and now, good-bye.'

The boy grasped the hand with which the Prince waved his farewell, and kissed it rapturously; and Charles, overcome at length by feelings he had repressed till then, threw his arms around the boy's neck, and pressed him to his bosom.

Fra Luke, terrified how such a moment might end, hurried the youth from the room, and retired.

CHAPTER VII

THE VILLA AT ORVIETO

IF the villa life of Italy might prove a severe trial of temper and spirits to most persons, to young Gerald, trained in all the asceticism of a convent, it was a perfect paradise. The wild and far-spreading landscape imparted a glorious sense of liberty, which grew with each day's enjoyment of it. It was a land of mountain and forest—those deep, dark woods of chestnut-trees traversed with the clear and rapid rivulets so common in the Roman States, with here and there, at rare intervals, the solitary hut of a charcoal-burner. In these vast solitudes, silent as the great savannahs of the South, he passed his days—now roaming in search of game, now dreamily lying, book in hand, beside a river's bank, or strolling list-lessly along, tasting, in the very waywardness of an untram-melled will, an ecstasy only known to those who have felt captivity.

Though there were several young people in the family of the Intendente, Gerald had no companionship with any of them: the boys were boorish, uneducated, and coarse-minded, and the girls, with one exception, were little better. Ninetta, it is true, was gentler; her voice was soft, and her silky hair and soft, dark eyes had a strange, subduing influence about them; but even she was far from that ideal his imagination had pictured, nor could he, by all his persuasions, induce her to share his raptures for Ariosto, or the still more passionate delight that Petrarch gave him. He was just opening that period of youth when the heart yearns for some object of affection—some centre around which its own hopes and fears, its wishes and aspirations, may revolve. It is wonderful how much imagination contributes in such cases, supplying graces and attractions where nature has been a niggard, and giving to the veriest commonplace character traits of distinctive charm.

Ninetta was quite pretty enough for all this, but she was no more. Without a particle of education, she had never raised her mind beyond the commonest daily cares; and what with the vines, the olives, the chestnuts, the festivals of the church, and little family gatherings, her life had its sphere of duties so full as to leave no time for the love-sick wanderings of an idle boy.

If she was disposed to admire him when, in fits of wild energy, he would pass nights and days in chase of the wild boar, or follow the track of a wolf, with the steadfast tenacity of a hound, she cared little for his intervals of dreamy fancy, nor lent any sympathy to joys or sorrows which had no basis in reality; and when her indifference had gone so far as to offend him, she would gently smile and say, 'Never mind, Gerald; the Contessina will come one of these days, and she'll be charmed with all these "moonings."' Whether piqued by the tone of this commiseration, or careless as to its meaning, he never thought of asking who the Contessina might be, until one morning a showily-dressed courier arrived at the villa to announce that, ere the end of the week, the Cardinal's niece and her governante were to arrive, and remain for, probably, several weeks there.

It was two years since her last visit, and great was the commotion to prepare a suitable reception for her. Saloons that had been carefully closed till now were immediately opened, and all the costly furniture uncovered. Within doors and without the work of preparation went briskly on. Troops of labourers were employed in the grounds and the gardens. Fresh parterres of flowers were planted beneath the windows; fountains long dried up were taught to play, and jets of many a fantastic kind threw their sportive showers on the grass.

Gerald took immense interest in all these details, to which his natural taste imparted many a happy suggestion. By his advice the statues were arranged in suitable spots, and a hundred little devices of ingenuity came from his quick intelligence. 'The Contessina will be delighted with this! How she will love that!' were exclamations that rewarded him for every fresh exertion; and, doubtless, he had fashioned to his own heart a Contessina, for he never asked a question, nor made one single inquiry about her, the real one. As little was he prepared for the great *cortège* which preceded her coming—troops of servants, saddle-horses, fourgons of luggage, even furniture kept pouring in, until the villa, so tranquil and deserted in its appearance, became like some vast and popular hotel. There was something almost regal in the state and preparation that went forward; and when, at the close of a long summer day, two mounted couriers dashed up to the door, all heated and dust-covered, quickly followed by two heavy coaches with scarlet panels, Gerald's curiosity at length got the upper hand, and he stole to a window to watch the descent of her for whom all these cares had been provided. What was his astonishment to see a little girl, apparently younger than himself, spring lightly to the ground, and, after a brief gesture of acknowledgment to the welcome tendered her, pass into the house. He had seen enough, however, to remark that her long and beautiful hair was almost golden in tint, and that her eyes, whatever their colour, were large and lustrous. He would have dwelt with more pleasure on her beauty had he not marked, in the haughty gestures she vouchsafed and the proud carriage of her head, a bearing he, not unfairly, ascribed to a character imperious and exacting—almost insolent, indeed, in its requirement of respect.

Guglia Ridolfi was, however, the greatest heiress in the Roman States: she was the niece of a cardinal, the granddaughter of a grandee of Spain, and, more than all, had been taught to reflect on these facts from the earliest years of her girlhood. It had been for years the policy of the Cardinal to increase the *prestige* of her position by every means in his power; and they who knew the ambitious nature of the man could easily see how, in the great game he played, his own future aggrandisement was as much included as was her elevation. Left without a father or mother when a mere infant, she had been confided to the care of her uncle. Surrounded with teachers of every kind, she only learned what and when she pleased, her education being, in fact, the result of certain impulses which swayed her from time to time. As she was gifted with great quickness, however, and a remarkable memory, she seemed to make the most astonishing progress, and her fame as a linguist and her reputation for accomplishments were the talk of Rome.

She had all the waywardness, caprice, and instability such a discipline might be supposed to produce, and so completely sated with amusement and pleasure was she that now, as a mere child, or little more, she actually pined away from sheer *ennui* of life. A momentary change of place afforded her a slight passing satisfaction, and so she had come down to Orvieto to stay some time, and persuade herself, if she could, that she enjoyed it. Strangely enough, nothing in either her general appearance or her gestures betrayed this weariness of the world : her eyes were bright, her look animated, her step active. It was only when watching her closely that one could see how estranged her thoughts were from what seemed to fill them ; and how, at times, a low, faint sigh would escape her, even when she was apparently occupied and interested.

It was rumoured that these very traits of her disposition were what had attached her uncle so fondly to her, and that he recognised in them the indications of a blood and a race which had always made their way in life, subjecting others to their rule, and using them as mere tools for their own advancement. One thing was certain : he curbed her in nothing; every wild weed of her heart grew up in all its own luxuriance, and she was the ideal of imperiousness and self-will.

Either from caprice or settled purpose—it were hard to say which—the Cardinal affected to submit his own plans to her, and he consulted her about many things which were clearly beyond the sphere of either her years or her knowledge, but to which her replies gave him the sort of guidance that gamblers are wont to accept for the accidents of play; and often and often had 'Da Guglia's' counsels decided him when his mind was wavering between two resolves. Whether from perceiving the ascendency she thus obtained over her uncle's mind, or that really, to her pleasure-sick heart, these sterner themes gave her a gleam of interest, but gradually she turned her thoughts to the great events of the day, and listened with eagerness only to subjects of State craft and intrigue.

Such was she to whose morning levee Gerald was summoned on the day after her arrival, when, in a sort of vassalage, the Intendente, followed by his family and the villagers, were admitted to pay their homage. It was not without a certain compulsion Gerald yielded to this customary act of deference; nor was his compliance more gracefully accorded when he learned that he was supposed to be a member of the steward's family, as, if he were known to be a stranger, it was almost certain the Contessina would not suffer him to remain there.

It solved much of his difficulty to be told that in all likelihood she would never notice nor remark him. She rarely did more than listen to the few words of routine gratulation the Intendente spoke, and with a slight nod of her head intimate that they might retire. 'Then, why am I needed at all? Why can't this ceremony go on without me?' cried he half peevishly.

'Because, if she were afterwards to see you about the grounds, she is quite capable of remembering that you had not presented yourself on her arrival. She forgets nothing.'

'That's true,' broke in the Intendente. 'It was but the last time she came here she remarked that the lace border of my hat was torn, and said to me, "Signor Maurizio, you must have lazy daughters, for I saw that piece of gold braid torn, as it is now, on the last two visits I made here."'

Gerald turned away in ill-humour, for he was vexed that any act of servitude should be required of him.

There is a strange mystery in that atmosphere of deference which arises from the united submission of many to one whom they would honour and reverence. The most stubborn asserter of equality has not failed to own this, as he has stood among the crowd before a throne. The sentiment of homage is quickly contagious, and few there are who can steel their hearts against the feelings of that homage which fills every breast about him. Gerald experienced this as he found himself moving slowly along in the procession toward the chamber where the Contessina held her court. The splendid suite of rooms, filled with objects of art, the massive candelabra of gilded bronze, the costly tables of malachite and agate, all obtained their full share of admiration from the simple villagers, whose whispered words almost savoured of worship, until, awe-stricken, they found themselves in a magnificent chamber, hung with pictures from floor to ceiling. In a deep window recess, from which a vast view opened over mountain and forest, the Contessina was standing, book in hand, gazing listlessly on the landscape, and never noticing in the slightest that dense throng which now gathered in the lower part of the room.

'Maurizio and the peasants have come to pay their duty,' whispered a thin, elderly lady, who acted as governante to the young countess.

'Well, be it so,' said she languidly. And now a very meanly-clad priest, poor and wretched in appearance, came crouchingly forward to kiss her hand. She gave it with averted head, and in a way that indicated little of courtesy, while he bent tremblingly over it, as beseemed one whose lips touched the fingers of a great cardinal's niece. Maurizio followed, and then the other members of his household. When it came to Gerald's turn to advance, 'You must, you must; it is your duty,' whispered the steward, as, rebel-like, the youth wished to pass on without the act of deference.

'Is this Tonino?' asked the Contessina, suddenly turning her head, for her quick ears had caught the words of remonstrance. 'Is this Tonino?'

'No, Eccelenza; Tonino was drawn in the conscription,' muttered the steward, in confusion. 'He knew your Excellency would have got him off, if you were here, but——'

'Which is this, then—your second son, or your third?'

'Neither, Eccelenza, neither; he is a sort of connection——'

'Nothing of the kind,' broke in Gerald. 'I'm of the blood of the Geraldines.'

'Native princes,' said the Contessina quickly. 'Irish, too! How came you here?'

'He has been living with us, Eccelenza, for some months back,' chimed in the steward; 'an honest Frate, one——'

'Let himself answer me,' said the Contessina.

'They took me from the Jesuit college and placed me here,' said the boy.

'Who do you mean by they?' asked she.

'The Frate, and the Count; perhaps, indeed, I owe the change more to him.'

'What is his name?'

'I never heard it. I only saw him once, and then for a short time.'

'How old are you?'

'I think, fifteen.'

'Indeed. I should have thought you younger than I am,' said she, half musingly.

'Oh, no; I look much, much older,' said Gerald, as he gazed at her bright and beautiful features.

'Don Cesare,' said she, turning to a pale old man beside her, 'you must write to the rector of the college, and let us learn about this boy—how he came there, and why he left. And so,' said she, addressing Gerald, 'you think it beneath your quality to kiss a lady's hand?'

'No, no!' cried he rapturously, as he knelt down and pressed her hand to his lips.

'It is not so you should do it, boy,' broke in the governante. 'Yours has been ill training, wherever you have got it.'

'Alas! I have had little or none,' said Gerald sorrowfully.

'Pass on, boy; move on,' said the governante, and Gerald's

head drooped as his heavy footsteps stole along. He never dared to look up as he went. Had he done so, what a thrill might his heart have felt to know that the Contessina's eyes had followed him to the very door.

'There, you have done for me and yourself too, with your stupid pride about your blood,' cried the Intendente, when they gained the courtyard. 'The next thing will be an order to send me to Rome, to explain why I have taken you to live here.'

'Well, I suppose you can give your reasons for it,' said Gerald gravely.

'Except that it was my evil fortune, I know of none other,' broke out the other angrily, and turned away. From each, in turn, of the family did he meet with some words of sarcasm and reproof; and though Ninetta said nothing, her tearful eyes and sorrow-stricken features were the hardest of all the reproaches he endured.

'What am I, that I should bring shame and sorrow to those who befriend me!' cried he, as with an almost bursting heart he threw himself upon his bed, and sobbed there till he fell asleep. When the first gleam of sunlight broke upon him he awoke, and as suddenly remembered all his griefs of the day before, and he sat down upon his bed to think over what he should do.

'If I could but find out the Conte at Rome, or even the Fra Luke,' thought he; but alas! he had no clue to either. 'I know it; I have it,' exclaimed he at last. 'There is a life which I can live without fearing reproach from those about me. I'll go and be a charcoal-burner in the Maremma. The Carbonari will not refuse to have me, and I'll set out for the forest at once.'

When Gerald had uttered this resolve it was in the bitterness of despair that he spoke, since of all the varied modes by which men earned a livelihood, none was in such universal disrepute as that of a charcoal-burner; and when the humblest creature of the streets said 'I'd as soon be a charcoal-burner,' he expressed the direst aspect of his misery.

It was not, indeed, that either the life or the labour had anything degrading in itself, but, generally, they who followed it were outcasts and vagabonds—the irreclaimable sweepings of towns, or the incorrigible youth of country districts, who sought in the wild and wandering existence a freedom from all ties of civilisation; the life of the forest in all its savagery, but in all its independence. The chief resort of these men was a certain district in those low-lying lands along the coast, called Maremmas, and where, from the undrained character of the soil and rapid decomposition of vegetable matter ever going on, disease of the most deadly form existed—ague and fever being the daily condition of all who dwelt there. Nothing but habits of wildest excess, and an utter indifference to life, could make men brave such an existence; but their recompense was, that this district was a species of sanctuary where the law never entered. Beyond certain well-known limits the hardiest carbineer never crossed; and it was well known that he who crossed that frontier came as fugitive, and not as foe. Many, it is true, of those who sojourned here were attainted with the deepest crimes—men for whom no hope of return to the world remained, outcasts branded with undying infamy; but others there were, mere victims of dissipation and folly—rash youths, who had so irretrievably compromised their fair fame that they had nothing left but to seek oblivion.

The terrible stories Gerald had heard of these outcasts from his school-fellows, the horror in which they were held by all honest villagers, inspired him with a strange interest to see them with his own eyes. It savoured, too, of courage; it smacked, to his heart, like bravery, to throw himself among such reckless and daredevil associates, and he felt a sort of hero to himself when he had determined on it. 'Ay,' said he, 'they have been taunting me here for some time back, that my friends take little trouble about me—that they half forget me, and so on. Let us see if I cannot make a path for myself, and spare them all future trouble.'

CHAPTER VIII

THE TANA IN THE MAREMMA

SIMPLY turning his steps westward, in the direction where he knew the Maremma lay, Gerald set out on his lonely journey. It was nothing new in his habits to be absent the entire day, and even night, so that no attention was drawn to his departure till late the following day; nor, perhaps, would it have been noticed then, if a summons had not come from the Contessina that she desired to speak with him. A search was at once made, inquiries instituted on every side, and soon the startling fact acknowledged, that he had gone away, none knew whither or why.

The Contessina at once ordered a pursuit; he was to be overtaken and brought back. Mounted couriers set off on every side, scouring the high-roads, interrogating hotel-keepers, giving descriptions of the fugitive at passport stations —taking, in short, all the palpable and evident means of discovery; while he—for whose benefit this solicitude was intended—was already deep among the dreary valleys to the west of the Lake of Bolseno. The country through which he journeyed was, indeed, sad-coloured as his own thoughts. Hills, not large enough to be called mountains, succeeded each other in unbroken succession, their sides covered with a poor and burned-up herbage, interspersed with masses of rock or long patches of shingle; no wood, no cultivation on any side. A few starved and wretched sheep, watched by one even more wretched still, were all that represented life; while in the valleys, a stray hut or two, generally on the borders of a swampy lake, offered the only thing in the shape of a village. After he had crossed the great post-road from Sienna to Rome, Gerald entered a tract of almost perfect desolation.

He bought two loaves of rye-bread and some apples at a

small house on the road, and with this humble provision slung in a handkerchief at his side, set out once more. At first it was rather a relief to him to be utterly alone; his own thoughts were his best companions, and he would have shrunk from the questionings his appearance was certain to elicit; but as the time wore on, and the noon of the second day was passed, he felt the dreariness of the solitude creeping over him, and would gladly have met with one with whom he could have interchanged even a few words of greeting. Not a human trace, however, was now to be seen; for he had gained that low-lying district which, stretching beneath the mountain of Bolseno, extends, in patches of alternate lake and land, to the verge of the Maremma. This tract is not even a sheep-walk, and although in mid-winter the sportsman may venture in pursuit of the wild duck or the mallard, the pestilential atmosphere produced by summer heat makes the spot a desert. Gerald was not long a stranger to the sickly influences of the place: a strange sense of dizziness would now and then come over him—something less than sickness, but usually leaving him confused and half stunned; great weariness, too, beset him; a desire to lie down and sleep, so strong as almost to be irresistible, seized him, but a dread of wild beasts—not unfrequent in these places—enabled him to conquer this tendency. The sun bore down with all its noonday force upon him, while an offensive odour from the stagnant waters oppressed him almost to choking.

He walked on, however, on and on, but almost like one in a dream. Thoughts of the past superseded all sensations of the present in his mind, and he fancied he was back once more in the old college of the Jesuit fathers. He heard the bell that summoned him to the schoolroom, and he hastened to put himself in his place, marching with crossed arms and bent-down head, in accustomed fashion. Then he heard his name called aloud, and one of the fathers told him to stand aside, for he was 'up' for punishment; and Fra Luke was there, wishing to speak to him, but not admitted; and then —how, he knew not—but he was gazing on grizzly bears and white-tusked boars, in great cages; and there they stood spell-bound and savage, but unable to spring out, though it was but glass confined them; and through all these scenes the wild strains of the tarantella sounded, and the light gestures and wistful looks of Marietta, whose hair, however, was no longer dark, but golden and bright, like the Contessina's. And as suddenly all changed, and there stood the Contessina herself, with one hand pressed to her eyes, and she was weeping, and Gerald felt—but how he did not know —he had offended her; and he trembled at his fault and hated himself, and, stooping down, he fell at last at her feet, and sobbed for pardon.

And there he lay, and there night found him sleeping— the long sleep that awakes to fever. Damp mists arose, charged with all the deadly vapours of the spot; foul airs steamed from the hot earth, to mingle with his blood, and thicken and corrupt it. Though the sky was freckled with stars, their light was dimmed by the dull atmosphere that prevailed, for the place was pestilential and deadly.

When day broke racking pains tortured him in every limb, and his head felt as though splitting with every throb of its arteries. A dreadful thirst, almost maddening in its craving, was on him, and though a rivulet rippled close by, he could not crawl to it; and now the hot sun beamed down upon him, and the piercing rays darted into his brain, penetrating it in all directions—sending wild fancies, horrible and ghastly visions, through his mind. And combats with wild beasts, and wounds, and suffering, and long days of agony and suspense, all came pouring in upon him, as vial after vial of misery bathed his poor, distracted intellect.

Three days of this half-conscious state—like so many long years of suffering they were—and then he sank into the low torpor that forms the last stage of the fever. It was thus, insensible and dying, a traveller found him, as the third evening was falling. The stranger stooped down to examine the almost lifeless figure, and it was long before he could convince himself that vitality yet lingered there: from the dried and livid lips no breath seemed to issue; the limbs fell heavily to either side as they were moved; and it was only after a most careful examination that he could detect a faint fluttering motion of the heart.

Whether it was that the case presented so little of hope, or that he was one not much given to movements of charity, but the traveller, after all these investigations, turned again to pursue his path. He had not gone far, however, when, gaining the rise of a hill, he cast his eyes back over the dreary landscape, and again they fell upon that small mound of human clay beside the lake. Moved by an impulse that, even to himself, was unaccountable, he returned to the spot and stood for some minutes contemplating Gerald. It might be that in the growing shades of the evening the gloomy desolation spoke more touchingly to his heart; it might be that a feeling of compassionate pity stirred him; as likely as either was it a mere caprice, as, stooping down, he raised the wasted form, and threw it loosely over one shoulder, and then strode out upon his way once more.

The stranger was a man of great size and personal strength, and though heavily framed, possessed considerable activity. His burden seemed little to impede his movements, and almost as little to engage his thoughts, and as he breasted the wild mountain, or waded the many streams that crossed his path, he went along without appearing to think more of him he was rescuing. It was a long road, too, and it was deep into the night ere he reached a solitary house, in a little slip of land between two lakes, and over whose door a withered bough denoted a cabaret.

'What, in the name of all the saints, have you brought us here?' said an old man who quickly responded to his knock at the door.

'I found him as you see beside the Lagoscuro,' said the other, laying down his burden. 'How he came there I can't tell you, and I don't suspect you'll ever get the report from himself.'

'He's not a contadino,' said the old man, as he examined

E

the boy's features, and then gazed upon the palms of his hands.

'No; nor is he a Roman, I take it: he's of German or English blood. That fair skin and blonde hair came from the north.'

'One of the Cavalrista, belike!'

'Just as likely one of the circus people; but why they should leave him there to die seems strange, except that strangers deem this Maremma fever a sort of plague, and, perhaps, when he was struck down they only thought of saving themselves from the contagion.'

'That wouldn't be human, Master Gabriel——'

'Wouldn't it, though!' cried Gerald's rescuer, with a bitter laugh. 'That's exactly the name for it, caro Pippo. It is the beasts of prey—the tiger and lion—that defend their young; it is the mild rabbit and the tender woman that destroy theirs.'

The innkeeper shook his head, as though the controversy were too subtle for him, and, bending down to examine the boy more closely, 'What's this, Master Gabriel?' said he, taking a peculiar medal that hung suspended round his neck.

'He was a colleger of some sort certainly,' cried Gabriel. 'It's clear, therefore, he wasn't, as we suspected, one of the Cavalrista. I'll tell you, Pippo; I have it: this lad has made his escape from some of the seminaries at Rome, and in his wanderings has been struck down by the fever. The worthy Frati have, ere this, told his parents that he died in all the hopes of the church, and is an angel already——'

'There, there,' interposed Pippo rebukingly; 'no luck ever came of mocking a priest. Let's try if we can do anything for the lad. Tina will be up presently, and look to him'; and with this he spread out some leaves beside the wall, and covering them with a cloak, laid the sick boy gently on them.

'There, see; his lips are moving — he has swallowed some of the water—he'll get about—I'll swear to it!' cried the other. 'A fellow that begins life in that fashion has always his mission for after years. At all events, Pippo, don't disturb me for the next twelve hours, for I mean to sleep so long ; and let me tell you, too, I have taken my last journey to Bon Convento. The letters may lie in the post-office till doomsday, ere I go in seach of them.'

' Well, well, have your sleep out, and then——'

' And then ? ' cried Gabriel, turning suddenly round, as he was about to quit the room. 'I wish to Heaven you could tell me, what then !'

Old Pippo shook his head mournfully, heaved a heavy sigh, and turned away.

Tina, a peasant girl, pale and sickly, but with that energy of soul that belongs to the Roman race, soon made her appearance, and at once addressed herself to nurse the sick boy. ' I ought to know this Maremma fever well,' said she, with a faint sigh ; 'it struck me down when a child, and has never left my blood since.' Making a polenta with some strong red wine, she gave him a spoonful from time to time, and by covering him up warmly induced perspiration, the first crisis of the disease. ' There,' cried she, after some hours of assiduous care ; 'there, he is safe ; and God knows if he 'll bless me for this night's work after all ! It is a sad, dreary life, even to the luckiest !'

While Gerald lay thus—and it was his fate in this fashion to pass some six long weeks, ere he had strength to sit up or move about the house—let us say a few words of those to whose kindness he owed his life. Old Pippo Baldi had kept the little inn of Borghetto all his life. It was his father's and grandfather's before him. Situated in this dreary, un-wholesome tract, with a mere mountain bridle-path—not a road—leading to it, there seemed no reason why a house of entertainment—even the humblest—could be wanted in such a spot ; and, indeed, the lack of all comfort and accommodation bespoke how little trade it drove. The ' Tana,' however, as it was called, had a brisk business in the long dark nights of winter, since it was here that the smugglers from the Tuscan frontier resorted, to dispose of their wares to the up-country dealers ; and bargains for many a thousand scudi went on in that dreary old kitchen, while bands of armed contrabandieri scoured the country. To keep off the Pope's carbineers—in case that redoubtable corps could persuade themselves to adventure so far—the Maremma fever, a malady that few ever eradicated from their constitution, was the best protection the smugglers possessed; and the Tana was thus a sanctuary as safe as the rocky islands that lay off St. Stephano. A disputed question of boundary also added to the safety of the spot, and continual litigation went on between the courts of Florence and Rome as to which the territory belonged—contests the scandal-mongering world implied might long since have been terminated, had not the cardinal-secretary Manini been suspected of being in secret league with the smugglers. The Tana was, therefore, a sort of refuge; and more than one, gravely compromised by crime, had sought out that humble hostel, as his last place of security. To the refugee from the north of Italy it was easily available, lying only a few miles beyond the Tuscan frontier, while it was no less open to those who gained any port of the shore near St. Stephano.

In a wild and melancholy waste, with two dark and motionless lakes girt in by low mountains, the Tana stood, the very ideal of desolation. The strip of land on which it was built was little wider than a mere bridge between the lakes, and had evidently been selected as a position capable of defence against the assault of a strong force, and two rude breastworks of stone yet bore witness that a military eye had scanned the place, and improved its advantages. Within, a stray loop-hole for musketry still showed that defence had occupied the spirits of those who held it, while a low, flat-bottomed boat, moored at a stake before the door, provided for escape in the last extremity. The great curiosity of the place, however, was a kind of large hall or chamber, where the smugglers transacted business with their customers, and the walls of which had been decorated with huge frescoes, in charcoal, by no less a hand than Franzoni himself, whose fate it had once been to pass months here. Taking for his subjects the lives of the various refugees who had sojourned

in the Tana, he had illustrated them in a series of bold
and vigorous sketches, and assuredly every breach of the
Decalogue had here its portraiture, with some accompanying
legend beneath to show in whose honour the picture had
been painted. Pippo, who had supplied from memory all
the incidents thus communicated, regarded these as perfect
treasures, and was wont to show them with all the pride of
a connoisseur. 'The maestro'—so he ever called Franzoni
—'the maestro,' said he, 'never saw Cimballi, who strangled
the Countess of Soissons, and yet, just from my description,
he has made a likeness his brother would swear to. And
there, look at that fellow asking alms of the Cardinal
Frescobaldi—that's Fornari. He's merely there to see the
cardinal, and he's sure he can recognise him; for he is
engaged to stab him on his way to the Quirinal, the day
of his election for Pope. The little fellow yonder with
the hump is the Piombino, who poisoned his mother. He
was drowned in the lake out there. I don't think it was
quite fair of the maestro to paint him in that fashion'; and
here he would point to a little humped-backed creature
rowing in a boat, with the devil steering, the flashing eyes
of the fiend seeming to feast on the tortures of fear depicted
in the other's face.

Several there were of a humorous kind. Here, a group
of murderous ruffians were kneeling to receive a pontifical
blessing. There, a party of Papal carbineers were in full
flight from the pursuit of a single horseman armed with a
bottle; while, in an excess of profanity that Pippo shuddered
to contemplate, there was a portrait of himself, as a saint,
offering the safeguard of the Tana to all persecuted sinners;
and what an ill-favoured assemblage were they who thus
congregated at his shrine!

Poor Gerald had lain for days gazing on the singular
groupings and strange scenes these walls presented. At
first, to his disordered intellect, they were but shapes of
horror, wild and incongruous. The savage faces that scowled
on him in paint sat, in his dreams, beside his pillow. The

terrible countenances and frantic gestures were carried into his sleeping thoughts, and often did he awake, with a cry of agony, at some fearful scene of crime thus suggested. As his mind acquired strength, however, they became a source of endless amusement. Innumerable stories grew out of them : romances, whose adventures embraced every land and sea; and his excited imagination revelled in inventing trials and miseries for some, while for others he sought out every possible escape from disaster. His solitude had no need of either companionship or books; his mind, stimulated by these sketches, could invent unweariedly, so that, at last, he really lived in an ideal world, peopled with daring adventurers, and abounding in accidents by flood and field.

One day, as Gerald lay musing on his bed of chestnut-leaves, the door of his room was opened quietly, and a large, powerfully-built man entered. He walked with noise-less steps forward, placed a chair in front of Gerald, and sat down. The boy gazed steadfastly at him, and so they remained a considerable time, each staring fixedly at the other. To one who, like Gerald, had passed weeks in weaving histories from the looks and expressions of the faces around him, the features on which he now gazed might well excite interest. Never was there, perhaps, a face in which adverse and conflicting passions were more palpably depicted. A noble and massive head, covered with a profusion of black hair, rose from temples of exquisite symmetry, greatly indented at either side, and forming the walls of two orbits of singular depth. His eyes were large, dark, and lustrous, the expression usually sad. Here, however, ended all that indicated good in the face. The nose was short, with wide expanded nostrils, and the mouth large, coarse, and sensual; but the lower jaw, which was of enor-mous breadth, and projected forward, gave a character of actual ferocity that recalled the image of a wild boar. The whole meaning of the face was power—power and indomit-able will. Whatever he meditated of good or evil, you could easily predict that nothing could divert him from attempting;

and there was in the carriage of his head, all his gestures, and his air, the calm self-possession of one that seemed to say to the world, 'I defy you.'

As Gerald gazed in a sort of fascination at these strange features, he was almost startled by the tone of a voice so utterly unlike what he was prepared for. The stranger spoke in a low, deep strain of exquisite modulation, and with that peculiar mellowness of accent that seems to leave its echo in the heart after it. He had merely asked him how he felt, and then, seeing the difficulty with which the boy replied, he went on to tell how he himself had discovered him on the side of the Lagoscuro at nightfall, and carried him all the way to the Tana. 'The luck was,' said he, 'that *you* happened to be light, and *I* strong.'

'Say, rather, that *you* were kind-hearted and *I* in trouble,' muttered the boy, as his eyes filled up.

'And who knows, boy, but you may be right!' cried he, as though a sudden thought had crossed him; 'your judgment has just as much grounds as that of the great world!' As he spoke, his voice rose out of its tone of former gentleness and swelled into a roll of deep, sonorous meaning; then changing again, he asked—'By what accident was it that you came there?'

Gerald drew a long sigh, as though recalling a sorrowful dream; and then, with many a faltering word, and many an effort to recall events as they occurred, told all that he remembered of his own history.

'A scholar of the Jesuit college; without father or mother; befriended by a great man, whose name he has never heard,' muttered the other to himself. 'No bad start in life for such a world as we have now before us. And your name?'

'Gerald Fitzgerald. I am Irish by birth.'

The stranger seemed to ponder long over these words, and then said: 'The Irish have a nationality of their own—a race—a language—traditions. Why have they suffered themselves to be ruled by England?'

'I suppose they couldn't help it,' said Gerald, half smiling.

'Which of us can say that? who has ever divined where the strength lay till the day of struggle called it forth? Chance, chance—she is the great goddess!'

'I'd be sorry to think so,' said Gerald resolutely.

'Indeed, boy!' cried the other, turning his large, full eyes upon the youth, and staring steadfastly at him; then passing his hand over his brow, he added, in a tone of much feeling: 'And yet it is as I have said. Look at the portraits around us on these walls. There they are, great or infamous, as accident has made them. That fellow yonder, with that noble forehead and generous look, he stabbed the confessor who gave the last rites to his father, just because the priest had heard some tales to his disadvantage; a scrupulous sense of delicacy moved him—there was a woman's name in it—and he preferred a murder to a scandal! There, too, there's Marocchi, who poisoned his mother the day of her second marriage. Ask old Pippo if he ever saw a gentler-hearted creature: he lived here two years, and died of the Maremma fever, that he caught from a peasant whom he was nursing. And there again, that wild-looking fellow with the scarlet cap—he it was who stole the Medici jewels out of the Pitti to give his mistress, and killed himself afterwards when she deserted him. Weigh the good and evil of these men's hearts, boy, and you have subtle weights if you can strike the balance for or against them. We are all but what good or evil fortune makes us, just as a landscape catches its tone from light; and what is glorious in sunshine is bleak and desolate and dreary beneath a leaden sky and lowering atmosphere!'

'I'll not believe it,' said the boy boldly. 'I have read of fellows that never showed the great stuff they were made of until adversity had called it forth. They were truly great!'

'Truly great!' repeated the other, with an intense mockery. 'The truly great we never hear of. They die in workhouses or garrets—poor, dreary optimists, working out of their fine-spun fancies hopeful destinies for those who sneer at them.

The idols men call great are but the types of Force—mere Force. One day it is courage; another, it is money; another day, political craft is the object of worship. Come, boy,' said he, in a lighter vein, 'what have these worthy Jesuits taught you?'

'Very different lessons from yours,' said the youth stoutly. 'They taught me to honour and reverence those set in authority over me.'

'Good; and then——'

'They taught me the principles of my faith; the creed of the Church.'

'What Church?'

'What but the one Church—the Catholic!'

'Why, there are fifty, child, and each with five hundred controversies within it. Popes denying Councils; Councils rejecting Popes; Synods against Bishops; Bishops against Presbyters. What a mockery is it all!' cried he passionately. 'We who, in our imperfect forms of language, have not even names for separate odours, but say, "this smells like the violet," and "that like the rose," presume to talk of eternity and that vast universe around us, as though our paltry vocabulary could compass such themes! But to come back: were you happy there?'

'No; I could not bear the life, nor did I wish to be a priest.'

'What would you be, then?'

'I wish I knew,' said the boy fervently.

'I'm a bad counsellor,' said the other, with a bitter smile; 'I have tried several things, and failed in all.'

'I never could have thought that you could fail,' said Gerald slowly, as in calm composure he gazed on the massive features before him.

'I have done with failure now,' said the other; 'I mean to achieve success next. It is something to have learned a great truth, and this is one, boy—our world is a huge hunting-ground, and it is better to play wolf than lamb. Don't turn your eyes to those walls, as if the fellows depicted there could gainsay me—they were but sorry scoundrels, the bad ones; the best were but weakly good.'

'You do but pain me when you speak thus,' said Gerald; 'you make me think that you are one who, having done some great crime, waits to avenge the penalty he has suffered on the world that inflicted it.'

'What if you were partly right, boy? Not but I would protest against the word crime, or even fault, as applied to me; still you are near enough to make your guess a good one. I have a debt to pay, and I mean to pay it.'

'I wish I had never quitted the college,' said the boy, and the tears rolled heavily down his cheeks.

'It is not too late to retrace your steps. The cell and the scourge—the fathers know the use of both—will soon condone your offence; and when they have sapped the last drop of manhood out of your nature, you will be all the fitter for your calling.'

With these harsh words, uttered in tones as cruel, the stranger left the room; while Gerald, covering his face with both hands, sobbed as though his heart were breaking.

'Ah! Gabriel has been talking to him. I know how it would be,' muttered old Pippo, as he cast a glance within the room. 'Poor child! better for him had he left him to die in the Maremma.'

CHAPTER IX

THE 'COUR' OF THE ALTIERI

A LONG autumn day was drawing to its close in Rome, and gradually here and there might be seen a few figures stealing listlessly along, or seated in melancholy mood before the shop-doors, trying to catch a momentary breath of air ere the hour of sunset should fall. All the great and noble of the capital had left a month before for the sea-side, or for Albano, or the shady valleys above Lucca. You might walk for days and never meet a carriage. It was a city in complete desolation. The grass sprang up between the stones, and troops of seared leaves, carried from the gardens, littered the empty streets. The palaces were barred up and fastened, the massive doors looking as if they had not opened for centuries. In one alone, throughout the entire city, did any signs of habitation linger, and here a single lamp threw its faint light over a wide courtyard, giving a ghost-like air to the vaulted corridors and dim distances around. All was still and silent within the walls; not a light gleamed from a window, not a sound issued. A solitary figure walked with weary footsteps up and down, stopping at times to listen, as if he heard the noise of one approaching, and then resuming his dreary round again.

As night closed in, a second stranger made his appearance, and timidly halting at the porter's lodge, asked leave to enter; but the porter had gone to refresh himself at a neighbouring café, and the visitor passed in of his own accord. He was in a friar's robe, and by his dusty dress and tired look showed that he had had a long journey; indeed, so overcome was he with fatigue that he sat down at once on a stone bench, depositing his heavy bag beside him. The oppressive heat, the fatigue, the silence of the lonesome spot, all combined, composed him to sleep; and poor Fra Luke, for it was he, crossed his arms before him, and snored away manfully.

Astonished by the deep-drawn breathing, the other stranger drew nigh, and, as well as the imperfect light permitted, examined him. He himself was a man of immense stature, and, though bowed and doubled by age, showed the remnant of a powerful frame: his dress was worn and shabby, but in its cut and in the fashion he wore it, bespoke the gentleman. He gazed long and attentively at the sleeping friar, and then approaching, he took up the bag that lay on the bench. It was weighty, and contained money—a considerable sum, too, as the stranger remarked, while he replaced it. The heavy bang of a door at this moment, and the sound of feet, how-

ever, recalled him from this contemplation, and at the same
time a low whistle was heard, and a voice, in a subdued tone,
called out, 'O'Sullivan!'

'Here!' cried the stranger, who was quickly joined by
another.

'I am sorry to have kept you so long, chief,' said the
latter; 'but he detained me, watching me so closely, too,
that I feared to leave the room.'

'And how is he—better?'

'Far from it; he seems to be sinking every hour. His
irritability is intense; eternally asking who have called to
inquire after him—if Boyer had been to ask, if the Cardinal
Caraffa had come. In fact, so eagerly set is his mind on
these things, I have been obliged to make the coachman
drive repeatedly into the courtyard, and by a loud uproar
without convey the notion of a press of visitors.'

'Has he asked after Barra or myself?' said the chieftain,
after a pause.

'Yes; he said twice, "We must have our old followers up
here—to-morrow or the next day." But his mind is scarcely
settled, for he talked of Florence and the duchess, and then
went off about the insult of that arrest in France, which
preys upon him incessantly.'

'And why should it not, Kelly? Was there ever such
baseness as that of Louis? Take my word for it, there's a
heavy day of reckoning to come to that house yet for this
iniquity. It's a sore trouble to me to think it will not be in
my time, but it is not far off.'

'Everything is possible now,' said Kelly. 'Heaven knows
what's in store for any of us! Men are talking in a way I
never heard before. Boyer told me, two days ago, that the
garrison of Paris was to be doubled, and Vincennes placed in
a perfect state of defence.'

A bitter laugh from the old chieftain showed how he
relished these symptoms of terror.

'It will be no laughing matter when it comes,' said Kelly
gravely.

'But who *have* called here? Tell me their names,' said O'Sullivan sternly.

'Not one, not one—stay, I am wrong. The cripple who sells the water-melons at the corner of the Babuino, he has been here; and Giacchino, the strolling actor, comes every morning and says, "Give my duty to his Royal Highness."'

A muttered curse broke from O'Sullivan, and Kelly went on: 'It was on Wednesday last he wished to have a mass in the chapel here, and I went to the Quirinal to say so. They should, of course, have sent a cardinal; but who came?—the Vicar of Santa Maria maggiore. I shut the door in his face, and told him that the highest of his masters might have been proud to come in his stead.'

'They are tired of us all, Kelly,' sighed the chieftain. 'I have walked every day of the eight long years I have passed here in the Vatican gardens, and it was only yesterday a guard stopped me to ask if I were noble?—ay, by Heaven, if I were noble! I gulped down my passion and answered, "I am a gentleman in the service of his Royal Highness of England"; and he said, "That may well be, and yet give you no right to enter here." The old Cardinal Balfi was passing, so I just said to his Eminence, "Give me your arm, for you are my junior by three good years." Ay, and he did it too, and I passed in; but I'll go there no more! no more!' muttered he sadly. 'Insults are hard to bear when one's arm is too feeble to resent them.'

Kelly sighed too; and neither spoke for some seconds. 'What heavy breathings are those I hear?' cried Kelly suddenly; 'some one has overheard us.'

'Have no fear of that,' replied the other; 'it is a stout friar, taking his evening nap, on the stone bench yonder.'

Kelly hastened to the spot, and by the struggling gleam of the lamp could just recognise Fra Luke as he lay sleeping, snoring heavily.

'You know him, then?' asked O'Sullivan.

'That do I: he is a countryman of ours, and as honest a. soul as lives; but yet I'd just as soon not see him here

Fra Luke,' said he, shaking the sleeper's shoulder, 'Fra Luke. By St. Joseph! they must have hard mattresses up there at the convent, or he'd not sleep so soundly here.'

The burly friar at last stirred, and shook himself like some great water-dog, and then turning his eyes on Kelly, gradually recalled where he was. 'Would he see me, Laurence? would he just let me say one word to him?' muttered he in Kelly's ear.

'Impossible, Fra Luke; he is on a bed of sickness. God alone knows if he is ever to rise up from it!'

The Fra bent his head, and for some minutes continued to pray with great fervour, then turning to Kelly, said: 'If it's dying he is, there's no good in disturbing his last moments; but if he was to get well enough to hear it, Laurence, will you promise to let me have two or three minutes beside his bed? Will you, at least, ask him if he'd see Fra Luke? He'll know why himself.'

'My poor fellow,' said Kelly kindly, 'like all the world, you fancy that the things which touch yourself must be nearest to the hearts of others. I don't want to learn your secret, Luke—Heaven knows I have more than I wish for in my keeping already!—but take my word for it, the Prince has cares enough on his mind without your asking him to hear yours.'

'Will you give him this, then?' said the Fra, handing him the bag with the money; 'there's a hundred crowns in it just as he gave it to me, Monday was a fortnight. Tell him that—' here he stopped and wiped his forehead, in confusion of thought; 'tell him that it's not wanting any more for—for what he knows; that it's all over now; not that he's dead, though—God be praised!—but what am I saying? Oh dear! oh dear! after my swearing never to speak of him!'

'You are safe with me, Luke, depend on that. Only, as to the money, take my advice, and just keep it. He'll never want to hear more of it. Many a hundred crowns have left this on a worse errand, whatever be its fate.'

'I wouldn't, to save my life! I wouldn't, if it was to keep me from the galleys!'

'Have your own way, then,' said Kelly sharply; 'I must not loiter here'; and so saying, took the bag from the friar's hand, and moved over toward where O'Sullivan was standing.

'Come along home with me, friar,' said O'Sullivan, as Kelly wished them good-night; 'I'll give you a glass of Vermouth, and we'll have a talk about the old country.'

CHAPTER X

GABRIEL DE ——

'I WISH I knew how I could ever repay you, Pippo, for all your kindness to me,' said Gerald, as he sat one fine evening with the old man at the door; 'but when I tell you that I am as poor and as friendless in the world as on that same night when Signor Gabriel found me beside the lake——'

'Not a whit poorer or more alone in the world than the rest of us,' said Pippo good-naturedly. 'We have all a rough journey before us in life, and the least we can do is to help one another.'

The youth grasped the old man's hand and pressed it to his heart.

'Besides,' continued Pippo, 'all your gratitude is owing to Signor Gabriel himself. Any little comforts you have had here have been of his procuring. He it was fetched that doctor from Bolseno, and his own hands carried the little jar of honey from St. Stephano.'

'What a kind heart he has!' cried Gerald eagerly.

'Well,' said Pippo, with a dry, odd smile, 'that's not exactly what people say of him; not but he can do a kind thing too, just as he can do anything.'

'Is he so clever, then?' asked Gerald curiously.

'Is he not!' exclaimed Pippo; 'where has he not travelled, what has he not seen! And then the books he has written—scores of them, they tell me: he's always writing still—whole nights through; after which, instead of going to his bed like any one else, he is off for a plunge in the lake there, though I've told him over and over, that the water that kills fish can never be healthy for a human being!'

'What a strange nature his must be! And what brings him here?'

'That's *his* secret, and it would be *mine* too, if I knew it; for, I promise you, he's not one it's over safe to talk about.'

'Where does he come from?'

'He's French, and that's all I can tell you.'

'It can't be for the *chasse* he comes here,' said Gerald musingly. 'There's no game in these mountains. It can scarcely be for seclusion, for he's always rambling away to some village or town near. It's now more than a week since we have seen him. I wish I could make out who or what he is!'

'Would you indeed?' cried a deep voice, as a large, heavy hand fell upon his shoulder; 'and what would the knowledge benefit you, boy?' Gerald looked up, and there stood Gabriel. He was dressed in a loose peasant's frock, and seemed by his mien as if he had come off a long day's march.

'Go in, Pippo, and make me a good salad. Grill me that old hen yonder, and I'll give you a share of a flask of Orvieto that was in the bishop's cellar last night.'

He threw off his knapsack as he spoke, and removing his hat, wiped his heated forehead, and then turning to the youth at his side, he said: 'So, boy, I am a sort of mystery to you, it seems—mayhap others share in that same sentiment—at least I have heard as much. But whence this curiosity on your part? You were a stranger to me, and you are so still. What can it signify to either of us what has happened before we met and knew each other? Life is not a river running in one bed, but a series of streams that follow fifty channels—some pure and limpid, some, perchance, turbid and foul enough. What you have been gives no guarantee to what you may be, remember that!'

He spoke with a tone of sternness that made his words sound like reproof, and the youth held down his head abashed.

'Don't suppose I am angry with you,' continued the other, but in the self-same tone as before; 'nor that I regard this curious desire of yours as ingratitude. You owe me nothing, or next to nothing, and you're a rare instance of such in life, if within the next ten years the wish will not occur to you at least twenty times, that I had left you to die beside the dark shores of Bolseno!'

'I can well believe it may be so,' said Gerald with a sigh.

'Not that this is my own philosophy,' said the other, in a voice of powerful meaning. 'I soon made the discovery that life was not a garden, but a hunting-ground, and that the wolves had the best of it! Ay, boy,' cried he, with a kind of savage exultation, 'there's the experience of one whose boast it is to know something of his fellows!'

Gerald was silent, and for some time Gabriel also did not speak. At last, looking steadfastly at the youth, he said: 'I have been up to Rome these last three days. My errand there was to learn something about *you*.'

'About *me*?' said Gerald, blushing deeply.

'Yes. It was a whim—(I am the slave of such caprices)—seized me to learn how you came among the Jesuit brothers, and why you left them.'

'I thought I had told you why myself,' said the youth proudly.

'So you had; but I am one of those who can only build on the foundation their own hands have laid, and so I went myself to learn your history.'

'And has the journey rewarded your exertions?' said the boy, half mockingly.

A sudden start, and a look of almost savage ferocity on Gabriel's features, made Gerald tremble for his own rashness;

F

and then, with a measured voice, he repeated the boy's
words :

'The journey *has* rewarded my exertions.'

'May I venture to ask what you have discovered ? ' said
Gerald timidly.

'I went to satisfy my own curiosity, not yours, boy.
What I have learned may suffice for the one, and not for the
other.　Here comes Pippo with pleasanter tidings than all
this gossip,' said he, rising, and entering the house.

'Won't you come in and have a bit of supper with us,
Gerald ? ' asked Pippo kindly.

'No, I cannot eat,' said the boy, as he wiped the tears
from his eyes.

'Come and taste a glass of the generous Orvieto, however.'

'No, Pippo ; I could not swallow it,' said he, in a half-
choking voice.

'Ah !' muttered the old man with a sigh, 'Signor Gabriel's
talk rarely makes one relish the meal they wait for,' and with
bent-down head he re-entered the house.

The feeling Gerald had long experienced toward Gabriel
was one of fear, almost verging upon terror.　There was
about the man's look, his voice, his manner, something that
portended danger.　Do what he would, the boy never could
make his sense of gratitude rise superior to his fear.　He
tried, over and over again, to think of him only as one who
had saved his life, and to whom he owed all the present
comforts he enjoyed; but above these thoughts there
triumphed a terrible dread of the man, and a strange,
mysterious belief that he possessed a sort of control over his
destiny.

'If it were indeed so,' muttered he to himself, 'and that
his shadow were to be over me through life, I'd curse the
day he carried me from the shore of the Lagoscuro !'

Night was rapidly closing in, and the dreary landscape
was every moment growing sadder and drearier.　As the
sun sank beneath the hills the heavy exhalations began to

well up from the damp earth, till a bluish haze of vapour rested over the plains and even partly up the mountain side. An odour, oppressive and sickening, accompanied this mist, which embarrassed the respiration, and made the senses dull and weary; and yet there sat Gerald, drinking in these noxious influences, careless of his fate, and half triumphing in his own indifference as to life. A drowsy stupor was rapidly gaining on him, when he felt his arm violently shaken, and, looking up, saw Gabriel at his side. In a gruff, rude voice, he chided him for his imprudence, and told him to go in.

'Isn't my life, at least, my own?' said Gerald boldly.

'That it is not,' said the other. 'Your priestly teachers might have told you that you hold it in trust for Him who gave it. I, and men like me, would say that each of us here has his allotted task to do in life; and that he is but a coward, or as bad as a coward, who skulks his share of it. Go in, I say, boy.'

Gerald obeyed without a word; and now a slavish sense of fear came over him, and he felt that this man swayed and controlled him as he pleased.

'There, Gerald, drink that,' said Gabriel, filling him out a goblet of red wine. 'That's the liquor inspires the pious sentiments of the Bishop of Orvieto. From that generous grape-juice spring his Christian charities and his heavenly precepts. Let us see what miracles it can work upon two such sinful mortals as you and me. Well done, boy; drain off another,' and he refilled his glass as he spoke.

Old Pippo had retired and left them alone together. The moon was slowly rising beyond the lake, and threw a long yellow stream upon the floor, the only light in the chamber where they sat, thus giving a sort of solemnity to a moment when each felt too deeply sunk in his own thoughts for much conversation.

'Do you remark how that streak of moonlight seems to separate us, Gerald?' said Gabriel. 'A superstitious mind would find food for speculation there, and trace some mysterious meaning—perhaps a warning—from it. Are you superstitious?'

'I can scarcely say I am not,' said the boy diffidently.

'None of us are,' said the other boldly. 'If we affect to despise spirits we are just as eager slaves of our own presentiments. What we dignify by the name of reason is just as often a mere prompting of instinct. It amuses us to believe that we steer the bark of our destiny; but the truth comes upon us at last, that the tiller was lashed when the voyage began.' After a long silence on both sides, Gabriel said: 'I have told you, Gerald, that I made a journey to Rome on your account. I have been to the Jesuit College; conversed with the superior; saw your cell, your torn schoolbooks, your little table carved over with your pen-knife; and, by a date scratched on a window-pane, was led to discover where you had passed the evening of the fifth of January.'

'And did you go *there* also?' asked Gerald eagerly.

'Ay, boy. I gave an afternoon to the Altieri and the café in front of it.'

'You saw the Count, then?'

'No, I have not seen him,' said Gabriel dryly. 'He was away from Rome at a villa, I believe; but I have learned that, indignant at your flight from the Cardinal's villa, he absolves himself of all further interest in you.'

'Have you seen Fra Luke?' asked the boy, who now talked as if the other had known every incident of his life.

'No; he too was away. In fact, Gerald, there was little to learn, and I came back very nearly as I went. I only know that you are about as much alone in the world as myself. We are meet companions. You said, a while ago, you were curious to know who and what I was. You shall hear. I am of a good Provençal family, originally derived from Italy. We are counts, from a date before the Medici; so much for blood. As to fortune, my grandfather was rich, and my own father enjoyed a reasonable fortune. I was, however, brought up to believe all men my brothers; all

interested alike in serving and aiding each other: helping in
the cause of that excellent thing we are pleased to call
HUMANITY; and as a creed firmly believing that, bating a
chance yielding to temptation, a little backsliding now and
then on the score of an evil passion, men and women were
wonderfully good, and were on the road to be better. We
were most ingenious in our devices to build up this belief.
My father wrote books and delivered lectures to prove it.
He did more: he squandered all his patrimony in support
of his theory, and he trained me up to be—what I am.'
And the last words were uttered in a voice of intense
solemnity.

'I am not going to give you a story of my life,' said he,
after some time; 'I mean only to let you hear its moral.
Till I was eighteen I was taught to believe that men were
honest, truthful, brave, and affectionate; and that women
were pure-hearted, gentle, forgiving, and trustful. Before I
was nineteen I knew men to be scoundrels; it took me about
a year more to think worse of the others. Then began my
real life. I ceased to be a dupe, and felt a man. I am a
quick learner, and I acquired their vices rapidly, all but one,
that is still my stumbling-block—hypocrisy. All that I have
done,' said he, in half soliloquy, 'might have passed harm-
lessly had I known but how to shroud it. Slander, theft,
and seduction must not walk naked in this well-dressed
world; but, with fine clothes on, they make very good
company. I was curious to see if other lands were the same
slaves of conventionalities, and I travelled. I went to
Holland and to England; I found both as bad—nay worse—
than France. If I obtained a momentary success in life I
was certain to be robbed of it by some allegation foreign to
the question. My book was clever; but I had deserted my
wife. My treatise was admirable; but I had seduced the
daughter of my protector. My views were just, right-
minded, and true; but I had robbed my father. Thus,
with a subtlety the stupidest possess, they were able to
detract from my genius by charging it with the defects of

my character, as if it behoved one to pay the debts of the other. I went on insisting that it was my opinions alone were before the world; they as steadily persisted in dragging myself there. At last they have had their will, and I wish them joy of the victory.' There was a savage triumph in his eyes as he spoke this that made Gerald tremble while he looked at him.

'If you care for my story, boy,' resumed he, 'old Pippo there will give it to you for a flask of Monte Pulciano. He'll tell you of all my cruelties in my first campaign in Corsica; how I won my wife by first blasting her reputation; how I left her; how I was imprisoned and fined, and how escaped from both by a seduction. If he forget the name, you may remind him of Sophie De Mounier. They beheaded me in effigy for this at Dole. But why go on with vulgar incidents which have happened to so many? It is the moral of it all I would impress, boy, which is this—take nothing from the world but solid gifts. Laugh at its praises, and drink deep of its indulgences! Those born great are able to do this by prerogative; you and I may succeed to it by skill. Remember, too, that my theory is a wide, a most catholic one; and to follow it you need assume no special discipline, but be priest, soldier, statesman, scholar, just as you will. I have been all these in turn, and may be so again; but whether I wear a cassock or a cuirass, my knowledge of men will guide me to but one mode of dealing with them.'

'There is nothing in what you have told me of your life to make me revere your principles,' said Gerald, with a courageous boldness.

'Because I have told you how I fell, and not how I was tempted; because I have stooped to say of myself that which none dare say to my face; because whatever I have been to the world it was that same world fashioned me to. What would it avail me that I made out a case of undeserving hardships and injustice, proved myself an injured, martyred saint: would your wondering sympathy heal any the least of those wounds that fester here, boy? Every man's course in life is but one swing of the pendulum. I have vowed that with mine I shall cleave the dense mob and scatter the vile multitude. As to you,' said he, suddenly turning his glaring eyes upon the youth, 'you are free to leave this to-morrow. I'll take care that you are safely restored to those you came from, if you wish to return. If you prefer it, you may remain here for a month or two; by that time I shall return.'

'Are you going, then, from this?' asked Gerald.

'Yes. I am on my trial at Aix, for cruelty and desertion of my wife. They have spread a report that I have no intention to appear; that, having fled France, I mean never to return to it. Ere the week's over they shall learn their mistake. I shall be there before them; and, if instances from the uses of court and courtiers are admissible, show, that when they prove me guilty, they must be ready to include Versailles in the next prosecution. Watch this case, boy; I'll send you the newspapers daily. Watch it closely, and you'll see that the file is at work noiselessly now, but still at work on those old fetters that have bound mankind so long. But first say if you desire to stay here.'

Gerald held down his head and muttered a half audible 'Yes.'

'To-night, then, I will jot down the names of certain books you ought to read. I shall leave you many others too, and take your choice among them. Read and think, and, if you are able, write too: I care not on what theme, so the thoughts be your own.'

Gerald wished to thank him, but even gratitude could not surmount the dread he felt for him. Gabriel saw the struggle that was engaged in the boy's heart, and, smiling half sadly, said, 'To our next meeting, lad!'

CHAPTER XI

LAST DAYS AT THE TANA

IF Gerald breathed more freely the next morning, on hearing that Signor Gabriel had departed, it is, perhaps, no great wonder. The Tana was not a very agreeable abode. Dreariness within doors and without, a poverty unredeemed by that graceful content which so often sheds its influence over humble fortune, a wearisome round of life—these were the characteristics of a spot which, in a manner, was associated in his mind with all the sufferings of a sickbed. Yet no sooner had he learned that Gabriel was gone, than he felt as if a load were removed from his heart, and that even by the shores of that gloomy lake, or on the sides of those barren hills, he might now indulge his own teeming fancies, and live in a world of his own thoughts.

It was no common terror that possessed him ; his studies as a child had stored his memory with many a dreadful story of satanic temptation. One in particular he remembered well, of St. Francis, who, accompanied by a chance traveller, had made a journey of several days ; but whenever the saint, passing some holy shrine or sacred spot, would kneel to pray, the most terrible blasphemies would issue from his lips instead of prayer ; for his fellow-traveller was the Evil One himself. What if Gabriel had some horrible mission of this kind ? There was enough in his look, his manner, and his conversation to warrant the belief. He half laughed when the thought first crossed his mind, but it came up again and again, gaining strength and consistency at each recurrence ; nor was the melancholy desolation of the scene itself ill suited to aid the dreary conjecture. Though Gabriel had confided to him the key of his chamber where all his books were kept, Gerald passed days before he could summon resolution to enter it. A vague terror—a dread to which he could not give shape or form—arrested his steps, and he would turn away from the door and creep noiselessly down the stairs, as though afraid of confessing, even to himself, what his errand had been.

At last, ashamed of yielding to this childish fear, he took a moment when old Pippo and his niece were at work in the garden, to explore the long-dreaded chamber. The room was very different from what he had anticipated, and presented a degree of comfort singularly in contrast to the rest of the Tana. Maps and book-shelves covered the walls, with here and there prints, mostly portraits of celebrated actresses. A large table was littered with letters and papers, left just as Gabriel had quitted the spot. Great piles of manuscript, too, showed what laborious hours had been spent there, while books of reference were strewn about, the pages marked by pencil-notes and interlineations. All indicated a life of study and labour. One trait alone gave another and different impression; it was a long rapier that hung over the fire-place, around whose blade, at about a foot from the point, was tied a small bow of sky-blue ribbon. As, curious to divine the meaning of this, Gerald examined the weapon closely, he perceived that the steel was stained with blood up to the place where the ribbon was attached. What strange, wild fancies did not the boy weave as he gazed on this curious relic! Some fatal encounter there had been. Doubtless the unwiped blood upon that blade had once welled in a human heart. Some murderous hand had grasped that strong hilt, and some silk tresses had once been fastened with that blue band which now marked where the blade had ceased to penetrate. 'A sad tale, surely, would it be to hear,' said he, as he sat down in deep thought.

Tired of these musings, he turned to the objects on the table. The writings that were scattered about showed that almost every species of composition had engaged his pen. Essays on education, a history of the Illuminati, love-songs, a sketch of Cagliostroa, a paper on the commerce of the

Scheldt, a life of Frederic, with portions of an unfinished novel, all indicated the habits of a daily labourer of literature ; while passages selected from classic authorities, with great care and research, evinced that much pains had been expended in cultivating that rich intelligence.

The last work which had occupied his hand—it still lay open, with an unfinished sentence in the pen—was a memoir of the Pretender's expedition in '45. The name of Charles Edward was like a spell to Gerald's heart. From the earliest day he could remember he was taught to call him his own Prince, and among the prayers his infant lips had syllabled, none were uttered with more intense devotion than for the return of that true and rightful sovereign to the land of his fathers. And now, how his eyes filled up, and his heart swelled, as a long-forgotten verse arose to his mind ! He had learned it when its meaning was all mystery, but the clink of the rhythm had left it stored in his memory :

' Though for a time we see Whitehall
With cobwebs hanging on the wall,
Instead of gold and silver bright,
That glanced with splendour day and night,
    With rich perfume
    In every room,
That did delight that princely train,
    These again shall be,
    When the time we see,
That the king shall enjoy his own again.'

Heavy and hot were the tears that rolled down the youth's cheeks, for he was thinking of home and long ago—of that far-away home where loving hearts had clustered round him. He could recall, too, the little room, the little bed he slept in, and he pondered over his strange, forlorn destiny. And yet, thought he suddenly, 'What is there in my fate equal to that poor Prince's ? I am a Geraldine, they say, but I have none to own or acknowledge me. Who knows in what condition of shame I came into the world, since none will call me theirs ? This noble name is little better than a scoff upon me.' The boy's heart felt bursting at this sad retrospect of his lot. 'Would that I had never left the college!' cried he in his misery. 'Another year or two had, doubtless, calmed down the rebellious longings of my heart for a life of action, and then I should have followed my calling humbly, calmly, perhaps contentedly.'

Partly to divert his thoughts from this theme, he turned to the memoir of the Prince's expedition, and soon became so deeply interested in its details as to forget himself and his own sorrows. Brief and sketchy as the narrative was, it displayed in all the warm colouring of a romance that glorious outburst of national chivalry which gathered the chieftains around their sovereign — all the graces, too, of his own captivating manner, his handsome person, his courtly address, were dwelt upon, exerting as they did an almost magical influence upon every one who came before him. The short and bloody struggle which began at Preston and ended at Culloden was before his eyes, with all its errors exposed, all its mistakes displayed; every fault of strategy dwelt upon, and every miscalculation criticised. All the train of events which might have occurred had this or that policy been adopted was set forth in most persuasive form; till, when the youth arose from the perusal, such a conviction was forced upon him that rashness alone had defeated the enterprise, that he sprang to his feet, and paced the room in passionate indignation. As he thought over the noble devotion of Charles Edward's followers, he felt as if such a cause could not die. 'The right is there,' muttered he, 'and there must yet be brave men who think so. It cannot, surely, be possible that for one defeat so great a claim could be abandoned for ever! Where is the Prince now? how is he occupied? who are his adherents and counsellors?' were the questions which quickly succeeded each other in his mind. 'Would I were a soldier, that I could lay my services at his feet, or that I had skill or ability to aid his cause in any way!'

He turned eagerly again to the memoir, whose concluding

words were, 'He landed once more in France, on the 20th of September.' 'And that is now many a year ago,' said he, and with a dreary sigh; 'mayhap, of his wrecked fortune, not a plank now remains. Who could guide me in this matter— who advise me?' He knew of but one, and yet he shuddered at the idea of seeking counsel from Gabriel. The more Gerald reflected on it, the more was he assured that if he could obtain access to the Prince, his Royal Highness would remember his name. 'It is impossible,' thought he, 'but that some of my family must have been engaged in his cause, or why should I, as a mere child, have been taught to pray each night for his success, and ask for a blessing on his head?' Yearning as his heart was for some high purpose in life, it sent a thrill of intense delight through him to think of such a destiny.

It was a part of the training in the Jesuit College, to induce the youth to select some saintly model for imitation in life, and while some chose St. Francis Xavier, or St. Vincent de Paul, others took St. Anthony of Padua, St. Francis d'Assisi, or any other illustrious martyr of the faith; each votary being from the hour of his selection a most strenuous upholder of the patron he assumed. Indeed, of the enthusiasm in this respect some strange and almost incredible stories ran, showing how, in their zeal, many had actually submitted to most painful self-tortures, to resemble the idols of their ambition. How easy was it now for Gerald to replace any of these grim saints and martyrs by an image that actually filled his whole heart—one who possessed every graceful attribute and every attractive quality. The seed of hero-worship thus sown in his nature ripened to a harvest very different from that it was intended to bear, and Charles Edward occupied the shrine some pious martyr should have held. He little knew, indeed, how easily affections, nurtured for one class of objects, are transferred to others totally unlike them, and how often are the temples we rear and mean to dedicate to our highest and holiest aspirations made homes for most worldly passions! And what a strange chaos did that poor boy's mind soon become! for now he read whole days, and almost whole nights long, hurrying from his meals back to that lonely chamber, where he loved to be. With the insatiable thirst for new acquirement he tasted of all about him: dramatists, historians, essay-writers, theologians; the wildest theories of the rights of man, the most uncompromising asserters of divine authority for royalty, the sufferings and sorrows of noble-hearted missionaries, the licentious lives of courtly debauchees—all poured in like a strong flood over the soil of his mind, enriching, corrupting, ennobling, and debasing it by turns. Like some great edifice reared without plan, his mind displayed the strangest and most opposite combinations, and thus the noble eloquence of Massillon, the wit of Molière, the epigrammatic pungency of Pascal, blended themselves with the caustic severity of Voltaire, the touching pathos of Rousseau, and the knowledge of life so eminently the gift of Le Sage. To see that world of which these great men presented such a picture, became now his all-absorbing passion. To mingle with his fellow-men as actor, and not spectator. To be one of that immense *dramatis personæ* who moved about the stage of life, seemed enough for all ambition. The strong spirit of adventure lay deeply in his heart, and he felt a kind of pride to think that if any future success was to greet him, he could recall the days at the Tana, and say, there never was one who started in life poorer or more friendless.

There was no exaggeration in this. His clothes were rags, his shoes barely held together, and the only covering he had for his head was the little skullcap he used to wear in school hours. Even old Pippo began to scoff at his miserable appearance, and hinted a hope, that before the season of the contraband begun Gerald would have taken his departure, or be able to make a more respectable figure. As Gabriel had now been gone many weeks, and no tidings whatever come of him, the old man's reserve and deference daily decreased. He grumbled at Gerald's habits of study, profitless and idle as they seemed to him, while there was many a thing to be done about the house and the garden. He was not weak or sickly now: he could help to chop the wood for winter firing; he could raise those heavy water-buckets that swung over the deep well in the garden; he could draw the net in the little stream behind the house, or trench about the few stunted olives that struggled for life on the hillside. Gerald would willingly have done any or all of these, if the idea had occurred to himself. He was not indolent by nature, and liked the very fact of active occupation. As a task, however, he rejected the notion at once. It savoured of servitude to his mind, and who was this same Pippo who aspired to be his master?

The more the boy's mind became stored with knowledge, the fuller his intelligence grew of great examples and noble instances—the more indignantly did he repulse the advances of Pippo's companionship. 'What!' he would mutter to himself, 'leave Bossuet and his divine teachings for his coarse converse! Quit the sarcastic intensity of Voltaire's ridicule for the vulgar jests of this illiterate boor! Exchange the glorious company of wits and sages, and poets and moralists, for a life of daily drudgery, with a mean peasant to talk to! Besides, I am not his guest, nor a burden upon his charity. It is to Gabriel I owe my shelter here.'

When driven by many a sarcasm to assume this position, Pippo gravely remarked: 'True enough, boy, so long as he was here; but he is gone now, and who'll tell us will he ever come back? He may have been sentenced by the tribunal. At the hour we are talking here he may be in prison—at the galleys, for aught we know; and I promise you one thing, there's many a better man there.'

'And I, too, promise one thing,' replied Gerald angrily, 'if he ever do come, he shall hear how you have dared to speak of him.'

Old Pippo started at the words, and his face became lividly pale, and muttering a few words beneath his breath, he left the spot. Nothing was further from Gerald's mind than any defence of Gabriel, for whom, do what he might, he could feel neither affection nor gratitude. In what he had said he merely yielded to a momentary impatience to sting the old man by an angry reply. For the remainder of that day not a word was exchanged between them. They met and parted without saluting; they sat silently opposite each other at their meals. The following day opened with the same cold distance between them, the old man barely eyeing Gerald, when the youth was not observing him, and casting toward him glances of doubtful meaning. Too deeply engaged in his books to pay much attention to these signs of displeasure, Gerald passed his hours as usual in Gabriel's room.

He was seated, reading, when the door opened gently, and the old man's niece entered : her step was so noiseless, that she was nearly beside Gerald's chair before he noticed her.

'What is it, Tina,' said he, starting; 'what makes you look so frightened ?'

She placed her finger on her lip, a sign of caution, and looked anxiously around her.

'He has not been cruel or angry with you, poor girl ?' asked the boy; 'tell me this.'

'No, Gerald,' said she, in a low and broken voice; 'but there is danger over you—ay, and near too, if you can't escape it. He sent me last night over to St. Stephano, twelve weary miles across the mountain, after nightfall, to fetch the Gobbino——'

'The Gobbino—who is he ?'

'The hunch-back, that was at the galleys in Messina,' said the girl, trembling all over; and then went on, 'and to tell him to come over to the Tana, for he wanted him.'

'Well, and then——'

'And then,' muttered the girl, 'and then,' and she made a pantomimic gesture of drawing a knife suddenly across the throat. 'It is so with him, they say ; he 'd think no more of it than do I of killing a hen !'

'No, no, Tina,' said the boy, smiling at her fears. 'You wrong old Pippo and the Gobbo too. Take my word for it, there is something else he wants him for; besides, why should he dislike *me*? What have I done to provoke such a vengeance?'

'Haven't you threatened him?' said the girl eagerly. 'Have you not said that when Signor Gabriel comes back you will tell him something Pippo said of him? Is that not enough? Is the Signor Gabriel one who ever forgives an injury?'

'I'll not believe, I can't believe it,' said Gerald musingly.

'But I tell you it is true; I tell you I know it,' cried the girl passionately.

'But what am I to do, then? How can I defend myself?'

'Fly—leave this—get over to Bolseno, or cross the frontier; neither of them can follow you into Tuscany.'

'Remember, Tina, I have no money. I am almost naked. I know no one.'

'What matters all that if you have life?' said she boldly.

'Well said, girl!' cried he, warmed by the same daring spirit that prompted her words. A slight noise in the garden underneath the window startled Tina, and she stepped quietly from the room and closed the door.

It was some time before Gerald could thoroughly take in the full force of the emergency that threatened him. He knew well that in the Italian nature the sentiment of vengeance occupies no low nor ignominious place, but is classed among high and generous qualities; and that he who submits tamely to an injury is infinitely meaner than the man who, at any cost of treachery, exacts his revenge for it.

That a terrible vengeance was often exacted for some casual slight, even a random word, the youth well knew. These were the points of honour in that strange national character of which, even to this hour, we know less than of any people's in Europe; and certainly, no crime could promise an easier accomplishment or less chance of discovery. 'Who is ever to *know* if I sunk under the Maremma fever,' said he, 'and who to *care*?'

He gazed out upon the lonesome waste of mountain and the black and stagnant lake at its foot, and thought the spot, at least, was well chosen for such an incident. If there were moments in which the dread of a terrible fate chilled his blood and made his heart cold with fear, there were others in which the sense of peril rallied and excited him. The stirring incidents of his readings were full of suchlike adventures, and he felt a sort of heroism in seeing himself thus summoned to meet an emergency. 'With this good rapier,' said he, taking down Gabriel's sword from its place, 'methinks I might offer a stout resistance. That blade, if I mistake not, already knows the way to a man's heart,' and he flourished the weapon so as to throw himself into an attitude of defence.

Too much excited to read, except by snatches, he imagined to his own mind every possible species of attack that might be made upon him. He knew that a fair fight would never enter into *their* thoughts; that even before the fate reserved for him would come the plan for their own security; and so he pictured the various ways in which he might be taken unawares and disposed of without even a chance of reprisal. As night drew near his anxieties increased. The book in which from time to time he had been reading was the *Life of Benvenuto Cellini*, an autobiography filled with the wildest incidents of personal encounter, and well suited to call up ideas of conflict and peril. Not less, however, was it calculated to suggest notions of daring and defiance; for in every perilous strait and hair-breadth emergency the great Florentine displayed the noblest traits of calm and reasoning courage. 'They shall not do it without cost,' said Gerald, as he stole up noiselessly to his room, never appearing at the supper-table, but retiring to concert his future steps. Gerald's first care on entering his room was to search it thoroughly, though there was not a corner nor a cupboard capable of concealing a child. He went through the process of investigation with all the diligence his readings prompted. He sounded the walls for secret panels, and the floor for trap-doors; but all was so far safe. He next proceeded to barricade his door with chairs; not, indeed, to prevent an entrance, but arrayed so skilfully that they must topple down

G

at the least touch, and thus apprise him of his peril if sleeping. He then trimmed and replenished his lamp, and with his trusty rapier at his side, lay down, all dressed as he was, to await what might happen.

He who has experienced in life what it is to lie watching for the dawn of a day full of Heaven-knows-what fatalities, patiently expecting the sun to rise upon what may prove his saddest, his last hour of existence, even he, however, will fall short of imagining the intense anxiety of one who with aching ears watches for the slightest sound, the lightest footfall, or the lowest word that may betoken the approach of danger. With the intensity of the emotion the senses become preternaturally acute, and the brain, overcharged with thought, suggests the wildest and strangest combinations. Through Gerald's mind, too, Cellini's daring adventures were passing. The dark and narrow streets of old Florence; the muffled 'sbirri' crowding in the dim doorways; the stealthy footsteps heard and lost again; the sudden clash of swords and the cries of combat; the shouts for succour, and the heavy plash into the dark waters of the Arno, all filled his waking, ay, and his dreamy thoughts, for he fell asleep at last and slept soundly. The day was just breaking, a grey, half-pinkish light faintly struggling through his window, when Gerald started up from his sleep. He had surely heard a sound. It was his name was called. Was it a human voice that uttered it? or was the warning from a more solemn world? He bent down his head to listen again; and now he distinctly heard a low, creaking sound, and as distinctly saw that the door was slightly moved, and then the words 'Gerald, Gerald,' whispered. He arose at once, and quickly recognising Tina's voice, drew nigh the door.

'You have no time to lose, Gerald,' said she rapidly. 'Pippo has taken the boat and is rowing across the lake; and even by this half light I can see a figure standing on the rock at the foot of the mountain waiting for him, just where the pathway from St. Stephano comes down to the water.'

'The Gobbo, I suppose,' said Gerald, half mockingly, as he showed the rapier he still held in his hand.

'And if it be he, boy, there is no need to laugh,' said Tina, shuddering. 'The dark waters of that lake there, that cover some of his handiwork, if they could speak, would tell you so.'

'Then what am I to do, Tina?' said he, throwing open the door. 'You'd not have me meet them on the shore there and begin the attack, would you?'

If Gerald threw out this suggestion as impracticable, it was yet precisely the course he was longing himself to follow, and most eager that she should assent to.

'The Blessed Virgin forbid it!' cried she, crossing herself. 'There is but one road to take, and that is yonder,' and she pointed to a little rugged footpath that wound its way over the mountain, which joined the frontier with Tuscany.

'And am I in meet condition to travel, Tina?' said he jestingly, as he showed his ragged dress and pulled out the lining of his empty pockets.

'There is Signor Gabriel's cape,' said she; 'it is almost as good as a cloak: he left it with me, but I have no need of it; and there is the crown-piece you gave me yourself when you were ill of the fever, and I want it just as little.'

The boy struggled hard to refuse both, but the sorrow Tina felt for the rejection at last overcame him, and, half in shame and half in pleasure—for the sense of exacting sacrifice is pleasure, deny it how we may—he yielded, and accepted her gift.

'Oh, Tina, will there ever come a day when I can repay this kindness?' said he. 'I almost think there will.'

'To be sure, Gerald, and you'll not forget me even if there should not. You who were taught by the pious Frati how to pray will surely say a good word in your devotions for a poor girl like Tina.'

The boy's heart overflowed with emotion at the trait of simple piety, and he kissed her twice with all the affection of a fond brother. 'Good-bye, Tina,' said he, sobbing; 'I feel stronger and stouter in heart, now that I know your kind wishes are going along with me—they are better to me, love, than a purse full of money.'

'Do not take that sword, Gerald,' said she, trying to take the weapon from him. 'If you enter a village with a rapier at your side, they'll call you a brigand, and give you up to the carabinieri.'

'I'll not quit the good blade so long as I can wear it,' said he resolutely; and then added to himself, 'I am nobly born, and have a right to a sword. "Cinctus gladio," says the old statute of knighthood; and if I be a Geraldine, I am noble!'

And with these words the boy bade his last farewell, and issued from the house.

CHAPTER XII

A FOREST SCENE

ONCE more did Gerald find himself alone and penniless upon the world. He was not, however, as when first he issued forth, timid, depressed, and diffident. Short as had been the interval since that time, his mind had made a considerable progress. His various readings had taught him much; and he had already learned that in the Mutual Assurance Company we call Life men are ever more or less dependent on their fellows. 'There must, then,' said he to himself, 'be surely some craft or calling to which I can bring skill or aptitude, and some one or other will certainly accept of services that only require the very humblest recognition.' He walked for hours without seeing a living thing: the barren mountain had not even a sheep-walk; and save the path worn by the track of smugglers, there was nothing to show that the foot of man had ever traversed its dreary solitudes. At last he gained the summit of the ridge, and could see the long line of coast to the westward, jagged and indented with many a bay and promontory. There lay St. Stephano: he could recognise it by the light cloud of pale blue smoke that floated over the valley, and marked where the town stood; and, beyond, he could catch the masts and yards of a few small craft that were sheltering in the offing. Beyond these again stretched the wide blue sea, marked at the horizon by some far-away sails. The whole was wrapped in that solemn calm, so striking in the noon of an Italian summer's day. Not a cloud moved, not a leaf was stirring; a faint foam-line on the beach told that there the waves crept softly in, but, except this, all nature was at rest.

In the dead stillness of night our thoughts turn inward, and we mingle memories with our present reveries; but in the stillness of noonday, when great shadows lie motion-less on the hillside, and all is hushed save the low murmur of the laden bee, our minds take the wide range of the world—visiting many lands—mingling with strange people. Action, rather than reflection, engages us; and we combine, and change, and fashion the mighty elements before us as we will. We people the plains with armed hosts; we fill the towns with busy multitudes—gay processions throng the squares, and banners wave from steeple and tower; over the blue sea proud fleets are seen to move, and thundering echoes send back their dread cannonading: and through these sights and sounds we have our especial part—lending our sympathies here, bearing our warmest wishes there. If we dream, it is of the real, the actual, and the true; and thus dreaming, we are but foreshadowing to ourselves the incidents and accidents of life, and garnering up the resources where-with to meet them.

Stored as was his mind with recent reading, Gerald's fancy supplied him with innumerable incidents, in every one of which he displayed the same heroic traits, the same aptitude to meet emergency, and the same high-hearted courage he had admired in others. Vain-gloriousness may be forgiven when it springs, as his did, out of thorough ignorance of the world. It is, indeed, but the warm outpouring of a generous temperament, where self-esteem predominates. The youth ardently desired that the good should prosper and the bad be punished: his only mistake was, that he claimed the chief place in effecting both one and the other.

Eagerly bent upon adventure, no matter where, how, or with whom, he stood on the mountain's peak, gazing at the scene beneath him. A waving tract of country, traversed by small streams, stretched away toward Tuscany, but where the boundary lay between the states he could not detect. No town or village could be descried; and, so far as he could see, miles and miles of journey yet lay before him ere he could arrive at a human dwelling. This was indeed the less matter, since Tina had fastened up in his handkerchief sufficient food for the day; and even were night to overtake him, there was no great hardship in passing it beneath that starry sky.

'Many there must be,' thought he, 'campaigning at this very hour, in far-away lands, mayhap amid the sand deserts of the East, or crouching beneath the shelter of the drifted snows in the North; and even here are troops of gypsies, who never know what means the comfort of a roof over them.' Just as he said these words to himself, his eyes chanced to rest upon a thin line of pale blue smoke that arose from a group of alders beside a stream in the valley. Faint and thin at first, it gradually grew darker and fuller, till it rose into the clear air, and was wafted slowly along toward the sea.

'Just as if I had conjured them up,' cried Gerald, 'there are the gypsies; and if there be a Strega in the company, she shall have this crown for telling me my fortune! What marvels will she not invent for this broad piece—what dragons shall I not slay—what princesses not marry; not but in reality they do possess some wondrous insight into the future! Signor Gabriel sneered at it, as he sneered at everything; but there's no denying they read destiny, as the sailor reads the coming storm in signs unseen by others. There is something fine, too, in their clanship; how, poor and houseless, despised as they are, they cling together, hoarding up their ancient rites and traditions—their only wealth—and wandering through the world, pilgrims of centuries old.'

As he descended the mountain path he continued thus to

exalt the gypsies in his estimation, and with that unfailing resource in similar cases, that what he was unable to praise he at least found picturesque. The path led through a wood of stunted chestnut-trees, on issuing from whose shade he could no longer detect the spot he was in search of; the fire had gone out, and the smoke ceased to linger over the place.

'Doubtless the encampment has broken up; they are trudging along toward the coast, where the villages lie,' thought he, 'and I may come up with them to-morrow or next day,' and he stepped out briskly on his way.

The day was intensely hot, and Gerald would gladly have availed himself of any shade, to lie down and enjoy the 'siesta' hours in true Italian fashion. The only spot, however, he could procure likely to offer such shelter was a little copse of olives, at a bend of the river, about a mile away. A solitary rock, with a few ruined walls upon it, rose above the trees, and marked the place as one once inhabited. Following the winding of the stream, he at length drew nigh, and quickly noticed that the grass was greener and deeper, with here and there a daffodil or a wild-flower, signs of a soil which, in some past time, had been cared for and cultivated. The river, too, as it swept around the base of the rock, deepened into a clear, calm pool, the very sight of which was intensely grateful and refreshing. As the youth stood in admiring contemplation of this fair bath, and inwardly vowing to himself the luxury of a plunge into it, a low rustling noise startled him, and a sound like the sharp stamp of a beast's foot. He quickly turned, and, tracing the noise, saw a very diminutive ass, who, tethered to an olive-tree, was busily munching a meal of thistles, and as busily stamping off the stray forest flies that settled on him. Two panniers, covered over with some tarnished scarlet cloth, and a drum of considerable size and very gaudy colouring, lay on the grass, with three or four painted poles, a roll of carpet, and a bright brass basin, such as conjurers use for their trade. There was also a curiously-shaped box, painted in checkers, doubtless some mysteriously gifted 'property.'

Curious to discover the owners of these interesting relics,
Gerald advanced into the copse, when his quick hearing was
arrested by the long-drawn breathings of several people fast
asleep—so, at least, they seemed, by the full-toned chorus
of their snorings; though the next moment showed him
that they consisted of but three persons, an old, stunted,
and very emaciated man; an equally old woman, immensely
fat and misshapen, to which her tawdry finery gave something indescribably ludicrous in effect; and a young girl,
whose face was buried in the bend of her arms, but whose
form, as she lay in the graceful abandonment of sleep, was
finely and beautifully proportioned. A coarse dress of brown
stuff was her only covering, leaving her arms bare, while
her legs, but for the sandals of some tawdry tinsel, were
naked to the knees and as brown as the skin of an Indian,
yet in shape and symmetry they might have vied with the
most faultless statue of the antique—indeed, to a sleeping
nymph in the gallery of the Altieri Palace was Gerald now
comparing her, as he stood gazing on her. The richly floating
hair, which, as a protection against the zanzari, she had let
fall over her neck and shoulders, only partially defended her,
and so she stirred at times, each motion displaying some
new charm, some fresh grace of form. At last, perhaps
startled by a thought of her dreams, she gave a sudden cry,
and sprang up to a sitting posture, her eyes widely staring
and her half-opened lips turned to where Gerald stood. As
for him, the amazement that seized him overcame him—for
she was no other than the tarantella dancer of the Piazza
di Spagna, the Marietta who had so fascinated him on the
night he left the convent.

'Babbo! Babbo!' screamed she, in terror, as she caught
sight of the naked rapier at the youth's side; and in a
moment both the old man and the woman were on their legs.

'We are poor, miserably poor, Signore!' cried the old
man piteously; 'mere "vagabonds," and no more.'

'We have not a Bajocclo among us, Signore mio,'
blubbered out the old woman.

An honest burst of laughter from Gerald, far more re-
assuring than words, soon satisfied them that their fears
were needless.

'Who are you, then?' cried the girl, as she darted her
piercing black eyes toward him; 'and why are you here?'

'The world is wide, and open to all of us, *cara mia*,' said
the youth good-humouredly. 'Don't be angry with me
because I'm not a brigand.'

'He says truly,' said the old man.

'*Sangue dei Santi*, but you have given me a hearty fright,
boy, what ever brought you here!' said the fat old woman,
as she wiped the hot drops from her steaming face.

There is some marvellous freemasonry in poverty—some
subtle sympathy links poor men together—for scarcely had
Gerald told that he was destitute and penniless as themselves,
than these poor outcasts bade him a frank welcome among
them, and invited him to a share of their little scanty
supper.

'I'll warrant me that you have drawn a low number in
the conscription, boy; and that's the reason you have fled
from home,' said the old woman; and Gerald laughed good-
humouredly, as though accepting the suggestion as a happy
guess; nor was he sorry to be spared the necessity of
recounting his story.

'But why not be a soldier?' broke in Marietta.

'Because it's a dog's life,' retorted the hag savagely.

'I don't think so,' said Gerald. 'When I saw the noble
guard of his Holiness prancing into the Piazza del Popolo,
I longed to be one of them. They were all glittering with
gold and polished steel, and their horses bounded and
caracoled as if impatient for a charge.'

'Ah!' sighed the old man drearily, 'there's only one
happy road in this life.'

'And what may that be, Babbo?' said Gerald, addressing
him by the familiar title the girl had given him.

'A Frate's, boy, a Frate's. I don't care whether he be a
Dominican or an Ignorantine. Though, myself, I like the

Ignorantines.   Theirs is truly a blessed existence : no wants
—no cares—no thoughts for the morrow !   I never watched
one of them stepping along, with firm foot and sack on his
arm, that I didn't say to myself, "There's freedom—there's
light-heartedness."'

'I should have called your own a pleasanter life.'

'Mine !' groaned he.

'Ay, Babbo, and so is it,' burst in the girl, in an excited
tone.   'Show me the Frate has such a time as we have !
Whenever the friar comes, men shuffle away to escape
giving him their "quattrini."   They know well there's no
such sturdy beggar as he who asks no alms, but shows you
the mouth of his long empty sack ; but where we appear
the crowds gather, mothers snatch up their babies and hurry
out to greet us ; hard-worked men cease their toil ; children
desert their games ; all press round eagerly at the first roll
of Gaetana's drum, and of poor Chico's fife, when he was
with us,' added she, dropping her head, while a heavy tear
rolled down her swarthy cheek.

'*Maladizione a Chico !*' screamed out the old man, lifting
up both his clenched hands in passion.

'What was it he did ?' asked Gerald of the old man.

'He fancied himself a patriot, boy, and he stabbed a spy
of the police at the St. Lucia one evening ; and they have him
now at the galleys, and they 'll keep him there for life.'

'Ah ! if you saw him on the two poles,' cried the girl,
'only strapped so, over his instep, and he could spring from
here to the tree yonder ; and then he 'd unfasten one, and
holding it on his forehead, balance Babbo's basin on the top,
all the while playing the tambourine !   And who could play
it like him ?   It was a drum with cymbals in his hands.'

'Was he handsome, too ?' asked Gerald, with a half-sly
glance toward her ; but she only hung her head in silence.

'He handsome !' cried the old woman, catching at the
words.   'Brutto ! brutto ! he had a hare-lip, with a dog's
jaw !'

'No, truly,' muttered Babbo ; 'he was not handsome,

though he could do many a thing well-favoured ones couldn't attempt. He was a sore loss to us,' said he, with a deep sigh.

'There wasn't a beast of the field nor a bird that flies he couldn't imitate,' broke in Marietta; 'and with some wondrous cunning, too, he could blend the sounds together, and you'd hear the cattle lowing and the rooks cawing all at the same time.'

'The owl was good; that was his best,' said Babbo.

'Oh, was it not fine!—the wild shriek of the owl, while the tide was breaking on the shore, and the waves came in plash, plash, in the still night.'

'May his toil be hard and his chains heavy!' exclaimed the hag; 'we have had nothing but misery and distress since the day he was taken.'

'Poor fellow,' said Gerald, 'his lot is harder still.' The girl's dark eyes turned fully upon him, with a look of grateful meaning, that well repaid his compassionate speech.

'So may it be,' chimed in the hag; 'and so with all who ill-treat those whose bread they've eaten,' and she turned a glance of fiery anger on the girl. 'What art doing there, old fool!' cried she to the Babbo, who, having turned his back to the company, was telling over his beads busily. He made no reply, and she went on: 'That's all he's good for now. There was a time he could sing Punch's carnival from beginning to end, keep four dancing on the stage, and two talking out of windows; but now he's ever at the litanies: he'd rather talk to you about St. Francis than of the Tombola, he would!'

As the old hag, with bitter words and savage energy, inveighed against her old associate, Gerald had sense to mark that, small as the company was, it yet consisted of ingredients that bore little resemblance, and were attached by the slenderest sympathies to each other. He was young and inexperienced enough in life to imagine that they who amuse the world by their gifts, whatever they be, carry with them to their homes the pleasant qualities which delight the audiences. He fancied that, through all their poverty, the light-hearted gaiety that marked them in public would abide with them when alone, and that the quips and jests they bandied were but the outpourings of a ready wit always in exercise.

The Babbo had been a servitor of a convent in the Abruzzi, and, dismissed for some misdemeanour, had wandered about the world in vagabondage till he became a conjurer, some talent or long-neglected gift of slight-of-hand coming to the rescue of his fortune. The woman, Donna Gaetana, had passed through all the stages of 'Street Ballet,' from the prodigy of six years old, with a wreath of violets on her brow, to the besotted old beldame, whose specialty was the drum. As for Marietta, where she came from, of what parentage, or even of what land, I know not. The Babbo called her his niece—his grandchild—his 'figliuola' at times, but she was none of these. In the wayward turns of their fortune these street performers are wont to join occasionally together in the larger capitals, that by their number they may attract more favourable audiences; and so, when Gerald first saw them at Rome, they were united with some Pifferari from Sicily; but the same destiny that decides more pre-tentious coalitions had separated theirs, and the three were now trudging northward in some vague hope that the land of promise lay in that direction. It is needless to say how Gerald felt attracted by the strange adventurous life of which they spoke. The Babbo, mingling his old convent traditions, his scraps of monkish Latin, his little fragments of a pious training, with the descriptions of his subtle craft, was a study the youth delighted in, while from his own early teaching, it was also a character he could thoroughly appreciate. Donna Gaetana, indeed, offered little in the way of interest, but did not Marietta alone compensate for more than this? The wild and fearless grace of this young girl, daring to the very verge of shamelessness, and yet with a strange instinctive sense of womanly delicacy about her, that lifted her, in her raggedness, to a sphere where deference was her due; her matchless symmetry, her easy motion, a mingled expression of energy and languor about her, all met happily in one who but needed culture to have become a great artiste. She possessed, besides, a voice of exquisite richness, one of those deep-toned organs whose thrilling expression seems to attain at once the highest triumph of musical art in the power of exciting the sensibilities : such was that poor neglected child, as she hovered over the brink where vice and wretchedness and crime run deep and fast below !

When the meal was over, and the little vessels used in preparing it were all duly washed and packed, old Gaetana lighted her pipe, and once in full puff proceeded to drag from a portentous-looking bag a mass of strange rags, dirty and particoloured, the slashed sleeves and spangled skirts proclaiming them as 'properties.'

'Clap that velvet cap on thy head, boy, and let's see what thou lookest like,' cried she, handing Gerald a velvet hat, looped up in front, and ornamented with an ostrich feather.

'What for?' cried he rudely; 'I am no mountebank.' And then, as he caught Marietta's eyes, a deep blush burned all over his face, and he said, in a voice of shame, 'To be sure! Anything you like. I'll wear this too,' and he snatched up a tawdry mantle and threw it over his shoulders.

'*Come e bellino!*' said Marietta, as she clasped her hands across her bosom, and gazed on him in a sort of rapture. 'He's like Paolo in the Francesca,' muttered she.

'He'll never be Chico,' growled out the hag. 'Birbante that he was, who'll ever jump through nine hoops with a lighted taper in his hand? Oh, *Assassino!* it won't serve you now !'

'Do you know Paolo's speech?' whispered Marietta.

'No,' said he, blushing, half angry, half ashamed.

'Then I'll teach it to you.'

'Thou shouldst have been an acolyte at San Giovanni di Laterano when the Pope says the high mass, boy,' cried Babbo enthusiastically. 'Thy figure and face would well become the beauteous spectacle.'

'Does not that suit him?' cried the girl, as she replaced the hat by a round cap, such as pages wear, with a single eagle's feather. 'Does not that become him?'

'Who cares for looks?' muttered the hag. 'Chico was ugly enough to bring bad luck; and when shall we see his like again?'

'Who knows! who knows?' said Babbo slowly. 'This lad may, if he join us, have many a good gift we suspect not. Canst sing?'

'Yes; at least the litanies.'

'Ah, bravo, Giovane!' cried the old man. 'Thou 'lt bring a blessing upon us.'

'Canst play the fife, the tambourine, the flute?' asked Gaetana.

'None of them.'

'Thou canst recite, I'm sure,' said Marietta. 'Thou knowest Tasso and Petrarch, surely, and Guarini?'

'Yes; and Dante by heart, if that be of any service to me,' said Gerald.

'Ah! I know nothing of him,' said she sorrowfully; 'but I could repeat the Orlando from beginning to end.'

'How art thou on the stilts or the slack-rope?' asked the old woman; 'for these other things never gave bread to any one.'

'If I must depend upon the slack-rope, then,' said Gerald, good-humouredly, 'I run a good chance of going supperless to bed.'

'How they neglect them when they're young, and their bones soft and pliant!' said Gaetana sternly. 'What parents are about nowadays I can't imagine. I used to crouch into a flower-pot when I was five years old; ay, and spring out of it too when the Fairy Queen touched the flower!'

Gerald could with great difficulty restrain the burst of laughter this anecdote of her early life provoked.

'Oh, come with us; stay with us,' whispered Marietta in his ear.

'If thou hast been taught the offices, boy,' said Babbo,

'thou deservest an honester life than ours. Leave us, then; go thy ways, and walk in better company.'

'*Corpo del diavolo!*' screamed out the hag. 'It's always so with him. He has nothing but hard words for the trade he lives by.'

'Stay with us; stay with us,' whispered the girl, more faintly.

'Thou mightst have a worse offer, lad; for who can tell what's in thee? I warrant me, thou'lt never be great at jumping tricks,' said Babbo.

'Wilt stay?' said Marietta, as her eyes swam in tears.

'I will,' said Gerald, with a glance that made her cheek crimson.

CHAPTER XIII

A CONTRACT

I AM not certain that a great 'Impressario' of Paris or London would have deemed the document which bound Gerald to his new master a very formal instrument. But there was a document. It was written on a fly-leaf of old Babbo's Breviary, and set forth duly that for certain services to be afterward detailed, '*un certo Gherardi*'—so was he called —was to eat, and drink, and be clothed; always providing that there was meat, and drink, and wearables to give him; with certain benefices — small contingent remainders — to accrue when times were prosperous and patrons generous, and all this for the term of a twelvemonth. Donna Gaetana stoutly fought for five years, then three, and then two: but she was beaten in all her amendments, though she argued her case ably. She showed, with a force derived from great experience, that theirs was a profession wherein there was much to learn; that the initial stages developed very few of those gifts which won popular applause; that, consequently, the neophyte was anything but a profitable colleague; and it

was only when his education was perfected that he could be
expected to repay the cost of his early instruction. 'At the
end of a year,' to borrow her own forcible language, 'he'll
have smashed a dozen basins and broken twenty poles, and
he'll just be as stiff in the back as you see him to-day.'

'He'll have had enough of a weary life ere that,' muttered
the Babbo.

'What have *you* to complain of, I'd like to know?' asked
she fiercely; 'you that sit there all day like a prince on a
throne, never so much as giving a blast of a horn or a beat
on the drum; but pulling a few cords for your puppets, and
making them patter about the stage while you tell over the
self-same story I heard forty years ago. Ah, if it was
Pierno! that was something indeed to hear! He came out
with something new every evening—droll fellow that he
was—and could make the people laugh till the Piazza rung
again.'

'Well, well,' sighed Babbo, 'his drollery has cost him
something. He cut a jest upon the Cardinal Balfi, and they
sent him to Molo di Gaeta, to work at the galleys. My
pulcinello may be stupid, but will not make me finish my
days in chains.'

Whether Marietta feared the effect these domestic dis-
cussions might produce upon Gerald, newly come as he was
among them, or that she desired to talk with him more at
her ease, she strolled away into the wood, giving one lingering
glance as she left the place to bid him follow. The youth
was not loth to accept the hint, and soon overtook her.

'And so,' said she, taking his hand between both her own,
'you *will* stay?'

'I have promised it,' replied Gerald.

'All for me, all for me, as the little song says.'

'I never heard it. Will you sing it, Marietta?' said he,
placing his arm around her waist.

'I'll go and fetch my guitar, then,' said she, and bounding
away, was soon once more beside him, sweeping her fingers
over the cords as she came.

'It's nothing of a song, either words or music; but I picked it up at Capri, and it reminds me of that sweet spot.' So saying, and after a little prelude, she sang the canzonette, of which the following words are a rude version :

> 'I know a bark on a moonlit sea,
> >   Pescator! Pescator!
> There's one in that bark a-thinking of me,
> >   Oh, Pescator!
> And while his light boat steals along,
> >   Pescator! Pescator!
> He murmurs my name in his evening song,
> >   Oh, Pescator!
> He prays the Madonna above my head,
> >   Pescator! Pescator!
> To bring sweet dreams around my bed,
> >   Oh, Pescator!
> And when the morning breaks on shore,
> I'll kneel and pray for my Pescator,
> Who ventures alone on the stormy sea,
> >   All for me! all for me!'

Simple as were the words, the wild beauty of the little air thrilled through Gerald's heart, and twice did he make her repeat it.

'Oh, if you like barcarolles,' said she, 'I'll sing you hundreds of them, and teach you, besides, to sing them with me. We shall be so happy, *Gherardi mio*, living thus together.

'And not regret Chico?' said Gerald gravely.

'Chico was very clever, but he was cruel. He would beat me when I would not learn quickly; and my life was very sad when he was with us. See,' said she, drawing down her sleeve from her shoulder, 'these stripes were of his giving.'

'*Briccone!*' muttered Gerald, 'if I had him here.'

'Ah, he was so treacherous! He'd have stabbed you at the altar-foot rather than let a vengeance escape him. He was a Corsican.'

'And are they so treacherous always?'

'Are they?' cried she. '*Per Dio*, I believe they are.'

H

'Well, let's talk of him no more. I only mentioned his name because I feared you loved him, Marietta.'

'And if I had?' asked she, with a half-malicious drollery in her dark eyes.

'Then I'd have hated him all the more—hated *you*, perhaps, too.'

'*Poverino!*' said she, with a sigh which ended in a laugh.

And now they walked along, side by side, while she told Gerald all about her life, her companions, their humours, their habits, and their ways. She liked Babbo. He was kind-hearted and affectionate; but Donna Gaetana was all that was cruel and unfeeling. Chico, indeed, had always resisted her tyranny, and she counselled Gerald to do the same. 'As for me,' added she sorrowfully, 'I am but a girl, and must bear with her.'

'But I'll stand by you, Marietta,' cried Gerald boldly. 'We'll see if the world won't go better with each of us as we meet it thus,' and he drew her arm around his waist, while he clasped hers with his own.

And what a happy hour was that as thus they rambled along under the leafy shade, no sound but the wild wood-pigeon's cry to break the silence! for often they were silent with thoughts deeper than words could render. She, full of that future where Gerald was to be the companion of all her games; he, too, ranging in fancy over adventures wherein, as her protector and defender, he confronted perils unceasingly. Then he bethought him how strangely destiny should have thus brought them together, two forsaken, friendless creatures.

One falls in love at eighteen, at eight-and-twenty, and at eight-and-forty, with very different reasons for the process. Silky hair, and long eye-lashes, and pearly teeth get jostled as we go on through life, with thoughts of good connections and the three per cents., and a strange compromise is effected between inclination and self-interest. To know, however, the true ecstasy of the passion, to feel it in all its impulsive force, and in the full strength of its irresponsibility, be very

young and very poor—young enough to doubt of nothing,
not even yourself; poor enough to despise riches most
heartily.

Gerald was young and poor. His mind, charged with deep
stores of sentiment, was eagerly seeking where to invest its
wealth. The tender pathos of St. Pierre, the more dangerous
promptings of Rousseau, were in his heart, and he yearned
for one to whom he could speak of the feelings that struggled
within him. As for Marietta, to listen to him was ecstasy.
The glowing language of poetry, its brilliant imagery, its
melting softness, came upon her like refreshing rain upon
some arid soil, scorched and sun-stricken: her spirit, half-
crushed beneath daily hardships, rose at once to the magic
touch of ennobling sentiment. Oh! what a new world
was that which now opened before them: how beautiful,
how bright, how full of tenderness, how rich in generous
emotions!

'Only think,' said she, looking into his eyes, 'but this
very morning we had not known each other, and now we are
bound together for ever and ever. Is it not so, *Gherardi mio*?'

'So swear I!' cried Gerald, as he pressed her to his heart;
and then, in the full current of his warm eloquence, he poured
forth a hundred schemes for their future career. They would
seek out some sweet spot of earth, far away and secluded,
like that wherein they rambled then, only more beautiful in
verdure, and more picturesque, and build themselves a hut;
there they would live together a life of bliss.

It was only by earnest persuasion she could turn him from
at once putting the project into execution. ' Why not now?'
cried he. 'Here we are free, beyond the wood; you cross a
little stream, and we are in Tuscany. I saw the frontier
from the mountain-top this morning.'

'And then,' said the girl, 'how are we to live? We shall
neither have the Babbo nor Donna Gaetana; I cannot dance
without her music, nor have you learned anything as yet to
do. *Mio Gherardi*, we must wait and study hard; you must
learn to be Paolo, and to declaim "Antonio," too. I'll teach

you these; besides, the Babbo has a volume full of things would suit you. Our songs, too, we have not practised them together; and in the towns where we are going, the public, they say, are harder to please than in these mountain villages.' And then she pictured forth a life of artistic triumph—success dear to her humble heart, the very memory of which brought tears of joy to her eyes. These she was longing to display before him, and to make him share in. Thus talking, they returned to the encampment, where, as the heat was past, the Babbo was now preparing to set out on his journey.

CHAPTER XIV

THE ACCIDENTS OF 'ARTIST' LIFE

AN autumnal night, in all its mellow softness, was just closing in upon the Lungo l'Arno of Florence. Toward the east and south the graceful outlines of San Miniato, with its tall cypresses, might be seen against the sky, while all the city, which lay between, was wrapped in deepest shadow. It was the season of the Ville-giatura, when the great nobles are leading country lives; still the various bridges, and the quays at either side of the river, were densely crowded with people. The denizens of the close and narrow streets came forth to catch the faint breath of air that floated along the Arno. Seated on benches and chairs, or gathered in little knots and groups, the citizens seemed to enjoy this hour al fresco with a zest only known to those who have basked in the still and heated atmosphere of a southern climate. Truly, no splendid salon, in all the gorgeous splendour of its gildings, ever presented a spot so luxurious as that river-side, while the fresh breeze came, borne along the water's track from the snow-clad heights of Vallombrosa, gathering perfume as it came. No loud voices, no boisterous mirth disturbed the delicious calm of the enjoyment, but a low murmur of human sounds, attuned as it were to the gentle ripple of the passing stream, and here and there a light and joyous laugh, were only heard. At the Pont St. Trinita and immediately below it the crowd was densest, attracted, not impossibly, by the lights and movement that went on in a great palace close by, the only one of all those on the Arno that showed signs of habitation. Of the others the owners were absent; but here, through the open windows, might be seen figures passing and repassing, and at times the sounds of music heard from within. With that strange sympathy—for it is not all curiosity—that attracts people to watch the concourse of some gay company, the ebb and flow of intercourse, the crowd gazed eagerly up at the windows, commenting on this or that personage as they passed, and discussing together what they fancied might form the charm of such society.

The faint tinkling of a guitar in the street beneath, and the motion of the crowd, showed that some sort of street performance had attracted attention; and soon the balcony of the palace was thronged with the gay company, not sorry, as it seemed, to have this pretext for loitering in the free night air. To the brief prelude of the guitar a roll of the drum succeeded, and then, when silence had been obtained, might be heard the voice of an old, infirm man, announcing a programme of the entertainment. First of all—and by 'torch-light, if the respectable public would vouchsafe the expense'—The adventures of Don Callemacho among the Moors of Barbary; his capture, imprisonment, and escape; his rescue of the Princess of Cordova, with their shipwreck afterward on the island of Ithica: the whole illustrated with panoramic scenery, accompanied by music, and expressed by appropriate dialogue and dancing. The declamation to be delivered by a youth of consummate genius—the action to be enunciated by a Signorina of esteemed merit. 'I do not draw attention to myself, nor to the gifts of that excellent lady who presides over the drum,' continued he. 'Enough that Naples has seen, Venice praised, Rome applauded us.

We have gathered laurels at Milan; wreathed flowers have
fallen on us at Mantua; our pleasant jests have awoke
laughter in the wild valleys of Calabria; our pathos has
dimmed many an eye in the gorgeous halls of Genoa; princes
and contadini alike have shared in the enjoyment of our
talents; and so, with your favour, may each of you, *Gentilis-
simi Signori.*'

Whether, however, the 'intelligent public' was not as
affluent as it was gifted, or that, to apply the ancient adage,
'Le jeu ne valait pas la chandelle,' but so was it, that the
old man had twice made the tour of the circle without
obtaining a single quatrino.

'At Bologna, *O Signori*, they deemed this representation
worthy of wax-light. We gave it in the Piazza before two
thousand spectators, who, if less great or beautiful than those
we see here, were yet bountiful in their generosity! Sound
the drum, *comare mia*,' said he, addressing the old woman,
'and let the spirit-rousing roll inspire heroic longings. A
blast of the tromb, *figlio mio*, will set these noble hearts high-
beating for a tale of chivalry.' The deafening clamour of
drum and trumpet resounded through the air, and came
back in many an echo from across the Arno; but, alas! they
awoke no responsive sympathies in the audience, who probably having deemed that the spectacle might be partly
gratuitous, showed already signs of thinning away. 'Are
you going, *Illustrissimi Signori*,' cried he, more energetically,
'going without one view, one passing glance at the castle on
the Guadalquivir, with its court of fountains, all playing
and splashing like real water; going without a look at the
high-pooped galleon, as she sailed forth at morn, with the
banner of the house of Callemacho waving from the mast,
while the signal guns are firing a salute, the high cliffs of
Carthagena reverberating with the sound?' A loud 'bom'
from the drum gave testimony to the life-like reality of the
description. 'Going,' screamed he, more eagerly still, 'without witnessing the palace of the Moorish king, lit up at
night—ten thousand lanterns glittering along its marble

terraces, while strains of soft music fill the air ?   A gentle melody, *figlio mio*,' whispered he to the boy beside him.

'Let them go, in the devil's name!' broke out the old woman, whose harsh accents at once proclaimed our old acquaintance Donna Gaetana.

'What says she—what says the Donna ?' cried three or four of the crowd in a breath.

'She says that we'll come back in the daylight, *Signori*,' broke in the old man, in terror, 'and sing our native songs of Calabria, and show our native dances.   We know well, O gentle public, that poor ignorant creatures like ourselves are but too rash to appear before you great Florentines, citizens of Michel Angelo, dwellers with Benvenuto, companions of Boccaccio!'

'And not a quatrino among ye!' yelled out the old hag, with a laugh of scorn.

A wild cry of anger burst from the crowd, who, breaking the circle, now rushed in upon the strollers.

In vain the Babbo protested, explained, begged, and entreated.   He declared the company to be the highest, the greatest, the richest, he had ever addressed; himself and his companions the vilest and least worthy of humanity.   He asseverated in frantic tones his belief, that from the hour when he should lose their favour no fortune would ever attend on him, either in this world or the next.

But of what avail was it that he employed every eloquence at his command, while the Donna, with words of insult, and gestures more offensive still, reviled the 'base rabble,' and with all the virulence of her coarse nature hurled their poverty in their teeth ?

'Famished curs!' cried she.   'How would ye have a *soldo*, when your nobles dine on parched beans, and drink the little sour wine of Ponteseive ?'

A kick from a strong foot, that sent it through the parchment of the drum with a loud report, answered this insolent taunt, and gave the signal for a general attack.   Down went the little wooden edifice, which embodied the life and fortunes of the Don and the fair Princess of Cordova; down went the Babbo himself over it, amid a crash of properties, that created a yell of laughter in the mob. All the varied insignia of the cunning craft, basins and bladders, juggling sticks, hoops, and baskets, flew right and left, in wild confusion. Up to this time Gerald had witnessed the wreck unmoved, his whole care being to keep the crowd from pressing too rudely upon Marietta, who clung to him for protection. Indeed, the frantic struggles of old Gaetana, as she laid about her with her drum-sticks, had already provoked the youth's laughter, when, at a cry from the girl, he turned quickly around.

'Here's the Princess herself, I'll be sworn,' said a coarse-looking fellow, as, seizing Marietta's arm, he tried to drag her forward.

With a blow of his clenched fist Gerald sent him reeling back, and then, drawing the short scimitar which he wore as part of his costume, he swept the space in front of him, while he grasped the girl with his other arm. So unlooked-for a defiance seemed for an instant to unman the mob, but the next moment a shower of missiles, the fragments of old Babbo's fortune, were showered upon them. Had he been assailed by wild beasts, Gerald's assault could not have been more wildly daring: he cut on every side, hurling back those that rushed in upon him, and even trampling them beneath his feet. ·

Bleeding and bruised, half-blinded, too, by the blood that flowed from a wound on his forehead, the youth still held his ground, not a word escaping him, not a cry; while the reviling of the mob filled the air around. At last, shamed at the miserable odds that had so long resisted them, the rabble, with a wild yell of vengeance, rushed forward in a mass, and though some of the foremost fell covered with blood, the youth was dashed to the ground, all eagerly pressing to trample on and crush him.

'Over the parapet with him! Into the Arno with them both!' cried the mob.

'Stand back, ye cowardly crew!' shouted a loud, strong voice, and a powerful man, with a heavy bludgeon in his hand, burst through the crowd, felling all that opposed him; a throng of livery servants armed in the same fashion followed; and the mob, far more in number though they were, shrank back abashed from the sight of one whose rank and station might exact a heavy vengeance.

'It is the Principe. It is the Conte himself,' muttered one or two, as they stole off, leaving in a few moments the space cleared of all, save the wounded and those who had come to the rescue. If the grief of Donna Gaetana was loudest, the injuries of poor Gerald were the gravest there. A deep cut had laid open his forehead, another had cleft his shoulder, while a terrible blow of a stone in the side made his respiration painful in the extreme.

'Safe, *Marietta mia*; art safe?' whispered he, as she assisted him to rise. 'My poor boy,' said the Count compassionately; 'she *is* safe, and owes it all to you. You behaved nobly, lad. The Don himself, with all his Castilian blood, could not show a more courageous front.'

Gerald looked at the speaker, and whether at the tone of his voice, or that the words seemed to convey an unseemly jest at such a moment, he flushed till his cheek was crimson, and drawing himself up said: 'And who are you? or by what right do you pronounce upon *my* blood?'

'*Gherardi mio, caro fratellino*,' whispered the girl. 'It was he that saved us, and he is a Prince!'

'For the first, I thank him,' said the youth. 'As to his rank, it is his own affair and not mine.'

'Well spoken, faith!' said the noble. 'I tell thee, Giorgio,' added he to a friend at his side, 'poets may well feel proud, when they see how the very utterance of their noble sentiments engenders noble thoughts. Look at that tatterdemalion, and think how came he by such notions.'

The abject expression of Babbo's gratitude, and the far more demonstrative enunciations of old Gaetana's misery, here interrupted the colloquy. In glowing terms she pictured the calamity that had befallen them—a disaster irreparable for evermore. Never again would human ingenuity construct such mechanism as that which illustrated Don Callemacho's life. The conjuring tools, too, were masterpieces, not to be replaced; and as to the drum, no contrivance of mere wood and ram-skin ever would give forth such sounds again.

'Who knows, worthy Donna?' said the Count, with a grave half-smile. 'Your own art might teach you, that even the great drama of antiquity has its imitators—some say superiors—in our day.'

'I'd say so for one!' cried Gerald, wiping the blood from his face.

'Would you so, indeed?' asked the Count.

'That would I, so long as glorious Alfieri lives,' said Gerald resolutely.

'What hast thou read of thy favourite poet, boy?' asked the Count.

'What have I not?—the Saul, the Agamemnon, Oreste, Maria Stuart.'

'Ah, Signor Principe, you should hear him in Oreste,' broke in Gaetana; 'and he plays a solo on the trombone after the second act: he sets every ass in the Campagna a-braying, when he comes to one part. Do it, *Gherardi mio*; do it for his Highness. *Ohi me!* we have no trombone left us,' and she burst out into a torrent of grief.

'Take these people to the inn at the Porta Rossa,' said the Count to one of his servants. 'Let them be well cared for and attended to. Fetch a surgeon to see this boy. *Adio*, my friends. I'll come and see you to-morrow, when you are well rested and refreshed.'

In a boisterous profusion of thanks, old Babbo and the Donna uttered their gratitude, while Gerald and Marietta kissed their benefactor's hand, and moved on.

'He's a noble Signor,' muttered old Gaetana; 'and I'd swear by the accent of his words he is no Florentine.'

'Thou art right for once, old lady,' said the servant, as he led the way; 'he's of the north, and the best blood of Piedmont.'

CHAPTER XV

A TUSCAN POLICE COURT

LONG before their generous patron had awoke the following morning, the little company of Babbo were standing as prisoners in the dread presence of the Prefetto. Conducted by a detachment of the carabinieri, and secured with manacles enough to have graced the limbs of galley-slaves, the 'vagabonds,' as they were politely called, were led along through the streets, amid the jokes and mockeries of a very unsympathising public.

Tuscan justice, we are informed by competent authority, has not made, either in its essence or externals, any remarkable progress since the time we are now speaking of. The same ruinous old edifice stands the Temple of Justice; the same dirt and squalor disgraces its avenues and approaches; the same filthy mob beset the doors—a ragged mob, in whose repulsive features a smashed decalogue is marked, amid whom, in hot and eager haste, are seen some others, a shadow better in dress, but more degraded still in look—the low advocates of these courts, 'Cavallochi,' as they are styled —a class whose lives of ignominy and subornation would comprise almost every known species of rascality. By these men are others goaded on and stimulated to prefer claims against the well-to-do and respectable; by them are charges devised, circumstances invented, perjuries provided, at the shortest notice. They have their company of false witnesses ready for any accusation—no impugnment upon their credit being the fact that they live by perjury, and have no other subsistence.

Meet president of such a court was the scowling, ill-dressed, and ill-favoured fellow who, with two squalid clerks at his side, sat judge of the tribunal. A few swaggering carabinieri, with their carbines on their arms, moved in and

out of the court, buffeting the crowd with rude gestures,
and deporting themselves like masters of the ignoble herd
around them. By these, as it seemed—for all was mere
conjecture here—were the cases chosen for adjudication, the
selection of the particular charges being their especial province. Elbowing their way through the filthy corridors,
where accusers and accused were inextricably mingled—the
prisoner, and the plaintiff, and the witness all jammed up
together, and not unfrequently discussing the vexed question
to be tried with all the virulence of partisans—the carabiniere
makes his choice among these, aided, not impossibly, by a
stimulant, which in Italy has its agency throughout all ranks
and gradations of men.

In this vile assemblage of all that was degrading and
wretched our poor strollers were now standing, their foreign
aspect and their title of vagabonds obtaining for them a
degree of notice the reverse of flattering. Sarcastic remarks
upon their looks, their means of life, and, stranger still, their
poverty, abounded; and these from a mob whose gaunt and
famished faces and tattered rags bespoke the last stage of
destitution.

The Babbo, indeed, was a picture of abject misery; bank-
rupt was written on every line of his poor old face, through
which the paint of forty years blended with the sickly hues
of hunger and fear. He turned upon the bystanders a
glance of mild entreaty, however, that in a less cruel company
could not have failed to meet some success. Not so Donna
Gaetana: *her* stare was an open defiance, and even through
her bleared eyes there shot sparks of fiery passion that
seemed only in search of a fitting object for their attack.

As for Gerald—his head bound up in a bloody rag, his
arm in a sling, and his face pale as death—he might have
disarmed the malice of sarcasm, had it not been that he held
his arm clasped close round Marietta's waist, and even thus,
in all his misery, seemed to assert that he was her protector
and defender. This was alone sufficient to afford scope for
mockery and derision, the fairer portion of the audience dis-

tinguishing themselves by the pungent sharpness of their criticisms; and Marietta's swarthy skin, her tinsel raggedness, and her wild, bold eyes, came in for their share of bitter commentary.

'What a brazen-faced minx it is!' cried one.

'What a young creature to have come to such wickedness!' exclaimed another.

'Look at the roundness of her shape, and you'll see she is not so very young neither,' whispered a third.

'That's her gypsy blood,' broke in another. 'There was one here t'other day, of thirteen, with an infant at her breast; and, more by token, she had just put a stiletto into its father.'

'The ragazza yonder looks quite equal to the same deed,' observed the former speaker, 'if _I_ know anything about what an eye means.'

'Vincenzio Bombici—where is Vincenzio Bombici?' cried a surly-looking brigadier, whose large cocked-hat, set squarely on, increased the apparent breadth of an immensely wide face.

'_Ecco mi, Eccelenza!_' whimpered out a wretched-looking object, who, with his face bound up, and himself all swathed like Lazarus from the tomb, came, helped forward by two assistants.

'Pass in, Vincenzio, and narrate your case,' said the brigadier, as he opened a door into the dread chamber of justice.

While public sympathy followed the Signor Bombici into the hall of justice, fresh expressions of anger were vented on the unhappy strollers. Any one conversant with Italy is aware that so divided is the peninsula by national jealousies —feuds that date from centuries back—the most opprobrious epithet that hate or passion can employ against any one is to stigmatise him as the native of some other town or city. And now the mob broke into such gibes as, 'Accursed Calabrians! Ah, vile assassins from Capri'—from Corsica, from the Abruzzi; from anywhere, in short, save the

favoured land they stood in. Donna Gaetana was not one
who suffered herself to be arraigned without reply, nor was
she remarkable for moderation in the style and manner of
her rejoinders. With a voluble ribaldry for which her nation
enjoys a proud pre-eminence, she assailed her opponents,
one and all. She ridiculed their pretensions, mocked their
poverty, jeered at their cowardice, and—last insult of all—
derided their personal appearance.

Passion fed her eloquence, and the old dame vented upon
them insult after insult with a volubility that was astounding.
There is no need to record the vindictive and indecorous
epithets she scattered broadcast around her; and even as her
enemies skulked craven from the field, her wrathful indignation tracked them as they went, sending words of outrage to
bear them company. The mere numerical odds was strong
against her, and the clamour that arose was deafening, drawing crowds to the doors and the street in front, and at last
gaining such a height as to invade the sacred precincts of
justice, overbearing the trembling accents of Bombici as he
narrated his tale of woe. Out rushed the valiant carabinieri
with the air of men hurrying to a storm, cleaving their
way through the crowd—striking, buffeting, trampling all
before them. At sight of the governmental power the crowd
quailed at once, all save one, the Donna. Standing to her
guns to the last, she now turned her sarcasms upon the
gendarmes, overwhelming them with a perfect torrent of
abuse, and with such success that the mob, so lately the mark
of her virulence, actually shook with laughter at the new
victims to her passion. For a moment discipline seemed like
to yield to anger. The warriors appeared to waver in their
impassive valour; but suddenly, with a gleam of wiser counsel, they formed a semi-circle behind the accused, and marched
them bodily into the presence of the judge.

Justice was apparently accustomed to similar interruptions;
at least, it neither seemed shocked nor disconcerted, but continued to listen with unbroken interest to Vincenzio Bombici's
sorrows—not, indeed, that he had arrived at the incident of

the night before. Far from it. He was merely preluding in that fashion which the exactitude of the Tuscan law requires, and replying to the interesting interrogatories regarding his former life, so essential to a due understanding of his present complaint.

'You are, then, the son of Matteo Friuli Bombici, by his wife Fiammetta?' read out the prefect solemnly, from the notes he was taking.

'No, Eccelenza. She was my father's second wife. My mother's name was Pacifica.'

'Pacifica,' wrote the prefect. 'Daughter of whom?'

'Of Felice Corsari, tin-worker in the Borgo St. Apostoli.'

'Not so fast, not so fast,' interposed the judge, as he took down the words, and then muttered to himself, 'in the Borgo St. Apostoli.'

'My mother was one of eight—three sons and five daughters. The eldest boy, Onofrio——'

'Irrelevant, irrelevant; or, if necessary, to be recorded hereafter,' said the prefect. 'You were bred and brought up in the Catholic faith?'

'Yes, Eccelenza. The Prete of San Gaetano has confessed me since I was eleven years old. I have taken out more than two hundred pauls in private masses, and paid for three novenas and a plenary, as the Prete will vouch.'

'I will note your character in this respect, Vincenzio,' said the judge approvingly.

'They will probably bring up before your worship the story against my father, that he stole the cloak of the Cancelliere Martelli, when he was performing the part of Pontius Pilate in the holy mysteries at Sienna; but we have the documents at home——'

'Are they registered?'

'I believe not, Eccelenza.'

'Are they stamped?'

'I'm afraid not, Eccelenza. The Cavallochio that defended my father couldn't write himself, and it was one Leonardo Capprini——'

'The sausage-maker,' broke in the judge, with a smack of his lips.

'The same, Eccelenza; you knew him, perhaps?'

'Knew him well, and liked his hog's puddings much.' Justice seemed half ashamed at this confession of a weakness, and in a more stern tone, told him to 'Go on.'

It was not very easy for honest Vincenzio to know at what part of his history he was to take up the thread; so he shuffled from foot to foot, and sighed despondingly.

'I said "go on,"' said the judge, more peremptorily than before.

'I was talking of my father, Eccelenza,' said he modestly.

'No, of your good mother Fiammetta,' said the judge, rather proud of the accuracy with which he retained the family history.

'She was my step-mother,' interposed Vincenzio humbly.

'Blockheads all!' broke in old Gaetana, with a hearty laugh.

'Silence!' cried the gendarmes, as, with their muskets dropped to the ground, they made the chamber ring again, while the judge, turning a glance of darkening anger on the speaker, said: 'Who is this old woman?'

'Let *me* tell him. Let myself speak,' cried Gaetana, pressing forward, while the gendarmes, with their instinct as to coming peril, prudently held her back.

'So then,' said the judge, in reply to a whisper of one of his assistants, 'she is the principal delinquent'; and referring to the written charge before him, read out: 'An infuriated woman, who presided over the drum.'

'They smashed it, the thieves!' cried Gaetana; 'they smashed my drum; but, *per Dio*, I beat a roll on their own skulls that astonished them! They'll not deny that I gave them an ear for music.' And the old hag laughed loud at her savage jest.

Again was silence commanded, and after some trouble obtained; and the judge, whose perceptions were evidently disturbed by these interruptions, betook himself to the pages

of the indictment, to refresh his mind on the case. Muttering to himself the lines, he came to the words, 'and with a
formidable weapon, of solid wood, with the use of which long
habit had rendered her familiar, and in this wise dangerous,
she, the aforesaid Gaetana, struck, beat, battered, and be-
laboured——'

'Didn't I!' broke in the hag.

What consequences might have ensued from this last interruption must be left to mere guess, for the door of the
chamber was now opened to its widest to admit a gentleman,
who came forward with the air of one in a certain authority.
He was no other than the Count of the night before, who
had so generously thrown his protection over the strollers.
Advancing to where the Prefetto sat, he leaned one arm on
the table, while he spoke to him in a low voice.

The judge listened with deference and attention, his
manner being suddenly converted into the very lowest
sycophancy. When it came to his turn to speak, 'Certainly,
Signor Conte; unquestionable,' muttered he. 'It is enough
that your Excellency deigns to express a wish on the subject,' and, with many a bow, he accompanied him to the
door. A brief nod to the youth Gerald was the only sign
of recognition he gave, and the Count withdrew.

'This case is prorogued,' said the Prefetto solemnly.
'The Court will inform itself upon its merits, and convoke
the parties on some future day.' And now the gendarmes
proceeded to clear the hall, huddling out together plaintiffs
and prisoners and witnesses, all loudly inveighing, pro-
testing, denouncing, and explaining what nobody listened
to or cared for.

'Eh viva!' exclaimed old Gaetana, as she reached the
open air, 'there's more justice here than I looked for.'

CHAPTER XVI

THE POET'S HOUSE

It was late on the evening of the same day that Gerald received a message to say the Count desired to see him. No little jealousy was occasioned among his companions by this invitation. The Babbo deemed that, as 'Impressario' of the company, he ought himself to have been selected. Donna Gaetana was indignant that a mere Giovane was to occupy the responsible station of representing their dramatic guild; and even Marietta felt her eyes to swim, as she thought over this mere passing separation, and in her heart foreboded some ill to come of it. She, however, did her very best to master these unworthy fears. She washed the bloody stains carefully off his forehead. She combed and oiled his long silky hair. She aided him to dress in the one only suit that now remained of all his wardrobe —a page's dress of light blue, with a little scarlet mantle, embroidered in silver, and a small bonnet surmounted by an ostrich feather. Nor was it without deep shame, and something very like open rebellion, that Gerald donned these motley habiliments.

'The Count has not said that he wants me to exhibit before him—why am I to masquerade in this fashion?'

'There is no choice for you between this "tinsel bravery" and the tattered rags, all blood-stained and torn, you wore last night.' There they were, scattered about, the crushed and crumpled hat, the doublet torn to ribbons, the rapier smashed—all a wreck. 'No, no, you could not appear in such a presence in rags like these.' Still was Gerald irritated and angry : a sudden sense of shame shot through him as he saw himself thus alone, which, had the others been joined with him, he had doubtless never felt ; and for the first time his station suggested the idea of humiliation.

'I will not go, Marietta,' said he at last, as he flung himself upon a chair, and threw his cap to the end of the room. 'So long as thou wert with me, sustaining the interest of the scene, replying to my words, answering every emotion of my heart, I loved Art—I cherished it as the fairest expression of what I felt, but could not speak. Now, alone and without thee, it is a mere mockery—it is more, it is a degradation!'

She knelt down beside him and took his hands in hers. She turned her full, moist eyes toward him, and in broken words besought him not to speak slightingly of that which bound them to each other, for, 'If the day comes, *Gherardi mio*, that thou thinkest meanly of our ART, so surely will come another when thou wilt be ashamed of *me*,' and she hid her face on his knees and sobbed bitterly. With what an honest-hearted sincerity did he swear that such a day could never come, or if it did, that he prayed it might be his last! And then he ran over, in eager tones, all that he owed to her teachings. How, but for her, he had not known the true tenderness of Metastasio, the fervour of Petrarch, or the chivalry of Ariosto. 'How much have we found out together we had never discovered if alone!'

And then they dried their tears; and he kissed her, and set out on his way.

It was with a look of haughty meaning, almost defiant, that Gerald ascended the marble stairs and passed between two lines of liveried servants, who smiled pitifully on the strolling player, nor put the slightest restraint upon this show of their contempt. Fortunately for him and them he had no time to mark it, for the folding doors suddenly opening, he found himself in a large chamber, brilliantly lighted, and with a numerous company assembled. Before the youth had well crossed the door-sill the Count was at his side, and having kindly taken him by the hand, expressed a hope that he no longer felt any bad effects of his late ill-treatment.

Gerald stammered out his acknowledgments, and tried to make some excuses for his costume, which ended, at last, by the blunt avowal, 'It was this or nothing, sir.

'The mishap is not without its advantage,' said the Count, in that calm voice which, but for a peculiar expression on his mouth when he spoke, had something almost severe about it. 'It was the resemblance you bear to a certain portrait was the reason of my sending for you to-night : your dress assists the likeness, for, strangely enough, it is of the very same style and colour as that of the picture. Come forward, and I will present you to a lady who is curious to see you.'

'Madame la Duchesse, this is the youth,' said the Count, as he bowed before a lady, who was seated in a deep chair, at either side of which some ladies and gentlemen were standing. She closed her fan and leaned forward, and Gerald beheld a countenance which, if not beautiful, was striking enough to be remembered for years after. She was a blonde of the purest type, with full blue eyes, and masses of light hair, which in long ringlets descended to her very shoulders; the features were youthful, though she herself was no longer young; and the same contradiction existed in their expression, for they were calm, without softness, and had a fixity almost to sternness, while their colouring and tint were actually girlish in freshness. There was in her air and demeanour, too, a similar discordance, for, though with a look of dignity, her gestures were abrupt, and her manner of speaking hurried.

'He *is* like,' said she, scanning him through her eye-glass. 'Come nearer, boy. Yes, strangely like,' said she, with a smile, rather indicating sarcasm than courtesy. 'Let us compare him with the portrait,' and she gave her hand languidly, as she spoke, to be assisted to rise. The Count aided her with every show of deference, respectfully offering his arm to conduct her; but she declined the attention with a slight motion of the head, and moved slowly on. As she went, the various persons who were seated arose, and they who stood in groups talking, hushed their voices, and stood in a respectful attitude as she passed. None followed her but the Count and Gerald, who at a signal walked slowly behind.

After traversing three rooms, whose costly furniture

amazed the youth, they reached a small chamber, where
two narrow windows opened upon a little terrace. A single
picture occupied the wall in front of these, to either side of
whose frame two small lamps were attached, with shades so
ingeniously contrived as to throw the light at will on any
part of the painting. The Duchess had seated herself
immediately on entering, with the air of one wearied and
exhausted, and the Count occupied himself in disposing the
lamps to most advantage.

'Stand yonder, boy, and hold your cap in your hand, as
you see it in the portrait,' and Gerald turned his eyes to the
picture, and actually started at the marvellous resemblance
to himself. The figure was that of a youth somewhat older,
perhaps, than himself, dressed in a suit of velvet, with a
deep lace collar and hanging ruffles; the long ringlets, which
fell in profusion on his neck, the expression of the eyes, a
look of sadness not unmixed with something stern, and a
haughty gathering of the lower lip, were all that a painter
might have given to Gerald, if endeavouring to impart to his
likeness some few additional traits of vigour and determination.

'It is wonderful!' said the Duchess, after a long pause.

'So, indeed, it strikes me,' said the Count. 'Mark, even
to the flattening of the upper lip, how the resemblance
holds.'

'What age are you—are you a Roman—what is your
name?' asked the Duchess, in a hurried but careless manner.

'My name is Fitzgerald. They call me here Gherardi, for
some of the race took that name in Italy.'

'So that you talk of blood and lineage, boy?' asked she
haughtily.

'I am of the Geraldines, lady, and they were princes!' said
the boy, as proudly.

'Came they from Scotland?' she asked eagerly.

'No, madam, they were Irish.'

'Irish! Irish!' muttered she twice or thrice, below her
breath; then, as her eyes caught sight of his features

suddenly, she started and exclaimed: 'It is nigh incredible! And how came you to Italy?'

With that brevity which distinguished Gerald when speaking of himself, he told of his having been a scholar with the Jesuits, where some—he knew not exactly which—of his relatives had placed him.

'And you left them; how, and wherefore?' inquired the Duchess.

'I know not by what right, madam, I am thus questioned. Is it because I wear such tinsel rags as these?'

'Bethink you in whose presence you stand, boy?' said the Count sternly; 'that lady is one before whom the haughtiest noble is proud to lay his homage.'

'Nay, nay,' broke she in gently, 'he will tell me all I ask in kindness, not in fear.'

'Not in fear, I promise you,' said he proudly, and he drew himself up to his highest.

'Was not that like him!' exclaimed the Duchess eagerly. 'It was his own voice! And what good Italian you speak, boy,' said she, addressing Gerald, with a pleasant smile. 'The Jesuit Fathers have given you the best Roman accent. Tell me, what were their teachings—what have you read?'

'Nothing regularly—nothing in actual study, madam; but, passingly, I have read, in French, some memoirs, plays, sermons, poems, romances, and suchlike; in English, very little; and in Italian, a few of the very good.'

'Which do you call the very good?'

'I call Dante.'

'So do I. Go on.'

'Sometimes I call Tasso, always Ariosto, so.'

She nodded an assent, and told him to continue.

'Then there is Metastasio.'

'What say you of him?' asked the Count.

'I like him: his rhymes flow gracefully, and the music of his verse floats sweetly in one's ear; but then, there is not that sentiment, that vigorous dash that stirs the heart, like a trumpet-call, such as we find, for instance, in Alfieri.'

The Duchess smiled assuringly, and a faint, very faint tinge of red coloured her pale cheek. 'It appears, then, he is your favourite of them all?' said she gently. 'Can you remember any of his verses?'

'That can I. I knew him, at one time, off by heart, but somehow, in this ignoble life of mine, I almost felt ashamed to recite his noble lines to those who heard me. To think, for example, of the great poet of the Oreste declaimed before a vile mob, impatient for some buffoonery, eager for the moment when the jugglery would begin!'

'But you forget, boy, this is true fame! It is little to the great poet that he is read and admired by those to whose natures he can appeal by all the emotions which are common to each—lasting sympathies, whose dwelling-places he knows; the great triumph is, to have softened the hearts seared by dusty toil—to have smitten the rock whose water is tears of joy and thankfulness. Is not Ariosto prouder as his verses float along the dark canals of Venice, than when they are recited under gilded ceilings?'

'You may be right,' said the boy thoughtfully, as he hung his head; 'am I not, myself, a proof of what the bright images of poetry have cheered and gladdened, out of depths of gloom and wretchedness? Not that I complain of this life of mine!' cried he suddenly.

'Tell us about it, boy; it must present strange scenes and events,' said the Count, and, taking Gerald's arm, he pressed him to a seat beside him. The Duchess, too, bent on him one of her kindest smiles, so that he felt encouraged in a moment.

And now Gerald talked away, as only the young can talk about themselves and their fortunes. Their happy gift it is to have a softly tempered tint over even their egotism, making it often not ungraceful. He sketched a picturesque description of the stroller's life: its freedom compensating for the hardships; its careless ease recompensing many a passing mishap; the strange blending of study with little quaint and commonplace preparation; the mind now charged with bright fancies, now busy in all the intricacies of costume;

the ever-watchful attention to the taste of that strange public
that formed their patron, and who, not unfrequently wearying
of Tasso and Guarini, called loudly for Punch and his ribald-
ries. The boy's account of the Babbo and Donna Gaetana
was not devoid of humour, and he painted cleverly the simple
old devotee giving every spare hour he could snatch to
penances for the life he was leading; while the Donna took
the world by storm, and started each day to the combat,
like a soldier mounting a breach. Lastly he came to
Marietta, and then his voice changed, his cheek grew red
and white by turns, and his chest heaved full and short, like
one oppressed. He did not mark the looks of intelligence
that passed between the Duchess and the Count: he never
saw how each turned to listen to him with the self-same
expression on their features; he was too full of his theme to
note these things, and yet he could not dilate upon it as he
had about Babbo and the Donna.

'I saw her,' said the Count, as Gerald came to a pause.
'I noticed her at the court, and she was, indeed, very handsome. Something Egyptian in the cast of features.'

'But not a gypsy!' broke in the boy quickly.

'No, perhaps not. The eyes and brow resembled the
Moorish race—the same character of fixity in expression.
Eyes, that carry—

'"I tesori d'amore e i suoi nasconde."'

There was a sly malice in the way the Count led the boy
on, opening the path, as it were, to his enthusiasm, and so
artfully, that Gerald never suspected it.

No longer restrained by fear or chilled by shame, he
launched out into praises of her beauty, her gracefulness, and
her genius. He told the Count that it was sufficient to read
for her once over a poem of Petrarch, and she could repeat it
word for word. With the same facility could she compose
music for words that struck her fancy. The silvery sweetness
of her voice—her light and graceful step—the power of expression she possessed by gesture, look, and mien—he went

over all these with a rapture that actually warmed into eloquence, and they who listened heard him with pleasure, and encouraged him to continue.

'We must see your Marietta,' said the Duchess at last. 'You shall bring her here.'

Gerald's cheek flushed, but whether with shame, or pride, or displeasure, or all three commingled, it were hard to say. In truth, many a hard conflict went on within him, when, out of his dream of art and its triumphs, he would suddenly awake, and bethink him in what humble estimation men held such as he was; how closely the world insisted on associating poverty with meanness; and how hopeless were the task of him who would try to make himself respected in rags.

As these thoughts arose in his mind, he lifted his eyes once more to the portrait, and in bitterness of heart he felt how little resemblance there was in the condition of the youth there represented and himself.

'I see what you are thinking of,' said the Duchess mildly. 'Shall I show you another picture? It is of one you profess to admire greatly—your favourite poet.'

'I pray you do, madam. I long to know his features. It is a face I have painted in fancy often and often.'

'Tell me, then, how you would portray him,' said she, smiling.

'Not regularly handsome; but noble-looking, with the traits of one who had such vigour of life and mind within, that he lived more for his own thoughts than the world, and thus would seem proud to sternness. A high, bold forehead, narrow and indented at the temples, and a deep brow over two fierce eyes. O! what wildly flashing eyes should Alfieri's be when stirred by passion and excitement!'

'And should you find him different from all this—a man of milder mould, more commonplace and less vigorous—will you still maintain that faith in his genius that now you profess?' said the Count, with slow and quiet utterance.

'That will I. How could I, in my presumption, doubt the power that has moved the hearts of thousands?'

'Come, then, and look at him,' said the Duchess, and she arose, and moved into a room fitted up as a library. Over the chimney was a large picture, covered by a silk curtain. To this Gerald eagerly turned his eyes, for he already marked that the gilded eagle that surmounted the frame held in his beak a wreath of flowers, interwoven with laurel leaves.

'One whose enthusiasm equals your own, boy, placed the wreath there, on the 17th of January last. It was the festa of Vittorio Alfieri,' said the Duchess, as she gently pulled the cord that drew back the curtain.

Gerald moved eagerly forward—gazed—passed his hand across his eyes, as if to dispel a fancy—gazed again and again—and then, turning round, stood steadfastly staring at the Count himself. A faint, sad smile was on the calm and haughty face; but, as it passed away, the boy dropped down upon his knees, and seizing the other's hand, kissed it rapturously, as he cried—

'Oh! that I should have ever known a moment like this! Tell me, I beseech thee, Signor Conte, is my brain wandering, or are you Alfieri?'

'Yes, boy,' said he, with a slight sigh, while he raised him from the ground, laying one hand gently on his shoulder.

'It is with reason, boy, you are proud of this event in your life,' said the Duchess. 'The truly great are few in this world of ours; and you now stand before one whose memory will be treasured when we are all dust.'

The poet did not seem to heed or hear these words, but stood calmly watching the boy, who continued to turn his eyes alternately from the picture to the original.

'I suspect, boy,' said he, with a smile, 'that your mind-drawn picture satisfied you better—is it not so?'

'O! you who can so read hearts, why will you not interpret mine?' cried Gerald, in rapture; for now to his memory in quick succession were rising the brilliant fancies, the splendid images, the heart-moving words of one whose genius had been a sort of worship to him.

'This, too, is fame!' said the poet, turning to the Duchess.

'But we are keeping you too long from your guests, madam; and Gherardi and I will have many an opportunity of meeting. Come up here to-morrow in the forenoon, and let me talk with you. The youth is more complimentary to me than was the cardinal yesterday.'

'What was it that he said?' asked she.

'He wondered I should have written the tragedy of "Saul," since we had it already in the Bible! To-morrow, Gherardi, about eleven, or even earlier—*a rivederlo!*'

As with slow steps, half in a dream, and scarce daring to credit his senses, Gerald moved down the stairs, the poet overtook him, and pressing a purse into his hand, said—

'You must have some more suitable dress than this, and remember to-morrow.'

CHAPTER XVII

A LOVER'S QUARREL

WHEN Gerald found himself once more in his little room at the Porta Rosa, it was past midnight. He opened his window and sat down at it to gaze out upon the starry sky and drink in the refreshing night air, but, more than even these, to calm down the excitement of his feelings, and endeavour to persuade himself that what he had passed through was not a dream. It is not easy for those who have access to every grade they wish in life—who, perhaps, confer honour where they go—to fashion to their minds the strange, wild conflict that raged within the youth's heart at this moment. Little as he had seen of the great poet, he could not help comparing him with Gabriel, his acquaintance at the Tana. They were both proud, cold, stern men — strong in conscious power, self-reliant and daring. Are all men of genius of that stamp? thought Gerald. Are they who diffuse through existence its most elevating influences, its most softening emotions—are

they hard of mould and stern in character? Does the force
with which they move the world require this impulse of
temperament, as rivers that traverse great continents come
down, at first, from lofty mountains? And if it be so, is not
this a heavy price for which to buy even fame? Then, again,
he bethought him, what a noble gift to bestow must be the
affection of such men—how proud must be they who owned
their love or shared their friendship! While he was thus
musing a round, warm arm clasped his neck, and Marietta
sat down beside him. She had waited hours for his return,
and now stole gently to his room to meet him.

'I could not sleep till I had seen you, *caro*,' said she fondly.
'It seemed as if in these few hours years had separated us.'

'And if they had, Marietta, they could scarcely have
brought about anything stranger. Guess where I have been
—with whom I have passed this entire evening?'

'How can I? Was he a prince?'

'Greater than any prince.'

'That must mean a king, then.'

'Kings die, and a few lines chronicle them; but I speak
of one whose memory will be graven in his language, and
whose noble sentiments will be texts to future generations.
What think you of Alfieri?'

'Alfieri!'

'Himself. He was the Count who rescued us from the
mob, and with him I have passed the hours since I saw
you. Not that I ever knew nor suspected it, Marietta: if
I had, I had never dared to speak as I did about ourselves
and our wayward lives in such a presence. I had felt these
themes ignoble.'

'How so?' cried she eagerly. 'You have ever told me
that art was an ennobling and a glorious thing; that after
those whose genius embodied grand conceptions, came he
who gave them utterance. How often have you said, the
poet lives but half in men's hearts whose verses have not
found some meet interpreter; with words like these have
you stimulated me to study, and now——'

'And now,' said he, sighing drearily, 'I wake to feel
what a mere mockery it is:

> " Tra l'ombra è bella
> L'istessa stella
> Che in faccia del sole
> Non si mirò."

Ah, *Marietta mia*, he who creates is alone an artist!'

The girl bent her head upon her bosom, and while her
long waving curls fell loosely over him, she sobbed bitterly.
Gerald clasped her closer to his heart, but never spoke a
syllable.

'I ever thought it would be so,' murmured she at last: 'I
felt that in this sense of birth and blood you boasted of,
would one day come a feeling of shame to be the companion
of such as me. It is not from art itself you turn away, it
is the company of the strolling actor that you shun.'

'And who or what am I that I should do so?' said Gerald
boldly. 'When, or where, have I known such happiness as
with you, Marietta? Bethink you of the hours we have
passed together, poring over these dear old books there,
enriching our hearts with noble thoughts, and making the
poet the interpreter between us? Telling, too, in the fervour
we spoke his lines, how tenderly we felt them; as Metastasio
says:

> " And as we lisped the verse along,
> Learning to love."'

'And now it is over,' said she, with a sigh of deep despondency.

'Why so? Shall I, in learning to know the great and
the illustrious—to feel how their own high thoughts sway
and rule them—be less worthy of your love? The poet
told me, to-night, that I declaimed his lines well; but who
taught me to feel them, *Marietta mia*?' And he kissed her
cheek, bathed as it was and seamed with hot tears. Again
he tried to bring back the dream of the past, and their oft-

projected scheme of life; but he urged the theme no longer as of old; and even when describing the world they were about to fly from, his words trembled with the emotion that swelled in his heart. In the midst of all these would he break off suddenly with some recollection of Alfieri, who filled every avenue of his thoughts: his proud but graceful demeanour, his low, deep-toned voice, his smile so kind and yet so sad withal; a gentleness, too, in his manner that invited confidence, seemed to dwell in Gerald's memory, and shed, as it were, a soft and pleasing light over all that had passed.

'And I am to see him again to-morrow, Marietta,' continued he proudly; 'he is to take me with him to the Galleries. I am to see the Pitti and the Offizzi, where in the Tribune the great triumphs of Raffael are placed, and the statue of Venus, too: he is to show me these, and the portraits of all the illustrious men who have made Italy glorious. How eager I am to know how they looked in life, and if their features revealed the consciousness of the fame they were to inherit! And when I come back at night to thee, Marietta, how full shall I be of all these, and how overjoyed if I can pour into your heart the pleasures that swell in my own! Is it not good, dearest, that I should go forth thus to bring back to you the glad tidings of so many beautiful things—will you not be happier for *yourself*, prouder in *me*? Will it not be better to have the love of one whose mind is daily expanding, straining to greater efforts, growing in knowledge and gaining in cultivation? Shall I not be more worthy of *you* if I win praise from others? And I am resolved to do this, Marietta. I will not be satisfied to be ever the mean, ignoble thing I now am.'

'Our life did not seem so unworthy in your eyes a day or two ago,' said she sighing. 'You told me, as we came up the Val d'Arno, that our wandering, wayward existence had a poetry of its own that you loved dearly. That to you ambition could never offer a path equal to that wayside

rambling life, over whose little accidents the softening influences of divine verse shed their mild light, so that the
ideal world dominated the actual.'

'All these will I realise, but in a higher sphere, Marietta.
The great Alfieri himself told me that a life without labour
is an ignominy and a shame. That he who strains his
faculties to attain a goal is nobler far than one whose higher
gifts lie rusting in disuse. Man lives not for himself, but
for his fellows, said he, nor is there such incarnate selfishness
as indolence.'

'And where, and how, and when is this wondrous life of
exertion to be begun?' said she half-scornfully. 'Can the
great poet pour into your heart out of the fulness of his
own, and make you as he is? Or are you suddenly become
rich and great, like *him*?'

The youth started, and an angry flush covered his face,
and even his forehead, as he arose and walked the room.

'I see well what is working within you,' said the girl.
'The contrast from that splendour to this misery—these
poor bleak walls, where no pictures are hanging, no gilding
glitters—is too great for you. It is the same shock to your
nature as from the beautiful princess in whose presence you
stood to that humble bench beside *me*.'

'No, by Heaven! Marietta,' cried he passionately, 'I have
not an ambition in my heart wherein your share is not
allotted. It is that you may walk with me to the goal——'

A scornful gesture of disbelief, one of those movements
which, with Italians, have a significance no words ever
convey, interrupted his protestation.

'This is too bad!' he cried; 'nor had you ever conceived
such distrust of me if your own heart did not give the
prompting. There, there,' cried he, as he pointed his finger
at her, while her eyes flashed and sparkled with a wild and
lustrous expression, 'your very looks betray you.'

'Betray me! this is no betrayal,' said she haughtily.
'I have no shame in declaring that I too covet fame, even
as you do. Were some mighty patron to condescend to

favour *me*—to fancy that *I* resembled, I know not what great personage—to imagine that in *my* traits of look and voice theirs were reflected, it is just as likely I should thank fortune for the accident, and bid adieu to *you*, as you intend, to-morrow or next day, to take leave of *me*.'

She spoke boldly and defiantly, her large, full eyes gazing at his with a steadfast and unflinching look, while Gerald held down his head in sorrow and in shame.

Nor was it alone with himself that Gerald was at war, for Marietta had shocked and startled him by qualities he had never suspected in her. In her passion she had declared that her heart was set upon ambitions daring as his own; and, even granting that much of what she said was prompted by wounded pride, there was in her wildly excited glances and her trembling lips the sign of a temperament that knew little of forgiveness. If he was then amazed by discovering Marietta to be different from all he had ever seen her, he was more in love with her than ever.

She had opened the window, and, with her face between her hands, gazed out upon the silent street. Gerald took his place at her side, and thus they remained for some time without a word. A low, faint sigh at last came from the girl, and, placing his arm around her, Gerald drew her gently to him, murmuring softly in her ear:

> ' L'onda che mormora,
> Tra sponda e sponda ;
> L'aura che tremola,
> Tra fronda e fronda.
> E meno instabile,
> Del vostro cor.'

She never spoke, but, averting her head still farther from him, screened herself from his view. At last a low, soft murmuring broke from her lips, and she sang, in accents scarcely above her breath, one of those little native songs she was so fond of. It was a wild but plaintive air, sounding like the wayward cadences of one who left her fancy free to give music to the verse, each stanza ending with the words:

> 'Non ho più remi,
> Non ho più vele,
> E al suo talento
> Mi porta il mar.'

With a touching tenderness that thrilled through Gerald's heart she sung, with many a faltering accent, and in a tremulous tone, the simple words:

> 'In a lone, frail bark, forsaken,
>   I float on a nameless sea,
> Nor care to what morrow I waken ;
>   I drift where the waves bear me.

> 'I look not up to the starry sky,
>   For I have no course to run,
> Nor eagerly wait, as the dawn draws nigh,
>   To watch for the rising sun.

> 'For noon is drear as the night to me,
>   To-day is as dark as to-morrow :
> Forsaken, I float on the nameless sea,
>   To think and weep over my sorrow.'

'Oh, Marietta, if thou wouldst not wring my heart, do not sing that sad air,' cried Gerald, pressing her tenderly to him. 'I bore it ill in our happiest hours, when all went well and hopefully with us.'

'It better suits the present, then,' said she calmly; then added, with a sudden energy—'at all events, it suits my humour !'

'Thou wouldst break with me, then, Marietta ?' said Gerald, relaxing his hold on her, and turning his eyes fully upon her face.

'Look down there,' cried she, pointing with her finger: 'that street beneath us is narrow enough, but it has two exits : why shouldn't *you* take one road, and *I* the other ?'

'Agreed : so be it, then !' said Gerald passionately, 'only remember, this project never came from *me*.'

K

'If there be blame for it, I accept it all,' said she calmly. 'These things come ever of caprice, and they go as they come. As your own poet has it :

> '"Si sente che diletta
> Ma non si sa perchè."'

And with a cold smile and a light motion of the hand, as in adieu, she turned away and left the room. Gerald buried his face between his hands and sobbed as though his heart was breaking. Alternately accusing Marietta and himself of cruelty and injustice, his mind was racked by a conflict, to which nothing offered consolation.

He tried to compose himself to sleep: he lay down on his bed, and endeavoured in many ways to induce that calm spirit which leads to slumber; he even murmured to himself the long-forgotten litanies he had learned, as a student, in the college; but the fever that raged within defied all these attempts, and, foiled in his efforts, he arose and left the house. The day was just dawning, and a pinkish streak of sky could be seen over the mountains of Vall' Ombrosa, while all the vale of the Arno and Florence itself lay in deep shadow, the great 'Duomo' and the tall tower at its side not yet catching the first gleam of the rising sun.

Gerald left the gates of the city, and strode on manfully till he gained the crest of the 'Bello Sguardo,' whence the view of the city and its environs is peculiarly fine. Here he sat down to gaze on the scene beneath him; that wondrous map, whose history contains records of mingled greatness, crime, genius, noble patriotism, and of treachery so base that all Europe cannot show its equal; and thus gazing, and thus musing, he sank into deep sleep.

CHAPTER XVIII

THE DROP

THE morning was already far advanced and the sun high when Gerald awoke. The heavy dews had penetrated his frail clothing and chilled him, while the hot gleam of the sun glowed fiercely on his face and temples. He was so confused besides, by his dream and by the objects about him, that he sat vainly endeavouring to remember how and why he had come there.

One by one, like stragglers falling into line, his wandering faculties came back, and he bethought him of the poet's house, Alfieri himself, the Duchess, and lastly, of his quarrel with Marietta—an incident which, do what he might, seemed utterly unaccountable to him. If he felt persuaded that he was in the right throughout, the persuasion gave him no pleasure—far from it. It had been infinitely easier for him now, if he had wronged her, to seek her forgiveness, than forgive himself for having offended her. She, so devoted to him! She, who had taken such pains to teach him all the excellences of the poets she loved; who had stored his mind with Petrarch, and filled his imagination with Ariosto; who taught him to recognise in himself feelings, and thoughts, and hopes akin to those their heroes felt, and thus elevated him in his own esteem. And what a genius was hers!—how easily she adapted herself to each passing mood, and was gay or sorrowful, volatile or passionate, as fancy inclined her. How instinctively her beautiful features caught up the expression of each passion; how wild the transports of her joy; how terrible the agonies of her hatred!

With what fine subtlety, too, she interpreted all she read, discovering hidden meanings, and eliciting springs of action from words apparently insignificant; and then her memory, was it not inexhaustible? An image, a passing simile from a poet she loved, was enough to bring up before her whole cantos; and thus, stored with rich gems of thought, her conversation acquired a grace and a charm that were actual fascination. And was he now to tear himself away from charms like these, and for ever, too? But why was she displeased with him? how had he offended her? Surely it was not the notice of the great poet had awakened her jealousy; and yet, when she thought over her own great gifts, the many attractions she herself possessed—claims to notice far greater than his could ever be—Gerald felt that she might well have resented this neglect.

'And how much of this is my own fault?' cried he aloud. 'Why did I not tell the poet of her great genius? Why not stimulate his curiosity to see and hear her? How soon would *he* have recognised the noble qualities of her nature!'

Angry with himself, and eager to repair the injustice he had done, he arose and set out for the city, resolved to see Alfieri, and proclaim all Marietta's accomplishments and talents.

'He praised *me* last night,' muttered he, as he went along; 'but what will he say of *her*? She shall recite for him the "Didone," the lines beginning,

'"No! sdegnata non sono!"

If his heart does not thrill as he listens, he is more or less than man! He shall hear, too, his own "Cleopatra" uttered in accents that he never dreamed of. And then she shall vary her mood, and sing him one of her Sicilian barcarolles, or dance the Tiranna. Ah, Signor Poeta,' said he aloud, 'even thy lofty imagination shall gain by gazing upon one gifted and beautiful as she is.'

When Gerald reached the Roman gate he found a large cavalcade making its exit through the deep archway, and the crowd, falling back, made way for the mounted party. Upward of twenty cavaliers and ladies rode past, each mounted and followed by a numerous suite, whose equipment proclaimed the party to be of rank and consideration. As

Gerald stood aside to make place for them to pass, a pair of dark eyes were darted keenly toward him, and a deep voice called out:

'There's my Cerretano, that I was telling you about! Gherardi, boy, what brings thee here?'

Gerald looked up and saw it was the poet who addressed him; but before he could summon courage to answer, Alfieri said:

'Thou didst promise to be with me this morning early, and hast forgotten it all, not to say that thou wert to equip thyself in something more suitable than this motley. Never mind, come along with us. Cesare, give him your pony; he is quiet and easy to ride. Fair ladies all,' added he, addressing the party, 'this youth declaims the verse of Alfieri as such a great poet merits. *Gherardi mio*, this is a public worthy of thy best efforts to please. Get into the saddle; it's the surest, not to say the pleasantest, way to jog toward Parnassus!'

Gerald was not exactly in the mood to like this bantering; he was ill at ease with himself, and not over well satisfied with the world at large, and he had half turned to decline the poet's invitation, when a gentle voice addressed him, saying:

'Pray be my cavalier, Signorino; you see I have none.'

'Not ours the fault, Madame la Marquise,' quickly retorted Alfieri; 'you rejected us each in turn. Felice was too dull, Adriano too lively, Giorgio was vain, and I—I forget what I was.'

'Worst of all, a great genius in the full blaze of his glory. No; I'll take Signor Gherardi—that is, if he will permit me.'

Gerald took off his cap and bowed deeply in reply; as he lifted his head he beheld for the first time the features of her who addressed him. She was a lady no longer young, past even the prime of life, but retaining still something more than the traces of what had once been great beauty: fair brown hair, and blue eyes shaded by long dark lashes, preserved to her face a semblance of youthfulness; and there was a coquetry in her riding-dress—the hat looped up with a richly jewelled band, and the front of her habit embroidered in gold—which showed that she maintained pretensions to be noticed and honoured.

As Gerald rode along at her side, she drew him gradually and easily into conversation, with the consummate art of one who had brought the gift to high perfection. She knew how to lead a timid talker on, to induce him to venture on opinions, and even try and sustain them. She understood well, besides, when and how, and how far, to offer a dissent, and at what moments to appear to yield convictions to another. She possessed all that graceful tact which supplies to mere chit-chat that much of epigram that elevates, without pedantry; a degree of point that stimulates, yet never wounds.

'The resemblance is marvellous!' whispered she to Alfieri, as he chanced to ride up beside her; 'and not only in look, but actually in voice, and in many a trick of gesture.'

'I knew you'd see it!' cried the poet triumphantly.

'And can nothing be known about his history? Surely we could trace him.'

'I like the episode better as it is,' said he carelessly. 'Some vulgar fact might, like a rude blow, demolish the whole edifice one's fancy had nigh completed. There he stands now, handsome, gifted, and a mystery. What could add to the combination?'

'The secret of an illustrious birth,' whispered the Marquise.

'I lean to the other view. I'd rather fancy nature had some subtle design of her own, some deep-wrought scheme to work out by this strange counterfeit.'

'Yes, Gherardi,' as the youth looked suddenly around; 'yes, Gherardi,' said she, 'we were talking of you, and of your likeness to one with whom we were both acquainted.'

'If it be to that prince whose picture I saw last night,' replied he, 'I suspect the resemblance goes no further than externals. There can be, indeed, little less like a princely station than mine.'

'Ah, boy!' broke in the poet, 'there will never be in all your history as sad a fate as has befallen him.'

'I envy one whose fortune admits of reverses!' said Gerald peevishly. 'Better be storm-tossed than never launched.'

'I declare,' whispered the Marquise, 'as he spoke there, I could have believed it was Monsieur de Saint George himself I was listening to. Those little wayward bursts of temper——'

'Summer lightnings,' broke in Alfieri.

'Just so: they mean nothing, they herald nothing:

> '"They flash like anger o'er the sky,
> And then dissolve in tears."'

'True,' said the poet; 'but, harmless as these elemental changes seem, we forget how they affect others—what blights they often leave in their track:

> '"The sport the gods delight in
> Makes mortals grieve below."'

'It was Fabri wrote that line,' said Gerald, catching at the quotation.

'Yes, Madame la Marquise,' said Alfieri, answering the quickly darted glances of the lady's eyes, 'this youth has read all sorts of authors. A certain Signor Gabriel, with whom he sojourned months long in the Maremma, introduced him to Voltaire, Diderot, and Rousseau: his own discursive tastes added others to the list.'

'Gabriel! Gabriel! It could not be that it was——' and here she bent over and whispered a word in Alfieri's ear.

A sudden start and an exclamation of surprise burst from the poet.

'Tell us what your friend Gabriel was like.'

'I can tell you how he described himself,' said Gerald. 'He said he was:

> "Un sanglier marqué de petite vérole."'

'Oh, then, it was he!' exclaimed the Marquise. 'Tell us,

I pray you, how fortune came to play you so heartless a trick as to make you this man's friend ?'

Half reluctantly, almost resentfully, Gerald replied to this question by relating the incidents that had befallen him in the Maremma, and how he had subsequently lived for months the companion of this strange associate.

'What marvellous lessons of evil, boy, has he not instilled into you! Tell me frankly, has he not made you suspectful of every one—distrusting all friendship, disowning all obligations, making affection seem a mockery, and woman a cheat ?'

'I have heard good and bad from his lips. If he spoke hastily of the world at times, mayhap it had not treated him with too much kindness. Indeed he said as much to me, and that it was not his fault that he thought so meanly of mankind.'

'What poison this to pour into a young heart !' broke in Alfieri. 'The cattle upon the thousand hills eat not of noxious herbage; their better instincts protect them, even where seductive fruits and flowers woo their tastes. It is man alone is beguiled by false appearances, and this out of the very subtlety of his own nature. The plague-spot of the heart is distrust !'

'These are better teachings, boy, than Signor Gabriel's,' said the lady.

'You know him, then ?' asked Gerald.

'I have little doubt that we are speaking of the same person ; and if so, not I alone, but all Europe knows him.'

Gerald burned to inquire further, to know who and what this mysterious man was, how he had earned the terrible reputation that attended him, and what charges were alleged against him. He could not dare, however, to put questions in such a presence, and he sat moodily thinking over the issue.

Diverging from the high-road, they now entered a pathway which led through the vineyards and the olive groves, and, being narrow, Gerald found himself side by side with the Marquise, without any other near. Here, at length, his

curiosity mastered all reserve, and plucking up courage for
the effort, he said—

'If my presumption were not too bold, madame, I would
deem it a great favour to be permitted to ask you something
of this Signor Gabriel. I know and feel that, do what I will,
reason how I may, reject what I can, yet still his words have
eaten down deep into my heart; and if I cannot put some
antidote there against their influence, that they will sway
me even against myself.'

'First, let me hear how he represented himself to you.
Was he as a good man grossly tricked and cheated by the
world, his candour imposed on, his generosity betrayed?
Did he picture a noble nature basely trifled with?'

'No, no,' broke in Gerald; 'he said, indeed, at first he
felt disposed to like his fellow-men, but that the impulse was
unprofitable; that the true philosophy was unbelief. Still
he avowed that he devoted himself to every indulgence; that
happiness meant pleasure, pleasure excess; that out of the
convulsive throes of the wildest debauchery, great and
glorious sensations, ennobling thoughts spring—just as the
volcano in full eruption throws up gold amid the lava: and
he bade me, if I would know myself, to taste of this same
existence.'

'Poor boy, these were trying temptations.'

'Not so,' broke in Gerald proudly; 'I wanted to be something better and greater than this.'

'And what would you be?' asked the Marquise, as she
turned a look of interest on him.

'Oh, if a heart's yearning could do it,' cried Gerald warmly,
'I would be like him who rides yonder; I would be one
whose words would give voice to many an unspoken emotion
—who could make sad men hopeful, and throw over the
dreariest waste of existence the soft, mild light of ideal
happiness.'

She shook her head, half-sorrowfully, and said, 'Genius
is the gift of one, or two, or three, in a whole century!'

'Then I would be a soldier,' cried the boy; 'I would shed

my blood for a good cause. A stout heart and a strong arm are not rare gifts, but they often win rare honours.'

'Count Alfieri has been thinking about you,' said she, in a tone half confidential. 'He told me that, if you showed a disposition for it, he would place you at the University of Sienna, where you could follow your studies until such time as a career should present itself.'

'To what do I owe this gracious interest in my fate, lady?' asked he eagerly. 'Is it my casual resemblance to the prince he was so fond of?'

'So fond!' exclaimed she; then, as quickly correcting herself, she added: 'No, not altogether that—though, perhaps, the likeness may have served you.'

'How kind and good of him to think of one so friendless!' muttered Gerald, half aloud.

'Is the proposal one you would like to close with? Tell me frankly, Gherardi, for we are speaking now in all frankness!'

'Perhaps I may only lose another friend if I say no!' said he timidly; and then, with bolder accents, added: 'Let me own it, madame, I have no taste for study—at least such studies as these. My heart is set upon the world of action: I would like to win a name, no matter how brief the time left me to enjoy it.'

'Shall I tell you *my* plan——'

'*Yours!*' broke he in. 'Surely you too have not deigned to remember me?'

'Yes; the Count interested me strongly in you. This morning we talked of little else at breakfast, and up to the moment we overtook you at the gate. His generous ardour in your behalf filled me with a like zeal, and we discussed together many a plan for your future; and mine was, that you should enter the service of the King——'

'What King?'

'What other than the King of France, boy, the heir of St. Louis?'

'He befriended the cause of Charles Edward, did he not?' asked Gerald eagerly.

'Yes,' said she, smiling at the ardour with which he asked the question. 'Do you feel deep interest in the fortunes of that Prince?'

The youth clasped his hands together and pressed them to his heart, without a word.

'Your family, perhaps, supported that cause?'

'They did, lady. When I was an infant, I prayed for its success; as I grew older, I learned to sorrow for its failure.'

There was something so true and so natural in the youth's expression as he spoke, that the Marquise was touched by it, and turned away her head to conceal her emotion.

'The game is not played out yet, boy,' said she at last; 'there are great men, and wise ones too, who say that the condition of Europe, the peace of the world, requires the recognition of rights so just as those of the Stuarts. They see, too, that in the denial of these claims the Church is wounded, and the triumph of a dangerous heresy proclaimed. Who can say at what moment it may be the policy of the Continent to renew the struggle?'

'Oh, speak on, lady: tell me more of what fills my heart with highest hope,' exclaimed he rapturously. 'Do not, I beseech you, look on me as the poor stroller, the thing of tinsel and spangles, but as one in whose veins generous blood is running. I am a Geraldine, and the Geraldines are all noble.'

The sudden change in the youth's aspect, the rich, full tones of his voice, as, gaining courage with each word, he asserted his claim to consideration, seemed to have produced an effect upon the Marquise, who pondered for some time without speaking.

'Mayhap, lady, I have offended you by this rash presumption,' said Gerald, as he watched her downcast eyes and steadfast expression; 'but forgive me, as one so little skilled in life, that he mistakes gentle forbearance for an interest in his fortunes.'

'But I *am* interested in you, Gherardi; I *do* wish to

befriend you. Let me hear about your kith. Who are these
Geraldines you speak of ?'

'I know not, lady,' said he, abashed ; 'but from my childhood I was ever taught to believe that, wherever my name
was spoken, men would acknowledge me as noble.'

'And from whom can we learn these things more accurately ?
have you friends or relations to whom we could write ?'

Just as she spoke, the head of the cavalcade passed beneath
a deep gateway into the court of an ancient palace, and the
echoing sounds of the horses' feet soon drowned the voices
of the speakers. 'This is "Camerotto," an old villa of the
Medici,' whispered the Marquise. 'We have come to see
the frescoes ; they are by Perugino, and of great repute.'

The party descended, and entering the villa, wandered
away in groups through the rooms. It was one of those
spacious edifices which were types of mediæval life, lofty,
splendid, but comfortless. Dropping behind the well-dressed
train as they passed on, Gerald strayed alone and at will
through the palace, and at last found himself in a small
chamber, whose one window looked out on a deep and lonely
valley. The hills which formed the boundaries were arid,
stony, and treeless, but tinted with those gorgeous colours
which, in Italian landscape, compensate in some sort for the
hues of verdure, and every angle and eminence on them
were marked out with that peculiar distinctness which objects
assume in this pure atmosphere. The full blaze of a noonday
sun lit up the scene, where not a trace of human habitation
nor a track of man's culture could be seen for miles.

'My own road in life should lie along that glen,' said
Gerald dreamily, as he leaned out of the window and gazed
on the silent landscape, and soon dropped into a deep reverie,
when past, present, and future were all blended together.
The unbroken stillness of the spot, the calm tranquillity of
the scene, steeped his spirit in a sort of dreamy lethargy,
scarcely beyond the verge of sleep itself. To his half-waking
state his restless night contributed, and hour by hour went
over unconsciously : now muttering verses of his old convent

hymns, now snatches of wild peasant legends, his mind lost itself in close-woven fancies.

Whether the solitary tract of country before him was a reality or a mere dreamland, he knew not. It needed an effort to resume consciousness, and that effort he could not make; long fasting, too, lent its influence to increase this state, and his brain balanced between fact and imagination weariedly and hopelessly. At moments he fancied himself in some palace of his ancestors, dwelling in a high but solitary state; then would he suddenly imagine that he was a prisoner, confined for some great treason—he had taken arms against his country—he had adhered to a cause, he knew not what or whose, but it was adjudged treasonable. Then, again, it was a monastery, and he was a novice, waiting and studying to assume his vows; and his heart struggled between a vague craving for active life and a strange longing for the death-like quiet of the cloister.

From these warring fancies he started suddenly, and, passing his hand across his forehead, tried to recall himself to reason. 'Where am I?' exclaimed he, and the very sound of his own voice, echoed by the deep-vaulted room, almost affrighted him. 'How came I here?' muttered he, hoping to extricate himself from the realm of fancy by the utterance of the words. He hastened to the door, but the handle was broken and would not turn; he tried to burst it open, but it was strong and firm as the deep wall at either side of it; he shouted aloud, he beat loudly on the oaken panels, but though the deep-arched ceiling made the noise seem like thunder, no answer was returned to his call. He next turned to the window, and saw to his dismay that it was at a great height from the ground, which was a flagged terrace beneath. He yelled and cried at the very top of his voice; he waved his cap, hoping that some one at a distance might catch the signal; but all in vain. Wearied at last by all his attempts to attract notice, he sat moodily down to think over his position and devise what was to be done. Wild thoughts flashed at times across him—that this was some deep-laid scheme to entrap him; that he had been enticed here that he might meet his death without marks of violence; that, somehow, his was a life of consequence enough to provoke a crime. The Prince that he resembled had some share in it—or Marietta had vowed a vengeance—or the Jesuit Fathers had sent an emissary to despatch him. What were not the wild and terrible fancies that filled his mind: all that he had read of cruel torturings, years' long suffering, lives passed in dreary dungeons, floated mistily before him, till reason at last gave way, and he lost himself in these sad imaginings.

The ringing of a church bell, faint and far away as it sounded, recalled him from his dreamings, and he remembered it was the 'Angelus,' when long ago he used to fall into line, and walk along to the chapel of the college. 'That, too, was imprisonment,' thought he, but how gladly would he have welcomed it now! He leaned from the window to try and make out whence the sounds came, but he could not find the spot. He fancied he could detect something moving up the hillside, but a low olive scrub shaded the path, and it was only as the branches stirred that he conjectured some one was passing underneath. The copse, however, extended but a short way, and Gerald gazed wistfully to see if anything should emerge from where it finished. His anxiety was intense as he waited; a feverish impatience thrilled through him, and he strained his eyes until they ached.

At last a long shadow was projected on the road; it was broken, irregular, and straggling. It must be more than one—several—a procession, perhaps, and yet not that—there was no uniformity in it. He leaned out as far as he could venture. It was coming. Yes, there it was! A donkey with heavy panniers at his side, driven by an old man; a woman followed, and after her a girl's figure. Yes, he knew them and her now! It was the Babbo! and there was Marietta herself, with bent-down head, creeping sadly along, her arms crossed upon her breast, her whole air unspeakably sad and melancholy. With a wild scream Gerald called to them to turn back, that he, their companion, their comrade, was a captive. He shouted till his hoarse throat grew raw with straining, but they heard him not.

A deep, narrow gorge lay between them, with a brawling rivulet far below, and though the boy shouted with all his might, the voice never reached them. There they walked along up the steep path, whither to, he knew not. That they meant to desert him was, however, clear enough. Already in that far-away land to which they journeyed no part was assigned him. And Marietta!—she to whom he had given his heart, she whom he bound up with all his future fortunes—she to leave him thus without a word of farewell, without one wish to meet again, without one prayer for his welfare! Half-maddened with grief and rage—for in his heart now each sentiment had a share—he sprang wildly to the window, and gazed downward at the terrace. Heaven knows what terrible thoughts ebbed and flowed within him as he looked! Life had little to attract him to it; his heart was well-nigh broken; a reckless indifference was momentarily gaining on him; and he crept farther and farther out upon the window-sill, till he seemed almost to hang over the depth beneath him. He wanted to remember a prayer, to recall some words of a litany he had often recited, but in his troubled brain, where confusion reigned supreme, no memory could prevail; thoughts came and went, clashing, mingling, conflicting, like the storm-tossed sea in a dark night, and already a stupid and fatalist indifference dulled his senses, and one only desire struggled with him—a wish for rest!

Once more, with an effort, he raised his eyes toward the mountain side. The little procession was still ascending, and nigh the top. At a short distance behind, however, he could see Marietta standing and looking apparently toward Florence. Was it that she was thus taking a last farewell of him, muttering, among some broken words of affection, some blessing upon him! A sudden thrill of joy—it was hope— darted through him as he gazed; and now bending over, he perceived that the steep wall beneath the window was broken by many a projection and architrave, the massive pediment of a large window projecting far, about six feet from where he sat. Could he gain this he might descend by the column which supported it, and reach a great belt of stonework that ran about fifteen feet from the ground, and whence he might safely venture to drop. If there was peril to life in every step of this dangerous exploit, there was, in the event of success, a meeting once more with Marietta—a meeting never to part again. Whatever the reasons for having deserted him he was determined to overbear. Some one must have calumniated him: he would meet the slander. Marietta herself would do him justice; he would soon show her that the passing vision of ambition had no hold upon his heart, that he only cared for her, wished for nothing beyond their own wayward life. As he thus reasoned, he tore his mantle into long strips, which he twisted and knotted together, testing its strength till assured that it would bear his weight. He then fastened one end to the window-bars, and grasping the cord in both hands, he prepared to descend. Could he but gain the pediment in this wise, the rest of the descent would not be difficult.

With one fervent prayer to Her whose protection he had learned to implore from very infancy, he glided softly from the window-sill and began the descent. For a second or two did he grasp the stone ledge with both hands, as if fearing to loose his hold, but at length, freeing one hand and then the other, he gave himself up to the cord. Scarcely had his full weight straightened the rope than the frail texture began to give way; a low sound, as of the fibres tearing, met his ear, and just as his feet touched the pediment the rope snapped in two, and the shock throwing him off his balance, he swayed forward. One inch more and his fate was certain; but his body recovered its equipoise, and he came back to the wall, where he stood motionless, and almost paralysed with terror. The ledge on which he stood, something less than two feet in width, was slightly sloped from the wall, and about forty feet from the ground. To crouch down upon this now and reach the column which supported it, was his next task, nor was it till after a long struggle with himself that he could once again peril life by such an attempt.

By immense caution he succeeded in so bending down that he at last gained a sitting position on the ledge, and then, with his face to the wall, he glided over the pediment and grasped one of the columns. Slipping along this, he arrived at the window-sill, from which the drop to the ground was all that now remained. Strange was it that this latter and easier part of all the danger affrighted him more than all he had gone through. It was as if his overtasked courage was exhausted; as though the daring energy had no more supplies to draw upon; for there he sat, hopelessly gazing at the ground beneath, unable to summon resolution to attempt it.

The brief season between day and dark, the flickering moments of half-light passed away, and a night calm and starlit spread over the scene. Except the wild and plaintive cry of an owl from an ivy-clad turret above him, not a sound broke the stillness, and there Gerald sat, stunned and scarce conscious. As darkness closed round him, and he could no longer measure the distance to the ground beneath, the peril of his position became more appalling, and he felt like one who must await the moment of an inevitable and dreadful fate. Already a sense of weariness warned him that at the slightest stir he might lose his balance, and then what a fate—mutilation perhaps, worse than any death! If he could maintain his present position till day broke, it was certain he must be rescued. Solitary as was the spot, some one would surely pass and see him, but then, if overcome by fatigue, sleep should seize him—even now a dreary lassitude swept over him: oftentimes his eyes would close, and fancies flit across him, that boded the approach of slumber! Tortured beyond endurance by this long conflict with his fears, he resolved, come what might, to try his fate, and, with a shrill cry for mercy upon his soul, he dropped from the ledge.

When the day broke he was there beneath the window,

his forehead bleeding and his ankle broken. He had tried
to move, but could not, and he waited calmly what fate
might befall him. He was now calm and self-confident. The
season of struggle was over; the period of sound thought
and reflection had begun.

CHAPTER XIX

THE PLAN

WHEN one looks back upon the story of his life, he is sure to
be struck by the reflection, that its uneventful periods, its
seasons of seeming repose, were precisely those which tended
most to confirm his character. It is in solitude—in the long
watches of a voyage at sea—in those watches more painful
still, of a sick-bed, that we make up our account with ourselves, own to our short-comings, and sorrow over our faults.
The mental culture that at such seasons we pursue, is equally
certain to exercise a powerful influence on us. Out of the
busy contest of life—removed, for the moment, from its
struggles and ambitions—the soil of our hearts is, as it were,
fresh turned, and rapidly matures the new-sown seed we
throw upon it. How many date the habits of concentration,
by which they have won success in after-life, to the thoughtful hours of a convalescence. It is not merely that isolation
and quiet have aided their minds; there is much more in the
fact that at such times the heart and the brain work together.
Every appeal to reason must be confirmed by a judgment in
the higher court of the affections, and out of our emotions
as much as out of our convictions do we bend ourselves to
believe.

How fresh and invigorated do we come forth from these
intervals of peace! less confident, it may be, of ourselves,
but far more trustful of others—better pleased with life,
and more sanguine of our fellow-men. And no matter how

often we may be deceived or disappointed, no matter how frequently our warmest affections have met no requital, let us cherish this hopeful spirit to the last—let us guard ourselves against doubting! There is no such bankruptcy of the heart as distrust.

Gerald was for weeks long a sufferer on a sick-bed. In a small room of the villa, kindly cared for, all his wants supplied by the directions of his wealthy friends, there he lay, pondering over the wayward accident of his life, and insensibly feeding his heart with the conviction that Fate, which had never failed to befriend him in difficulty, had yet some worthy destiny in store for him. He read unceasingly, and of everything. The Marquise constantly sent him her books, and what now interested him no less, the newspapers and pamphlets of the time. It was the first real glimpse he had obtained of the actual world about him; and with avidity he read of the ambitions and rivalries which disturbed Europe —the pretensions of this State, the fears and jealousies of that. Stored as his mind was with poetic images, imbued with a rapturous love for the glowing pictures thus presented, he yet hesitated to decide whether the life of action was not a higher and nobler ambition than the wondrous dreamland of imagination.

In the convent Gerald's mind had received its first lessons of religion and morality. His sojourn at the Tana had imparted his earliest advances into the world of knowledge through books, and now his captivity at the 'Camerotto' opened to him a glance of the real world, its stirring scenes, its deep intrigues, and all the incidents of that stormy sea on which men charter the vessels of their hope. Was it that he forgot Marietta? Had pain and suffering effaced her image; had ambition obliterated it? No; she was ever in his thoughts—the most beautiful and most gifted creature he had ever seen. If he read, it was always with the thought, what would she have said of it? If he sank into a reverie, she was the centre round which his dreams revolved. Her large, mild eyes, her glowing cheek, her full lips, tremulous

with feeling, were ever before him; and what would he
not have given to be her companion again, wandering the
world; blending all that was fascinating in poetic description
with scenes wayward enough to have been conjured up by
fancy! Why had they deserted him? he asked himself over
and over. Had the passing dispute with Marietta determined her to meet him no more? And if so, what influence
could she have exercised over the others to induce them to
take this step? There was but one of whom he could hope
to gain this knowledge—Alfieri himself, whose generosity had
succoured them, and in the few and brief moments of the
poet's visit to the villa he had not courage to venture on the
question.

The Marquise came frequently to see him, and seemed
pleased to talk with him, and lighten the hours of his solitude
by engaging him in conversation. Dare he ask her? Could
he presume to inquire, from one so high-born and so great,
what had befallen his humble comrades of the road? How
entreat her to trace their steps, or to learn their plans? Had
she, indeed, seen Marietta, there would have been no difficulty
in the inquiry. Who could have beheld her without feeling
an interest in her fate? Brief, however, as had been his
intercourse with great people, he had already marked the
tone of indolent condescension with which they treated the
lives of the very poor. The pity they gave them cost no
emotion: if they sorrowed, it was with a grief that had no
pang. Their very generosity had more reference to their
own sensations than to the feelings of those they befriended.
Already, young as he was, did he catch a glimpse of that
deep gulf that divides affluence from misery, and in the
bitterness of his grief for her who had left him, he exaggerated the callousness of the rich and the sufferings of
the poor.

Every comfort was supplied to him, all that care could
bestow, or kindness remember, was around him; and yet,
why was it his gratitude flowed not in a pure, unsullied
stream, but came with uncertain gushes, fitfully, unequally:

now sluggish, now turbid; clogged with many a foul weed, eddying with many an uncertain current?

The poison Gabriel had instilled into his heart, if insufficient to kill its nobler influences, was yet enough to render them unsound. The great lesson of that tempter was to 'distrust,' never to accept a benefit in life without inquiring what subtle design had prompted it, what deep-laid scheme it might denote. 'None but a fool bestows without an object,' was a maxim he had often heard from his lips. Not all the generosity of the youth's nature—and it was a noble one—could lessen the foul venom of this teaching! To reject it seemed like decrying the wisdom of one who knew life in all its aspects. How could he, a mere boy, ignorant, untravelled, unlettered, place his knowledge of mankind in competition with that of one so universally accomplished as Gabriel? His precepts, too, were uttered so calmly, so dispassionately—a tone of regret even softened them at times, as though he had far rather have spoken well and kindly of the world, if truth would have suffered him. And then he would insidiously add: 'Don't accept these opinions, but go out and test them for yourself. The laboratory is before you, experiment at your will.' As if he had not already put corruption in the crucible, and defiled the vessel wherein the ore should be assayed!

For some days Gerald had seen neither the Count nor the Marquise. A brief note, a few lines, from the latter, once came to say that they continued to take an interest in his welfare, and hoped soon to see him able to move about and leave his room; but that the arrival of a young relative from Rome would probably prevent her being able to visit the Camerotto for some time.

'They have grown weary of the pleasure of benevolence,' thought Gerald peevishly; 'they want some other and more rewarding excitement. The season of the Carnival is drawing nigh, and doubtless fêtes and theatres will be more gratifying resources than the patronage of such as I.'

It was in a spirit resentful and rebellious that he arose and dressed himself. The very clothes he had to wear were given him—the stick he leaned on was an alms; and his indignation scoffed at his mendicancy, as though it were a wrong against himself.

'After all,' said he mockingly, 'if it were not that I chanced to resemble some dear prince or other, they had left me to starve. I wonder who my prototype may be: what would he say if I proposed to change coats with him? Should I have more difficulty in performing the part of prince, or he that of vagabond?'

In resentful reflections like this he showed how the seeds of Gabriel's teaching matured and ripened in his heart, darkening hope, stifling even gratitude. To impute to mere caprice, a passing whim, the benevolence of the rich was a favourite theory of Gabriel; and if, when Gerald listened first to such maxims, they made little or no impression upon him, now, in the long silent hours of his solitude, they came up to agitate and excite him. One startling illustration Gabriel had employed, that would occur again and again to the boy's mind, in spite of himself.

'These benefactors,' said he, 'are like men who help a drowning swimmer to sustain himself a little longer: they never carry him to the shore. Their mission is not rescue, it is only to prolong a struggle, to protract a fate.'

The snow lay on the Apennines, and even on the lower hills around Florence, ere Gerald was sufficiently recovered to move about his room. The great dreary house, silent and tenantless, was a dominion over which he wandered at will, sitting hours long in contemplation of frescoed walls and ceilings, richly carved architraves, and finely chiselled traceries over door and window. Had they who reared such glorious edifices left no heirs nor successors behind them? Why were such splendours left to rot and decay? Why were patches of damp and mildew suffered to injure these marvellous designs? Why were the floors littered with carved and golden fretwork? What new civilisation had usurped the place of the old one, that men preferred lowly dwellings

—tasteless, vulgar, and inconvenient—to those noble abodes, elegant and spacious ? Could it possibly be that the change in men's minds, the growing assertion of equality, had tended to suppress whatever too boldly indicated superiority of station ? Already distinctions of dress were fading away. The embroidered jabot, the rich falling ruffle, the ample peruke, and the slashed and braided coat, were less and less often seen abroad. A simpler and more uniform taste in costume began to prevail, the insignia of rank were seldom paraded in public, and even the liveries of the rich displayed less of costliness and show than in times past. Over and over had Gabriel directed the youth's attention to these signs, saying, with his own stern significance—

'You will see, boy, that men will not any longer wait for equality till the churchyard.'

Was the struggle, then, really approaching ?—were the real armies, indeed, marshalling their forces for the fight ? And if so, with which should he claim brotherhood ? His birth and blood inclined him to the noble, but his want and destitution gave him common cause with the miserable.

It was a dreary day of December, a low, leaden sky, heavily charged with rain or snow, stretched over a landscape inexpressibly sad and wretched-looking. The very character of Italian husbandry is one to add greatly to the rueful aspect of a day in winter : dreary fields of maize left to rot on the tall stalks ; scrubby olive-trees, in all the deformity of their leafless existence ; straggling vine branches, stretching from tree to tree, or hanging carelessly about—all these damp and dripping, in a scene desolate as a desert, with no inhabitants, and no cattle to be seen.

Such was the landscape that Gerald gazed on from a window, and, weary with reading now, stood long to contemplate.

'How little great folk care for those seasons of gloom !' thought he. 'Their indoor life has its thousand resources of luxury and enjoyment : their palaces stored with every appliance of comfort for them—pictures, books, music—all

that can charm in converse, all that can elevate by taste
about them.   What do they know of the trials of those who
plod heavily along through mire and rain, weary, footsore,
and famishing?'   And Marietta rose to his mind, and he
pictured her toiling drearily along, her dress draggled, her
garments dripping.   He thought he could mark how her
proud look seemed to fire with indignation at an unworthy
fate, and that a feverish spot on her cheek glowed passionately at the slavery she suffered.   'And why am I not there
to share with her these hardships?' cried he aloud.   'Is not
this a coward's part in me to sit here in idolence, and worse
again, in mere dependence?   I am able to travel: I can, at
least, crawl along a few miles a day; strength will come by
the effort to regain it.   I will seek her through the wide
world till I find her.   In her companionship alone has my
heart ever met response, and my nature been understood.'

A low, soft laugh interrupted these words.   He turned,
and it was the Abbé Girardon, a friend of the Marquise de
Bauffremont's, who always accompanied her, and acted as a
sort of secretary in her household.   There was a certain half-
mocking subtlety, a sort of fine raillery in the manner of the
polished Abbé which Gerald always hated; and never was
he less in the humour to enjoy the society of one whom even
friends called 'malin.'

'I believed I was alone, sir,' said Gerald, half haughtily,
as the other continued to show his whole teeth in ridicule of
the youth's speech.

'It was chance gave me the honour of overhearing you,'
replied the Abbé, smiling.   'I opened this door by mere
accident, and without expecting to find you here.'

Gerald's cheek grew crimson.   The exceeding courtesy of
the other's manner seemed to him a studied impertinence,
and he stared steadfastly at him, without knowing how to
reply.

'And yet,' resumed the Abbé, 'it was in search of you I
came out from Florence this dreary day.   I had no other
object, I assure you.'

'Too much honour, Monsieur,' said Gerald, with a haughty bend of the head; for the raillery, as he deemed it, was becoming insupportable.

'Not but the tidings I bear would reward me for even a rougher journey,' said the Abbé courteously. 'You are aware of the deep interest the Marquise de Bauffremont has ever taken in your fortunes. To her care and kindness you owe, indeed, all the attentions your long illness stood in need of. Well, her only difficulty in obtaining a career for you was her inability to learn to what rank in life to ascribe you. You believed yourself noble, and she was most willing to accept the belief. Now, a mere accident has tended to confirm this assumption.'

'Let me hear what you call this accident, Monsieur l'Abbé,' broke in Gerald anxiously.

'It was an observation made yesterday at dinner by Sir Horace Mann. In speaking of the Geraldines, and addressing Count Gherardini for confirmation, he said: "The earldom of Desmond, which is held by a branch of the family, is yet the youngest title of the house." And the Count answered quickly: "Your Excellency is right; we date from a long time back. There's an insolent proverb in our house that says, '*Meglio un Gherardini bastardo che un Corsini ben nato.*'" Madame de Bauffremont caught at the phrase, and made him repeat it. In a word, Monsieur, she was but too happy to avail herself of what aided a foregone conclusion. She wished you to be noble, and you were so.'

'But I am noble!' cried Gerald boldly. 'I want no hazards like these to establish my station. Let them inquire how I am enrolled in the college.'

'Of what college do you speak?' asked the Abbé quickly.

'It matters not,' stammered out Gerald, in confusion at thus having betrayed himself into a reference to his past. 'None have the right to question me on these things.'

'A student enrolled with his due title,' suggested the wily Abbé, 'would at once stand independent of all generous interpretation.'

'You will learn no more from *me*, Monsieur l'Abbé,' said the youth disdainfully. 'I shall not seek to prove a rank from which I ask to derive no advantage. They called me t'other day, at the tribunal, a "vagabond": that is the only title the law of Tuscany gives me.'

The Abbé, with a tact skilled to overcome far greater difficulties, strove to allay the youth's irritation, and smooth down the asperity which recent illness, as well as temperament, excited, and at last succeeded so far that Gerald seated himself at his side, and listened calmly to the plan which the Marquise had formed for his future life. At some length, and with a degree of address that deprived the subject of anything that could alarm the jealous susceptibility of the boy's nature, the Abbé related that a custom prevailed in certain great houses (whose alliances with royalty favoured the privilege) of attaching to their household young cadets of noble families, who served in a capacity similar to that of courtier to the person of the king. They were 'gentlemen of the presence,' pages or equerries, as their age or pretensions decided; and, in fact, from the followers of such houses as the De Rohan, the Noailles, the Tavannes, and the Bauffremont, did royalty itself recruit its personal attendants. Monsieur de Girardon was too shrewd a reader of character not to perceive that any description of the splendours and fascinations of a life of voluptuous ease would be less captivating to such a youth than a picture of a career full of incident and adventure, and so he dwelt almost exclusively on all that such a career could offer of high ambition, the army being chiefly officered by the private influence of the great families of France.

'You will thus,' said he, at the close of a clever description; 'you will thus, at the very threshold of life, enjoy what the luckiest rarely attain till later on—the choice of what road you will take. If the splendour of a court life attract you, you can be a courtier; if the ambitions of statesmanship engross your mind, you are sure of office; if you aspire to military glory, here is your shortest road to it; or if,' said he, with a graceful melancholy, 'you can submit yourself to be a mere guest at the banquet of life, and never a host—one whose place at the table is assigned him, not taken by right—such, in a word, as I am—why, then, the Abbé's frock is an easy dress, and a safe passport besides.'

With a sort of unintentional carelessness, that seemed frankness itself, the Abbé glided into a little narrative of his own early life, and how, with a wide choice of a career before him, he had, half in indolence, half in self-indulgence, adopted the gown.

'Stern thinkers call men like me mere idlers in the vineyard, drones in the great human hive: but we are not; we have our uses just as every other luxury. We are to society what the bouquet is to the desert; our influence on mankind is not the less real, that its exercise attracts little notice.'

'And what am I to be, what to do?' asked Gerald proudly.

'Imagine the Marquise de Bauffremont to be Royalty, and you are a courtier; you are of her household, in attendance on her great receptions; you accompany her on visits of ceremony—your rank securing you all the deference that is accorded to birth, and admission to the first circles in Paris.'

'Is not this service menial?' asked he quickly.

'It is not thus the world regards it. The Melcours, the Frontignards, the Montrouilles are to be found at this moment in these ranks.'

'But they are recognised by these very names,' cried Gerald; 'but who knows *me*, or what title do *I* bear?'

'You will be the Chevalier de Fitzgerald; the Marquise has influence enough at court to have the title confirmed. Believe me,' added he, smiling blandly, 'everything has been provided for—all forethought taken already.'

'But shall I be free to abandon this—servitude' (the word would out, though he hesitated to utter it)—'if I find it onerous or unpleasant? Am I under no obligation or pledge?'

'None; you are the arbiter of your own fortune at any moment you wish.'

'You smile, sir, and naturally enough, that one poor and friendless as I am should make such conditions; but remember, my liberty is all my wealth—so long as I have that, so long am I master of myself: free to come and go, I am not lost to self-esteem. I accept,' and so saying, he gave his hand to the Abbé, who pressed it cordially, in ratification of the compact.

'You will return with me to Florence, Monsieur le Chevalier,' said the Abbé, rising, and assuming a degree of courteous respect which Gerald at once saw was to be his right for the future.

BOOK THE SECOND

CHAPTER I

IN a large salon of the palace at Versailles, opening upon a
terrace, and with a view of the vast forest beneath it, were
assembled a number of officers, whose splendid uniforms and
costly equipments proclaimed them to be of the bodyguard
of the king. They had just risen from table, and were
either enjoying their coffee in easy indolence, gathered in
little knots for conversation, or arranging themselves into
parties for play.

The most casual glance at them would have shown what
it is but fair to confess they never sought to conceal—that
they were the pampered favourites of their master. It was
not alone the richness of their embroidered dress, the boundless extravagance that all around them displayed, but, more
than even these, a certain air of haughty pretension, the
carriage and bearing of a privileged class, proclaimed that
they took their rank from the high charge that assigned
them the guard of the person of the sovereign.

When the power and sway of the monarchy suffered no
check—so long as the nation was content to be grateful for
the virtues of royalty, and indulgent to its faults—while
yet the prestige of past reigns of splendour prevailed, the
'Garde du Corps' were great favourites with the public:
their handsome appearance, the grace of their horsemanship,
their personal elegance, even their very waste and extravagance had its meed of praise from those who felt a reflected

pride from the glittering display of the court. Already,
however, signs of an approaching change evidenced themselves: a graver tone of reprehension was used in discussing
the abandoned habits of the nobility; painfully drawn pictures of the poor were contrasted with the boundless waste
of princely households; the flatteries that once followed
every new caprice of royal extravagance, and which imparted to the festivities of the Trianon the gorgeous colours
of a romance, were now exchanged for bare recitals, wherein
splendour had a cold and chilling lustre. If the cloud were
no bigger than a man's hand, it was charged with deadliest
lightning.

The lack of that deference which they had so long regarded
as their due, made these haughty satraps but haughtier and
more insolent in their manner toward the citizens. Every
day saw the breach widen between them; and what formerly
had been oppression on one side and yielding on the other,
were now occasions of actual collision, wherein the proud
soldier was not always the victor. If the newspapers were
strong on one side, the language of society was less measured
on the other. The whole tone of conversation caught its
temper from the times; and 'the bourgeois' was ridiculed
and laughed at unceasingly. The witty talker sought no
other theme; the courtly epigrammatist selected no other
subject; and even royalty itself was made to laugh at the
stage exhibitions of those whose loyalty had once, at least,
been the bulwark of the monarchy.

In the spacious apartment already mentioned, and at a
small table before an open window, sat a party of three, over
their wine. One was a tall, spare, dark-complexioned man,
with something Spanish in his look, the Duc de Bourguignon,
a captain in the Garde; the second was a handsome but
over-conceited-looking youth, of about twenty-two or three,
the Marquis de Maurepas. The third was Gerald, or as he
was then and there called, Le Chevalier de Fitzgerald.
Though the two latter were simple soldiers, all their equipment was as costly as that of the officer at their side. As

little was there any difference in their manner of addressing him. Maurepas, indeed, seemed rather disposed to take the lead in conversation, and assumed a sort of authority in all he said, to which the Duke gave the kind of assent usually accorded to the 'talkers by privilege.' The young Marquis had all the easy flippancy of a practised narrator, and talked like one who rarely fell upon an unwilling audience.

'It needs but this, Duke,' said he, after a very energetic burst of eloquence; 'it needs but this, and our corps will be like a regiment of the line.'

'*Parbleu!*' said the Duke, as he stroked his chin with the puzzled air of a man who saw a difficulty, but could not imagine any means of escape.

'I should like to know what your father or mine would have said to such pretension,' resumed the Marquis. 'You remember what the great monarch said to Colonna, when he asked a place for his son ?—"You must ask Honoré if he has a vacancy in the kitchen!" And right, too. Are we to be all mixed up together? Are the employments of the State to be filled by men whose fathers were lackeys? Is France going to reject the traditions that have guided her for centuries ?'

'To what is all this àpropos, Gaston?' asked Fitzgerald calmly.

'Haven't you heard that M. Lescour has made interest with the king to have his son appointed to the Garde ?'

'And who is M. Lescour ?'

'I'll tell you what he is, which is more to the purpose: he himself would be puzzled to say who. M. Lescour is a fermier-general—very rich, doubtless, but of an origin the lowest.'

'And his son ?'

'His son! What do I know about his son? I conclude he resembles his father: at all events, he cannot be one of us.'

'Pardon me if I am not able to see why,' said Gerald calmly. 'There is nothing in the station of a fermier-

general that should not have opened to his son the approach
to the very highest order of education, all that liberal
means could bestow——'

'But, *mon cher*, what do we care for all that? We want
good blood and good names among our comrades; we want
to know that our friendships and our intimacies are with
those whose fathers were the associates of our fathers. Ask
the Duke here, how he would fancy companionship with the
descendants of the rabble. Ask yourself, is it from such a
class you would select your bosom friends?'

'Grant all you say to be correct: is not the king himself
a good judge of those to whom he would intrust the guardianship of his person?' interposed Gerald. 'The annals of the
world have shown that loyalty and courage are not peculiar
to a class.'

'A'nt they—*parbleu!*' cried Maurepas. 'Why, those sentiments are worthy of the Rue Montmartre. Messieurs,'
added he, rising, and addressing the others, scattered in
groups through the room, 'congratulate yourselves that the
enlightened opinions of the age have penetrated the darkness
of our benighted corps. Here is the Chevalier de Fitzgerald
enunciating opinions that the most advanced democracy
would be proud of.'

The company thus addressed rose from their several places
and came crowding around the table where the three were
seated. Gerald knew not very accurately the words he had
just uttered, and turned from one face to the other of those
around to catch something like sympathy or encouragement
in this moment of trial, but none such was there. Astonishment and surprise were, perhaps, the most favourable among
the expressions of those who now regarded him.

'I was telling the Duc de Bourguignon of the danger that
impended our corps,' began Maurepas, addressing the company generally. 'I was alluding to what rumour has been
threatening us with some time back, the introduction into
the Garde of men of ignoble birth. I mentioned specifi-
cally one case, which, if carried through, dissolves for ever

the prestige of that bond that has always united us, when our comrade here interposes and tells me that the person of his Majesty will be as safe in the guardianship of the vile " Roturier" as in that of our best and purest blood. I will not for an instant dispute with him as to knowledge of the class whose merits he upholds.' A faint murmur, half astonishment, half reproof, arose throughout the room at these words; but Gerald never moved a muscle, but sat calm and still awaiting the conclusion of the speech.

'I say this without offence,' resumed Maurepas, who quickly saw that he had not the sympathy of his hearers in his last sally; 'without the slightest offence, for, in good truth, I have no acquaintanceship outside the world of my equals. Our comrade's views are doubtless, therefore, wider and broader; but I will also say that these used not to be the traditions of our corps, and that not only our duty, but our very existence, was involved in the idea that we were a noble guard.'

'Well said!' 'True!' 'Maurepas is right!' resounded through the room.

'We are, then, agreed in this,' resumed Maurepas, following up his success with vigour; 'and there is only one among us who deems that the blood of the plebeian is wanting to lend us chivalry and devotion.'

'Shame! shame!' cried several together, and looks of disapprobation were now turned on Fitzgerald.

'If I have unintentionally misrepresented the Chevalier,' resumed Maurepas, 'he is here to correct me.'

Gerald arose, his face crimson, the flush spreading over his forehead and his temples. There was a wild energy in his glance that showed the passion that worked within him; but though his chest heaved with high indignation and his heart swelled, his tongue could not utter a word, and he stood there mute and confounded.

'There, there—enough of it!' exclaimed an old officer, whose venerable appearance imparted authority to his words. 'The Chevalier retracts, and there is an end to it.'

'I do not. I withdraw nothing—not a syllable of what I said,' cried Gerald wildly.

'It is far better thus, then,' cried Maurepas; 'let the corps decide between us.'

'Decide what?' exclaimed Gerald passionately. 'Monsieur de Maurepas would limit the courage and bravery of France to the number of those who wear our uniform. I am disposed to believe that there are some hundreds of thousands just as valiant and just as loyal who carry less lace on their coats, and some even——' here he stopped confused and abashed, when a deep voice called out—

'And some even who have no coats at all. Is it not so you would say, Chevalier?'

'I accept the words as my own, though I did not use them,' cried Gerald boldly.

'There is but one explanation of such opinions as these,' broke in Maurepas; 'the Chevalier de Fitzgerald has been keeping other company than ours of late.'

Gerald rose angrily to reply, but ere he could utter a word an arm was slipped within his own, and a deep voice said—

'Come away from this—come to my quarters, Gerald, and let us talk over the matter.' It was Count Dillon, the oldest captain of the corps, who spoke, and Gerald obeyed him without a word of remonstrance.

'Don't you perceive, boy,' said the Count, as soon as they reached the open air, 'that we Irish are in a position of no common difficulty here? They expect us to stand by an order of nobility that we do not belong to. To the king and the royal family you and I will be as loyal and true as the best among them; but what do we care—what can we care —for the feuds between noble and bourgeois? If this breach grows wider every day, it was none of our making; as little does it concern us how to repair it.'

'I never sought for admission into this corps,' said Gerald angrily. 'Madame de Bauffremont promised me my grade in the dragoons, and then I should have seen service. Two squadrons of the very regiment I should have joined are already off to America, and instead of that I am here to lounge away my life, less a soldier than a lackey!'

'Say nothing to disparage the Garde, young fellow, or I shall forget we are countrymen,' said Dillon sternly; and then, as if sorry for the severity of the rebuke, added, 'Have only a little patience, and you can effect an exchange. It is what I have long desired myself.'

'You too, Count?' cried Gerald eagerly.

'Ay, boy. This costly life just suits my pocket as ill as its indolence agrees with my taste. As soldiers, we can be as good men as they, but neither you nor I have three hundred thousand livres a year, like Maurepas or Noailles. We cannot lose ten rouleaux of Louis every evening at ombre, and sleep soundly after; our valets do not drink Pomard at dinner, nor leave our service rich with two years of robbery.'

'I never play,' said Gerald gravely.

'So I remarked,' continued Dillon; 'you lived like one whose means did not warrant waste, nor whose principles permitted debt.'

By this time they had reached a small pavilion in the wood, at the door of which a sentry was stationed.

'Here we are,' cried Dillon; 'this is my quarter: come up and see how luxuriously a Chef d'Escadron is lodged.'

Nothing, indeed, could be more simple or less pretentious than the apartment into which Gerald was now ushered. The furniture was of a dark nut-wood, and the articles few and inexpensive.

'I know you are astonished at this humble home. You have heard many a story of the luxury and splendour of the superior officers of our corps, how they walk on Persian carpets and lounge on ottomans covered with Oriental silks. Well, it's all true, Gerald; the only exception is this poor quarter before you. I, too, might do like them. I might tell the royal commissary to furnish these rooms as luxuriously as I pleased. The civil list never questions or cavils—it only pays. Perhaps, were I a Frenchman born, I should have little scruple about this; but, like you, Fitzgerald, I am an alien—only a guest, no more.'

The Count, without summoning a servant, produced a bottle and glasses from a small cupboard in the wall, and drawing a table to the window, whence a view extended over the forest, motioned to Gerald to be seated.

'This is not the first time words have passed between you and Maurepas,' said Dillon, after they had filled and emptied their glasses.

'It happens too frequently,' said Gerald, with warmth. 'From the day I bought that Limousin horse of his we have never been true friends.'

'I heard as much. He thought him unrideable, and you mounted him on parade, and that within a week.'

'But I offered to let him have the animal back when I subdued him. I knew what ailed the horse; he wanted courage—all his supposed vice was only fear.'

'You only made bad worse by reflecting on Maurepas's riding,' said Dillon, smiling.

'*Par Dieu!* I never thought of that,' broke in Fitzgerald.

'Then there was something occurred at court, wasn't there?'

'Oh, a mere trifle. He could not dance the second figure in the minuet with the Princesse de Clèves, and the Queen called me to take his place.'

'Worse than the affair of the horse, far worse,' muttered Dillon; 'Maurepas cannot forgive you either.'

'I shall assuredly not ask him, sir,' was the prompt rejoinder.

'And then you laughed at his Italian, didn't you? The "Nonce" said that you caught him up in a line he had misquoted.'

'He asked me himself if he were right, and I told him he was not; but I never laughed at his mistake.'

'They said you did, and that the Princesse de Lamballe made you repeat the story. No matter, it was still another item in the score he owes you.'

'I am led by these remarks of yours to suppose that you have latterly bestowed some interest in what has befallen me, Count: am I justified in this belief?'

'You have guessed aright, Fitzgerald. Thirty-eight years and seven months ago I entered this service, knowing less of the world than you do now. So little aware was I what was meant by a provocation, that I attributed to my own deficiency in the language and my ignorance of life what were intended as direct insults. They read me differently, and went so far as to deliberate whether I ought not to be called on to leave the corps. This at last aroused my indolence. I fought four of them one morning, and three the next—two fell fatally wounded. I never got but this'—and he showed a deep scar on the wrist of his sword-arm. 'From that time I have had no trouble.'

'And this is an ordeal I must pass also,' said Gerald calmly.

'I scarcely know how it is to be avoided, nor yet complied with. The king has declared so positively against duelling, that he who sends a challenge must consent to forgo his career in the service.'

'But, surely, not he who only accepts a provocation?'

'That is a difficulty none seems to have answered. Many think that all will be treated alike—the challenger and the challenged, and even the seconds. My own opinion is different.'

'It is not impossible, then, that M. de Maurepas desired to push me to demand satisfaction,' said Gerald slowly, for the light was beginning to break upon his mind.

Dillon nodded in silence.

'And *you* saw this, Count?'

Another nod was the reply.

'And, doubtless, the rest also?'

'Doubtless!' said Dillon slowly.

Fitzgerald leaned his head on his hand, and sat in deep reflection for some time.

'This is a puzzle,' said he at last. 'I must be frank with

you, Count Dillon. Madame de Bauffremont cautioned me, on my entrance into the corps, against whatever might involve me in any quarrel. There are circumstances, family circumstances, which might provoke publicity, and be painful—so, at least, she said—to others, whose fame and happiness should be dearer to me than my own. Now, I know nothing of these. I only know that there are no ties nor obligations which impose the necessity of bearing insult. If you tell me, then, that Maurepas seeks a quarrel with me, that he has been carrying a grudge against me for weeks back, I will ask of you—and, as my countryman, you'll not refuse me—to call on him for satisfaction.'

'It can't be helped,' said Dillon, speaking to himself.

'Why should it be helped?' rejoined Gerald, overhearing him.

'And then, Maurepas is the very man to do it,' muttered the Count again. Then lifting his head suddenly, he said: 'The Marquise de Bauffremont is at Paris, I believe. I'll set off there to-night; meanwhile do you remain where you are. Promise me this; for it is above all essential that you should take no step till I return.'

CHAPTER II

A NIGHT ON DUTY

SCARCELY had the Count set out for Paris when Gerald remembered that it was his night for duty, he was *de service* in the antechamber of the king, and had but time to hasten to his quarters and equip himself in full uniform. When he reached the foot of the grand staircase he found several dismounted dragoons, splashed and travel-stained, the centres of little groups, all eagerly questioning and listening to them. They had arrived in hot haste from Paris, where a tremendous revolt had broken out. Some said the Prince of

Lambesi's regiment, the 'Royal Allemand,' were cut to pieces; others, that the military were capitulating everywhere; and one averred that when he passed the barrier the Bastille had just fallen. While the veterans of the Swiss Guard and the household troops conversed in low and anxious whispers together, exchanging gloomy forebodings of what was to come, the two or three courtiers whom curiosity had attracted to the spot spoke in tones of contempt and scorn of the mob.

'They are shedding their blood freely, though, I assure you,' said a young sous-lieutenant, whose arm was in a sling. 'The fellow who smashed my wrist had his face laid open by a sabre-cut, but seemed never to heed it in the least.'

'Have you despatches, Monsieur de Serrans?' asked a very daintily-dressed and soft-voiced gentleman, with a wand of office as chamberlain.

'No, Monsieur le Marquis. I have a verbal message for his Majesty from the Duc de Bassompierre, and I crave an early audience.'

'His Majesty is going to supper,' replied the chamberlain. 'I will try and obtain admission for you to-morrow.'

'The Duc's orders were very pressing, Monsieur le Marquis. He was retiring for want of reinforcements, but would still hold his ground if his Majesty ordered it.'

'I regret it infinitely, but what is to be done, Monsieur?' said the other, with a slight shrug of the shoulders.

'At the hazard of spoiling his Majesty's appetite, I'd like to see him at once, Monsieur de Brezé,' said the officer boldly.

The polished courtier turned a look of half astonishment, half rebuke, on the soldier, and tripped up the stairs without a word.

'I am *de service*, sir,' whispered Gerald to the young officer. 'Could I possibly be of any use to you?'

'I am afraid not,' replied the other courteously. 'I have a message to be delivered to his Majesty's own ear, and the answer to which I was to carry to my general. What I have just mentioned to M. de Brezé was not of the importance of that with which I am charged.'

'And will it be too late to-morrow?'

'To-morrow! I ought to have been half-way back toward Paris already. You don't know that a battle is raging there, and fifty thousand men are engaged in deadly conflict.'

'The king *must* hear of it,' said Gerald, as he mounted the stairs.

Very different was the scene in the splendid salons from that which presented itself below. Groups of richly attired ladies and followers of the court were conversing in all the easy gaiety their pleasant lives suggested. Of the rumours from the capital they made matter of jest and raillery; they ridiculed the absurd pretensions of the popular leaders, and treated the rising as something too contemptible for grave remark. As Gerald drew nigh, he saw, or fancied he saw, a sort of coldness in the manner of those around. The conversation changed from its tone of light flippancy to one of more guarded and more commonplace meaning. It was no longer doubtful to him that the story of his late altercation had got abroad, with, not impossibly, very exaggerated accounts of the opinions he professed. Indeed, the remark of an old Maréchal du Palais caught his ear as he passed, while the sidelong glances of the hearers told that it was intended for himself—'It is too bad to find the sentiments of the Breton Club from the lips of a Garde du Corps.'

It was all that Gerald could do to restrain the impulse that urged him to confront the speaker, and ask him directly if the words were applied to *him*. The decorous etiquette of the spot, the rigid observance of all that respect that surrounds the vicinity of a king, checked his purpose, and, having satisfied himself that he should know the speaker again, he moved on. It was on the stroke of ten, the hour that he was to relieve the soldier on guard, a duty which, in the etiquette of the Garde du Corps, was always performed by the relief appearing at the proper moment, without the usual military ceremony of a guard.

Alone at last, in that vast chamber where he had passed many an hour of sentinel's watch, Gerald had time to compose his thoughts, and calm down the passionate impulses that swayed him. He walked for above an hour his weary round, stopping at times to gaze on the splendid tapestries which, on the walls, represented certain incidents of the *Æneid*. The faint, far-away sounds of the band, which performed during the supper of the king, occasionally met his ear, and he could not help contrasting the scene which they accompanied with the wild and terrible incidents then going forward at Paris. His mind ever balanced and vacillated between two opinions. Were they right who maintained the supremacy of the royal cause, and the inviolability of that princely state whose splendours were such a shock to misery? Or had the grievances of the people a real ground —were there great wrongs to be redressed, cruel inequalities to be at least compromised? How much had he listened to on either side? What instincts and prejudices were urged for this! what strength of argument enlisted to support that! And he himself, what a position was his!—one of a corps whose very boast it was to reject all save of ancient lineage! What could he adduce as his claim to high descent? If they questioned him to-morrow, how should he reply? What meant his title of Chevalier? might he not be arraigned as a pretender, a mere impostor for assuming it? If the Count Dillon decided that he should challenge Maurepas, might not his claim to gentle blood be litigated? And what a history should he give if asked for the story of his life! From these thoughts he rambled on to others, scarcely less depressing: the cause of the king, of the very monarchy itself. Bold as the pretensions, high as the language was of those about the court, the members of the royal family exhibited the most intense anxiety. Within view of the palace windows, in that same week, tumultuous assemblages had taken place, and thousands of men passed in solemn procession to the place where the 'States General' had appointed for their meeting. The menacing gestures, the wild and passionate words, all so unlike what formerly had marked such demonstrations, were terribly significant of the change that had come over public opinion. Over and over had Gabriel predicted all this to him. Again and again had he impressed upon him that a time was coming when the hard evils of poverty would arouse men to ask the terrible question, Why are we in wretchedness while others revel in excess? 'On that day, and coming it is,' said he, 'all the brain-spun theories of statecraft will be thrown aside like rubbish, and they alone will be listened to who are men of action.' Was this dark prophecy now drawing nigh to accomplishment? were these the signs of that dread consummation? Gabriel had told him that the insane folly and confidence of those about the court would be the greatest peril of the monarchy. 'Mark my words,' said he, 'it will be all insolence and contempt at first, abject terror and mean concession after.' Was not the conduct of De Brezé a very type of the former? he had not even a word of passing courtesy for the brave fellow who wounded and exhausted, stood there waiting like a lackey.

Gerald was startled by the sudden opening of a door; and, as he turned, he saw a figure which he speedily recognised as the brother of the king, or, as he was called in court phrase, 'Monsieur.'

'Are you Maurice de Courcel?' asked he, addressing Gerald hastily.

'No, Monseigneur; I am Fitzgerald.'

'Where is De Courcel, can you tell me?'

'He went on leave this morning, Monseigneur, to shoot in the forest of Soissons.'

'Peste!' muttered he angrily. 'Methinks you gentlemen of the Garde du Corps have little other idea of duty than in plotting how to evade it. It was De Courcel's night of duty, was it not?'

'Yes, sir; I took it in his place.'

'Who relieves you?'

'The Chevalier de Monteroue, sir.'

'You are l'Écossais—at least they call you so, eh?'

'Yes, Monseigneur, they call me so,' said Gerald, flushing.

The Prince hesitated, turned to speak, and then moved away again. It was evident that he laboured under some irresolution that he could not master.

Resolved not to lose an opportunity so little likely to recur, Gerald advanced toward him, and, with an air of deep respect, said : 'If I might dare to approach your Royal Highness on such a pretext, I would say that some tidings of deepest moment have been brought this evening by an officer from Paris, charged to deliver them to the king; and that he yet waits unable to see his Majesty.'

'How—what—why has he not sent up his despatches ?'

'He had none, sir ; he was the bearer of a verbal message from the Duc de Bassompierre.'

'Impossible, sir ; none could have dared to assume this responsibility. Who told you this story ?'

'I was present, sir, when the officer arrived—spoke with him—and heard M. de Brezé say, "You can, perhaps, have an audience to-morrow."'

'He deserves the Bastille for this !'

'He would have deserved it, sir, yesterday.'

'How do you mean, sir ?'

'That there is no Bastille to-day. The officer I mentioned saw it carried by the populace as he left Paris : the garrison are all cut to pieces.'

With something like a cry of agony, half-smothered by an effort, the Prince hurried from the room.

While the clock was yet striking, the sentinel in relief arrived, and Gerald was released from duty. As he wended his way along through room after room, he was struck by the air of silence and desertion around ; nowhere were to be seen the groups of lounging courtiers and 'officiers de service.' A few inferior members of the household rose and saluted him, and even they wore something ominous and sad in their look, as though evil tidings were abroad.

A light, soft rain was falling as Gerald left the palace toward the pavilion, where Count Dillon's quarters were established. He knew it was impossible that the Count could yet have returned from Paris, but somehow he found himself repairing to the spot without well knowing why.

As he drew nigh he perceived a light in the little salon, and could distinguish the figure of a man writing at the table. Curious to learn if the Count had unexpectedly turned back, Gerald opened the door and entered. The person at the table turned quickly about, and to his utter confusion Gerald saw it was Monsieur.

'Come in, come in; you will, perhaps, spare me some writing,' cried he, in an easy, familiar tone : 'you may indeed read what I have just written,' and so saying he handed him a paper with these lines :

'DEAR COUNT DILLON,—Give me the earliest and fullest information with respect to a young countryman of yours, Fitzgerald, called "L'Écossais." May we employ him on a mission of secrecy and importance ? It is of consequence— that is, it were far better—that the person intrusted with our commands were not a Frenchman——'

The Prince had but written so much as Gerald entered, and he now sat calmly watching the effect produced upon the young soldier as he read it.

'Am I to answer for myself, Monseigneur ?' said he modestly.

'It is exactly what I intended,' was the calm reply.

'I can pledge for my fidelity and devotion, sir, but not for any skill or ability to execute your orders.'

'They will require little beyond speed and exactitude. You know Paris well ?'

'Perfectly, sir.'

'At the Rue de Turenne there is a small street called l'Avenue aux Abois—do you know it ?—well, the second or third house, I am not sure which, is inhabited by a gentleman called the Count Mirabeau.'

'He who spoke so lately at the Assembly ?'

'The same. You will see him, and induce him to repair

with you to St. Cloud. Haste is everything. If your mission speed well, you can be at St. Cloud by noon to-morrow. It is possible that the Count may distrust your authority to make this appointment, for I dare not give you anything in writing; you will then show him this ring, which he will recognise as mine. Spare no entreaties to accomplish the object, nor, so far as you are able, permit anything to thwart it. Let nothing that you see or hear divert you from your purpose. Pay no attention to the events at Paris, whatever they be. You have one object—only one—that Count Mirabeau reach the Château de St. Cloud by the earliest moment possible, and in secrecy. Remember that, sir—in secrecy.'

'I cannot wear my uniform,' began Gerald.

'Of course not, nor suffer any trace of powder to remain in your hair. I will send you clothes which will disguise you perfectly; and, if questioned, you can call yourself a peasant on the estate of the Mirabeaus, come up from Provence to see the Count. You must stain your hands, and be particular about every detail of your behaviour. There is but one thing more,' said he, after a moment's reflection; 'if Monsieur de Mirabeau refuse, if he even seek to defer the interview I seek for—but he will not, he dare not.'

'Still, Monseigneur, let me be provided for every emergency possible—what if he should refuse?'

'You will be armed, you will have your pistols—but no, no, under no circumstances,' muttered he below his breath. 'There will be then nothing for you to do, but to hasten back to me with the tidings.' Monsieur arose as he said these words, and stood in apparently deep thought. 'I believe,' said he at last, 'that I have not forgotten anything. Ah, it were well to take one of the remount horses that are not branded—I will look to that.'

'If the Count should be from home, am I to seek for him elsewhere, sir?'

'That will depend upon your own address; if you are satisfied that you can defy detection. I leave all to yourself, Chevalier. It is a great and a holy cause you serve, and no words of mine can add to what your own heart will teach you. Only remember, that hours are like weeks, and time is everything.'

Gerald kissed the hand that Monsieur extended to him; and lighting him down the little stairs, saw him take his way across the park.

CHAPTER III

THE MISSION

THE day had not yet dawned when Gerald, admirably disguised as a Provençal peasant, arrived at the Avenue aux Abois. The night had been hot and sultry, and many of the windows of the houses were left open; but from none save one were any lights seen to gleam. This one was brilliant with the glare of wax-lights; and the sounds of merriment from within showed it was the scene of some festivity. Light muslin curtains filled the spaces of the open casements, through which at moments the shadowy traces of figures could be detected.

While Gerald stood watching, with some curiosity, this strange contrast to the unbroken silence around, a rich deep voice caught his ear, and seemed to awaken within him some singular memory. Where, and when, and how he had heard it before, he knew not; but every accent and every tone struck him as well known.

'No, no, Mirabeau,' broke in another; 'when men throw down their houses, it is not to rebuild them with the old material.'

'I did not speak of throwing down,' interposed the same deep voice; 'I suggested some safe and easy alteration. I would have the doors larger, for easy access; the windows wider, for more light.'

'And more wood, generally, in the construction, for easy burning, I hope,' chimed in a third.

'Make your best provisions for stability : destruction will always be a simple task,' cried the deep voice. 'You talk of burning,' cried he, in a louder tone ; ' what do you mean to do when your fire goes out ? materials must fail you at last. What then ? You will have heaped many a good and useful thing upon that pile you will live to regret the loss of. What will you do, besides, with those you have taught to dance round these bonfires ? '

' Langeac says it is an experiment we are trying,' replied another ; ' and, for my part, I am satisfied to accept it as such.'

' Nay, nay,' interposed a soft, low voice ; ' I said that untried elements in government are an experiment only warrantable in extreme cases ; just as the physician essays even a dangerous remedy, when he deems his patient hopeless.'

' But it 's your own quackeries here have made all the mischief,' broke in the deep voice. ' If the sick man sink, it is yourselves have been the cause.'

' Was there ever a royal cause that had not its own fatal influences ? ' said another.

' There is an absurd reliance on prestige, a trust in that phantom called Divine right, that blinds men against their better reason. This holiday faith is but a sorry creed in times of trouble.'

' Far from this being the case,' said the deep voice, ' you will not concede to kings what you would freely grant to your equals. You reject their word, you distrust their oath, you prejudge their intentions, and suspect their honour.'

' Why, Mirabeau, you ought to be at Versailles,' said another, laughing. ' The pavilion of the Queen is more your place than the table of the Tiers-État.'

' So thinks he himself,' broke in the low voice. ' He expects to pilot the wreck after we have gone off on the raft.'

' Four o'clock,' exclaimed another, pushing his chair hastily back as he arose ; ' and here is D'Entraigues fast asleep these two hours.'

'No, *parbleu!*' muttered a drowsy voice. 'I closed my eyes when the Bordeaux was finished, and began to reflect on Lafayette's breakfast. Isn't this the day?'

'To be sure. You are coming, Mirabeau?'

'Of course, we will all be there.'

'I must be at St. Frotin by seven o'clock,' said one.

'And I have to see Marigni at the mill of Montmorency, by the same hour.'

'A duel?'

'Yes; they are both Vendéans, and may kill each other without damage to the State.'

'He was going to say Republic!' cried another, laughing.

'Who talks of a Republic?' interposed a rough voice angrily.

'Be calm, messieurs—all religions are to be respected.'

'True, Mirabeau; but this is to proclaim none.'

'Who knows? They never excavate near Rome but they discover some long-forgotten deity! Can you or I venture to say what new faith may not arise out of these ashes?'

'Let it but repudiate the law of debt and discountenance marriage,' said another, 'and I am its first convert.'

'Good-bye, Mirabeau, adieu,' cried several together, and they were now heard descending the stairs. Meanwhile, Mirabeau drew back the curtain and looked out upon the street.

'Whom have we got here?' said the first who issued forth from the door, and saw Gerald standing before him.

'What is it? who does he want?' cried Mirabeau, as he saw them in conversation.

'One of your peasants, Mirabeau, with, doubtless, a Provençal cheese and some olives for you.'

'Or a letter of loving tidings from that dear uncle,' cried another; 'the only one who ever knew the real goodness of your nature.'

'Let him come up,' said Mirabeau, as he closed the window.

When Gerald reached the top of the stair, he saw in front

of him a large, powerfully-built man, who, standing with his back to the light, had his features in deep shadow.

'You are the Count de Mirabeau?' began Gerald.

'And you—who are you?' responded he quickly.

'That you shall know, when I am certain of whom I am addressing.'

'Come in,' said the Count, and walked before him into the room. He turned about just as the door closed, and Gerald, fixing his eyes upon him, cried out, 'Good heavens! is it possible? Signor Gabriel!'

'Now for your own name, my friend,' said Mirabeau calmly.

'Don't you know me, then? don't you remember the boy you saved years ago from death in the Roman Maremma—Fitzgerald?'

'What!' said Mirabeau, in the same calm voice, 'you Fitzgerald? I should never have recognised you.'

'And are you really the Count de Mirabeau?'

'Gabriel Riquetti, Count de Mirabeau, is my name,' replied he slowly. 'How did you find me out? What chance led you here?'

'No chance, nor accident. I have come expressly to see and speak with you. I am a Garde du Corps, and have assumed this disguise to gain access to you unremarked.'

'A Garde du Corps!' said the Count, in some surprise.

'Yes, Signor Gabriel. My life has had its turns of good and ill fortune since we parted—the best being that I serve a great prince and a kind master.'

'Well said, but not over-prudent words to utter in the Faubourg St. Antoine,' rejoined the Count, smiling. 'Go on.'

'I have come with a message from Monsieur, to desire you will hasten immediately to St. Cloud, where he will meet you. Secrecy and speed are both essential, for which reasons he intrusted me with a mere verbal message, but to secure me your confidence he gave me this ring.'

Mirabeau smiled, and with such a scoffing significance that Gerald stopped, unable to proceed further.

'And then ?' said Mirabeau.

'I have no more to add, Monsieur,' said Gerald haughtily. 'My commission is fulfilled already.'

'Take some wine; you are heated with your long ride,' said the Count, filling out a large goblet, while he motioned to Gerald to be seated.

'Nay, sir; it is not of *me* there is time to think now. Pray, let me have your answer to my message, for Monsieur told me, if I either failed to find you, or from any casualty you were unable to repair to St. Cloud, that I should come back with all speed to apprise him, my not returning being the sign that all went well.'

'All went well,' muttered Mirabeau to himself. 'How could it go worse ?'

Gerald sat gazing in wonderment at the massive, stern features before him, calling up all that he could remember of their first meeting, and scarcely able, even yet, to persuade himself that he had been the companion of that great Count de Mirabeau whose fame filled all France.

'In the event of my compliance, you were then to accompany me to St. Cloud ?' said the Count, in a tone of inquiry.

'Yes, sir; so I understood my orders.'

'There is mention in history of a certain Duc de Guise——' He stopped short, and walked to and fro for some time in silence; then, turning abruptly around, he asked: 'How came it that you stood so high in Monsieur's confidence that he selected you for this mission ?'

'By mere accident,' said Gerald, and he recounted how the incident had occurred.

'And your horse—what has become of him ?' asked the Count.

'He is fastened to the ring of the large *porte cochère*—the third house from this.'

Mirabeau leaned out of the window as if to satisfy himself that this statement was true.

'Supposing, then, that I agree to your request, what

means have you to convey me to St. Cloud?—what preparations are made?'

'None, sir. There was no time for preparation. It was, as I have told you, late last night when Monsieur gave me this order. It was in the briefest of words.'

'"Tell Monsieur de Mirabeau that his Majesty would speak with him,"' said the Count, suggesting to Gerald's memory the tenor of his message.

'No, sir. "Tell Monsieur de Mirabeau to hasten to St. Cloud, where I will meet him."'

'How did you become a noble guard?' asked he quickly. 'They say abroad that the difficulties to admission are great?'

'I owe my admission to the favour of Madame de Bauffremont, sir.'

'A great patron, none more so. She would have befriended me once,' added he, with an insolent sneer, 'but that my ugliness displeased the Queen. Since that time, however, her Majesty has condescended to accustom herself to these harsh features, and even smiles benignly on them. There is little time to criticise the visage of your pilot, while the breakers are before and the rocks beside you. I will go, Gerald. Give me that ring.'

Gerald hesitated for a second; the Prince had not bestowed the ring on him, but only confided it to his care.

'I will not compromise you, young man,' said Mirabeau gravely: 'I will simply enclose that ring in a letter which you shall see, when I have written it,' and he immediately sat down to a table, and in a rapid hand dashed off some lines, which he threw across to Gerald to read. They ran thus:

'DEAR FRIEND AND NEPHEW,—I am summoned to a meeting at St. Cloud, by the owner of the ring which I enclose. If I do not return to Paris by noon on Saturday, it is because ill has befallen yours,

'GABRIEL RIQUETTI, Count de Mirabeau.

'To MONS. DU SAILLANT, Rue d'Ascour, 170.
'Friday, 3 A.M.'

'There is the ring,' said Gerald, as he took it from his finger.

Mirabeau sealed the note, enclosing it in a strong envelope, and placing it on the table among other letters, ready sealed and addressed.

'You will carry this letter to its address, Gerald, and you will remain there till—till my return.'

'I understand,' said Gerald; 'I am a hostage.'

'*You* a hostage for *me*!' cried the other haughtily. 'Do you fancy, young man, that the whole corps you belong to could requite the loss of Gabriel Riquetti? Would the Court —would the Assembly—would France accept such a price? Go, sir, and tell Monsieur du Saillant that if any evil befall his uncle, he is to make use of you as the clue to trace it, and be sure that you discharge this trust well.'

'And if I refuse this mission?'

'If you refuse, you shall bear back to Monseigneur the reasons for which I have not obeyed his commands,' said Mirabeau coldly. 'Methought you remembered me better. I had fancied you knew me as one who had such confidence in himself, that he believed his own counsels the wisest, and who never turned from them. There is the letter—yes or no?'

'Yes—I will take it.'

'I will, with your leave, avail myself of your horse till I pass the barrier. You can meanwhile take some rest here. You will be early enough with Du Saillant by eight o'clock,' and with this the Count withdrew into a room adjoining to complete his preparations for the road. While thus occupied, he left the door partly open, and continued to converse with Gerald, asking him various questions as to what had befallen him after having quitted the Tana, and eagerly entering into the strange vicissitudes of his life as a stroller.

'I met your poet, I think it was at Milan. We were rivals at the time, and I the victor. A double insult to him, since he hated France and Frenchmen,' said the Count carelessly. 'There was a story of his having cut the fingers of his right hand to the bone with a razor, to prevent his assassinating me. What strange stuff your men of imagination are made of—ordinary good sense had reserved the razor for the enemy!'

'His is a great and noble nature,' exclaimed Gerald enthusiastically.

'So much the better, then, is it exercised upon fiction : real events and real men are sore tests to such temperaments. There, I am ready now; one glass to our next meeting, and good-bye.'

With a hearty shake-hands they parted, and as Gerald looked from the window, he saw the Count ride slowly down the street. Closing the window, he threw himself upon a couch and slept soundly.

CHAPTER IV

A SALON UNDER THE MONARCHY

LONG after the events which heralded the great Revolution in France had assumed proportions of ominous magnitude, after even great reverses to the cause of monarchy, the nobles, whether from motives of hardihood or from downright ignorance of the peril, continued to display in their equipages, their mode of living, and their costly retinues, an amount of splendour terribly in contrast with the privations of the people.

Many of the old families deemed it a point of honour to abate nothing of the haughty pretensions they had exhibited for centuries; and treating the widespread discontent as a mere passing irritation, they scoffed at the fears of those who would regard it as of any moment. Indeed, to their eyes, the only danger lay in the weak, submissive policy of the court—a line of action based on the gentle and tender qualities of the king's own nature, which made him prefer an injury to his own influence, to even the slightest attack on those who assailed him. Truthfully or not, it is somewhat hard to say, a certain section of the nobles asserted that the Queen was very differently minded; that she not only took a just measure of the difficulty, but saw how it was to be met and combated. Far from any paltering with the men of the movement, it was alleged that she would at once have counselled force, and, throwing the weight of the royal cause upon the loyalty of the army, have risked the issue without a fear. Around Marie Antoinette were, therefore, grouped those who took the highest ground in the cause of monarchy, and who resisted almost the bare thought of what savoured of compromise or concession.

Among those who were conspicuous for adherence to these opinions, was the Marquise de Bauffremont. To high rank, a large fortune, no inconsiderable share of court favour, she added a passion for everything like political intrigue. She was one of a school—of which some disciples have been seen in our own day—who deem that there are questions of statecraft too fine and too delicate for the rough handling of men, and where the finer touch of woman is essentially needed. So far as matters of policy are moulded by the tempers of those who treat them, and so far as it is of moment to appreciate finer traits of character—to trace their origin, their leanings and their sympathies—there is no doubt that the quicker and more subtle instincts of a woman have an immense advantage over the less painstaking and less minute habits of a manly mind. If the Marquise did not inaugurate this school, she gave a great development to its principles, and, assuredly, she practised her art at a period when its resources were to be submitted to the severest of all tests. Her spacious 'hotel' in the Place Louis Quinze was the centre of all those who assumed to be the last bulwark of the monarchy, and there might be found the Rochejaquelins, the Noailles, the Tavannes, the Valmys, and a host of others not less distinguished, while the ministers and envoys of various foreign courts resorted to these salons as the most authentic source of news to be transmitted to their govern-

ments. Partly from predilection, partly from that policy
which affected to despise popular dictation, these receptions
were conducted with considerable display and ostentation, and
all that costly luxury and expense could impart lent its aid
to give them an air of almost princely state. For a while
there was a pretence of treating the passing events as incidents too slight and too vulgar for notice, but after a time
this affectation gave way to another scarcely less absurd : of
alluding to them in a tone of scoff and derision, ridiculing
those who were their chief actors, and actually making them
subjects of witty pasquinade and caricature. As each new
actor on the popular scene appeared, he was certain to be the
mark of their insulting comments ; and traits of low origin,
and vulgarity of manner, were dwelt on with a significance
that showed how contemptuously they regarded all whose
condition was beneath their own. How little did they suspect, as they mocked Rabaut St. Etienne, Petion, and
Robespierre, that this 'ill-dressed and ill-mannered crew '—
these 'noisy screamers of vapid nonsense'—these 'men of
sinister aspect and ignoble look,' would one day become the
scourge of their order, and the masters of France ! So far
was this thought from all their speculation, that their indignation knew no bounds in discussing those who admitted
this *canaille* to anything like consideration ; and thus the
Bishop of Autun and Lafayette were the constant subjects
of sarcasm and attack.

'What do they want, Madame la Marquise !' exclaimed
the old Marquis de Ribaupierre, as he stood, one evening,
the centre of a group eagerly discussing the views and objects
of these innovators. 'I ask, what do they want? It cannot
be the destruction of the *noblesse*, for they are noble. It
cannot be the extinction of property, for they are rich.
It cannot be—surely it cannot be—that they believe the
monarchy would be more faithfully guarded by a rabble than
by the best chivalry of France. If Monseigneur Maurice
Talleyrand were here now, I would simply ask him——'

The door opened as he uttered these words. and a servant,

in a loud voice, announced, 'Monseigneur the Bishop of Autun.'

Small of stature and lame, there was yet in the massive head, the broad full brow, and the large orbits of the eyes, a certain command and dignity that marked him for no ordinary man ; and, though the suddenness of his entrance at this moment had created a sensation, half painful, half ludicrous, there was a calm self-possession in his manner, as he advanced to kiss the hand of the Marquise, that quickly changed the feeling for one of deference and respect.

'I was fortunate enough to be the subject of discussion as I came into the room—will my esteemed friend the Marquis de Ribaupierre inform me to what I owe this honour ? '

'Rather let me become the interpreter,' broke in the Marquise, who saw the speechless misery that now covered the old Marquis's countenance. 'Distressed at the length of time that had elapsed since we saw you among us here— grieved at what we could not but imagine a desertion of us —pained, above all, Monseigneur, by indications that you had sought and found friends in other ranks than those of your own high station——'

'A bishop, Madame la Marquise—forgive my interruption —a bishop only knows mankind as his brethren.' There was a malignant twinkle in his eye as he spoke, that deprived the sentiment of all its charitable meaning.

'Fortune has been very unkind to you in certain members of your family, Monseigneur,' said the Count de Noailles tartly.

'Younger branches, somewhat ill-cared-for and neglected,' said Talleyrand dryly.

'Nay, Monseigneur, your Christian charity goes too far and too fast,' said De Noailles. 'Our lackeys were never called our *frères cadets* before.'

'What a charming dress, Madame de Langeac!' said the bishop, touching a fold of the rich silk with a veneration he might have bestowed on a sacred relic.

'The favourite colour of the Queen, Monseigneur,' said she pointedly.

'Lilac is the emblem of hope; her Majesty is right to adopt it,' was the quick response.

'Is that like Monsieur de Mirabeau, Monseigneur?' said the Duc de Valmy, as he handed a coarse engraving to the bishop.

'There is a certain resemblance, unquestionably. It is about as like him—as—as—what shall I say—as the general estimate of the man is to the vast resources of his immense intelligence!'

'Immense intelligence!' exclaimed the Marquise de Bauffremont. 'I could more readily believe in his immense profligacy.'

'You might assent to both, Madame, and yet make no great mistake, save only that the one is passing away, the other coming,' said Talleyrand courteously.

'Which is the rising, which the setting sun, Monseigneur?' said De Valmy.

'I sincerely trust it may not shock this distinguished company if I say that it is the dawn of intellect, and the last night of incapacity, we are now witnessing. You have heard that this gentleman has seen the king?'

'Mirabeau been received by his Majesty!' 'Mirabeau admitted to the presence!' exclaimed three or four, in tones of utter incredulity.

'I can be positive as to the fact,' resumed the bishop. 'I can be even more—I can tell this honourable company what passed at the interview. It was, then, last night—(thank you, Monsieur le Duc, I accept your chair, since it allows me a more convenient spot to speak from)—it was last night, at a late hour, that a messenger arrived at the Avenue aux Abois with an order—I suppose it is etiquette I should call it order—for Monsieur de Mirabeau to hasten to St. Cloud, where the king desired to confer with him.'

'I'll never believe it!' cried the Marquis de Ribaupierre impetuously.

'If I had the happiness of being confessor to the Marquis, I would enjoin an extension of faith—particularly in the times we live in,' said Talleyrand, with a dry humour in his look. 'At all events, it is as I have the honour to acquaint you. Monsieur de Mirabeau received this message and obeyed it.'

'Par St. Louis, I can believe he obeyed it!' exclaimed the Duc de Valmy.

'And yet, Monsieur,' said the bishop, 'it was not till after very grave reflection the Count de Mirabeau determined to accept that same invitation.'

'Ah, Monseigneur, you would presume upon our credulity,' broke in De Valmy.

'Far from it, Duc; I cherish every crumb of faith that falls from a table so scantily dressed; but once more I repeat, the Count de Mirabeau weighed well the perils on either side, and then decided on accepting those which attached to the court.'

'The perils which attached to the court!' cried the Marquis de Langeac scoffingly. 'Monseigneur doubtless alludes to all the seductive temptations that would assail the cold, impassive temperament of his friend.'

'My friend! I accept the phrase, and wish it might be mutually acknowledged. My friend has little to boast of on the score of impassiveness, nor would the quality stand him in great stead just now. What the king wants he has got, however.'

'And pray what may that be, Monseigneur?'

'I will tell you, Monsieur: great promptitude, great eloquence, great foresight, and, better than all these, great contempt for a pretentious class, whose vanity would lead them to believe that a wound to themselves must be the death-blow to the monarchy. Now, sir, Monsieur de Mirabeau has these gifts, and by their influence he has persuaded the king to accept his services——'

'Oh, Monseigneur, if any one has dared to make you the subject of a mystification!'

'I have been the subject of many, my dear Marquis, and

may live to be the subject of more,' said the bishop, with great suavity and good-humour; 'but I see I must not presume upon my credit with this honourable company.' Then, changing his tone quickly, he added : 'Can any one give me information about a young Garde du Corps called Fitzgerald—Gerald Fitzgerald ?'

'I believe I am the only one he is known to,' said Madame de Bauffremont.

'As, next to the honour of offering you my homage, Madame la Marquise, that was the reason of my coming here this evening, may I trespass upon you to give me a few minutes alone ?'

Madame de Bauffremont arose, and, taking the bishop's arm, retired into a small room adjoining, and closed the door.

'Who is this Chevalier de Fitzgerald, Madame ?' said he abruptly.

'I can give you very little insight into his history,' replied the Marquise; 'but dare I presume to ask how are you interested about him ?'

'You shall hear, Madame la Marquise. About six or eight months back, the Queen's almoner, l'Abbé Jostinard, forwarded, of course by order of her Majesty, certain names of individuals in the royal household to Rome, imploring on their behalf the benediction of the Holy Father—a very laudable measure, not unfrequent in former reigns, but somehow lamentably fallen into disuse.' There was a strange, quaint expression in his eye as he uttered these last words, which did not escape the attention of the Marquise. 'Among these,' resumed he, 'there was included the Chevalier de Fitzgerald. Now, Madame, you are well aware that His Holiness takes especial pains to know that the recipients of the holy favour are persons worthy, by their lives and habits, of this precious blessing: while, therefore, for each of the others so recommended there were friends and relatives in abundance to vouch—the Rochemards, the Gueselins, the Tresignés can always find sufficient bail—this poor Chevalier stood friendless and alone, none to answer for, none to acknowledge him. Now, Madame, this might seem bad enough, but it was not all, for, not satisfied with excluding him from the sacred benediction, the consulta began speculating who and what he might be, whence he came, and so on. The most absurd conjectures, the wildest speculations, grew out of these researches : some tracing him to this, others to that origin, but all agreeing that he belonged to that marvellous order whom people are pleased to call adventurers. In the midst of this controversy distinguished names became entangled, some one would have said too high for the breath of scandal to attain—your own, Madame la Marquise——'

'Mine! how mine?' cried she eagerly.

'A romantic story of a sojourn in a remote villa in the Apennines—a tale positively interesting of a youth rescued from brigands or Bohemians, I forget which—pray assist me.'

'Continue, sir,' said the Marquise, whose compressed lips and sparkling eyes denoted the anger she could barely control.

'I am a most inadequate narrator, Madame—in fact, I am not sure that I should have lent much attention to this story at all if the Queen's name and your own had not been interwoven with it.'

'And how the Queen's, sir?' cried she haughtily.

'Ah, Madame la Marquise, ask yourself how, in this terrible time in which we live, the purest and the best are sullied by the stain of that calumny the world sows broadcast! Is it not a feature of our age that none can claim privilege nor immunity? Popular orators have no more fertile theme than when showing that station, rank, high duties, even holy cares are all maintained by creatures of mere flesh and blood, inheritors of human frailties, heirs of mortal weakness. Cardinals have lived whose hearts have known ambition—empresses have felt even love.'

'Monseigneur, this is enough,' said the Marquise, rising, and darting at him a look of haughty indignation.

'Not altogether, Madame,' said he calmly, motioning her to be reseated. 'To-morrow, or next day, this scandal—for

it is a scandal—will be the talk of Paris.   Whence came this
youth? who is he? how came he by his title of Chevalier?
will be asked in every salon, in every café, at every corner.
Madame de Bauffremont's name, and one even yet higher,
will figure in these recitals.   Some will suppose this, others
suggest that, and the world—the world, Madame la Marquise
—will believe all!'

'My Lord Bishop,' she began, but passion so overwhelmed
her that she could not continue.   Meanwhile he resumed—

'The vulgar herd, who know nothing, nor can know anything, of the emotions, noble and generous, that sway high-
born natures, who must needs measure the highest in station
by the paltry standards that apply to their own class, will
easily credit that even a Marquise may have been interested
for a youth to whom, certainly, rumour attributes considerable merit.   One word more, Madame; for as this youth,
educated, some say by no less gifted a tutor than Jean
Jacques Rousseau—others pretend by the watchful care of
Count Mirabeau himself——'

'Whence have you derived this most ingenious tissue of
falsehood, Monseigneur?' cried she passionately.

'Nay, Madame, I speak "from book" now.   The Chevalier
is intimately known to Monsieur de Mirabeau—lived at one
time in close companionship with him—and is, indeed, deeply
indebted to his kindness.'

'How glad I am, Monseigneur,' said she quickly, 'at
length to undeceive you!'

A knock at the door here interrupted the Marquise.   It
was a servant with a letter from Versailles that demanded
immediate attention.

'Here is more of it, Monseigneur,' cried she passionately.
'Her Majesty's ears have been outraged by these base
calumnies, and I am summoned to her presence in all haste.'

'I foresaw it, Madame,' said the Bishop, as he arose to
withdraw.   'I wish you a most pleasant journey, Madame
la Marquise, and all that can render the conclusion of it
agreeable.'

CHAPTER V

A SUDDEN REVERSE

'WHAT is it?—what has happened?' cried Gerald, as he awoke suddenly from a deep sleep, the first he had enjoyed after some nights of pain.   'Oh, it is you, Count Dillon,' and he tried to smile an apology for his abruptness.

'Lie down again, my lad, and listen to me, patiently too, if you can, for I have tidings that might try your patience.'

'I see you *have* bad news for me,' said Gerald calmly; 'out with it at once.'

The other made no reply, but turned toward him a look of compassionate tenderness.

'Come, Count, uncertainty is the worst of penalties—what are your tidings?'

'Tell me, first of all, Gerald, is it true that you supped on Friday last at Paris with a party, at the house of a certain Monsieur du Saillant, and there met Desmoulins, Rivarol, and several others of that party?'

'Yes, quite true.'

'And they drank patriotic toasts—which means that they pledged bumpers in insult to the court?'

'They made an attempt to do so, which I resisted.   I said that I would not sit there and hear one word to disparage my sovereign or his cause, on which one of them cried out, "And who are you who dares to prescribe to us how we are to speak, or what to toast?"   "He is *my* friend," said Du Saillant, "and that is enough."   "Nay," broke in the others, "it is not enough.   We have placed our necks in a halter, if this youth should turn out a spy of the court, or a Garde du Corps."   "And I am a Garde du Corps," said I.   "*Parbleu!*" said one, "I know him well now; he is the fellow they call the Ecossais—the Queen's minion."   With that I struck him across the face—the others fell upon me, and pressed me toward the window, I believe, to throw me out; at all events there was a severe struggle, from which I escaped, roughly handled and bruised, into an adjoining room. Here they followed and arranged that meeting of which you have heard.'

'You ran him through?'

'Yes, a bad wound, I fear; but it was no time to measure consequences; besides, three others claimed to fight me.'

'And did they?'

'No, the affair stands over; for Carcassone—that's his name—they thought was dying, and all their care was turned to him. Meanwhile I was bleeding tremendously, for he had cut a blood-vessel in my arm.'

'Well, and then——?'

'Then I can't well tell you what happened. I found myself in the street, with my cravat bound round my arm, and one man, they called Boulet, beside me. He said all he could to cheer me, bade me be of good heart, and that if I liked to make my fortune he would show me the way. "Come with me," said he, "to the 'Trois Étoiles,' declare yourself for us: you are well known in Paris—every one has heard how the Queen likes you." I tried to strike him, but I only tore off the bandage by my effort, and fell all bathed in blood on the pavement.'

'And it was in that state you were found underneath the Queen's window?'

'I know no more,' said Gerald drearily, as he lay back, and crossed his eyes with his hand. 'I have a hundred confused memories of what followed, but can trust none of them. I can recall something of a calèche driven furiously along, while I lay half-fainting within; something of wine or brandy poured down my throat; something of being carried in men's arms, but through all these are drifting other thoughts, vague, incoherent, almost impossible.'

'Is it true that the Queen, with one of her ladies, found you still lying in the garden when day broke?'

'It may have been the Queen—I did not know her,' said he despondently. 'Now, then, for your tidings.'

'You remember, of course, the events which have occurred

since your illness, that you have been examined by a military commission, in presence of two persons deputed by the " States-General ? " '

' Yes—yes, I have had two weary days of it ; ten minutes might have sufficed for all I was going to tell them.'

' So you really did refuse to answer the questions asked of you ? '

' I refused to speak of what was intrusted to my honour to preserve secret.'

' Or even to tell by whom you were so intrusted ? '

' Of course.'

' And you thus encountered the far worse peril of involving in an infamous slander the highest and purest name in France.'

' I do not understand you,' cried Gerald wildly.

' Surely you know the drift of all this inquiry—you cannot be ignorant that it was to assail her Majesty with a base scandal that you were placed beneath her window, and so discovered in the morning, at the very moment of her finding you there. Are you not aware that no falsehood is too gross nor too barefaced not to meet credence if she be its object ? Do not all they who plan the downfall of the monarchy despair of success while her graceful virtues adorn her high station ? Is not every effort of the vile faction directed solely against her ? Have you not witnessed how, one by one, have been abandoned all the innocent pleasures to which scandal attached a blame ? The Trianon deserted — the graceful amusements she loved so well—all given up. Unable to meet slander face to face, she has tried to make it impossible, as if one yet could obliterate the venomous poison of this rancorous hate ! '

' And now,' said Gerald, drawing a long breath, ' and now for my part in this infernal web of falsehood ? '

' If you refused to state where you had passed the evening — why you wore a disguise, how you came by your wound—you must allow you furnished matter for whatever suspicion they desired to attach to you.'

'They are free to believe of me what they may.'

'Ay, but not to include others in the imputation.'

'I never so much as dreamed of that!' said Gerald, with a weary sigh.

'Well, boy, it is just what has happened; not that there lives one base enough to believe this slander, though ten thousand are ready to repeat it. There, see how the *Gazette de Paris* treats it, a journal that once held a high place in public favour. Read that.'

Gerald bent over the paper, and read, half aloud, the following paragraph :—

'The young officer of the Garde du Corps examined by the Special Commission as to the extraordinary circumstances under which he was lately discovered in the garden of her Majesty, having refused all explanation either as to his disguise, his recent wound, or any reason for his presence there, has been adjudged guilty under the following heads: First, breach of military duty in absence from the Garde without leave; secondly, infraction of discipline in exchanging his uniform.'

'Well, well,' cried Gerald, 'what is the end of all this ?'

'You are dismissed the service, boy !' said Dillon sternly.

'Dismissed the service !' echoed he, in a broken voice.

'Your comrades bore you no goodwill, Gerald; even that last scene in the Salle des Gardes had its unhappy influence on your lot. It was to the comment of the journalist, however, I had directed your attention. See there !'

And Gerald read :—

'France will not, we assert, accept the degradation of this young officer as a sufficient expiation for what, if it means anything at all, implies a grave insult to the Majesty of the realm. In the name of an outraged public, we demand more than this. We insist on knowing how this youth, so devoid of friends, family, and fortune, became a soldier of the Garde —whence his title—who his patrons. To these questions, if not satisfactorily answered within a week, we purpose to

O

append such explanations as mere rumour affords; and we dare promise our readers, if not all the rigid accuracy of an attested document, some compensation in what may fairly claim the interest of a very romantic story. Not ours the blame if our narrative comprise names of more exalted station than that of this fortunate adventurer.'

'Fortunate adventurer! I am well called by such a title,' exclaimed he bitterly. 'And so I am dismissed the service!'

'The sentence was pronounced yesterday, but they thought you too ill to hear it. I have, however, appealed against it. I have promised that if re-examined——'

'Promise nothing for me, Count; I should reject the boon if they reinstated me to-morrow,' said Gerald haughtily.

'But remember, too, you must have other thoughts here than for yourself.'

'I will leave France; I will seek my fortune elsewhere; I cannot live in a network of intrigue; I have no head for plots, no heart for subtleties. Leave me, therefore, Count, to my fate.'

In broken, unconnected sentences the youth declined all aid or counsel. There are moments of such misery that all the offices of friendship bring less comfort to the heart than a stern self-reliance. A rugged sense of independence supplies at such times both energy and determination. Mayhap it is in moments like these more of real character is formed than even years accomplish in the slower accidents of fortune.

'This journalist, at least, shall render me satisfaction for his words,' thought he to himself. 'I cannot meet the whole array of these slanderers, but upon this one I will fix.'

'By what mischance, Gerald, have you made Monsieur your enemy?' asked the Count.

'Monsieur my enemy!' repeated Gerald, in utter amazement.

'Yes. The rumour goes that when the commission returned their report to the King, his Majesty was mercifully inclined, and might have felt disposed to inflict a mere reprimand, or some slight arrest, when Monsieur's persuasions prevailed on him to take a severer course.'

'I cannot bring myself to credit this!' cried Fitzgerald.

'It is generally believed, nay, it is doubted by none, and all are speculating how you came to incur this dislike.'

'It is hard to say,' muttered Gerald bitterly.

'This is for you, Fitzgerald,' said a sergeant of the Corps, entering the room hastily. 'You are to appear on the parade to-morrow, and hear it read at the head of your company,' and with these words he threw an open paper on the table and withdrew.

'Open shame and insult—this is too much,' said Gerald.

'You must appeal, Gerald; I insist upon it,' cried Dillon.

'No, sir. I have done with princes and royal guards. I could not put on their livery again with the sense of loyalty that once stirred my heart. Leave me, I pray, an hour or two to collect my thoughts and grow calm again. Good-bye for a short while.'

CHAPTER VI

A WANDERER

AFTER many vicissitudes and hazards, Fitzgerald succeeded in making his escape from France, and reaching Coblentz, where a small knot of devoted Royalists lived, sharing their little resources in common, and generously contributing every aid in their power to their poorer brethren. This life, if one of painful and unceasing anxiety, was yet singularly devoid of incident. To watch the terrible course of that torrent that now devastated their native country; to see how in that resistless deluge all was submerged—throne, villa, home, and family; to sit motionless on the shore, as it were, and survey the shipwreck, was their sad fate.

According to the various temperaments they possessed

did men bear this season of probation. To some it was like
a dreary nightmare, a long half sleep of suffering and oppression, leaving them devoid of all energy, or all will for
exertion. Others felt stimulated to be up and doing, to write
and plot, and intrigue with their fellow-exiles in Italy and
the north of Germany. The very transmission of the sad
tidings which came from Paris became an accustomed task;
while some few, half resigned to a ruin whose widespread
limits seemed to menace the whole of Europe, began to weave
plans for emigrating to a new world beyond the seas.

Gerald halted, and deliberated to which of these two latter
he would attach himself. If the idea of a new colony and
a new existence, where each should stamp his fate with his
own impress, had its attractions, there was also much that
fascinated in the heroism that bound men to a losing cause,
and held them faithful and true where so many fell off in
defection. Perhaps it was the personal character of the men
who professed these opinions ultimately decided his choice;
for D'Allonville, Caumartin, and Lessieux, who then lived
at Coblentz, gave to these sentiments all the glowing ardour
of a high and noble chivalry. Nor was it without a certain
charm for a young mind to see himself, as it were, a partici-
pator and agent in the cause of great events. By zeal to
encounter any difficulty, readiness to go anywhere, or dare
any peril, Fitzgerald had won the esteem and confidence of
men high in the exiled Prince's favour. They grew to talk
with him and confide in him, showing him private letters
from exalted personages, and even at times to take his counsel
in affairs which required prompt action. Young, active, able
to endure fatigue without inconvenience, he offered himself
for every charge where such qualities might be available;
and thus he traversed Europe, from Hamburg to Italy, from
the Rhine to the Vistula, bearing despatches, or as often
himself charged with some special communication too delicate
to commit to writing, and wherein his tact was intrusted with
the details.

At last it was deemed essential to have a number of agents

in France itself—men capable of watching and recording the changes of public opinion, who might note the rising discontents of the popular mind, and observe where they had their source. It was a rooted faith in the Royalist party that sooner or later the nation would react against the terrible doctrines of the anarchists, and welcome back to France the men whose very names and titles were part of her glory : the mistake was in supposing that the time for this reaction was at hand, and in believing that every passing shadow was its herald.

Gerald's personal courage, his adroitness in the use of disguise, his unfailing resources in every difficulty, pointed him out as one well adapted for this employ ; and he was constantly intrusted with secret missions to this or that part of France, occasions on which he as invariably distinguished himself by his capacity. The very isolation in which he stood, without family or connections, favoured him, removing him from the sphere of those jealousies which oftentimes marred and defeated the wisest plans of the Royalists. He was not a Rohan nor a Courcelles—a Grammont nor a Tavanne—whose family influence was one day or other to be dreaded. Let him win what fame he might, gain what credit, attract what notice, he carried with him no train of followers to profit by his success and bar up the avenues of promotion ; for so was it—strange and scarce credible though it seems—men were already quarrelling over the spoils ere the victory was won ; ere, indeed, the battle was engaged, or the enemy encountered.

BOOK THE THIRD

CHAPTER I

A CARDINAL'S CHAMBER

WE must ask of our reader to pass over both time and space, and accompany us, as night is falling, to a small chamber in the house of the Cardinal Caraffa at Rome, where his Eminence is now closeted in secret converse with a tall, sickly, but still handsome man, in a long robe of black serge, buttoned almost to his feet, and wearing on his head a low square cap, of the same coarse material; he is the Père Massoni, superior of the College of Jesuits.

The Cardinal had but just returned from a conclave, and had not taken time to change a dress, whose splendour formed a strong contrast with the simple attire of his guest.

'It is, happily, the last council for the season,' said his Eminence, as he seated himself in a deep easy-chair. 'His Holiness leaves for Gaeta to-morrow, the Cardinal Secretary Piombino retires to Albano during the hot weather, and I am free to confer with my esteemed friend the Père Massoni, and discuss deeper themes than the medallions in the nave of San Giovanni di Laterano. There were to have been fourteen on either side last Tuesday; on Friday, we came down to twelve; to-day, we deemed eleven enough; in fact, Massoni, we are less speculative as to the future, and have left but four spaces to be filled up; but enough of this,—have your letters arrived?'

'Yes, your Eminence, the Priest Carroll from Ireland has brought me several, and much information besides of events in England.'

214

'It is of France I want to hear,' broke in the Cardinal impatiently. 'It is of the man in the throes of death I would learn tidings, not of him lingering in the long stages of a chronic malady. Did this priest pass through Paris?'

'He did, your Eminence; he was two days there. The fever of blood still rages. 'Twas but Monday week, thirty-two nobles of La Vendée were guillotined, and, worse still, eight priests, old and venerable men, curés of the several parishes. They met their death as became true sons of the holy Church, declaring with their last breath that the sacrifice would bring a blessing on the faith.'

'So it will—they are right—truth must triumph at last, Massoni,' said the Cardinal hurriedly; 'but we are passing through a fiery ordeal; sparks of the same fire have been seen among ourselves too. Grave fears exist that all is not well at Viterbo.'

'The flame must be trodden out quickly and completely, your Eminence; deal with traitors with speed, and you can treat true men with justice. The Abbé Guescard, whose book on private judgments you have seen, was buried this morning.'

'I had not heard that he was ill.'

'It was a sudden seizure, your Eminence, but the convulsions resisted all treatment, and death closed his sufferings about midnight. The doctrines of Diderot and Jean Jacques form but sorry homilies. They who preach them go to a heavy reckoning hereafter.'

'And meet with sudden deaths besides,' said the Cardinal, with a glance in which there was fully as much jollity as gloom.

The Jesuit Father's pale face remained calm and passionless as before, nor did a syllable escape from him in reply. At length the Cardinal said, 'All accounts agree in one thing, the pestilence is spreading. At Aranguez, in Spain, a secret society has been discovered in correspondence with Desmoulins. At Leipsic a record for future proscription throughout Germany has been found, exactly fashioned after the

true Paris model; and even in sluggish England the mutterings of discontent are heard, but with them we have less
sympathy—or rather we might say, God speed the hand
that would pull down the heretic Church!'

'Carroll tells me that Ireland is ripe, though for what, it
is yet hard to pronounce. The cry of "Liberty" in France
has awakened her to the memory of all her hatred to
England. Men of great ability and daring are eagerly
feeding the flame; the difficulty will be to direct its ravages
when once it breaks out. If the principles of France sway
them, the torrent that will overwhelm the heretic will also
sweep away the faith.'

'Much will depend upon the men who direct the movement.'

'No, no,' said the Jesuit, 'next to nothing. Each in his
turn will be the victim of the event he seems to control. It
is not the riven tree carried along by the current that directs
the stream. It is to human passions and their working we
must look, to see the issue out of these troubles. Once men
emerge out of the storm-tossed ocean of their excesses, they
strain their eyes to catch some haven—some resting-place.
Some find it in religion; some in ambition, which is the
religion of this world. The crime of France has been that
no such goal has ever existed. In their lust to destroy, they
have forfeited the power to rebuild. As well endeavour to
reanimate the cold corpses beneath the guillotine as revive
that glorious monarchy. For men like these there is no
hope—no hereafter. Have no trust in them.'

'But you yourself told me,' cried the Cardinal, 'how vain
it were to pledge men to the cause of the Church.'

'And truly did I say so. Men will serve no cause but
that which secures them a safe recompense. In France they
have that recompense—there is vengeance and there is
pillage; but both will be exhausted after a time—there will
be satiety for one and starvation for the other, and then
woe to those who spirited them on to this pursuit. The
convulsion in Ireland, if it should come, need not have this

peril; there, there is a race to expel and a heresy to exter-
minate; in both the prospect of the future is implied. Let
us aid this project.'

'Ah! it is your old project lurks there,' cried the Cardinal; 'I see a glimpse of it already; but what a dream is
the restoration of that house!'

'Nor do I mean it should be more; the phantom of a
Stuart in the procession is all I ask for. By that dynasty
the Church is typified. Instead of encountering the thousand
enemies of a faith, we rally to us the adherents of a
monarchy. If we build up this throne, he who sits on it is
our viceroy; we have made, and can unmake him.'

'And how can the Cardinal York serve these plans?'

'I never intended that he should; his gown alone would
exempt him, even had he—which he has not—personal qualities for such a cause.'

'Yet with him the race is extinct.'

'Of that I am not so certain, and it is precisely the point
on which I want to confer with you.' So saying, the Père
drew a packet of papers from the breast of his robe, and
placed it on the table. 'I have there beneath my hand,'
said he, 'the copy of a marriage certificate between Charles
Edward, Prince of Wales, and Grace Geraldine, of Cappa
Glyn, County Kildare, Ireland. It is formally drawn up,
dated, signed, and witnessed with due accuracy. The Father
Ignatius, in whose hand the document is, is dead; but there
are many alive who could recognise his writing. One of the
witnesses, too, is believed still to be living in a remote part
of Ireland; I have his name and can trace him; but even
better than this, the Cardinal York admits the fact, and
owns that he retains in his possession a last legacy of the
Prince for the child born of this marriage.

'Your Eminence smiles incredulously; but what will you
say when I add that the same child was inscribed in our
College under the name of Gerald Fitzgerald; was well
known to my predecessor, the present Bishop of Orvieto;
quitted the College to acquire the protection of the Prince,

from which he most unaccountably strayed or was withdrawn, and ultimately reached France.'

'Where he has, doubtless, been guillotined for his royal
blood,' broke in the Cardinal.

'No, your Eminence; he lives, and I have traced him.
Nay, more, I have found that he is one in every way adapted
for such an enterprise as I speak of; possessed of the most
heroic courage, with a character fertile in resources; all the
winning graces of his father are united in him, with a
steadfast energy that few of the Stuarts could ever have laid
claim to. In a life of struggle and adversity—for he has
never known his rank, nor has the slightest suspicion of his
birth—he has never once descended to a single act that
could impugn the highest station. In a word, to declare him
a Prince to-morrow needs not that we should obliterate his
past life or conceal its vicissitudes.'

'Be it so as you say. Is it such pretensions you would
oppose to the recognised and established monarchy of England? A youth of at least highly questionable legitimacy,
friendless and penniless; and this, too, in an age when
thrones propped up by all that can aid their prestige are
tottering to their fall!'

'We want him but as the banner to rally around; we
need him as the standard which will draw Scotland to the
side of Ireland, and both for one cause—the Church. A
Prince of the House of Stuart is the emblem of all that
defies the heresy when the day of trouble comes. It is
vital that Ireland should not follow in the steps of France,
and Christian blood be shed to establish the reign of the
infidel! If the pestilence that now rages in France extend
through Europe, as many wise heads predict it will, the day
will come that the last resting-place of our faith will be that
small island in the west. Think, then, how important it is
that we should give to the struggle that is approaching a
guidance and direction. If the Irish insurrection be capable
of a royalist colouring, we can take advantage of that feature
to awaken the dormant chivalry of those who would risk

nothing in the cause of a Republic. The old Catholic families of England, the Scottish chiefs, men who can bring into the field the fiercest partisans and the most intrepid followers; all Ireland, save that small garrison which assumes to subject it to English rule, will rally round a Stuart: and that Stuart will be in our hands to deal with—to elevate to a throne on the claim of his birth; or, if need be, to proclaim an illegitimate pretender!'

The soft, mild eyes of the Jesuit grew darker and deeper in colour, and his pale cheeks flushed, while the last words came from him with an utterance thick and almost guttural from passion. Nor was the Cardinal unmoved: partly in sympathy with the emotion of the speaker, partly stimulated by the great proportions of the scheme displayed before him, he sat, with hurried breathing and a heated brow, gazing steadfastly at the other.

'There are immense difficulties, Father,' he began.

'I know them all,' broke in Massoni. 'For some I have provided, for many more I am still reflecting; but still remember, that to launch the project is our great care. When the rock is riven from its base, no man can tell by what course it will descend the mountain, over what precipice gain new force, or in what hollow lie spent and motionless. Let us be satisfied if we start the game, and leave to destiny the pursuit!'

'Much money will be needed——'

'The great families of England are rich. It will not require deep calculation to satisfy them that the cost of supporting a loyalist cause will be little in comparison with the consequences of a revolution to end in a republic; a loan is ever lighter than confiscation!'

'There is much in that if the alternative be well put and well understood.'

'From what I learn,' continued the Père, 'men of influence and fortune will grasp eagerly at what offers any issue to the coming trouble, save to follow in the footsteps of France. The Terror there has done us good service, and the lesson

may be still further improved. They who would imitate
Marat and Robespierre will have a short reign.'

'Better they should have none ! '

'There must be the baptism of blood,' said the Père, in a
low but firm voice.

'And who is to prepare the plan of this great campaign,
to gather together the leaders, to applot the several duties,
to arrange details, conciliate interests, and reconcile rivalries ?
He must be one, doubtless, of commanding ability and vast
resources.'

Massoni bowed a deep and reverential assent.

'A man of station sufficient to make his influence felt
without dispute—one whose counsel none dare gainsay.'

Again did a humble bow give acquiescence.

'Nor,' continued the speaker, 'must it be from his exalted
station alone that men yield deference to him. He must
needs be one well versed in human nature; who can read
the heart in its mood of strength or weakness ; a master of
all the secret springs that sway motives ; in a word, he ought
to combine the wide views and grand conceptions of the
politician with the deep and subtle knowledge of a churchman—where will you find such ?

'He can be found,' was the calm reply. 'I know of one
who answers to each demand of your description.'

'You are mistaken, Père Massoni,' said the Cardinal in a
voice slightly tremulous with agitation. 'I know his
Eminence of York well, and he is ill fitted for a charge so
vast and momentous.'

'I never thought of him, sir,' was the prompt answer.
'My eyes were fixed upon one scarcely his inferior in high
descent, infinitely above him in all the qualities of mind and
intellect, one whose name in the cause would half ensure
success, and whose vast resources of thought would be a
more precious mine than the wealth of Peru.'

'And he—who is this great and transcendent genius ?'
asked the Cardinal, half angrily.

'His Eminence the Cardinal Leo Gonzales Caraffa ! ' said

the Père, as he dropped on his knees and pressed his lips fervently to the other's hand.

The Cardinal's florid features flushed till they were crimson; and though he tried to speak, no sound came from his lips. A sense of overwhelming astonishment, even more than gratified vanity, had mastered him, and, with a gesture of modest dissent, he raised the priest from the ground.

'No, no, Massoni,' said he, in a soft, low tone; 'these are the promptings of your own affectionate regard for me, not the fruit of that calm reason with which you know so well how to judge your fellow-men.'

'Read these letters, then, sir,' said Massoni, placing a packet on the table, 'and see if my sentiments are not as strong in the hearts of others.'

The Cardinal hesitated to open the documents before him; there was a sort of modest reluctance in his manner which Massoni seemed to understand; for, taking up one of the letters himself, he glanced his eyes along the lines till he came to a particular passage, pointing out which with his finger, he read: '"You have among the Cardinals, however, one fully equal to this great task, the Cardinal Caraffa, a man whose political sagacity is not surpassed in Europe, and who, by a good fortune, rare among churchmen, possesses a mind capable of comprehending and directing great military measures. I am informed that he served in Spain."'

'Who writes this?' broke in the Cardinal.

'The writer is Prince Charles of Hesse.'

'A brave soldier and an honest man,' said the Cardinal, with evident pleasure in the words.

'This is from the Viscount de Noe,' resumed Massoni, opening another letter and reading: '"It is essentially the cause of the Church, and demands a churchman at its head. Who, then, so fit as he who may, one day or other, occupy the throne of St. Peter!"' Here he paused as if having concluded.

'The expression is vague, nor has it any the least application to me,' said Caraffa, reddening.

'Then hear what follows,' cried Massoni. '"Even if there were personal peril, which there is not, the Cardinal Caraffa would not refuse us his aid, nor must he remain the only man in Europe unconscious of the great qualities which stamp him as our leader." This,' continued the priest, with increased rapidity, 'this is from Sir Godefry Wharton, an English Catholic noble of great wealth and influence. "From all that I can learn it must be Caraffa, not York, to lead us in this enterprise; all agree in representing him as a man of resolute action, gifted with every quality of statesmanship." Troverini writes thus from Venice: "When the day of restoration"—it is of the Church he speaks—"when the day of restoration arrives, we shall need a man equal to the great task of reconstructing society, without employing too ostentatiously the old materials. I am assured that Caraffa is such a man; tell me your opinion of him." This,' resumed Massoni, holding up a large letter in a strange, rough, and irregular hand, 'this is from the Marquis d'Allonville, secretary to the Count d'Artois. "We all feel that if it be our fate to return, it must be as following in the procession of the Church. Nothing but the faith can successfully combat this infidelity baptized in crime. To give, therefore, the impulse of religion to any of these movements, no matter among what people, must be the first care of those who look forward to better things. Legitimacy is the doctrine of the Gospel." . . . This is what I was in search of. "Ireland is well adapted for the experiment. A people of believers under the sway of a nation they detest will eagerly grasp at what will alike establish the Church they revere and the nationality they covet. If you really have a legitimate descendant of the Stuarts, and if he be one equal to the demands of the crisis, it signifies little in what quarter of Europe the first essay be made, and we will throw all our efforts into the scale with you, always provided that you can show us some great political head, some man of foresight and reflection, among your party concurring in this view—such a one, for example, as the Cardinal Caraffa. We have money, men of action and daring, only longing for occasions to employ them, but we are sadly in want of such capacities as Caraffa represents ; so at least the Prince tells us, for I have no personal knowledge of the Cardinal."'

'I am flattered by his Royal Highness's remembrance of me,' said Caraffa proudly.

'And this,' said Massoni, showing a few lines on a simple slip of paper, 'this came enclosed within D'Allonville's letter. "I am willing to open direct relations with his Eminence the Cardinal Caraffa on the subjects herein discussed.—D'Artois." Are these enough, sir ?'

'More than enough to gratify a loftier pride than mine,' said Caraffa, with a flushed cheek ; 'but let us turn to a worthier theme. What is it that is proposed ?'

'The project, in one word, is this—to make the rising now about to take place in Ireland a royalist, and not a revolutionary movement ; to overbear the men of destruction by the influence of wiser and safer guides ; to direct the wild energies of revolt into the salutary channels of a restoration ; and to build up once more, in all its plenitude, the power of the Church.'

'Remember, Massoni, what Mirabeau said ; and though I do not love the authority, the words are those of wisdom : "Revolutions are not the work of men—they make themselves."'

'It is from men's hands, however, they receive their first impulses. It is also by a secret and firm alliance of men— steady to one purpose, and constant to one idea—that revolutions catch their tone and colour. None of us could expect that, in a great national struggle, there will not be many acts to deplore—grievous crimes committed gratuitously— vain and useless cruelties. To every great vicissitude in this world there is an amount of power applied totally disproportioned to the effect produced. To wreck one solitary ship, a whole ocean is convulsed, and desolate shores in faraway lands are storm-lashed for days. So is it in revolutions The unchained winds of men's passions sweep over a larger space than is needed. This must be borne. Let us remember, too, that the blood thus, to all seeming, gratuitously shed has also its profit. Terror is a great agency of revolt. Many must be intimidated. It is when people are paralysed by fear that they who are to reconstruct society have time to mature their plans, just as the surgeon awaits the moments of his patient's insensibility to commence his operation. But, above all, your Eminence, bear in mind that where the object is good and great, a blessing goes with those who sustain it.'

If the Cardinal bowed a submissive assent to this devout assertion, there was something like a half motion of impatience in his manner as he said—

'And the men who are to lead this movement?'

'The details are somewhat lengthy, your Eminence, but I have them here,' said Massoni, as he laid his hand on the papers before him.

'And this is Ireland?' said Caraffa, as he bent over a map and gazed on the small spot which represented the island. 'How small it looks, and how far away!'

CHAPTER II

A DEATH-BED

It was at the close of a sultry day that a sick man, wan, pale, and almost voiceless, sat propped up by pillows, and seeming to drink in with a sort of effort the faint breeze that entered by an open window. A large bouquet of fresh flowers stood in a vase beside him, and on the bed itself moss-roses and carnations were scattered, their gorgeous tints terribly in contrast to the sickly pallor of that visage on which death had already placed its stamp. It would have puzzled the wiliest physiognomist to have read that strange and strongly-marked face; for while the massive head and strong brow, the yet brilliant eye and contracted eyebrow, denoted energy and daring, there was a faint smile, inexpressibly sad and weary-looking, on the mouth, that seemed to bespeak a heart that had experienced many an emotion, and ended by finding 'all barren.'

A long, low sigh escaped him as he lay, and in his utter weariness his hands dropped listlessly, one falling over the side of the bed. The watchful nurse, who, in the dress of her order as a Sister of Charity, sat nigh, arose and leaned over to regard him.

'No, Constance, not yet,' said he, smiling faintly, and answering the unspoken thought that was passing in her mind; 'not yet; but very near—very near indeed. What hour is it?'

'St. Roch has just chimed half-past seven,' replied she calmly.

'Open the window wider; there is a little air stirring.'

'No; the evening is very still, but it will be fresher by and by.'

'I shall not need it,' said he, more faintly, though with perfect calm. 'Before midnight, Constance—before midnight it will be the same to me if it breathed a zephyr or blew a gale: where I am going it will do neither.'

'Oh, Citizen, can I not persuade you to see the Père Dulaque or the Curé of St. Roch? Your minutes are few here now, and I implore you not to waste them.'

''Tis so that I intend, my worthy friend,' said he calmly. 'Had either of these excellent men you mention made the voyage I am now going, I would speak to them willingly; but remember, Constance, it is a sea without a chart.'

'Say not so in the face of that blessed Book——'

'Nay, nay, do not disturb my few moments of calm. How sweet those flowers are! How balmy that little air that now stirs the leaves! Oh, what a fair world it is, or rather it might be! Do not sigh so heavily, Constance; remember what I told you yesterday; our belief is like our loyalty—it is independent of us.'

'Let some holy man at least speak to you.'

P

'Why should I shock his honest faith? Why should he disturb my peace? Know, woman,' added he, more energetically, 'that I have striven harder to attain this same faith than ever you have done to resist a heresy. I needed it a thousand times more than you; I'd have done more to gain it—clung closer to it when won too.'

'What did you do?' asked she boldly.

'I read, reflected, pondered years long—disputed, discussed, read more—inquired wherever I hoped to meet enlightenment.'

'You never prayed,' said she meekly.

'Prayed! How should I—not knowing for what, or to whom?'

An exclamation—almost a cry—escaped the woman, and her lips were seen to move rapidly, as if in prayer. The sick man seemed to respect the sentiment of devotion that he could not bring himself to feel, and was silent. At last he said, in a voice of much sweetness, 'Your patient care and kindness are not the less dear to me that I ascribe them to a source your humility would reject. I believe in human nature, my good Constance, though of a verity it has given me strong lessons not to be over-sanguine.'

'Who has had more friends?' began she; but he stopped her short at once by a contemptuous gesture with his hand, while he said—

'Men are your friends in life as they are your companions on a journey—so long as your road lies in the same direction they will travel with you. To bear with your infirmities, to take count of your trials, and make allowance for your hardships; to find out what of good there is in you, and teach you to fertilise it for yourself; to discern the soil of your nature, expel its weeds, and still to be hopeful—this is friendship. But it never comes from a brother man; it is a woman alone can render it. Who is it that knocks there?' asked he quickly.

She went to the door, and speedily returned with the answer—

'It is the same youth who was here yesterday, and refused to give his name. He is still most urgent in his demand to see you.'

'Does he know what he asks—that I am on the eve of a long journey, and must needs have my thoughts engaged about the road before me ?'

'I told him you were very ill—very ill_indeed ; that even your dearest friends only saw you for a few minutes at a time ; but he persisted in asserting that if you knew he was there, you would surely see him.'

'Let his perseverance have its reward. Tell him to come in.'

The sister returned to the door, and after a whispered word to the stranger, enforcing caution in his interview, admitted him, and pointing to the bed where the sick man lay, she retired.

If the features and gestures of the stranger, as he moved silently across the room, denoted the delicacy of a certain refinement, his dress bespoke great poverty ; his clothes were ragged, his shoes in tatters, and even the red woollen cap which he had just removed from his head was patched in several places.

The sick man motioned to him to stand where the light would fall upon him strongly ; and then, having stared steadfastly at him for several minutes, he sighed drearily, and said, 'What have you with me ?'

'Don't you remember me, then, Signor Gabriel ?' asked the young man, in a tone of deep agitation. 'Don't you remember Fitzgerald ?'

'The boy of the Maremma—the Garde du Corps—the favourite of the Queen—the postilion on the flight to Varennes—the secret letter-carrier to the Temple——'

'Speak lower, Monsieur! speak lower, I beseech you,' interposed the other. 'If I were betrayed, my life is not worth an hour's purchase.'

'And is it worth preserving in such a garb as that ? I thought you had been an apter scholar, Gerald, and that ere this you had found your way to fortune. The Prince de Condé wrote me that you were his trustiest agent.'

'And it is on a mission from him that I am here this day. I have been waiting for weeks long to see and speak with you. I knew that you were ill, and could find no means to approach you.'

'You come too late, my friend—too late,' said Mirabeau, sighing: 'Royalist, Girondin, Bourbon, or the Mountain, they are all illusions now!'

'The great principles of justice are not an illusion, sir; the idea of Right is immutable and immortal!'

'I know of nothing that does not change and die,' said Mirabeau gravely; then added, 'But what would you with me?'

'I have not courage to disturb your suffering sick-bed with cares you can no longer feel. I had not imagined I should have found you so ill as this.'

'Sick unto death—if you can tell me what death means,' said the other with a strange smile.

'They who sent me,' resumed Gerald, not heeding his last remark, 'believed you in all the vigour of health as of intellect. They have watched with almost breathless interest the glorious conflict you have long maintained against the men of anarchy and the guillotine; they have recognised in you the one sole man, of all the nation, who can save France——'

The sick man smiled sadly, and laying his wasted fingers on Gerald's arm, said, 'It is not to be done!'

'Do you mean, sir, that it is the will of the great Providence who rules us that this mighty people should sink under the tyranny of a few bloodthirsty wretches?'

'I spoke not of France; I spoke of the Monarchy,' said Mirabeau. 'Look at those flowers there: in a few hours hence they will have lost their odour and their colour. Now, all your memory—be it ever so good—will not replace these to your senses. Go tell your master that his hour has struck. Monarchy was once a Faith; it will henceforth be but a Superstition.'

'And is a just right like this to be abandoned?'

'No. The stranger may place them on the throne they have lost; and if they be wise enough to repay the service with ingratitude, a few more years of this mock rule may be eked out.'

'Would that I had power to tell you all our plans, and you the strength to listen to me!' cried Gerald: 'you would see that what they purpose is no puny enterprise; nor what they aim at, a selfish conquest.'

'You came to me once before—I remember the incident well; I was living in the Avenue aux Abois when you summoned me to a meeting at St. Cloud. The Monarchy might have been saved even then. It was late, but not too late. I advised a ministry of such materials as the people might trust and the court corrupt—men of low origin, violent, exacting, but venal. Six months of such rule would have sent France back to all her ancient traditions, and the king been more popular than ever. But they would not hear me: they talked of walking in the high path of duty; and it has led some to the scaffold, and the rest to exile! But what concern have I with these things? Do you know, young man, that all your king could promise, all the mighty people themselves could bestow upon me as I lie here, could not equal the pleasure that moss-rose yields me, nor the ecstasy of delight I feel when a gentle wind blows fresh upon my cheek. Say it out, sir; say out what that supercilious smile implies,' cried he, his eyes lighting up with all their ancient fire. 'Tell me at once it was Mirabeau the voluptuary that spoke there! Ay, and I'll not gainsay you! If to exult in the perfection of the senses nature has given me; to drink in with ecstasy what others imbibe in apathy; to feel a godlike enjoyment where less keenly gifted temperaments had scarcely known a pleasure—if this is to be a voluptuary, I am one.'

'But why, with powers like yours, limit your enjoyment to mere sensual pleasures? Why not taste the higher and purer delight of succouring misfortune and defending the powerless?'

'I *did* try it,' said the sick man, sighing. 'I essayed to discover the pleasures of what you would call morality. I was generous; I forgave injuries; I pardoned ingratitude; I aided struggling misery; but the reward was not forthcoming;—these things gave me no happiness.'

'No happiness!'

'None. I tried to forget I was a dupe; I did my best to believe myself a benefactor of my species; I stopped my ear against any praises from those I had befriended; but nothing in my heart responded to their joy. I was not happier. Remember, boy,' cried he, 'that even your own moralists only promise the recompense for virtue in another world. I looked for smaller profits and prompter payment.' The mockery of his smile, as he spoke, seemed to wound Gerald; for, as he turned away his head, a deep flush covered his face. 'Forgive me,' said the sick man; 'I ought to have remembered that your early training was derived from those worthy men, the Jesuit Fathers; and if I cannot participate in your consolations, I would not insult your convictions.' Then, raising himself on one arm, he added, with a stronger effort: 'Your mission to me is a failure, Fitzgerald. I cannot aid your cause: he whoso trembling hand cannot carry the glass of water to his lips can scarce replace a fallen dynasty. I will not even deceive you by saying what, if health and strength were mine, I might do—perhaps I do not know it myself. Go back and tell your Prince that he and his must wait—wait like wise physicians—till nature bring the crisis of the malady; that all they could do now would but hurt the cause they mean to serve. When France needs her princes, she will seek them even out of exile. Let them beware how they destroy the prestige of their high estate by accepting equality meanwhile. They are the priests of a religion, and can never descend to the charges of the laity. As for you, yourself, it is well that I have seen you; I have long desired to speak to you of your own fortunes. I had written to Alfieri about you, and his answer—to *you* an important

document—is in that box. You will find the key yonder
on the ring.'

As Gerald rose to obey this direction, Mirabeau fell back
exhausted on the bed, a clammy sweat breaking out over his
cheeks and forehead. The cry which unconsciously escaped
the youth, quickly summoned the 'sister' to the bedside.

'This is death,' said she, in the calm, solemn voice of one
long inured to such scenes. She tried to make him swallow
a teaspoonful of some restorative, but the liquid dropped
over his lips, and fell upon his chin. 'Death—and what a
death!' muttered the sister, half to herself.

'See — see — he is coming back to himself,' whispered
Gerald; 'his eyes are opening, and his lips move,' while
a faint effort of the muscles around the mouth seemed to
essay a smile.

Again she moistened his lips with the cordial, and this
time he was able to swallow some drops of it. He made a
slight attempt to speak, and as the sister bent her ear to
his lips, he whispered faintly, 'Tell him to come back—to-
morrow—to-morrow!'

She repeated the words to Gerald, who, feeling that his
presence any longer there might be hurtful, slowly and
silently stepped from the room, and descended to the street.

Late as it was, a considerable crowd was assembled before
the door in front of the house; their attitude of silent and
respectful anxiety showed the deep interest felt in the sick
man's state; and although no name was spoken, the frequent
recurrence of the words 'he' and 'his' evinced how absorb-
ingly all thoughts were concentrated upon one individual.
Nor was it only of one class in society the crowd was
composed. Mirabeau's admirers and followers were of every
rank and every section of politicians; and, strangely enough,
men whose public animosities had set them widely apart
from each other were here seen exchanging their last
tidings of the sick-room, and alternating and balancing their
hopes and fears of his condition.

'Jostinard calls the malady cerebral absorption,' said one,

'as though intense application had produced an organic change.'

'Lessieux holds that the disease was produced by those mercurial baths he used to take to stimulate him on occasions of great public display,' said another.

'There is reason to believe it a family complaint of some sort,' broke in a third; 'the Bailli de Mirabeau sank under pure exhaustion, as if the machine had actually worn out.'

'*Pardie!*' cried out a rough-looking man in a working dress; 'it is hard that we cannot repair him with the strong materials the useless fellows are made of; there are full fifty in the Assembly we could give for one like *him*.'

'You talk of maladies,' broke in a loud, full voice, 'and I tell you that the Citizen Riquetti is dying of poison—ay, start, or murmur if you will—I repeat it, of poison. Do we not all know how his power is feared, and his eloquence dreaded? Are we strangers to those who hate this great and good man?'

'Great and good he is,' murmured another; 'when shall we see his equal?'

'See, here is one who has been lately with him; let us learn his news.'

This speech was uttered by a poorly-clad man, with a red cap on his head, as Gerald was endeavouring to pierce the crowd.

'Who is the citizen who has this privilege of speaking with Gabriel Riquetti?' said Cabrot, an over-dressed man, who stood the centre of a group of talkers.

Without paying any attention to this summons, Gerald tried to pursue his way and pass on; but several already barred the passage, and seemed to insist, as on a right, to hear the last account of the sick man. For a moment a haughty impulse to refuse all information thus demanded seemed to sway Gerald; then, suddenly changing his resolution, he calmly answered that Mirabeau appeared to him so ill as to preclude all hope of recovery, and that his state portended but few hours of life.

'Ask him who he himself is?'—'Why and how he came there?'—'What medicine is Riquetti taking?'—'Who administers it?'—'Let this man give an account of himself!' Such, and such like, were the cries that now resounded on all sides, and Gerald saw himself at once surrounded by a mob, whose demands were uttered in no doubtful tone.

'The Citizen Riquetti is one whose life is dear to the Republic,' broke in Cabrot; 'all Frenchmen have a right to investigate whatever affects that life. Some aver that he is the victim of assassination——'

'I say, and will maintain it,' broke in the man who had made this assertion before; 'they have given him some stuff that causes a gradual decay.'

'Let this man declare himself. Who are you, Citizen, and whence?' asked another, confronting Fitzgerald. 'What business came you here to transact with the Citizen Riquetti?'

'Have I asked you, or you, or you,' said Gerald, turning proudly from one to the other of those around him, 'of your private affairs? Have I dared to interrogate you as to who you are, whence you came, whither you go? and by what presumption do you take this liberty with me?'

'By that which a care of the public safety imposes,' said Cabrot. 'As Commissary of the fifth "arrondissement," I demand this citizen's name.'

'You are right to be boastful of your liberty!' said Gerald insolently, 'when a man cannot walk the streets, nor even visit a dying friend, without submitting himself to the treatment of a criminal.'

'He a friend of Gabriel Riquetti!' burst in Cabrot. 'Look, I beseech you, at the appearance of the man who gives himself this title.'

'So, then, it is to my humble dress you object. Citizens, this speaks well for your fraternity and equality.'

'You shall not evade a reckoning with us in this wise,' said Cabrot. 'Let us take him to the Corps du Garde, citizens.'

'Ay! away with him to the Corps du Garde!' cried several together.

Gerald became suddenly struck by the rashness of his momentary loss of temper, and quietly said, 'I'll not give you such trouble, citizens. What is it you wish to hear?'

'Your compliance comes too late,' said Cabrot; 'we will do the thing in order; off with us to the Corps du Garde!'

'I appeal to you all, why am I to be subjected to this insult?' asked Gerald, addressing the crowd. 'You deliver me to the Commissary, not for any crime or for any accusation of one; you compel me to speak about matters purely personal—circumstances which I could have no right to extort from any of *you*. Is this fair—is it just—is it decent?'

While he thus pleaded, the crowd was obliged to separate suddenly, and make way for a handsome equipage, which came up at full trot, and stopped before the door of Mirabeau's house; and a murmur ran quickly around, 'It is The Gabrielle come to ask after Riquetti'; and Cabrot, forgetting his part of public prosecutor, now approached the window of the carriage with an almost servile affectation of courtesy. Had Gerald been so disposed, nothing would have been easier for him than to make his escape in the diversion caused by this new incident, so eager was the crowd to press around and catch a glimpse of her whose gloved hand now rested on the door of the carriage.

'She is Riquetti's mistress,' cried one; 'is not she?'

'Not a bit of it. Riquetti declared he would have no other mistress than France; and though she yonder changed her name to Gabrielle to flatter him, though she has sought and followed him for more than a year, it avails her nothing.'

'Less than nothing I'd call it,' said another, 'since she pays for all those flowers that come up from the banks of the Var—the rarest roses and orange buds—just to please him.'

'More than that too; she has paid all his debts—in Paris some six hundred thousand livres—all for a man who will not look at her.'

'That is to be a "veritable" woman !' said a foppish-looking man, who was for some time endeavouring to attract the attention of the fair occupant of the carriage.

Meanwhile, Gerald had pressed his way through the crowd, curious to catch one look of her whose devotion seemed so romantic.

'You see me in despair—in utter despair, Belle Gabrielle. There was no place to be had at the Français last night, and I missed your glorious "Phèdre."'

Her reply was inaudible, but the other went on—

'Of course, the effort must have cost you deeply, yet even in that counterfeit of another's sorrow who knows if you did not interpolate some portion of your own grief !'

'Is he better ? Can I not see the Sister Constance ?' asked she, in a low and liquid voice.

'He is no better; I believe he is far worse than yesterday. There was a young man here this moment who saw him, and whose interview, by the way, gave rise to grave speculation. There he is yonder—a strange-looking figure to call himself the friend of Gabriel Riquetti.'

'Who or what is he ?' asked she eagerly.

'It is what none of us know, though, indeed, at the moment you came up, we had some thoughts of compelling him to declare. Need I tell you that there is grave suspicion of foul play here ; many are minded to believe that Mirabeau has been poisoned. See how that fellow continues to stare at you, Gabrielle. Do you know him ?'

Step by step, slowly, but with eyes riveted upon the object before him, Gerald had now approached the carriage, and stood within a few yards of it, his eyeballs staring wildly, his lips apart, and every line of his face betraying the most intense astonishment. Nor was Gabrielle less moved: with her head protruded beyond the carriage-window, and her hair pushed suddenly back by some passing impulse, she gazed wildly at the stranger.

'Gherardi, Gherardi mio !' cried she at last. 'Speak, and tell me if it be you.'

'Marietta, oh, Marietta!' said he, with a sigh, whose heart-felt cadence seemed eloquent in sorrow.

'Come with me. Come home with me, and you shall hear all,' said she, in Italian, answering as it were the accents of his words.

The young man shook his head mournfully in reply, but never spoke.

'I tell you,' cried she, more passionately, 'that you shall hear all. It is more than I have said to a confessor. Come, come,' and she flung open the door as she spoke.

'If you but knew how I have longed to see you, Marietta!' whispered he, in broken accents; 'but not thus, oh, not thus!'

'How, then, do you dare to judge me?' cried she, with flashing eyes; 'how presume to scoff at *my* affluence, while *I* have not dared to reflect upon *your* poverty? Once, and for the last time, I say, come with me!'

Without another word he sprang to her side, the door was closed, and the carriage drove rapidly away, ere the staring crowd could express their amazement at what they had witnessed.

CHAPTER III

'LA GABRIELLE'

BY one of those inconsistencies which sway the popular mind in times of trouble, the gorgeous splendour and wasteful extravagance which were not permitted to an ancient nobility were willingly conceded to those who now ministered to public amusement, and the costly magnificence which aided the downfall of a monarchy was deemed pardonable in one whose early years had been passed in misery and in want.

It was in the ancient hotel of the Duc de Noailles that Gabrielle was lodged, and all the splendour of that princely residence remained as in the time of its former owners; even to the portraits of the haughty ancestry upon the walls, and the proud emblazonry of armorial bearings over doors and chimneys, nothing was changed; the embroidered crests upon chairs and tablecovers, the gilded coronets that ornamented every architrave and cornice, stood forth in testimony of those in whose honour those insignia were fashioned.

Preceding Gerald, and walking at a rapid pace, Gabrielle passed through several splendid rooms, till she came to one whose walls, hung in purple velvet with a deep gold fringe, had an air of almost sombre magnificence, the furniture being all of the same grave tint, and even the solitary lamp which lighted the apartment having a glass shade of a deep purple colour.

'This is my chamber of study, Gherardi,' said she, as they entered. 'None ever come to disturb me when here. Here, therefore, we are alone to question and to reply to each other —to render account of the past and speculate on the future— and, first of all, tell me, am I changed?'

As she spoke she tossed aside her bonnet, and loosening her long hair from its bands, suffered it to fall upon her neck and shoulders in the wild masses it assumed in girlhood. She crossed her arms, too, upon her breast in imitation of a gesture familiar to her, and stood motionless before him.

Long and steadfastly did Gerald continue to stare at her. It was like the look of one who would read if he might every trait and lineament before him, and satisfy his mind what characters had time written upon a nature he had once known so well.

'You do not answer me,' said she at last; 'am I then changed?'

A faint low sigh escaped him, but he uttered no word.

'Be frank with me as a brother ought; tell me wherein is this change? You thought me handsome once; am I less so?'

'Oh! no, no! not that, not that!' cried he passionately; 'you are more beautiful than ever.'

'Is there in my expression aught that gives you grief? has the world written boldness upon my brow? or do you fancy that you can trace the cost of all the splendour around us in some faint lines of shame and sorrow? Speak, sir, and be honest with me.'

'I have no right to call you to such a reckoning, Marietta,' said he, half proudly.

'I know it, and would have resented had you dared to do it of a right; but I stand here as one equal to such questioning. It will be your own turn soon,' added she, smiling, 'and it will be well if you can stand the test so bravely.'

'I accept the challenge,' cried Gerald eagerly; 'I take you at your word. Some years back, Marietta, I left you poor, friendless, and a wayworn wanderer through the world. Our fortunes were alike in those days, and I can remember when we deemed the day a lucky one that did not send us supperless to bed. We had sore trials, and we felt them, though we bore them bravely. When we parted, our lot was misery, and now, what do I see? I find you in the splendour of a princely house; your dress that which might become the highest rank; the very jewels on your wrist and on your fingers a fortune. I know well,' added he, bitterly, 'that in this brief interval of time destiny has changed many a lot; great and glorious men have fallen; and mean, ignoble, and unworthy ones have taken their places. You, however, as a woman, could have taken no share in these convulsions. How is it, then, that I see you thus?'

'Say on, sir,' said she, with a disdainful gesture; 'these words mean nothing, or more than they ought.'

He did not speak, but he bent his eyes upon her in reproachful silence.

'You lack the courage to say the word. Well, I'll say it for you: Whose mistress are you to be thus splendidly attired? What generous patron has purchased this princely house—given you equipage, servants, diamonds? Against how much have you bartered your heart? Who has paid the price? Ay, confess it, these were the generous thoughts that filled your mind—these the delicate questions your timidity could not master. Well, as I have spoken, so will I answer them. Only remember this,' added she solemnly, 'when I have made this explanation, when all is told, there is an end for ever between us of that old tie that once bound us: we trust each other no more. It is for you to say if you accept this contract.'

Gerald was silent; if he could not master the suspicions that impressed him, as little could he resolve to forget for ever his hold upon Marietta. That she was one to keep her word he well knew; and if she decided to part, he felt that the separation was final. She watched him calmly, as he sat in this conflict with himself; so far from showing any sense of impatience at the struggle, she seemed rather to enjoy the painful difficulty of his position.

'Well, have you made your choice?' cried she at length, as with a slight smile she stood in front of him.

'It would be a treachery to my own heart, and to you, too, were I to say that all this magnificence I see here suggested no thought of evil. We were poor even to misery once, Marietta—I am still so; and well I know that in such wretchedness as ours temptation is triply dangerous. To tell me that you have yielded is, then, no more than to confess you were like others.'

'Of what, then, do you accuse me? Is it that I am Mirabeau's mistress? Would that I were!' cried she passionately; 'would that by my devotion I could share his love and give him all my own! You would cry shame upon me for this avowal. You think more highly of your own petty contrivances, your miserable attempts to sustain a mock morality—your boasted tie of marriage—than of the emotions that are born with you, that move your infancy, sway your manhood, and temper your old age. You hold that by such small cheats you supply the insatiable longings of the human heart. But the age of priestcraft is over; throne, altar, purple, sceptre, incense and all, have fled; and in the stead of man's mummeries we have installed Man himself, in the might of his intellect, the glorious grandeur of his great conceptions, and the noble breadth of his philanthropy; and who is the type of these, if not Gabriel Riquetti? His mistress! what have I not done to win the proud name? Have I not striven hard for it? These triumphs, as they call them, my great successes, had no other promptings. If my fame as an actress stands highest in Europe, it was gained but in his cause. Your great Alfieri himself has taught me no emotions I have not learned in my own deep love; and how shadowy and weak the poet's words beside the throbbing ecstasies of one true heart! You ask for a confession: you shall have one. But why do you go? Would you leave me?'

'Would that we had never met again!' said Gerald sadly. 'Through many a dark and sad hour have I looked back upon our life, when, as little more than children, we journeyed days long together. I pictured to myself how the same teachings that nerved my own heart in trouble must have supported and sustained yours. If you knew how I used to dwell upon the memory of that time; its very privations were hallowed in my memory, telling how through all our little cares and sorrows our love sufficed us!'

'Our love,' broke she in scoffingly. 'What a mockery! The poor offspring of some weak sentimentality, the sickly cant of some dreamy sonneteer. These men never knew what love was, or they had not dared to profane it by their tawdry sentiments. Is it in nature,' cried she wildly, 'to declare trumpet-tongued to the world the secrets on which the heart feeds to live, the precious thoughts that to the dearest could not be revealed? These are your poets! Over and over have I wished for you to tell you this—to tear out of your memory that wretched heresy we then believed a faith.'

'You have done your work well,' said he sorrowfully. 'Good-bye for ever!'

'I wish you would not go, Gherardi,' said she, laying her hand on his arm, and gazing at him with a look of the deepest meaning. 'To me, alone and orphaned, you represent a family and kindred. The old ties are tender ones.'

'Why will you thus trifle with me?' said he, half angrily.

'Is it to rekindle the flame you would extinguish afterward?'

'And why not return to that ancient faith? You were happier when you loved me—when I learned my verses by your side, and sang the wild songs of my own wild land. Do you remember this one; it was a favourite once with you?' And, turning to the piano, she struck a few chords, and in a voice of liquid melody sang a little Calabrese peasant song, whose refrain ended with the words—

> 'Ti am' ancor, ti am' ancor.'

'After the avowal you have made me, Marietta, it were base in me to be beguiled thus,' said he, moving away. 'You love another: be it so. Live in that love, and be happy.'

'This, too, Gherardi, we used to sing together,' said she, beginning another air. 'Let us see if your memory, of which you boast so much, equals mine. Come, this is your verse,' said she caressingly. 'Ah, fratello mio, how much more lovable you were long ago! I remember a certain evening, that glided into a long night, when we leaned together, with arms around each other's necks, out of a little window; it was a poor, melancholy street beneath, but to us it was like an alley between cedar-trees. Well, on that same night, you swore to me a vow of eternal love; you told me a miraculous story: that, though poor and friendless, you were of birth and blood; and that birth and blood meant rank and fortune in some long hereafter, for which neither of us was impatient. It was on that same night you drew a picture to my mind of our life of happiness—a bright and gorgeous picture it was too—ay, and I believed it all; and yet, and yet—on the very day after you deserted me.' As she uttered the last words, her head fell upon his shoulder, and her long hair in waving masses dropped down over his chest and on his arm; a violent sobbing seemed to choke her utterance, and her frame shook with a strong tremor.

Gerald sank into a chair, and pressed her gently to his heart. Oh, what a wild conflict raged within him; what

Q

hopes and fears, wishes and dreads, warred there with each
other! At one moment all his former love came back, and
she was the same Marietta he had wandered with through
the chestnut groves, reciting in boyish ardour the verses he
had learned to master; at the next, a shuddering shame
reminded him that she had just confessed she loved another,
making a very mockery of the memory of their former
passion. What, too, was she—what her life—that she did
not dare to reveal it?

'And you,' cried she, suddenly springing up, 'what do
you know of Riquetti? How came you to be with him?'

'I have known him long, Marietta. Would that I had
never known him! Without him and his teachings I had
thought better of the world—been less prone to suspect—
less ready to distrust. You may remember how, long ago,
I told you of a certain Gabriel——'

'It was he, then, who befriended you in the Maremma?
Oh, the noble nature that can do generous things, yet seem
to think them weakness! How widely different from your
poets this—your men of high sentiment and sordid action—
your coiners of fine phrases, hollow-hearted and empty!'

'True enough,' said Gerald bitterly; 'Gabriel de Mirabeau
is at least consistent; his sentiments are all in harmony with
his life—he is no hypocrite.'

It was with a quick gesture, like a tigress about to spring,
that she now turned on him, her eyeballs staring wildly,
and her fingers closely clutched. 'Is it,' cried she in passion,
'is it given to creatures like you or me to judge of a man
like this? Do you imagine that by any strain of your
fancy you can conceive the trials, the doubts, the difficulties,
which beset him? To intellects like his what we call excess
may give that repose which to sluggish natures comes of
mere apathy. I, too,' said she, drawing herself proudly up,
'I, too, have been his pupil; he saw me in the Cleopatra;
he told me how I had misconceived the poet—or rather, how
the poet had mistaken the character—for he loves not your
Alfieri.'

'How should he? Whence could he draw upon the noble fund of emotions that fill that great heart?'

A smile of proud, ineffable scorn was all her reply.

'Tell me rather of yourself, Marietta mia,' said he, taking her hand, and placing her at his side. 'I long to hear how you became great and distinguished, as I see you.'

'The human heart throbs alike beneath rags or purple. When I could make tears course down the rude cheeks that were gaunt with famine, the task was easy to move those whose natures yielded to lighter impulse. For a whole winter—it was the first after we parted—I was the actress of a little theatre in the cité. We dramatised the events of the day; and they whose hard toil estranged them from the world of active life, could see at evening the sorrows and sufferings of the nobility they hated on "the scène." The sack of chateau and the guillotine were favourite themes; and mine was to portray some woman of the people, seduced, wronged, deserted, but avenged! A chance—a caprice of the moment—brought Riquetti one night to our theatre. He came behind the scenes and talked with me. My accent betrayed my birth, and we talked Italian. He questioned me closely, how and where I had learned to declaim. I spoke of you, though not by name. "Ah!" cried he, "a lover already!" The look which he gave me at the words was like a stab; I felt it here, in my heart. It was the careless scoff of one who deemed that to such as me no sense of delicacy need be observed. He might think and say as he pleased, my station was too ignoble to suggest respect. I hated him, and turned away, vowing, if occasion served, to be revenged upon him. He came a few nights after, accompanied by several others—there were ladies too, handsome and splendidly dressed. This splendour shocked the meanness of our misery, and even outraged the meanly clad audience around. I saw this, and seized it as the opportunity of my vengeance. Our piece was, as usual, the story of our daily life; I represented a seduced peasant girl, left to starve in a chateau, from which the owners had gone to enjoy the delights of Paris. I had wandered on foot to the capital, and was supposed to be in search of my seducer through the streets. I sat famished and shivering upon a door-sill, watching with half-listless gaze the rich tide of humanity that swept past. I heeded not the proud display of equipages; the gay groups; the gorgeous procession of life before me; till suddenly, as if on a balcony, I beheld him I sought, the centre of a knot of beautiful women, who, leaning over the balustrade, seemed to criticise the world below. Addressing myself at once to where Riquetti sat, I made him part of the scene. I knew nothing of him, nor of his history; but in blind chance I actually invented some of the chief incidents of his life. I made him a profligate, a duellist, and a seducer. I represented how he had won the affections of his friend's wife, eloped with, and deserted her; and yet, covered with crime, debased by every iniquity, and degraded by every vice, there he sat, successful, triumphant, and esteemed.

'What was my amazement, as the curtain fell, to see him at my side. "I have come," said he, in that rich, deep voice of his—"I have come to make you my compliments; you have your country's gift, and can 'improvise' well!" I blushed deeply, and could not answer him; but he went on: "These, however, are not wise themes to dwell upon. Popular passions are dangerous seas, and will often shipwreck even those whose breath has stirred them; besides, this is not art"; and with these words he launched forth into a grand description of what really should constitute the artist's realm, to what his teachings might extend, where should be their limits. He showed how the strict imitation of nature was an essential, yet, that the true criterion of success in art lay in the combination of such ingredients as best suited the impression to be conveyed; no mean or petty detail, however truthful or accurate, being suffered to detract from the whole conception. He then warned me against exaggeration, the prime fault of all inexperienced minds. "Even this very moment," said he, "you marred a fine

effect when you spoke of me as one capable of parricide."
"Of you," said I, blushing, and trying to disown the per-
sonality. " Yes," said he, "of me. Your biography was
often very accurate—to any but myself it might seem painfully accurate : I have done all that you ascribe to me, and
more ! "—"But I never knew it," cried I; "I never heard
it ; my improvisation was pure chance. I owed you a
vendetta for some cruel words you had spoken to me."—" I
remember them," said he, smiling ; " you may live to believe
that such phrases are a flattery ! But to yourself, come to
me to-morrow ; bring your books with you, that you may
read me something I will select. I can and may befriend
you !" And he did befriend me.

'There was with him a tall, dark man, of sombre aspect,
and a deep voice, who questioned me long and closely as to
my early studies, and who undertook from that hour to
teach me. This was Talma.

'And now a life of glorious labour opened upon me. I
worked unceasingly, with such ardour, indeed, as to affect
my health, which at last gave way, and I was obliged to
retire into the country, on the Loire, to recruit. Riquetti
came to see me once there; he was coming up from the
south, and happened to stop at Tours. His visit was scarcely
an hour, but it left me with memories that endured for
months. But why should I weary you with a recital which
can only interest when all its daily chances and changes are
duly weighed ? I came out at the "Français" as Zaire ; my
success was a triumph ! Roxane followed, and was even a
greater success. You do not care to hear by what flatteries
I was surrounded, what temptations assailed me, what wealth
laid at my feet, what protestations of devotion, what offers
of splendour met me. We were in a world that, repudiating
all its old traditions, had sworn allegiance to a new code !
Nobility, birth, title, were as nothing ; genius alone could
sway men's minds. Eloquence was deemed the grand ex-
ponent of intellect ; and next after the splendid oratory of
the Constituent came the declamation of the drama. You

must know France in its aspect of generous youth—in this, its brightest hour of destiny—to understand how much of influence is wielded by those who once were deemed the mere creatures of a pampered civilisation.   The artist is now a "puissance," as is every power that can move the passions, influence the motives, and direct the actions of mankind. The choice of the piece we played at night was in accordance with the political exigency of the day; and often has it been my lot to complete by some grand declamation the eloquent appeal by which Mirabeau had moved the Assembly.   Oh, what a glorious life it was to feel no longer the mere mouth-piece of mock passion, but a real, actual, living influence on men's hearts; what a triumph was it then to hear that wild outburst of applause, that seemed to say: "Here are we, ready at your call; speak but the word and the blade shall flash and the brand flare; denounce the treason, and leave the traitors to us!"   It was in this life, as in an orgie, I have lived.   If you fancy that I exaggerate this power, or overrate its extent, listen to one fact.

'I was one night at Mirabeau's—at one of those small, select receptions which none but his most intimate friends frequented.   D'Entraiques was there, Lavastocque, Maurice de Talleyrand, De Noe, and a few more.   We were talking of the fall of the Monarchy, and discussing whether there was in the story anything that future dramatists might successfully avail themselves of.   The majority thought not, and gave their reasons.   I was not able to controvert by argument such subtle critics, but I replied by improvising a scene in the Temple of Marie Antoinette writing a last letter to her children.   There was no incident to give story, no accessory of scenery to suggest a picture; but I felt that the theme had its own pathetic power, and I was right. D'Entraiques shed tears; Charles de Noe sobbed aloud.   "She must never repeat this," muttered Riquetti.—"Not for a while at least," said Talleyrand, smiling, as he took a pinch of snuff. From that hour I felt what it was to stir men's hearts.   Then, success became real; for it was certain and assured.

CHAPTER IV

SOME OF TIME'S CHANGES

RESISTING all Marietta's entreaties to stay and sup with her —resisting blandishments that might have subjugated sterner moralists—Gerald quitted her to seek out his humble lodging in the 'Rue de Marais.' Like all men who have gained a victory over themselves, he was proud of his triumph, and almost boastfully contrasted his tattered dress and lowly condition with the splendour he had just left behind him.

'I suppose,' muttered he, 'I too might win success if I could stifle all sense of conscience within me, and be the slave of the vile thing they call the world. It is what men would call my own fault if I be poor and friendless—so, assuredly, Mirabeau would say.'

'Mirabeau will not say so any more then,' said a voice close beside him in the dark street.

'Why so?' asked Gerald fiercely.

'Simply because that great moralist is dead.'

Not noticing the half sarcasm of the epithet, Gerald eagerly asked when the event occurred.

'I can tell you almost to a minute,' said the other. 'We were just coming to the close of the third act of the piece "L'Amour le veut," where I was playing Jostard, when the news came; and the public at once called out, "Drop the curtain."'

As the speaker had just concluded these words, the light of a street lamp fell full upon his figure, and Gerald beheld a meanly clad but good-looking man of about eight-and-twenty, whose features were not unfamiliar to him.

'We have met before, sir,' said he.

'It was because I recognised your voice I ventured to address you; you were a Garde du Corps once?'

'And you?'

'I was once upon a time the Viscount Alfred de Noe,' said the other lightly. 'It was a part my ancestors performed for some seven or eight centuries. Now I change my *rôle* every night.'

Through all the levity of this remark there was also what savoured of courage, that bold defiance of the turns of fortune which sounded haughtily.

'I, too, have had my reverses ; but not so great as yours,' said Gerald modestly.

'When a man is killed by a fall, what signifies it if the drop has been fifty feet or five hundred! *Mon cher*,' said the other, 'you and I were once gentlemen—we talked, ate, drank, and dressed as such; we have now the *canaille* life, and the past is scarcely even a dream.'

'It is the present I would call a dream,' said Gerald.

'I'd do so too if its cursed reality would let me,' said De Noe, laughing, 'or if I could throw off the cast of shop for one brief hour, and feel myself the man I once was.'

'What are you counting? Have you lost anything?' asked Gerald, as the other turned over some pieces of money in his hand, and then hastily searched pocket after pocket.

'No ; I was just seeing if I had wherewithal to ask you to sup with me, and I find that I have.'

'Rather, come and share mine—I live here,' said Gerald, as he pushed a door which lay ajar. 'It's a very humble meal I invite you to partake of; but we'll drink to the good time coming.'

'I accept frankly,' said the other, as he followed Gerald up the dark and narrow stairs.

'A bed and a looking-glass, as I live!' exclaimed De Noe, as he entered the room. 'What a sybarite! Why, my friend, you outrage the noble precepts of our glorious Revolution by these luxurious pretensions—you insult equality and fraternity together.'

'Let me at least conciliate liberty then,' said Gerald gaily, 'and ask you to feel yourself at home.'

'How am I to call thee, *mon cher*?' said De Noe, assuming

the familiar second person, which I beg the reader to supply in the remainder of the interview.

'Gerald Fitzgerald is my name.'

'Le Chevalier Fitzgerald was just becoming a celebrity when they changed the spectacle. Ah, what a splendid engagement we all had, if we only knew how to keep it!'

'The fault was not entirely ours,' protested Gerald.

'Perhaps not. The good public were growing tired of being always spectators; they wanted, besides, to see what was behind the scenes; and they found the whole machinery even more a sham than they expected, and so they smashed the stage and scattered the actors.'

Gerald had now covered the table with the materials of his frugal meal, and brought forth his last two bottles of Bordeaux, long reserved to celebrate the first piece of good fortune that might betide him.

'It is easy to see,' cried De Noc, 'that you serve a Prince; your fare is worthy of Royalty, my dear Fitzgerald. If you had supped with me, your meal had been a mess of *haricot*, washed down with the light wines of the "Pays Latin."'

'And why, or how, do you suspect in whose service I am?' asked Gerald eagerly.

'My dear friend, every man of the emigration is known to the police, and I am one of its agents. I am frank with you, just to show you that you may be as candid with me. Like you, I came to Paris as a secret agent of "the family." I plotted, and schemed, and intrigued to obtain access to information. All my reports, however, were discouraging. I had no tidings to tell but such as boded ill. I saw the game was up; and I was honest enough or foolish enough to say so. The orgies of the Revolution were only beginning, and no one wished to come back to the rigid decency and decorous propriety of the Monarchy. These were not pleasant things to write back; they were less pleasant, too, to read; besides that, a man who spent some three thousand francs a month ought, surely, to have had something more agreeable to report, and they intimated as much to me. Well, I endeavoured to obey. I frequented certain coteries at the Abbé Clery's; I went of an evening to D'Allonville's; and I even used to pass a Sunday at St. Germains with old Madame de St. Leon. I familiarised my mind with all the favourite expressions, and filled my letters with the same glowing fallacies that they ever repeated to each other. This finished me; they called me a knave, and dismissed me. I had then to choose between becoming a secret agent of the police, or throwing myself into the Seine. I took the humbler part, and became a spy. They assigned me the theatres, the small, low "spectacles" of the populace, and for this I had to become an actor. It was a vow of poverty I took, my dear Chevalier; but I always hoped I was to rise to a higher order, which did not enjoin fasts nor disclaim clean linen. Seventeen long months has this slavery now endured, and during this time have I had seventeen hundred temptations to pitch my career to the devil, who invented it, and take the consequences, whatever they were; but somehow—shall I own it?—the chances and changes of this strange time have grown to assume to my mind the vicissitudes of a game. Even from the humble place I occupied have I seen those that seemed fortune's first favourites ruined, and many a one as poor and needy and friendless as—as you or myself—rise to eminence, wealth, and power. This thought has given such an interest to events that I am reluctant to quit the table. What depressed me was that I was alone. Our old friends looked coldly on me, for I was no longer "of them." Among the others, I knew not whom to trust, for in my heart of hearts I have no faith in the Revolution. Now I have watched you for months back. I knew your purpose, the places you frequented, the themes that interested you; and I often said to myself, that man "Gerard"—for so we called you in the police roll—would suit me. He was a Royalist, like me; his sympathies are like my own, so are his present necessities. I could, besides, give him much information of value to his party. In a word, I wanted you, Fitzgerald, and I felt that if I could not make *my own* fortune, I could certainly aid *yours.*'

There are men whose influence upon certain others is like a charm; without any seeming effort—without apparently a care on the subject—the words sink deep into the heart and carry persuasion with them. Of these was De Noe. Poor and miserable as he was, the stamp of gentleman was indelibly on him; and as Gerald sat and listened, the other's opinions and views stole gradually into his mind with a power scarcely conceivable.

The ranges of his knowledge, too, seemed marvellous. He knew not only the theory of each pretender to popular favour, but the names and plans of their opponents. His firm conviction was that Mirabeau not only could, but would have saved the monarchy.

'And now?' cried Gerald, eager to hear what he had to predict.

'And now the cards are shuffling for a new deal, Gerald, but the game will be a stormy one. The men who have convulsed France have not received their wages; they are growing hourly more and more impatient, and the end will be they'll murder the paymasters.'

By a long but not wearisome line of argument he went on to show that the Revolution would consume itself. Out of anarchy and blood men would seek the deliverance of a dictator, and the real hope of the monarchists was in making terms with him.

'You will meet no acceptance for those opinions from your friends; they are too lukewarm for sanguine loyalty; they are, besides, to be the work of time. But think and ponder them, Fitzgerald. Go out to-morrow into the streets, and count how many heads must fall before men will condescend to reason; the gaunt and famished faces you will meet are scarcely the guarantees of a long tranquillity. If the Monarchy is ever to come back to France, it is the mob must restore it.'

''These are Mirabeau's words,' said Gerald quickly.

'It was a craftier than Mirabeau explained them, though,' broke in De Noe, 'the shrewd and subtle Maurice de Talleyrand! But let us turn to ourselves and our own fortunes. What are we to do that France may benefit by our valuable services? How are our grand intelligences to redound to the advantage of the nation?'

'I confess I have no plans. I grow weary of this inglorious life I lead. If there was an army in whose ranks I could fight, I'd turn a soldier, and care little in what cause.'

'I guess the secret of your recklessness, Gerald; I read it in every word you speak.'

'How so? What do you mean?'

'You are in love, *mon cher*. These are the promptings of a hopeless passion.'

'You were never more wrong in your life,' said Gerald, blushing till his face and forehead were crimson.

'Would you try to deceive a man trained to the subtleties of such a life as mine? Do you fancy that a "mouchard" cannot read the thoughts that men have scarcely confessed to themselves? It is not their privilege to win confidences, but to extort them; and so, I tell you again, Gerald, you are in love.'

'And again I say, you are mistaken; I have but to remind you of the life I lead—its cares and duties—to show you how unlikely, if not impossible, is such an event.'

'Bah!' said the other scoffingly. 'You stand at the door of the opera. As the crowd pours out, a shawled and muffled figure hastily passes to her carriage; she speaks a word or two, and the tones are in your heart for years after. The diligence drives at daybreak through some country village; a curtain is hastily withdrawn, and a pair of eyes meet yours, in which there is no expression save a pleased surprise; and yet you think of them in far-away lands, and across seas, as dear remembrances. Something more than these, an impression a little stronger, will oftentimes give the motive to a whole life. You doubt it; well, listen to a confession of my own.

'When I first took service under my present masters, they assigned to me, as the sphere of duty, a small and miserable theatre in the cité. When I tell you that the entrance was four sous, you have the measure of its pretensions. What singular destiny brought our strange corps together I cannot think; we were of every class and condition of life, and of every shade of temperament and character. There was a Catalonian condemned for life to the galleys in Spain; a Swiss, who had poisoned a whole family; a monk, whose convent had been burned, and he himself the only one escaped; a court lady, who had been betrothed to an ambassador; and a gipsy girl, who had exhibited her native dances through all the towns of Italy. These were but a few of our incongruous elements, and it is with the last of them only I have to deal —the gipsy. Whence she came, or with whom, I never could learn. I only know that one evening, from some illness of our first actress, we were driven upon our own resources to amuse the public. Each, after his fashion, delivered some specimen of his talents, by repeating some well-known part, some oft-recited speech or song. When it came to her turn to appear, she evinced no fear or trepidation; she did not even ask a question of advice or counsel, but walked boldly on, stood for a second or two contemplating the dense crowd before her, and then began a strange, wild rhapsody, illustrating the events of the time. She told of the nobles living in splendour, ignoring the sorrows of the poor, forgetting their very existence. She described their life of luxury and pleasure, how they beguiled their leisure hours with enjoyments. She counterfeited their polished intercourse. She was a duchess; her ragged, tattered shawl swept the ground as a train, and she curtsied with a grace and dignity the highest might have envied. She presented her daughter to some great noble: the young girl was asked to sing; and then, taking her guitar, she sang a troubadour melody, and with a touching tenderness that brought tears over cheeks seared and sorrow-worn. Her aim was evidently to throw over the haughty existence of a hated class the softened light of a home; to show that among that proud order the same sympathies lived and reigned, the same affections grew, the same joys and griefs prevailed. Therein lay the power of vengeance. "They despise and reject you!" cried she; "they hold themselves apart from you, as beings of another destiny; of all this fair world contains they will not share with you, save in the air and sunlight; and yet their passions are your passions—their hates, loves, and jealousies are all your own. All their wealth teaches no new affection, all their civilisation can stifle no old pang. If you be like them, then, in all these, why not resemble them in their cruelties? Down with them! down with them!" she cried, "for the brand to burn, and the axe to cleave." She shrieked the wild scream of an incensed populace. The chateau was attacked on every side—but why do I continue? The terrible roar of the famished crowd before her is still in my ears, as she sank dying on the stage, the martyred girl of the people, pouring out her blood for her brethren.

'As the curtain fell I rushed forward to raise her; she was fainting. The emotion was not all unreal. I had seen her a hundred times before; we used to salute each other as we met, and perhaps exchange a word or two; and though struck by her uncommon beauty, I only deemed her one of those unhappy shreds that hang on the draggled robe of humanity, without intellect or mind—of those who are unfortunate without pity; but now as I lifted her up, and carried her to a seat, I saw before me the marvellous artist—one whose genius could conceive the highest flights of passion, and who had powers also to portray it. It was some time before she came to herself; her faculties seemed to wander in a sort of dreamy vagueness. She dropped words of Italian too, and muttered strange rhymes to herself. I tried to soothe her and calm her. I told her of the immense success she had achieved, and that even in that rude audience there reigned a fervour of enthusiasm that would have carried them to any excesses. "Poor wretches," muttered she, "who are insensible to real wrongs, and can yet be moved by a mockery of woe."

This was all she said, and turned from me with a gesture of aversion. Half stung by the insult of her manner, half wounded in the instincts of my class—for it is hard to forget that one was born noble—I stooped down and whispered in her ear some bitter words of reproach. She started like one bitten by a serpent, and stared at me with wide eyeballs and half-opened mouth. I saw my advantage, and used it. I told her that those she insulted were incomparably above the base herd she dared to place above them; that in self-devotion, courage, and single-heartedness the world had never yet displayed their equals. The perils that others encountered in pursuit of vengeance or plunder were dared by them in the assertion of a noble cause and to avenge a glorious martyrdom. With a fierce look she scanned my features for above a minute, and then said, "I know it, and hate them for it." You might imagine that such a speech so uttered had made her odious to my eyes for ever; and yet, Gerald, from that very moment my heart was all her own. Some would explain this by saying we live in times when every human sentiment is inverted; when, having confounded right and wrong, made peace seem death, and anarchy a blessing, that men are fascinated by what should repel, and deterred by what should attract them. There may be truth in this manner of reconciling the strange caprices which seem to urge us even to what we have hitherto shown repugnance. I have neither taste nor patience for the inquiry; enough for me the fact that I loved her, with an ardour intense as it was sudden.

'I will not weary you with any story of my passion. It was the old narrative of a hopeless love, affection unreturned, a whole heart's devotion given without the shadow of requital. There was not an artifice I did not practise to cure myself of this baleful infatuation. I reasoned, I pondered, I even prayed against it. I tried to invest her with all the "traits" of that "canaille" multitude I hated. I endeavoured to believe her the very type of that base herd who exulted over our ruin and downfall; but no sooner did I see her,

and hear her voice, than I forgot all my self-deceptions, and
loved her more ardently, ay, more abjectly than ever. We
live in strange times, Gerald,' said he, with a deep sigh, 'and
we learn hard lessons. That this poor and friendless girl
of the people should despise a Count de Noe tells to what
depths we have fallen.'

Gerald listened with deep interest to this story. He never
doubted in his own mind that this girl was Marietta, nor
did he wonder at the fascination she exercised; still was he
careful to conceal this knowledge from De Noe, and affecting
a mere curiosity in the adventure, asked him to continue.

'I have little more to tell you,' said the other. 'I know
not if my attentions persecuted her, or that the promptings
of a higher ambition moved her, but she left us, some said,
to become the mistress of Mirabeau; others declared that
Collot d'Herbois was her lover. The truth was soon apparent
when she appeared at the Français under the name of Gabrielle.
Ay, Gerald, the great genius of the French stage, the gifted
pupil of Talma, the marvellous artiste whose triumphs are
trumpeted through Europe, was the other day but the gipsy
actress of the Trou de Taupe, as our little stage was politely
named.'

De Noe described with enthusiasm the fervour of admiration La Gabrielle had excited; how the foremost men of the
time had offered to share fortune with her; that she had but
to choose throughout France the man who would be her
protector—from Dumourier to Tinaille, there is not one
would not make her his wife to-morrow.

'I see,' added he, 'that you account all this exaggeration
on my part. Well, there is happily a way to test the faith-
fulness of my report.'

'How so?'

'To-morrow evening is Madame Roland's night of reception. You have heard of her as the great leader of the
advanced reformers—they who would strip the nation of
everything to clothe it in rags of their own pattern. Come
with me there; I will present you as a young friend from

the provinces, or better still, an exile fled from Italian tyranny.
You will meet the most distinguished men of that extreme
party; you will hear their sentiments and their hopes. A
stray phrase about despotism, a passing word of execration
on kingly rule, will be enough to make you free of the
guild, and you will not fail to glean information from them.
At all events, there is a great chance that you may see
"Gabrielle;" she rarely misses one of these evenings, and
you will see her in the sphere she loves best to move in, and
where her influence is unbounded. It may be she will give
me leave to present you.'

'I will not ask so much,' said Gerald, with an affected
humility.

'You cannot say so till you have seen her,' cried the other.
'I tell you, Gerald, that the men whose pride would scorn
the notice of royalty would kneel with devotion to do her
homage. She is not one of those whose eminence is a recognised conventionality, but one whose sway is an indisputable
influence, greater as she is in real life than when depicting
imaginary sorrows; and then that wondrous gift, the heritage
of her gipsy blood, perhaps heightens the power she possesses
to something almost terrible.'

'Of what do you speak?' asked Gerald eagerly.

'I scarcely know how or what to call it. It savours of
the old Egyptian art called "fate-reading." I am sceptical
enough on most things; and had I not seen with my eyes,
and heard with my ears, I had scouted the very thought of
such revelations.'

'And what have you seen?'

De Noe paused for a few seconds, and in a voice slightly
tremulous for agitation, said: 'I will tell you what I myself
witnessed. It was one night late at Madame Roland's: the
company had all gone, save the Gabrielle, Brissot, Guidet,
and myself, and we only waited for carriages to fetch us
away, as the rain was falling in torrents. The Gabrielle,
shawled and muffled, ready to depart, seated herself in the
antechamber; and refusing all entreaties to return to the

saloon, remained in a sort of reverie, with closed eyes and
clasped hands—the attitude bespeaking one who would not
be disturbed. Madame Roland said it was an "extase," and
would not suffer any one to speak. After a long pause,
during which her countenance was perfectly motionless, she
slowly raised her arm and pointed with her finger toward
one corner of the room. 'There, there,' whispered she, in
a low voice, 'what a number of them! There are more than
fifty; and see, they are saddling more! The black one will
not let himself be bridled. Ah! he has kicked the groom;
poor fellow! they are carrying him away. Hush! take care,
take care, or the secret will be out. Silly man,' said she,
with a mocking smile, 'he would paint out the arms, as if
any one could be deceived by such a cavalcade.' At this,
Brissot whispered in my ear: 'It is the royal stable that she
sees. I will soon test the truth of this vision'; and he
stepped unnoticed from the room. He had not gone many
minutes, when with a long-drawn sigh she opened her eyes
and looked about her. "How late my carriage is to-night,"
said she to Madame Roland, "and how ashamed am I to
keep you up to such an hour!" While Madame Roland
answered her in tones of kindness and affection, I watched
the Gabrielle closely. There was not a line in that pale
face that indicated the slightest emotion; perhaps the most
marked expression was a look of weariness and exhaustion.
At length the carriage arrived, and she drove away. We,
however, all remained, for Brissot had promised me to return,
and I told them whither he had gone. It was past two
when he came back, pale as death, and covered with a cold
perspiration. "It is as she said," cried he, in terror: "two
commissaries have brought the news to Bailly that the king
was about to fly to De Bouilly's camp; and all the horses at
Versailles were ready for the start. Two hundred mounted
royalists were in the Cour when the commissaries arrived."
I could tell you of other and more striking scenes than this,'
said De Noe; 'some are yet unaccomplished; but I believe
in them as I believe in my own existence.'

Gerald sat without uttering a word for some time.   At last he said, 'You have given me a great curiosity to see your priestess, if I could but do so unobserved.'

'Nothing is easier.   Come early to-morrow evening; and I will take care, after your presentation to the hostess, to secrete you where none will remark you.'

'I agree, then, and will ask you to come and fetch me at the proper hour.'

'Remember, Gerald, that in your dress you must adopt the mode of the Jacobins.'

'Marat himself could not be more accurate in costume than you will find me,' said Gerald, as he squeezed his friend's hand to say adieu.

CHAPTER V

A RECEPTION AT MADAME ROLAND'S

IF it be matter of wonderment that at such a time as we now speak of De Noe should have opened his heart thus freely to one he had never met before, the simple explanation lies in the fact that periods of "espionage" are precisely those when men make the rashest confederacies.   Wearied and worn out, as it were, by everlasting chicanery and trick, they seize with avidity on the first occasion that presents itself to relieve the weight of an overburdened heart.   To feel a sense of trust is sufficient to make them reveal their most secret feelings; and it was thus that De Noe no sooner found himself alone with Gerald than he told him the whole story of his love.

Gerald not only read his motives aright, but saw also something of the man himself.   He perceived in him a type of a class by no means unfrequent at the time—royalists by birth and instinct, and yet so stripped of all the prestige of their once condition, and so destitute of hope, that they really lived on the contingency of each day, not knowing

by what stratagem the morrow was to be met, nor to what
straits future fate might subject them.   Besides this, he saw
how the supporters of the 'cause' had gradually degenerated
from the great names and nobles of France to men of ruined
hopes and blasted fortunes, whose intrigues were conceived
in the lowest places, and carried on by the meanest associates.
The more he reflected on these things, the more was he
convinced that Mirabeau was right when he said the 'Revolution was a fire that must burn out.'

'And how long will the flames last?' cried he to himself;
'they will not assuredly be extinguished in my time.
The great convulsions of nations will bear proportion to the
vast materials they deal with.   France will not rally from
this shock for half a century to come; and ere that I shall
have passed away.'

When doubt or despondency weighed upon his mind, all the
crafty reasoning of Mirabeau and all the sensual teachings
of Rousseau came freshly to his memory.   They told him
of a world of conflict and struggle, but also a world of
voluptuous pleasure and abandonment.   They sneered at
the ideal pretexts men called loyalty and fidelity, and they
counselled the enjoyment of the present as the only true
philosophy.   'Tell me you are sure of being alone to-morrow,'
said Diderot, 'and I will listen to how you mean to spend it.'
Like evil spirits that love the night, these dark thoughts
were sure to seek him in his hours of gloomy depression.

There was, with all this, a sense of pique as he compared
his own position with that which Marietta had already won
for herself.   'We started together in the race,' thought he,
'and see where she has distanced me!   That poor friendless
girl is already a social influence and a power, while I am a
mere hanger-on of men, who use me in dangers that show
how little they regard me.   What rare abilities must she
possess!   What a marvellous insight into the human heart
and all its varied workings!   How ingeniously, too, has
she contrived to interweave with her dramatic power the
stranger and more mysterious workings of a supernatural

influence! How far is she the dupe of her own deceptions?' This was a thought not easily solved, knowing her well as he did, and knowing how often she was the slave of her own passionate impulses. 'I will see her to-night with my own eyes, and mayhap be able to read her aright.'

The receptions of Madame Roland were among the 'events' of the day. They were the rendezvous of all that was most advanced and extravagant in republicanism. Thoroughly true-hearted and single-minded herself, she was rapidly attracted to those men who declaimed against courts and courtly vices, and sincerely believed that virtue only resided beneath lowly roofs and among narrow fortunes. Her sincere enthusiasm—the genuine ardour of a character that had no duplicity in it—added to considerable personal charms, gave her a vast influence in the society wherein she moved. She was not strictly handsome, but her features were of extreme delicacy, and capable of expression the most refined and captivating; but her voice was the spell which, it is said, never failed to fascinate those who heard it.

In the management of this marvellous instrument of captivation was, perhaps, the solitary evidence of anything like study or artifice about her. She knew how to attune and modulate it to perfection; and even they who pronounced her conversational powers as inferior to Madame de Stael's, were ready to confess that the melody and softness of her utterance gave her an unquestionable advantage. Married to a man more than double her age, she exercised a complete independence in all the arrangements of her household, inviting whom she pleased, bringing together in her salons ingredients the most dissimilar, and representatives of classes the widest apart.

Gerald had more than once heard of these receptions, and was curious to witness them; he wished, besides, to see some of the men whom the popular will declared to be the great leaders of party, and whose legislative ability was regarded as the hope of France.

'Do not flatter yourself that you are about to be struck by

any intellectual display,' whispered De Noe, as he led him up the stairs. 'For the most part, you will hear nothing but violent tirades against royalty, and coarse abuse of a society of which the speaker knows nothing.'

The salons, which were small, were crammed with company, so that for some time Gerald had little other occupation than to scrutinise the appearance of the guests, and the strange extravagances of that costume which they had come to assume distinctively.

'Look yonder,' whispered De Noe, 'at the tall, dark man, like a Spaniard, with his long hair combed back and falling on his neck. That is Lanthenas, *l'ami de la maison*; he lives here. Were she any one else, people would call him her lover; but "La Manon," as they style her, has no heart to bestow on such emotion; she is with her whole soul in politics, and only cares for humanity when counted by millions.'

'Who is the pert-looking, conceited fellow he is talking to?' asked Gerald.

'That is Louvet, the great literary hero of the day. Seven editions of an indecent novel, sold in as many weeks, have made him rich as well as famous; and the author of *Faublas* is now courted and sought after on all sides.'

As the crowd thickened, De Noe could but just tell the names of the more remarkable characters without time for more. There was Pelleport, a marquis by birth, but now a spy, and libelist of the lowest class, side by side with Condorcet, the optimist philosopher, and Brissot, the wildest enunciator of republicanism. Carsu, with a dozen penal sentences over his head, was talking familiarly with old Monsieur Roland himself, a simple-hearted old egotist, vain, harmless, and conceited. Yonder, entertaining a group of ladies by the last scandals of the day, told as none but himself could tell them, was Gaudet, a young lawyer from Lyons, his dress the exaggeration of all that constituted the republican mode; while looking on, and with air at once rebuking and amused, stood Dumont, his staid features and simple attire the modest contrast to the other's finery.

'A young friend of mine, just come from Italy, Madame,' said De Noe, suddenly perceiving Madame Roland's eyes fixed on Fitzgerald.

'And ",of us"?' said she significantly.

'Assuredly, Madame, or I had not dared to present him,' said De Noe, bowing.

'You must not say so, sir. Do you know,' said she, addressing Gerald, 'that it was only last week he brought a bishop here, Monseigneur de Blois.'

'Ah! but be just, Madame; he had been degraded for immorality,' broke in De Noe, laughing.

'You should have shared his penalty, Monsieur De Noe,' said she, half coldly, and moved on.

'Come, Gerald, let me present you to some of my illustrious friends. Whom will you know? That choleric old lady there, a dismissed court lady, and the sworn enemy of the queen; or her daughter, the pretty widow, playing trictrac with Fabre d'Églantine? Or shall I introduce you to that dark-eyed beauty, whose foot you are not the first man that ever admired? She is, or was, La Comtesse de Ratignolles, but calls herself Julie Servan on her books.

'Why don't you answer me? What are you thinking of? Ah, parbleu! I see well enough. It is the Gabrielle; and the tall, pale man she leans upon is Talma. Is not that enough of homage, _mon cher_? See how they rise to let her pass. We have been courtiers in our day, Gerald, but did you ever see a more queenly presence than that?'

It was truly, as De Noe described, like the passage of royalty. Marietta swept by, bowing slightly to either side, and by an easy gesture of her hand seeming half to decline, half accept, the honours that were paid her. Refusing with a sort of haughty indifference the seat prepared for her at the end of the room, she moved on toward a small boudoir, and was lost to Gerald's view. Indeed, his attention was rapidly directed elsewhere, as a small, dark-eyed man in the centre of the room proceeded to entertain the company with an account of Mirabeau's last moments. It was the Doctor

Cabanis, who had tended his sickbed with such devotional affection, and whose real attachment had soothed the last sufferings of his patient. If there was something in Gerald's estimation more than questionable in this exposure of all that might be deemed most sacred and private, the narrative was full of little details that interested him.

The dreadful mockery by which Mirabeau endeavoured to cheat death of his terrors, as, dressed, perfumed, and essenced, he lay upon his last bed, all surrounded with flowers, was told with a thrilling minuteness. Through all the assumed calm, through all the acted philosophy, there crept out the agonising eagerness for life, that even *his* dissimulation could not smother. His incessant questioning as to this symptom or that, whether it indicated good or evil; the intense anxiety with which he scrutinised the faces around his bed, to read the thoughts their words belied, were all related; and, strangely enough, assumed to imply that they were the last desires of a patriot who only longed for life to serve his country. Of those who listened, many doubted the honesty and good faith of his character; some thought him a royalist in disguise; some deemed him a lukewarm patriot; some even regarded him as so destitute of principle, that his professions were good for nothing; and yet amid all these disparaging estimates, they regarded this deathbed, where no consolations of religion were breathed, where no murmur of prayer was heard, nor one supplication for mercy raised, as a glorious triumph! It was to *their* eyes the dawning of that transcendent brightness which was to succeed the long night of priestcraft and superstition; and however ready to cavil at his doctrines or dispute his theories, there was but one voice—to honour *him* who with his last breath had defied the Church.

'*Ah, que c'est beau!*' '*Ah, que c'est magnifique!*' were the mutterings on every side. One only circumstance detracted in any way from the effect of these revelations; it was, that he who made them momentarily gave vent to his feelings and shed tears. This homage to human frailty jarred upon the classic instincts of the assembly. It was an ignoble weakness, unworthy of such a theme ; and in a tone of stern rebuke, Fabre d'Églantine interrupted the speaker, and said—

'Your grief is unbecoming, sir ; such sorrow insults the memory you mean to hallow ! If you would learn how the death of Mirabeau should be accepted, go yonder, and you will see.' He pointed as he spoke toward the boudoir, and thither with a common impulse the crowd now moved.

A warning gesture from Talma, as he stood in the doorway, and with uplifted hand motioned silence, arrested their steps, and, awestruck by the imposing attitude of one whose slightest gesture was eloquent, they halted. Mixed in the throng, Gerald could barely catch a glimpse of the scene beyond. He could, however, perceive that Marietta was lying in a sort of trance ; a crown of 'immortelles' that she had been weaving had fallen from her hand, and lay at her feet ; her hair, too, had burst its bands, and fell in large waving masses over her neck and arms ; the faintest trace of colour marked her cheeks, and sufficed to show that she had not fainted.

Lanthenas laid his finger softly on her wrist, and in a cautious whisper said, 'The pulse is intermittent, the "accés" will be brief.'

'We were talking of the death of Cæsar,' said Talma, 'when the attack came on. She would not have it that Brutus was a patriot. She tried to show that in such natures—stern, cold, and self-denying—patriotism can no more take root than love. I asked her then if Gabriel Riquetti were such a man——'

'Hush ! she is about to speak,' broke in Madame Roland.

A few soft murmuring sounds escaped Marietta's lips, and her fingers moved convulsively.

'What is it she says,' cried Louvet, 'of crime and poison ?'

'Hush ! listen.'

'Examine Comps,' muttered she ; 'he knows all.'

'It is Mirabeau's secretary she speaks of,' said Louvet· 'he committed suicide last night.'

'No; he is not dead, though his wound may prove fatal,' said Cabanis.

'He will live,' said Marietta solemnly, and then seemed to sink into a deep stupor.

'Yes, trust me, I will tell him,' cried she suddenly, with a voice as assured and an accent as firm as though awake. 'Come here and let me whisper it.'

One after another bent down beside the couch, but she repulsed them sharply, and with a half-angry gesture motioned them away.

Madame Roland knelt down and took her hand, but with the same abrupt movement the other pushed her away, muttering, 'No, not you—not you.'

Again and again did they who knew her best present themselves, but with the same ill success. Some she drove rudely back, to others she made a sign to retire.

'Mayhap the person is not present that you wish for,' said Madame Roland softly.

'He is here,' said she gently.

Name after name of those around did Madame Roland whisper, but all without avail. At last, as Langrés presented himself, Marietta turned with a sort of aversion from him and said—

'I am in search of a prince, and you bring me a butcher.'

This insulting speech was not heard without a smile by some who knew this man's origin, and detested the coarse ruffianism of his address.

'*Parbleau*, Madame! if you want princes you must go and seek them at the Français,' said Langrés angrily, as he dropped back into the crowd.

Meanwhile, impelled by a strong desire to test the reality of her vision, Gerald made his way through the throng, and dropping on one knee, took her hand in his own.

A start and a faint exclamation—half surprise, half joy—broke from her as she felt his touch. She passed her hand over his face, and through his long hair, and then bending down kissed him on the forehead. She whispered a few words rapidly in his ear, and sank back exhausted.

'She has fainted! Bring water quickly,' cried Lanthenas.

For a few minutes every attention was directed toward her; and it was only as she showed signs of recovery, some one asked—

'What has become of De Noe and his friend?'

They were gone.

CHAPTER VI

'LA GRUE'

WHEN Gerald gained the street, it was to find it crammed with a dense mob, whose wild cries and screams filled the air. No sooner was he perceived by some of the multitude than a hundred yells saluted him, with shouts of 'Down with the aristocrat; down with the tyrant, who insults the friend of the people.' It was a mob who, in fervour of enthusiasm for Mirabeau's memory, had closed each of the theatres in succession, dispersed all meetings of public festivity, and even invaded the precincts of private houses, to dictate a more becoming observance toward the illustrious dead. Few men could bear such prescription less patiently than Fitzgerald. The very thought of being ruled and directed by the 'canaille' was insupportably offensive, and he drove back those who rudely pressed upon him, and answered with contempt their words of insult and outrage.

'Who is it that insults the majesty of the people?' cried one; 'let us hear his name.'

'It is Louvet'—'It is Plessard'—'It is Lestocq'—'It is that miserable Custine'—shouted several together.

'You are all wrong. I am a stranger, whose name not one of you has ever heard——'

'A spy! an emissary of Pitt and Cobourg!'

'I am a foreigner, with whose sentiments you have no concern. I do not obtrude my opinions upon you.'

'What do we care for that?' shouted a deep voice. 'You have dared to offend the most sacred sentiments of a nation, and to riot in a festive orgie while we weep over the death-bed of a patriot.'

'*A la Grue! à la Grue!*' screamed the wild mass in a yell of passion.

Now the Grue was an immense crane—used in some repairs of the Pont Neuf—which still held its place at the approach to the bridge. It was here that a sort of public tribunal held its nightly sittings by the light of a gigantic lantern, suspended from the crane; and which, report alleged, had more than once given way to a very different pendant. It is certain that two men, taken in the act of robbery, had been hanged by the sentence of this self-constituted tribunal, which, in open defiance of the authorities, continued to assemble there. The cry, '*A la Grue! à la Grue!*' had, therefore, a dreadful significance; and there was a terrible import in the savage roar of the mob as they ratified the proposal.

'We will try him fairly. He shall be judged deliberately, and be allowed to speak in his own defence,' said several, who believed that their words were those of moderation and equity.

Powerless against the overwhelming mass, and too indignant to proffer one single word of palliation, Gerald was hurried along towards the quay.

There was something singularly solemn in the measured tread of that vast multitude, as, in a mockery of justice, they marched along. At first not a word was spoken; but suddenly a deep voice in the front rank began one of the popular chants of the day, the whole dense mass joining in the refrain. Nothing could be ruder than the verses, save the accents that intoned them; but there was in the very roar and resonance a depth that imparted a sense of force and power.

We offer a rough version of the unpolished chant—

'The Cour Royale has a princely hall,
  And many come there to sue ;
But I love the sight of a stilly night,
  And the crowd beneath the Grue.

No lawyer clown, with his cap and gown,
  Has complex work to do ;
For the horny hand and the face that's tanned
  Are the judges beneath the Grue.

At best, this life is a fleeting strife,
  For me as well as for you ;
But our work is brief with a rogue or thief
  When he stands beneath the Grue.

No bribes resort to our humble court,
  All is open and plain to view ;
And the people's voice and the people's choice
  Are the law beneath the Grue.

The Grue ! the Grue ! the Grue !
  I ween there are but few
Who have hearts for hope as they see the rope
  That dangles beneath the Grue.'

As they sang a number of voices in front of them took up the strain, till the crowd seemed to make the very air ring with their hoarse chant. In this way they reached the Seine, over whose dark and rapid flood the fatal crane seemed to droop sadly. Several hundred people were assembled here, a confused murmur showing that they were engaged in conversing rather than in that judicial function it was their pride to discharge.

'A rebel against the majesty of the people and the fame of its greatest martyr,' said a deep voice, as he announced the crime of Fitzgerald, and pushed him forward to the place reserved for the accused. 'While a nation humbles itself in sorrow, this man chooses the hour for riotous dissipation and excess. We met him as he issued forth from the woman Roland's house, so that he cannot deny the charge.'

'Accused, stand forward,' said a coarse-looking man, in a mechanic's dress, but whose manner was not devoid of a certain dignity. 'You are here before the French people, who will judge you fairly.'

'Were I even conscious of a crime, I would deny your right to try me.'

'Young man, you do but injury to yourself in insulting us, was the grave rebuke, delivered with a calm decorum which seemed to have its influence on Fitzgerald.

'Who accuses him ?' asked the judge aloud.

'I'—'and I'—'and I'—'all of us,' shouted a number together, followed by a burst of, 'Let Lamarc do it; let Lamarc speak'; and a pale, very young man, of gentle look and slight figure, came forward at the call.

With the ease of one thoroughly accustomed to address public assemblies, and with an eloquence evidently cultivated in very different spheres, the young man pronounced a glowing panegyric on Mirabeau. It was really a fine and scarce exaggerated appreciation of that great man. Haughtily disclaiming the right of any less illustrious than Riquetti himself to sit in judgment upon the excesses of his turbulent youth, the orator even declared that it was in the passionate commotion of such temperaments that grand ideas were fostered, just as preternatural fertility is the gift of countries where earthquakes and volcanoes have convulsed them.

'Deplore, if you will,' cried he, 'his faults, for his own sake; sorrow over the terrible necessities of a nature whose excitements must be sought for even in crime; mourn over one whose mysterious being demanded for mere sustenance the poisoned draughts of intemperance; but for yourselves and for your own sakes, rejoice that the age has given you Gabriel Riquetti de Mirabeau.'

'Who is it dares to say such words as these ?' cried a hoarse, discordant voice, as forcing his way through the dense mass, a small, misshapen figure stood forward. Though bespeaking in his appearance a condition considerably above those around him, his dress was disordered, his cravat awry, and his features trembling with recent excitement. As the strong light fell upon him, Gerald could mark a countenance whose features once seen were never forgotten. The forehead was high, but retreating, and the eyes so sunk within their sockets that their colour could not be known, and their only expression a look of wolfish ferocity; to this, too, a haggard cheek and long, lean jaw contributed. All these signs of a harsh and cruel nature were greatly heightened by his mode of speaking, for his mouth opened wide, exposing two immense rows of teeth, a display which they who knew him well said he was inordinately vain of.

'Is it to men and Frenchmen that any dares to speak thus?' yelled he, in a voice that overtopped the others, and was heard far and wide through the crowd. 'Listen to me, people,' screamed he again, as, ascending the sort of bench on which the judge was seated, he waved his hand to enforce silence. 'Kneel down and thank the gods that your direst enemy is dead!'

A low murmur—it was almost like the growl of a wild beast —ran through the assembly; but such was the courage of the speaker that he waited till it had subsided, and then in accents shriller than before repeated the same words. The hum of the multitude was now reduced to a mere murmuring sound, and he went on. It was soon evident how inferior the polished eloquence of the other must prove before such an audience to the stormy passion of this man's speech. Like the voice of a destroying angel scattering ruin and destruction, he poured out over the memory of Mirabeau the flood of his invective. He reproduced the vices of his youth to account for the crimes of his age, and saw the treason to his party explained in his falsehood to his friends. There was in his words and in all he said the force of a mad mountain torrent, bounding wildly from crag to crag, sweeping all before it as it went, and yet ever pouring its flood deeper, fuller, and stronger. From a narrative of Riquetti's early life, with every incident of which he was familiar, he turned suddenly to show how such a man must, in the very nature of his being, be an enemy to the people. A noble by birth, an aristocrat in all his instincts, he could never have frankly lent himself to the cause of liberty. It was only a traitor he was, then, within their camp; he was there to learn their strength.

and their weakness, to delude them by mock concessions. It was, as he expressed it, by the heat of their own passions that he welded the fetters for their own limbs.

'If you ask who should mourn this man, the answer is, His own order; and it is they, and they alone, who sorrow over the lost leader. Not you, nor I, nor that youth yonder, whom you pretend to arraign; but whom you should honour with words of praise and encouragement. Is it not brave of him, in this hour of bastard grief, that he should stand forth to tell you how mean and dastardly ye are! I tell you, once more, that he who dares to stem the false sentiments of mis-guided enthusiasm has a courage grander than his who storms a breach. My friendship is his own from this hour,' and as he said, he descended from the bench, and flung his arms around Fitzgerald.

Shouts of 'Well done, Marat, bravely spoken!' rent the air, and a hundred voices told how the current of public favour had changed its course.

'Let us not tarry here, young man,' said Marat. 'Come along with me; there is much to be done yet.'

While Gerald was not sorry to be relieved from a position of difficulty and danger, he was also eager to undeceive his new ally, and avow that he had no sympathy with the opin-ions attributed to him. It was no time, however, for ex-planations, nor was the temper of the mob to be long trusted. He therefore suffered himself to be led along by the friends of Marat, who, speedily making way for their chief, issued into the open street.

'Whither now?' cried one aloud.

'To the Bureau—to the Bureau!' said another.

'Be it so,' said Marat. 'The *Ami du Peuple*'—so was his journal called—'must render an account of this night to its readers. I have addressed seven assemblies since eleven o'clock, and save that one in the Rue de Grenelle, all success-fully. By the way, who is our friend? What is he called? Fitzgerald—a foreign name—all the better; we can turn this incident to good account. Are Frenchmen to be taught the path to liberty by a stranger, eh, Favart? That's the key-note for your overture!'

'The article is written—it is half-printed already,' said Favart. 'It begins better—"The impostor is dead: the juggler who gathered your liberties into a bundle and gave them back to you as fetters, is no more!"'

'*Ah, que c'est beau*, that phrase!' cried two or three to-gether.

'I will not have it,' said Marat impetuously; 'these are not moments for grotesque imagery. Open thus: "Who are the men that have constituted themselves the judges of im-mortality? Who are these, clad in shame and cloaked in ignominy, who assume to dispense the glory of a nation? Are these mean tricksters—these fawners on a corrupted court—these slaves of the basest tyranny that ever defaced a nation's image, to be guardians at the gate of civic honours?'

'Ah! there it is. It was Marat himself spoke there,' said one.

'That was the clink of the true metal,' said Chaptal.

And now, in the wildest vein of rhapsody, Marat continued to pour forth a strange confused flood of savage invective. For the most part the language was coarse and ill-chosen and the reasoning faulty in the expression, but here and there would pierce through a phrase or an image so graphic or so true as actually to startle and amaze. It was these improvisations, caught up and reproduced by his followers, which constituted the leading articles of his journal. Too much immersed in the active career of his demagogue life to spare time for writing, he gave himself the habit of this high-flown and exaggerated style, which wore, so to say, a mock air of composition.

Pointing to the immense quantity of this sort of matter which his journal contained, Marat would boast to the people of his unceasing labours in their cause, his days of hard toil, his nights of unbroken exertion. He artfully contrasted a life thus spent with the luxurious existence of the pampered 'rich.' Such were the first steps of one who journeyed after-

ward far in crime—such the initial teachings of one who
subsequently helped mainly to corrupt a whole people.

A strange impulse of curiosity to see something of these
men of whom he had heard so much, influenced Gerald, while
he was also in part swayed by the marvellous force of that
torrent which never ceased to flow from Marat's lips. It was
a sort of fascination, not the less strong that it imparted a
sense of pain.

'I will see this night's adventure to the end,' said he to
himself, and he went along with them.

CHAPTER VII

A SUPPER WITH THE 'FRIENDS OF THE PEOPLE'

THERE is a strange similarity between the moral and the
physical evils of life, which extends even to the modes by
which they are propagated. We talk of the infection of a
fever, but we often forget that prejudices are infinitely more
infectious. The poor man, ill-fed, ill-housed, ill-clad, destitute, heart-sick, and weary, falls victim to the first epidemic
that crosses his path. So with the youth of unfixed faith
and unsettled pursuits: he adopts any creed of thought or
opinion warm enough to stimulate his imagination and fix
his ambition. How few are they in life who have chosen for
themselves their political convictions; what a vast majority
is it that has adopted the impressions that float around
them!

Gerald Fitzgerald supped with Marat at the Rue de
Moulins: he sat down with Fauchet, Etienne, Chaptal,
Favart and the rest—all writers for the *Ami du Peuple*—all
henchmen of the one great and terrible leader.

Gerald had often taken his part in the wild excesses of a
youthful origin; he had borne a share in those scenes where
passion stimulated by debauch becomes madness, and where

a frantic impetuosity usurps the place of all reason and judgment; but it was new to him to witness a scene where the excesses were those of minds worked up by the wildest flights of political ambition, the frantic denunciations of political adversaries, and the maddest anticipations of a dreadful vengeance. They talked before him with a freedom which, in that time, was rarely heard. They never scrupled to discuss all the chances of their party, and the casualties of that eventful future that lay before them.

How the monarchy must fall—how the whole social edifice of France must be overthrown—how nobility was to be annihilated, and a new code of distinction created, were discussed with a seriousness, mingled with the wildest levity. That the road to these changes lay through blood, never for a moment seemed to check the torrent of their speculations. Some amused themselves by imaginary lists of proscriptions, giving the names and titles of those they would recommend for the honours of the guillotine.

'Everything,' cried Guadet, 'everything that calls itself Duke, Marquis, or Count.'

'Do not include the Barons, Henri, for *my* cook is of that degree, and I could not spare him,' cried Viennet.

'Down with the aristocrat,' said several; 'he stands by his order, even in his kitchen.'

'Nay,' broke in Viennet, 'I am the first of you all to reduce these people to their becoming station.'

'Do not say so,' said Gensonné: 'the Marquis de Trillac has been a gamekeeper on my property this year back.'

'Your property!' said Marat contemptuously. 'Your paternal estate was a vegetable stall in the Marché aux Bois; and your ancestral chateau, a room in the Pays Latin, five stories high.'

'You lived at the same house, in the cellar, Marat; and, by your own account, it was I that descended to know you!'

'If he talks of property, I'll put him in *my* list,' said Laroche. 'He whose existence is secure is unworthy to live.'

'A grand sentiment that,' said another; 'let us drink it!' and they arose and drained their glasses to the toast.

'The Duc de Dampierre, has any one got him down?' asked Guadet.

'I have'—'and I'—'and I,' said several together.

'I demand a reprieve for the Duke,' said another. 'I was at college with him at Nantes, and he is a good fellow, and kind-hearted.'

'Miserable patriot,' said Guadet, laughing, 'that can place his personal sympathies against the interests of the State.'

'*Parbleu!*' cried Laroche, looking over his neighbour's arm. 'Gensonné has got Robespierre's name down!'

'And why not? I detest him. Menard was right when he called him a "*Loup en toilette de bal!*"'

'What a list Menard has here!' said Guadet, holding it up, as he read aloud. 'All who have served the court, or whose families have, for the last three generations—all who employ court tailors, barbers, shoemakers, or armourers——'

'Pray add, all whose names can be traced to baptismal registries, or who are alleged to have been born in wedlock,' said Lescour. 'Let us efface the vile aristocracy effectually!'

'Your sneer is a weak sarcasm,' said Marat savagely. 'Menard is right: it is not man by man, but in platoons, that our vengeance must be executed.'

'I have an uncle and five cousins, whom, from motives of delicacy, I have not denounced. Will any one do me the favour to write the Count de Rochegarde and his sons?'

'I adopt them with pleasure. I wanted a count or two among my barons.'

'I drink to all patriots,' said Marat, draining his glass, and turning a full look on Fitzgerald.

'I accept the toast,' said Gerald, drinking.

'And I too,' cried Louvet, 'though I do not understand it.'

'By patriot, I mean one who adores liberty,' said Marat

'And hates the tyrant,' cried another.

'For the liberty to send my enemy to the guillotine, I am ready to fight to-morrow,' said Guadet.

'For whom, let me ask, are we to make ourselves hangmen and headsmen?' cried a pale, sickly youth, whose voice trembled as he spoke. 'The furious populace will not thank you that you have usurped their hunting-grounds. If you run down *their* game, they will one day turn and rend you!'

'Ah, Brissot, are you there, with your bland notions stolen from Plato!' cried Guadet. 'It is pleasant even to hear your flute-stop in the wild concert of our hoarse voices!'

'As to liberty, who can define it?' exclaimed Brissot.

'I can,' cried Lescour. 'The right to guillotine one's neighbour!'

'Who ever understood the meaning of equality?' continued Brissot, unheeding him. 'Procrustes was the inventor of it!'

'And for fraternity: what is it—who has ever practised it?'

'Cain is the only instance that occurs to me,' said Guadet gravely.

'I drink to America,' said Marat. 'May the infant republic live by the death of the mother that bore her!'

A wild hurrah followed the toast, which was welcomed with mad enthusiasm.

'The beacon of liberty we are lighting here,' continued he, 'will be soon answered from every hill-top and mountain throughout Europe—from the snow-peaks of Norway to the olive-crowned heights of the Apennines—from the bleak cliffs of Scotland to the rocky summits of the Carpathians.'

In a strain bombastic and turgid, but marked at times by flashes of real eloquence, he launched out into one of those rhapsodies which formed the staple of his popular addresses. The glorious picture of a people free, happy, and prosperous was so mingled with a scene of vengeance and retribution, that the work of the guillotine was made to seem the chief agent of civilisation. The social condition of the nation was described, in the state of a man whose life could only be preserved at the cost of a terrible amputation. The operation once over, the body would recover its functions of health and stability. This was the image daily reproduced, till the public mind grew to regard it as a truism. The noblesse represented the diseased and rotten limb, whose removal was so imperative, and there were but too many circumstances which served to favour the comparison.

Gerald was of an age when fervour and daring exercised a deeper influence than calm conviction. The men of warm and glowing impulses, of passionate words and desperate achievements, are sure to exercise a powerful sway over the young, especially when they themselves are from the accident of fortune in the position of adventurers. The language he now heard was bold and definite: there was nothing of subterfuge or concealment about it. The men who spoke were ready to pledge their lives to their words; they were even more willing to fight than preach. There was, besides, a splendid assertion of self-devotion in their plans; personal advancement had no place in their speculations. All was for France and Frenchmen: nothing for a party; nothing for a class. Their aspirations were the highest too; the liberty they contended for was to be the birthright of every man. Brissot, beside whom Gerald sat, was one well adapted to captivate his youthful admiration. His long fair hair, his soft blue eyes, an almost girlish gentleness of look, contrasting with the intense fervour with which he uttered his convictions, imparted an amount of interest to him that Gerald was not slow to appreciate. He spoke, besides, with—what never fails in its effect—the force of an intense conviction. That they were to regenerate France; that the nation long enslaved, corrupted and degraded was to be emancipated, enlightened, and elevated by *them*, was his heartfelt belief. The material advantages of a great revolution to those who should effect it, he would not stop to consider. In his own phrase: 'It was not to a mere land flowing with milk and honey Moses led the Israelites, but to a land promised to their forefathers, to be a heritage to their children !'

It is true his companions regarded him as a wild and dreamy enthusiast, impracticable in his notions, and too hopeful of humanity ; but they wisely saw how useful such an element of 'optimism' was in flavouring the mass of their dangerous doctrines, and how the sentiments of such a man served to exalt the tone of their opinions. While the conversation went on around the table, the speakers, warming with the themes, growing each moment more bold and more animated, Brissot turned his attentions entirely to Fitzgerald. He not only sketched off to him the men around the board, but, in a few light touches, characterised their opinions and views.

At the conclusion of a description in which he had spoken with the most unguarded frankness, Gerald could not help asking him how it was that he could venture to declare so openly his opinions to a perfect stranger like himself.

Brissot only smiled, but did not answer.

'For, after all,' continued Gerald, 'I am here in the camp of the enemy ! I *was* a Royalist ; I am so still.'

'But there are none left, *mon cher* ; the King himself is not one.'

'Ready to die for the throne——'

'There is no throne ; there is an old arm-chair, with the gilding rubbed away !'

'At all events there was a right to defend——'

'The right to live has an earlier date than the right to rule,' said Brissot gravely ; and seeing that he had caught the other's attention, he launched forth into the favourite theme of his party, the wrongs of the people. Unlike the generality of his friends, Brissot did not dwell on the vices and corruptions of the nobles. It was the evils of poverty he pictured ; the hopeless condition of those whose misery made them friendless.

'If you but knew the suffering patience of the poor,' said he, 'the stubbornness of their devotion to those above them in station; the tacit submission with which they accept hardship as their birthright, you would despair of humanity —infinitely, more from men's humility than from their cruelty! We cannot stir them; we cannot move them,' cried he. '"They are no worse off than their fathers were," that is their reply. If the hour come, however, that they rise up of themselves——'

Once more did Gerald revert to the hardihood of such confessions to a stranger, when the other broke in—

'Does the shipwrecked sailor on the raft hesitate to stretch out his hand to the sinking swimmer beside him. Come home with me from this, and let me speak to you. You will learn nothing from these men. There is Marat again! he has but one note in his voice, and it is to utter the cry of Blood!'

While the stormy speaker revelled wildly in the chaos of his incoherent thoughts, conjuring up scenes of massacre and destruction, the others madly applauding him, Brissot stole away, and beckoned Gerald to follow him.

It was daybreak ere they separated, and as Gerald gained his chambers he tore the white cockade he had long treasured as a souvenir of his days of Garde du Corps in pieces, and scattered the fragments from his window to the winds.

CHAPTER VIII

THE DÉPÔT DE LA PRÉFECTURE

GERALD had scarcely fallen asleep when he was aroused by a rude crash at his door, and looking up, saw the room filled with *gendarmerie* in full uniform. A man in plain black meanwhile approached the bed where he lay, and asked if he were called Gerald Fitzgerald.

'A *ci-devant* Garde du Corps and a refugee too?' said the questioner, who was the substitute of the Procureur du Roi. 'This is the order to arrest you, Monsieur,' said he.

'On what charge, may I ask ?' said Gerald indolently.

'It is a grave one,' said the other in a solemn voice, while he pointed to certain words in the warrant.

Gerald started as he read them, and, with a smile of scornful meaning, said—

'Is it alleged that I poisoned the Count de Mirabeau ?'

'You are included among those suspected of that crime.'

'And was he poisoned, then ?'

'The report of the surgeons who have examined the body is not conclusive. There are, however, sufficient grounds for investigation and inquiry. You will see, sir, that I have told you as much as I may—perhaps more than I ought.'

Left alone in his chamber that he might dress, Gerald proceeded to make his preparations with becoming speed. The order committed him to St. Pélagie, a prison then reserved for those accused of great crimes against the state. Weighty as such a charge was, he felt in the fact of an unjust accusation a degree of courageous energy that he had not known for many a previous day. In the midst of one's self-accusings and misgivings, an ill-founded allegation brings a certain sense of relief: if this be the extent of my culpability, I may be proud of my conduct, is such satisfactory judgment to address to one's own heart. He would have felt more comfort, it is true, in the reflection, if he did not remember that it was a frequent artifice of the day to accuse men of crimes of which they were innocent, to afford time and opportunity to involve them in some more grounded charge. Many were sent to Vincennes who were never afterwards heard of; and what easier, if needed, than to dispose of one like himself, without family or friends?

Though nominally committed to St. Pélagie, such was the crowded condition of that prison that Gerald was conducted to the 'Dépôt de la Préfecture,' a horrible den, into which murderers, malefactors, political offenders, and thieves were indiscriminately huddled, until time offered the opportunity to sift and divide them. It was a long hall, supported on two ranges of stone pillars, with wooden guard-beds on each

side, and between them a space technically called 'the street.'
Four narrow windows, close to the roof, admitted a scanty
light into this dreary abyss, where upward of eighty prisoners
were already confined.   By a sort of understanding among
themselves, for no other direction existed, the prisoners
had divided themselves into three distinct classes, each of
which maintained itself apart from the others.   Such as had
committed capital offences or were accused of them, held the
first rank, and exercised a species of general sway over all.
The place occupied by them was called 'Le Nid'; they
themselves were styled the 'Birds of Passage.'   The political
criminals gathered in a corner named 'L'Opinion'; the rest,
a large majority, were known as 'Les Âmes de boue.'

Gerald had but crossed the threshold of this darksome
dungeon when the door closed behind him, leaving him
almost in total obscurity.   The heavy breathing of a number
of people asleep, and the low mutterings of others suddenly
awakened, showed him that the place was crowded, although
as yet he could distinguish nothing.   Not venturing to stir
from the spot he occupied, he waited patiently till by the
cold grey light of breaking day he could look at the scene
before him.   He was not suffered to indulge this contemplation long, for as the sleepers awoke and beheld him, a general
cry was raised to pass him on to the Prévôt to be classed.
Gerald obeyed the order, moving slowly up the narrow
'street' to the end of the hall, where sat or rather lay an
old man, whose imprisonment dated upward of forty years
back.   He was perfectly blind, and so crippled by age and
rheumatism as to be utterly helpless ; but notwithstanding
his infirmities his voice was loud and commanding, and its tones
resounded throughout the length and breadth of the prison.
After a brief routine address, informing the new arrival that
for the due administration of that discipline which all societies
of men demanded, he must pledge obedience to the laws of
the place, and after duly promising the same, and swearing
it by placing a handful of straw upon his head, Gerald was
told to be seated while he was interrogated.

'Not know where you were born,' said the Prévôt, 'and yet you call yourself noble! Be it so; and now your charge —what is it?'

'They accuse me of having poisoned Mirabeau.'

'And would that be called a crime?' said one.

'Against whom, I would like to know, could that be an offence?' said another. 'Not against the King, whom he had deserted, nor against the people whom he betrayed.'

'Silence!—silence in the court!' said the Prévôt; then, addressing Gerald, he went on: 'with what object did you kill him?'

'I did not poison him—I am innocent,' said Gerald calmly.

'So are we all,' said the Prévôt devoutly—'spotless as the snowdrift. Who was she that persuaded you to act?—tell us her name.'

'There was no act, and could have been no suggester.'

'Young man,' said the Prévôt solemnly, 'we know of but one capital crime here, that is, concealment. Be frank, therefore, and fearless.'

'I cannot be sure, if I had done this crime, that I would have confessed it here, but as I have not even imagined it, I repeat to you once more I know nothing of it.'

With an acuteness perfectly wonderful at his age, and with an intellect that retained much of its former subtlety— for the Prévôt had been the first lawyer at the Lyons bar— he questioned Gerald as to what had led to the accusation. Partly to display his own powers of cross-examination, and partly that the youth's answers imparted an interest to his story, he prolonged the inquiry considerably. Nor was Gerald indisposed to speak openly about himself; it was a species of relief out of the dreary isolation in which he had recently passed his days.

To one point the old man would, however, continue to recur without success—had some womanly influence not swayed him? Whether his heart had not been touched, and some secret spring of love had given the impulse to his character, remained a mystery.

'No man,' said the Prévôt, 'ever lived as you allege. He who reads Jean Jacques lives like Rousseau; he who pores over Diderot acts the fatalist.'

'Enough of this,' cried a rough, rude voice. 'Is he of us or not?'

It was a 'Bird of Passage' that spoke, impatient for the moment when the new-comer should pay his entrance fee.

'He is not of you, be assured of that,' said the Prévôt, 'and for the present his place shall be "L'Opinion."'

By chance—a mere chance—a death on the day before had left a vacancy in that section, and thither Gerald was now with due solemnity conducted.

If his present associates were the 'best of the bad' around him, they were still far from being to his taste. They were the lowest emissaries of every party—the agents employed for all purposes of espionage and corruption. They affected a sort of fidelity to the cause they served while sober, but once filled with wine, avowed their utter indifference to every party, as they avowed that they took bribes from each in turn. Many, it is true, had moved in the better classes of society, were well-mannered and educated; but even through these there ran the same vein of profligacy, a tone of utter distrust, and a scepticism as to all good here and hereafter.

One or two of these remembered to have seen Gerald in his days of Garde du Corps, and were more than disposed to connect him with the scandals circulated about the Queen; others inclined to regard him as a revolutionist in the garb of the court party; none trusted him, and he lived in a kind of haughty estrangement from all. The Prévôt, indeed, liked him, and would talk with him for hours long; and to the old man himself the companionship seemed a boon. He now learned for the first time a true account of the great changes 'without,' as he called the world, and heard with an approach to accuracy the condition in which France then stood.

The sense of indignation at a groundless charge, the cruelty of an imprisonment upon mere suspicion, had long ceased to weigh upon Fitzgerald, and a dreamy apathy, the true

lethargy of the prison, stole over him. To lie half sleeping
on his hard bed, to sit crouched down, gazing listlessly at
the small patch of sky seen through the window, to spell
over the names scratched by former prisoners on the plaster,
to count for the thousandth time the fissures in the damp
walls—these filled his days. His nights were drearier still,
tormented with distressing dreams, to be dispelled only by
the gloom of awaking in a dungeon.

At intervals of a week or two, orders would come for this
or that prisoner to be delivered to the care of the Marshal
of the Temple—none knew for what, though all surmised
the worst, since not one was seen to return; and so time
sped on, month after month, death and removal doing their
work, till at last Gerald was the oldest *détenu* in the section
of 'L'Opinion.'

The fatuous vacuity of his mind was such that though he
heard the voices around him, and even tried at times to
follow what they said, he could collect nothing of it: sometimes the sounds would simply seem to weary and fatigue
him—they acted as some deep monotonous noise might have
done on a tired brain; sometimes they would cause the most
intense irritation, exciting him to a sense of anger he could
with difficulty control; and at others, again, they would
overcome him so thoroughly with sorrow, that he would
weep for hours. How time passed, what he had himself
been in former years, where and how and with whom he
lived, only recurred to him in short fitful passages, like the
scenes of some moving panorama, present for a moment and
then lost to view. He would fancy, too, that he had many
distinct and separate existences, as many deaths; and then
marvel to himself in which of these states he was at that
moment.

His wild talk; his absurd answers when questioned; the
incoherent things he would say, stamped him among his
fellow-prisoners as one bereft of reason; nor was there, to
all seeming, much injustice in the suspicion. If the chance
mention of some name he once knew would start and arouse

him, his very observations would appear those of a wandering
intellect, since he seemed to have been acquainted with
persons the most opposite and incongruous; and it even
became a jest—a sort of prison 'plaisanterie'—to ask him
whether he was not intimate with this man or that, mention-
ing persons the least likely for him ever to have met.

'There goes another of your friends, Maître,' said one to
him : 'they have guillotined Brissot this morning; you surely
knew him, he edited the *Droit du Peuple.*'

'Yes, I knew him. Poor Brissot!' said Gerald, with a
sigh.

'What was he like, Maître ? was he short and thick, with
a beard like mine ?'

'No, he was fair and gentle-looking.'

'*Parbleu !* that was a good guess : so he was.'

'And kind-hearted as he looked,' muttered Gerald.

'He died with Gaudet, Gensonné, Louvet, and four other
Maratists. You have seen most of them, I 'm sure.'

'Yes. Gaudet and Gensonné I remember; I forget
Louvet. Had he a scar on his temple ?'

'That he had; it was a sabre-cut in a duel,' cried one,
who added in a whisper, 'he 's not the mad fool you take
him for.'

'You used to be Gabriel Riquetti in times past ?' asked
another gravely.

'No—that is—not I ; but—I forget how it was—we were
—I 'll remember it by and by.'

'Why, you told me a few days back that you were
Mirabeau.'

'No, no,' said another, 'he said he was Alfieri ; I was
present.'

'Mirabeau's hair was long and wiry. It was not soft like
mine,' said Gerald. 'When he shook it back, he used to say,
"I 'll show them the boar's head."'

'Yes. He 's right, that was a favourite saying of Mirabeau's,' whispered another.

'And they are all gone now,' said Gerald with a deep sigh.

'Ay, Maître, every man of them. All the Girondins; all the friends of liberty; all the kind spirits who loved men as their brothers; and the guillotine better than the men.'

'And Vergniaud and Fonfréde, you surely knew them?' Gerald shook his head.

'It was your friend Robespierre sent them to the knife.' Gerald started, and tried to understand what was said.

'Ask him about La Gabrielle,' whispered another.

'What of La Gabrielle? she was Marietta,' cried Gerald wildly.

'She might have been. We only knew her as she figured before our own eyes. In November last she was the Goddess of Reason.'

'No, no; I deny it,' cried another; 'La Gabrielle had fled from France before.'

'She was the Goddess of Reason, I repeat,' said the other. 'She that used to blush scarlet, when they led her out, after the scene, to receive the plaudits of the audience, stood shameless before the mob on the steps of the Pantheon.'

'And I tell you her name was Maillard; it was easy enough to mistake her for La Gabrielle, for she had the same long, waving, light-brown hair.'

'Marietta's hair was black as night,' muttered Gerald; 'her complexion, too, was the deep olive of the far south, and of her own peculiar race. *I* ought to know,' added he aloud; 'we wandered many a pleasant mile together through the valleys of the Apennines.'

The glance of compassionate pity they turned upon him showed how they read these remembrances of the past.

'Which of you has dared to speak ill of her?' cried he suddenly, as a gleam of intelligence shot through his reverie. 'Was it you? or you? or you?'

'Far be it from *me*,' said Courtel, a young debauchee of the Jacobin party; 'I admire her much. She has limbs for a statuary to match; and though this poor picture gives but a sorry idea of such perfections, it is not all unlike!'

As he spoke, he drew forth a coarse print of the Goddess of Reason, as she stood unveiled, almost unclad, before the populace.

Gerald caught but one glance at the ribald portrait, and then with a spring he seized and tore it into atoms. The action seemed to arouse in him all the dormant passion of his nature; for in an instant he clutched Courtel by the throat, and tried to strangle him. It was not without a severe struggle that he was rescued by the others, and Gerald thrown back, bruised and beaten, on his bed.

From this unlucky hour forth Gerald's comrades held themselves all aloof from him. He was no longer in their eyes the poor and harmless object they had believed, but a wild and dangerous maniac. His life henceforth was one unbroken solitude; not a word of kindness or sympathy met his ear. The little fragments of cheering tidings others interchanged, none shared with him, and he sank into a state of almost sleep. Nor was it a small privilege to sleep, while millions around him were keeping their orgie of blood; when the cries of the dying and the shouts of vengeance were mingled in one long, loud strain, and the monotonous stroke of the guillotine never ceased its beat. Sleep was, indeed, a boon, when the wakeful ear and eye had nought but sounds and sights of horror before them. What a blessing not to watch the street as it trembled before the fatal car, groaning under its crowd of victims. To see them, with drooped heads and hanging arms, swaying as the rude plank shook them, not lifting an eye upon that cruel mob, whose ribald cries assailed them, and who had words of welcome but for *him* who followed on a low, red-coloured cart, pale, stern, and still—the headsman. The thirsty earth was so drunk with carnage that, in the words of one of the Convention, it was said: 'We shall soon fear to drink the water of the wells, lest it be mixed with the blood of our brothers!'

Out of this deep slumber, in which no measure of time was kept, a loud and deafening shock aroused him. It was the force of the mob, who had broken-in the prison-doors, and proclaimed liberty to the captives. Robespierre had been guillotined that morning; the 'Terror' was over, and all Paris, in a frenzy of delight, awoke from its terrible orgie of blood, and dared to breathe with freedom. The burst of joy that broke forth was like the wild cry of delight uttered by a reprieved criminal.

Few in that vast multitude had less sympathy with that joy than Gerald Fitzgerald. Of the prisoners there was not one except himself who had not either home or friends to welcome him. Many were met as they issued forth, and clasped in the arms of loving relatives. Mothers and wives, sisters and brothers were there; children sprang wildly to their fathers' breasts, and words of love and blessing were heard on every side.

'Who is that yonder: the poor, sickly youth, that creeps along by himself, with his head down?' whispered a happy girl at her brother's side.

'That is the "Maître Fou!"' said he carelessly; 'I think he scarcely knows whither he is going.'

CHAPTER IX

THE PÈRE MASSONI IN HIS CELL

LET us now return to Rome. The Père Massoni sat alone in his small study; a single lamp, covered with a shade, stood beside him, throwing its light only on his thin, attenuated figure, dressed in the long robe of black serge, and buttoned to the very feet. One wasted, blue-veined hand rested on his knee, the other was in the breast of his robe. It was a wild and stormy night without: long, swooping dashes of rain came from time to time against the windows, with blasts of strong wind borne over the wide expanse of the Campagna. The blue lightning, too, flashed

T

through the half-darkened room, while the thunder rolled
unceasingly amid the stupendous ruins of old Rome. For
a long time had the Père sat thus motionless, and to all
seeming, in expectancy. Some books and an open map lay
on the table beside him, but he never turned to them, but
remained in this selfsame attitude ; only changing when he
bent his head to listen more attentively to the noises without.
At length he arose, and passing into a small octagonal tower
that opened from the corner of his chamber, closed the door
behind him. For a second or two he stood in perfect darkness, but suddenly a wide flash of lightning lit up the whole
air, displaying the bleak Campagna for miles and miles,
while it depicted every detail of the little tower around him.
Taking advantage of the light, he advanced and opened the
windows, carefully fastening them to the walls as he did so.
He now seated himself by the open casement, gathering his
robe well about him, and drawing the hood over his face.
The storm increased as the night went on. Many an
ancient pillar rocked to its base ; many a stern old ruin
shook, as in distinct blasts, like the report of cannon, the
wind hurled all its force upon them. In the same fitful
gusts the rain dashed down, seething across the wide plain,
where it hissed with a sound like a breaking sea borne away
on the wild blast. The sound of the bells through the city
was not heard : all except St. Peter's were dissipated and
lost. The great bell of the mighty dome, however, rose
proudly above the crash of elements, and struck three, and
as the Père counted the strokes, he sighed drearily. For
the last hour the lightning had been less and less frequent ;
and instead of that wide-spreading scene of open Campagna,
dotted with villages, and traversed by roads, suddenly
flashing upon him with a clearness more marked than at
noonday, all was now wrapped in an impenetrable darkness,
only broken at rare intervals, and by weak and uncertain
gleams.

Why does he peer so earnestly through the gloom, why
in every lull of the gale, does he bend his ear to listen, and

why, in the lightning flashes, are his eyes ever turned to
the winding road that leads to Viterbo ? For him, surely,
no ties of kindred, no affections of the heart are the motives
which hold him thus spell-bound : nor wife nor child are
his, for whose coming he watches thus eagerly. What can
it be, then, that has awakened this feverish anxiety within
him, that with every swell of the storm he starts and listens
with more intense eagerness ?

'He will not come to-night,' muttered he at length to
himself; 'he will not come to-night, and to-morrow it will
be too late. On Wednesday they leave this for Gaeta, and
ere they return it may be weeks, ay, months. So is it ever :
we strive, and plot, and plan ; and yet it is a mere question
of seconds whether the mine explode at the right instant.
The delay is inexplicable,' said he, after a pause. 'They
left Sienna on Sunday last; and, even granting that they
must travel slowly, they should have been here yesterday
morning. What misfortune is this ? I left the Cardinal
last night, at length—and after how much labour—persuaded
and convinced. He agreed to all and every thing. Had
the youth arrived to-night, therefore, his Eminence must
have pledged himself to the enterprise ; indeed he rarely
changes his mind under two days ! ' He paused for a while,
and then in a voice of deeper emotion, said : 'If we needed
to be taught how small is all our wisdom—how poor, and
weak, and powerless we are—we can read the lesson in the
fact that minutes decide destinies, while whole lives of
watching cannot control the smallest event ! ' A brilliant
flash of lightning at this instant illuminated the entire plain,
showing every object in the wide expanse for miles. The
Père started, and leaned eagerly upon the window, his eyes
fixed on the Viterbo road. Another minute, ay, a second
more, had been enough to assure him if he had seen aright;
but already it was dark again, and the dense thunder-clouds
seemed to descend to the very earth. As the low growling
sounds died away at last, the air seemed somewhat thinner,
and now the Père could make out a faintly twinkling light

that flickered through the gloom, appearing and disappearing at intervals, as the ground rose or fell: he quickly recognised it for a carriage-lamp, and with a fervently uttered entreaty to Heaven, that it might prove the herald of those he watched for, he closed the window and returned to his study.

If the law that condemns the priest to a life of isolation and estrangement from all human affections be severe and pitiless, there is what many would deem a proud compensation in the immensity of that ambition offered to men thus separated from their fellows. Soaring above the cares and anxieties, whose very egotism renders them little, these men fix their contemplation upon the great events of the world, and, in a spirit that embraces ages yet unborn, uninfluenced by the emotions that sway others, untouched by the yearnings that control them, they alone of all mankind can address themselves to the objects of their ambition without selfish interests. The aggrandisement of the Church, the spread and pre-eminence of the Catholic faith, formed a cause which for centuries engaged the greatest intellects and the most devoted hearts of her followers. Among these were many of more eminence, in point of station, than Massoni; many more learned, many more eloquent, many whose influence extended further and wider, but not one who threw more steadfast devotion into the cause, nor who was readier to peril all—even to life itself—in its support. He had been for years employed by the Papal Government as a secret agent at the different courts of Europe. He had been in Spain, in Austria, in France, and the Low Countries; he had travelled through England, and passed nearly a year in Ireland. Well versed in modern languages, and equally acquainted with the various forms of European government, he was one whose opinion had a great weight upon every question of political bearing. Far too crafty to employ this knowledge in self-advancement, where, at the very utmost, it might have led to some inferior dignity at home, or some small 'Nunciate' abroad, he devoted himself to the service of the Cardinal Caraffa, a man of immense wealth, high family, overweening pretensions, but of an intellect the very weakest, and so assailable by flattery, as to be the slave of those who had access to him. His Eminence saw all the advantages to be derived from such a connection. Whatever the point that occupied the Consulta, he was sure to be thoroughly informed upon it by his secret adviser; and so faithfully and so adroitly was he served, that the mystery of their intimacy was unfathomed by his brother cardinals. Caraffa spoke of Massoni as a person of whom 'he had heard, indeed'; a man trustworthy, and of some attainments, but that was all; 'he had seen him, too, and spoken with him occasionally!'

As for the Père, the name of his Eminence never passed his lips, except in company with those of other cardinals. In fact, he knew few great people; their ways and habits little suited his humble mode of life, and he never frequented the grand receptions of the princes of the Church, nor showed himself at their salons. Such, in brief, was the Jesuit father, who now walked up and down the little study, in a state of feverish impatience it was rarely his lot to suffer. At last the heavy roll of a carriage resounded in the court beneath, the clank of descending steps was heard, and soon after the sound of approaching feet along the corridor.

'Are they come? is it Carrol?' cried the Père, flinging wide the door of his chamber.

'Yes, most reverend rector,' said a full, rich voice; and a short, rosy-faced little man, in the prime of life, entered and obsequiously kissed Massoni's extended hand.

'What an anxious time you have given me, Carrol!' said the Père hastily. 'Have you brought him? Is he with you?'

'Yes; he's in the carriage below at this moment, but so wearied and exhausted that it were better you should not see him to-night.'

Massoni paused to reflect, and after a moment said—

'We have no time, not even an hour, to throw away, Carrol; the sooner I see this youth, the better prepared shall I be to speak of him to his Eminence. A few words to

welcome him will be enough for me. Yes, let him come; it
is for the best.'

Carrol left the room, and after some delay, was heard returning, his slow steps being accompanied by the wearied
foot-falls of one who walked with difficulty. Massoni threw
the door wide, and as the light streamed out he almost
started at the figure before him. Pale, wan, and worn-look-
ing as the stranger appeared, the resemblance to Charles
Edward was positively startling. The same lustrous gleam
of the deep blue eyes: the same refinement of brow; the
same almost womanly softness of expression in the mouth;
and stronger than all these, the mode in which he carried
his head somewhat back, and with the chin slightly elevated,
were all marks of the Prince.

Massoni welcomed him with a courteous and respectful
tone, and conducted him to a seat.

'This is a meeting I have long and ardently desired, sir,'
said the Père, in the voice of one to whom the arts of the
courtier were not unknown; 'nor am I the only one here
who has cherished this wish.'

A faint smile, half gracious half surprised, acknowledged
this speech, and Carrol watched with a painful anxiety even
this mark of recognition.

'The Chevalier is fatigued to-night, reverend father,' said
he; 'his endeavours to fulfil our wishes have cost him much
exertion and weariness. We have journeyed day and night
from Geneva.'

'In this ardour he has only given us a deeper pledge of his
high deservings. May I offer you some refreshments, sir?'
said he, hastily, struck by the weak pallor of the young
man's countenance.

A gentle gesture of refusal declined the offer.

'Shall I show you to your room, then?' said the Père,
rising and opening a door into a small chamber adjoining;
'my servant will attend you.'

'No,' said the youth faintly. 'Let us proceed with our
journey; I will not rest till I reach Rome.'

'But you are at Rome, sir; we are at our journey's end,' said Carrol.

The young man heard the words without emotion—the same sad smile upon his lips.

'He must have rest and care,' whispered Massoni to Carrol; and then turning to the youth, he took him by the hand and led him away.

Having consigned him to the care of a faithful servant, the Père re-entered the room, his face flushed, and his dark eyes flashing.

'What miserable deception is this?' cried he. 'Is this the daring, headlong spirit I have been hearing of? Are these the parts to confront an enterprise of peril?'

'He is——'

'He is dying,' broke in the Père passionately.

'Confess, at least, he is a Stuart, in every line and lineament.'

'Ay, Carrol, even to the word FAILURE, written in capitals on his brow.'

'But you see him wasted by fever and long suffering; he rose from a sick-bed to undertake this wearisome journey.'

'Better had he kept his bed till death released him. I tell you it is not of such stuff as this adventurers are made. His very appearance would dash men with discouragement.'

'Bethink you what he has gone through, Père; the sights and scenes of horror that have met his eyes—the daily carnage amid which he lived—himself, twice rescued from the scaffold, by what seems like a miracle—his days and nights of suffering in friendless misery too. Remember, also, how little of hope there was to cheer him through all this. If ever there was one forlorn and destitute, it was he.'

'I think not of *him*, but of the cause he should have served,' said the Père; 'and once more I say, this youth is unequal to "the event." His father had faults enough to have wrecked a dozen enterprises: he was rash, reckless, and unstable; but his rashness took the form of courage, and his very fickleness had a false air of versatility. Men regarded it as an element full of resources; but this sickly boy only recalls in his features every weakness of his race. What can we do with *him* ?'

'Men have fought valiantly for royalties that offered less to their regard,' said Carrol.

'Ay, Carrol, when the throne is fixed, men will rally to maintain it, even though he who wears the crown be little worthy of their reverence; but when the question is to re-establish a fallen dynasty—to replace one branch by another, the individual becomes of immense importance; personal qualities assume then all the proportions of claims, and men calculate on the future by the promises of the present. Tell me frankly what could you augur for a cause of which this youth was to be the champion ?'

Carrol did not break silence for some time; at length he said—

'You told me once, and I have never forgotten it, a re-markable story of Monsignor Saffi, the Bishop of Volterra——'

'I know what you allude to—how the simple-minded bishop became the craftiest of cardinals. Ay, elevation will now and then work such miracles; but it is because they are miracles we are not to calculate on their recurrence.'

'I would not say that this is not the case to hope for a similar transformation. They who knew Fitzgerald in his better, stronger days, describe him as one capable of the most daring exploits, full of heroism and of a boundless ambition, fed by some mysterious sentiment that whispers within him that he was destined for high achievement. These are inspirations that usually only die with ourselves.

'When I look at him,' said the Père sadly, 'I distrust them all.'

'You are not wont to be so easily discouraged.'

'Easily discouraged—easily discouraged! It is a strange reproach to bring against me,' said the Père, with a calm collectedness; 'nor is that the character all Rome would give me. But why am I steadfast of purpose and firm of plan ? Because, ere I engage in an enterprise, I weigh well the means of success, and canvass all its agencies. The smallest stream that ever dashed down a mountain has strength in the impulse of its course, while if it meandered through a plain it had been a rivulet. This is a lesson we may reap profit from.'

Carrol did not answer, and Massoni, covering his face with his hands, seemed lost in deep thought; at last he said—

'What was your pretext to induce him to come back here ?'

'To hear tidings of his family and kindred.'

'Did you intimate to him that they were of rank and station ?'

'Yes, of the very highest.'

'How did the news affect him ?'

'It was hard at first to convince him that they could be true. He had, besides, been so often tricked and deceived by false intelligence, and made the sport of craftier heads, that it was difficult to win his confidence; nor did I succeed until I told him certain facts about his early life, whose correctness he acknowledged.'

'I had imagined him most unlike what I see. If Charles Edward had left a daughter she might have resembled this.'

'Still that very resemblance is of great value.'

'What signifies that a thing may look like gold, when at the first touch of the chemist's test it blackens and betrays itself ?'

'He may be more of a Stuart even than he looks. It is too rash to judge of him as we see him now.'

'Be it so,' said the Père, with a sort of resignation; 'but if I have not lost my skill in reading temperament, this youth is not to our purpose. At all events,' resumed he, more rapidly, 'his Eminence need not see him yet. Enough when I say that the fatigues of the road have brought on some fever, and that he is confined to bed. Within a week, or even less, I shall be able to pronounce if we may employ him. I have no mind to hear your news to-night; this disappointment has unmanned me; but to-morrow, Carrol, to-morrow the day will be all our own, and I all myself. And so good-night, and good rest.'

CHAPTER X

THE CARDINAL AT HIS DEVOTIONS

If the night which followed the interview of the Père Massoni with Carrol was one of deep anxiety, the morning did not bring any relief to his cares. His first duty was to ask after Fitzgerald. The youth had slept little, but lay tranquil and uncomplaining, and to all seeming indifferent either as to the strange place or the strange faces around him. The keen-eyed servant, Giacomo, himself an humble member of the order, quickly detected that he was suffering under some mental shock, and that the case was one where the mere physician could afford but little benefit.

'He lies there quiet as a child,' said he, 'never speaking nor moving, his eyelids half drooped over his eyes, and save that now and then, at long intervals, he breathes a low, faint sigh, you would scarce believe he was alive.'

'I will see him,' said the Père, as he gently opened the door, and stole noiselessly across the room. A faint streak of light peering between the drawn window-curtains, fell directly on the youth's face, showing it pale and emotionless, as Giacomo described it. As the Père seated himself by the bedside, he purposely made a slight noise, to attract the other's attention, but Gerald did not notice him, not even turning a look toward him. Massoni laid his finger on the pulse, the action was weak but regular; nothing to denote fever or excitement, only the evidence of great exhaustion or debility.

'I have come to hear how you have rested,' said the Père, in an accent he could render soft as a woman's, 'and to welcome you to Rome.'

A faint, very faint, smile was all the reply to this speech.

'I am aware that you have gone through much suffering and peril,' continued the Père, 'but with rest and kind care you will soon be well again. You are among friends, who are devoted to you.'

A gentle movement of the brows, as if in assent, replied.

'It may be that speaking would distress you ; perhaps even my own words fatigue you. If so I will be satisfied to come and sit silently beside you, till you are stronger and better.'

'Si—si,' muttered Gerald faintly, and at the same time he essayed to smile as it were in recognition.

A quick convulsive twitch of impatience passed across the Père's pale face, but so rapidly that it seemed a spasm, and the features were the next moment calm as before ; and now Massoni sat silently gazing on the tranquil lineaments before him. Among the various studies of his laborious life medicine had not been neglected, and now he addressed himself to examine the condition and study the symptoms of the youth. The case was not of much bodily ailment, at least save in the exhaustion which previous illness had left. There was nothing like malady, but there were signs of a mischief far deeper, more subtle, and less curable than mere physical ills. The look of vacancy—the half-meaning smile—the dull languor, not alone in feature but in the way he lay—all presented matter for grave and weighty fears. The very presence of these signs, unaccompanied by ailment, gave a gloomier aspect to the case, and led the Père to reflect whether such traits had any connection with descent. The strong resemblance which the young man bore to the Stuarts —and there were few families where the distinctive traits were more marked—induced Massoni to consider the question with reference to *them*. They are indeed a race whose wayward impulses and rash resolves took oftentimes but little guidance of reason ; but these were mere signs of eccentricity and not insanity. But might not the one be precursor to the other ; might not the frail judgment, which sufficed for the every-day cares of life, utterly give way in seasons of greater trial ? Thus reasoning and communing with himself he sat till the hour struck which apprised him of his audience with the Cardinal.

It was not yet the season when Rome was filled by its higher classes, and Massoni could repair to the palace of the Cardinal without any of the secrecy observable at other periods. Still he deemed it more in accordance with the humility he affected to seek admission by a small garden gate, which opened on the Pincian hill. The little portal admitted him into a garden such as only Italy possesses. The gardens of England are unrivalled for their peculiar excellence, for the exquisite flavour of their fruit, and in their perfection of order and neatness they stand unequalled in the world; the trim quaintness of the Dutch taste has also its special beauty, and nowhere can be seen such gorgeous colouring in flower-pots, such splendour of tulip and ranunculus : but there is in Italy a rich blending of culture and wildness—a mingled splendour and simplicity, just as in the great halls of the marble palace on the Neva, where the haughtiest noble in his diamond pelisse, stands side by side with the simple Boyard in his furs : so in the 'golden land,' the cactus and the mimosa, the orange and the pear-tree, the cedar of Lebanon and the stone-pine of the north, are commingled and interleaved ; all signs of a soil which can supply nourishment to the rarest and most delicate, as well as to the hardiest of plants.

In this lovely wilderness, with many a group in marble, many a beautifully-carved fountain, many an ornamental shrine, half hidden in its leafy recesses, the Père now walked, screening his steps as he went, from that great range of windows which opened on a grand terrace—a precaution rather the result of habit than called for by the circumstance of the time. A fish-pond of some extent, with a small island, occupied the centre of the garden ; the island itself being ornamented by a beautiful little shrine dedicated to our Lady of Rimini, the birth-place of the Cardinal. To this sacred spot his Eminence was accustomed to repair for secret worship each morning of his life. As a measure of respectful reverence for the great man's devotions, the place was studiously secluded from all intrusion, and even strangers—

admitted, as at rare intervals they were, to visit the gardens—were never suffered to invade the sacred precincts of the island.

A strangely contrived piece of mechanism appended to the little wicket that formed the entrance always sufficed to show if his Eminence was engaged in prayer, and consequently removed from all pretext of interruption. This was an apparatus, by which the face of a beautifully painted Madonna became suddenly covered by a veil, a signal that none of the Cardinal's nearest of blood would have dared to violate. It was, indeed, to the hours of daily seclusion thus piously passed the Cardinal owed that character for sanctity which eminently distinguished him in the Church. A day never went over in which he did not devote at the least an hour to this sacred duty, and the air of absorption, as he repaired to the shrine, and the look of intense pre-occupation he brought away, vouched for the depth of his pious musings.

As Massoni arrived at the narrow causeway which led over to the island, he perceived that the veil of the Madonna was lowered. He knew, therefore, at once that the Cardinal was there, and he stopped to consider what course he should adopt, whether to loiter about the garden till his Eminence should appear, or repair to the palace and await him. The Père knew that the Cardinal was to leave Rome by midday, to reach Albano to dinner, and he mused over the shortness of the time their interview must last.

'This is no common emergency,' thought he at last; 'here is a case fraught with the most tremendous consequences. If this scheme be engaged in, the whole of Europe may soon be in arms—the greatest convulsion that ever shook the Continent may result; and out of the struggle who is to foresee what principles may be the victors!

'I will go to him at once,' said he resolutely. 'Events succeed each other too rapidly nowadays for more delay. The "Terror" in France has once more turned men's minds to the peaceful security of a monarchy. Let us profit by the moment'; and with this he traversed the narrow bridge and reached the island.

A thick copse of ornamental planting screened the front of the little shrine. Hastily passing through this, he stood within a few yards of the building, when his steps were quickly arrested by the sound of a voice whose accents could not be mistaken for the Cardinal's. There was besides something distinctively foreign in the pronunciation that marked the speaker for a stranger. Curious to ascertain who might be the intruder in a spot so sacred, Massoni stepped noiselessly through the brushwood, and gained a little loop-holed aperture beside the altar, from which the whole interior of the shrine could be seen. Seated on one of the marble steps below the altar was the Cardinal, a loose dressing-gown of rich fur wrapped round him, and a cap of the same material on his head. Directly in front of him, and also seated on the pedestal of a column, was a man in a Carthusian robe, patched and discoloured, and showing many signs of age and poverty. The wearer, however, was rubicund and jovial-looking, though the angles of the mouth were somewhat dragged, and the wrinkles at the eyes were deep-worn. The general expression, however, was that of one whose nature accepted the struggles of life manfully and cheerfully. It was not till after some minutes of close scrutiny that Massoni could recall the features, but at length he remembered that it was the well-known Carthusian friar, George Kelly, the former companion of Prince Charles Edward. If their positions in life were widely different, Kelly did not suffer the disparity to influence his manner, but talked with all the ease and familiarity of an equal.

Whatever interest the scene might have had for Massoni was speedily increased by the first words which met his ears. It was the Cardinal who said—

'I own to you, Kelly, until what you have told me I had put little faith in the whole story of this youth; and there is then really such?'

'There is, or at least there was, your Eminence. I remember as well as if it was yesterday the evening he came to the palace to see the Prince. A poor countryman of my own, a Carthusian, brought him, and took him back again to the college. The boy was afterward sent to a villa somewhere near Orvieto.'

'Was the youth acknowledged by his Royal Highness as his son ?' asked the Cardinal.

'The Prince never spoke of him to me till the day before his death. He then said, "Can you find out that Carthusian for me, Kelly?—I should like to speak with him." I told him that he had long since left Rome and even Italy. The last tidings of him came from Ireland, where he was living as a dependant on some reduced family.

'"There is no time to fetch him from Ireland," said his Highness; "and yet, Kelly, I'd give a thousand pounds that he were here." He then asked me if I remembered a certain boy, dressed like a colleger of the Jesuits, who came one night long ago to the palace with this same Carthusian.

'I said, yes; that though his Royal Highness believed that I was away from Rome that night, I came back post-haste from Albano; and finding myself in one of the corridors, I waited till Fra Luke came out from his interview, with the boy beside him.

'"True, true, Kelly; I meant you to have known nothing of this visit. So then you saw the boy? What thought you of him ?"

'"I saw and marked him well, for his fair hair and skin were so distinctively English, they made a deep impression upon me."

'"He had the mouth, too, Kelly—a little pouting and over full-lipped. Did you mark that ?"

'"No, sire; I did not observe him so closely."

'"How poor and ragged the child was! his very shoes were broken. Did you see his shoes ?—and that frail bit of serge was all his covering against the keen blast. O George," cried he, as his lip shook with emotion, "what would you say if that poor boy, all wretched and wayworn as you saw him, were the true heir of a throne, and that the proudest in Europe? What a lesson for human greatness that! It was a scurvy trick you played me that night, sir," said he, quickly changing, for his moods were ever thus, and you never could guess how long any theme would engage him—"a scurvy trick, sir, to pry into what your master desired you should not know. I had my own good reasons for what I did, and it ill became you to contravene them; but it was like your cloth—ay, sirrah, it was the trick of all your kind."

'Out of this he fell a-weeping over the fallen fortunes of his house, asking again and again if history contained anything its equal; and saying that other dynasties had fallen through their crimes and cruelties, but that his house had been ruined by trustfulness and generosity; and so he forgot the boy and all about him.'

'And think you it was to this youth that his Royal Highness bequeathed the sum mentioned in his will, together with his George, the Grand Cross of Malta, and the St. John of Jerusalem, for so the Cardinal York tells me the bequest runs?'

'As to that I can say nothing,' Kelly replied.

'I have heard,' said the Cardinal again, 'that in a sealed letter to his brother York the Prince acknowledges this boy as his son, born in wedlock, his mother being of an ancient and noble house.' Then quickly changing his tone, he asked, 'How are we to find him, Kelly? Do you believe that he still lives?'

'I have no means of knowing; but if I wished to trace a man, not merely in Europe, but through the globe itself, I am aware of but one police to trust to.'

'And that?'

'The Jesuits: they are everywhere; and everywhere cautious, painstaking, and trustworthy; they are well skilled in pursuits like these; and even when they fail—and they seldom fail—they never compromise those who employ them.'

'Well,' said the Cardinal, 'they have failed here. They have been on the track of this young fellow for years back; and when I tell you that the craftiest of them all, Massoni, has not been able to find a clue to him, what will you say ?'

'Why, that he must be dead and buried, your Eminence,' broke in Kelly.

'To that conclusion have I come myself, Fra Kelly. Had he been alive he had come long since to claim this costly inheritance. Seven hundred thousand Roman scudi, the Palazzo Albuquerque, at Albano, with all its splendid pictures and jewels, worth double the whole——'

'Egad, I had come out of my grave to assert my right to such a bequest,' said Kelly, laughing. 'Has the Cardinal York made search for him, your Eminence ?' said he, hastily correcting his levity.

'The Cardinal York is not likely to disturb himself with such cares ; and as the legacy lapses, in default of claimant, to the convent of St. Lazarus of Medina, he probably deems that it will be as well bestowed.'

'Lazarus will have fallen upon some savory crumbs this time,' muttered Kelly, whose disposition to jest seemed beyond all his self-control.

'It was this very day Massoni hoped to have brought me some tidings of the youth,' said the Cardinal, rising, 'and he has not appeared. It must be as you have said, Kelly ; the grave has closed over him. There is now, therefore, a great danger to guard against : substitution of some other for him —not by Massoni ; he is a man of probity and honour ; but he may be imposed on by others. It is a fraud which would well repay all its trouble.'

'There is but one could detect the trick—that Luke M'Manus, the Carthusian I have mentioned to your Eminence. He knew the boy well, and was intrusted by the Prince to take charge of him ; but he is away in Ireland.'

'But could be fetched, if necessary,' said Caraffa, half musing, as he moved toward the door.

Massoni did not wait to hear more, but stealthily threading his way through the copse, he gained the garden, and retracing his steps, returned to the convent. Ascending to his chamber by a private stair, he gave his servant orders to say that he was indisposed, and could not receive any one.

'So, then, your Eminence,' said he bitterly, as he sank into a chair, 'you would underplot me here. Let us see who can play his cards best.'

CHAPTER XI

AN AUDIENCE

WITHIN less than half an hour after his arrival at home, Massoni received an order from the Cardinal to repair to the palace. It was a verbal message, and couched in terms to make the communication seem scarcely important.

Massoni smiled as he prepared to obey; it amused him to think, that in a game of craft and subtlety his Eminence should dare to confront him, and yet this was evidently his policy.

The Cardinal's carriage stood ready horsed in the court-yard as the Père passed through, and a certain air of impatience in the servants showed that the time of departure had been inconveniently delayed.

'That thunder-storm will break over us before we are half way across the Campagna,' cried one.

'We were ordered for one, and it is now past three, and though the horses were taken from their feed to get in readiness, here we are still.'

'And all because a Jesuit is at his devotions!'

The look of haughty rebuke Massoni turned upon them as he caught these words, made them shrink back abashed and terrified; and none knew when nor in what shape might come the punishment for this insolence.

'You have forgotten an appointment, Père Massoni,' said the Cardinal as the other entered his chamber, with a deep and respectful reverence, 'an appointment too, of your own making. There is an opinion abroad, that we Cardinals are men of leisure, whose idle hours are at the discretion of all; I had hoped, that to this novel theory the Père Massoni would not have been a convert.'

'Nor am I, your Eminence. It would ill become one who wears such a frock as this to deny the rights of discipline and the benefits of obedience.'

'But you are late, sir?'

'If I am so, your Eminence will pardon me when I give the reason. The entire of last night was passed by me in watching for the arrival of a certain youth, who did not come till nigh daybreak, and even then, so ill, so worn out and exhausted, that I have been in constant care of him ever since.'

'And he is come—he is actually here?' cried the Cardinal eagerly.

'He is, at this moment, in the college.'

'How have you been able to authenticate his identity,— the rumour goes that he died years ago?'

'It is a somewhat entangled skein, your Eminence, but will stand the test of unravelment. Intervals there are, indeed, in his story, unfilled up; lapses of time, in which I am left to mere conjecture, but his career is traceable throughout; and I can track him from the days in which he stood an acolyte beside our altars to the hour we now talk in.'

'It is to your sanguine hopes you have been listening rather than cold reason, Père.'

'Look at me, Eminence—scan me well, and say, do I look like those who are slaves to their own enthusiasm?'

'The strongest currents are often calm on the surface.'

The Père sighed heavily, but did not answer.

'The youth himself, too, may have aided the delusion: he is, probably, one well suited to inspire interest: in a varied and adventurous life, men of this stamp acquire, amid their other worldly gifts, a marvellous power of persuasiveness.'

The Père smiled half sadly.

'You would tell me, by that smile, Père Massoni, that you

are not to be the victim of such seductions; that you understand mankind in a spirit that excludes such error.'

'Far be it from me to indulge such boastfulness,' said the
other meekly.

'At all events,' said the Cardinal, half peevishly, 'he who
has courage and ambition enough to play this game is,
doubtless, a fellow of infinite resource and readiness, and
will have, at least, plausibility on his side.'

'Would that it were so!' exclaimed Massoni eagerly.

'What do you mean by that?'

'Would that he were one who could boldly assert his own
proud cause, and vindicate his own high claims; would that
he had come through the terrible years of his suffering life
with a spirit hardened by trials, and a courage matured by
exercise; would, above all, that he had not come from the
conflict broken in health, shattered and down-stricken! Ay,
sir, this youth of bold pretensions, of winning manners, and
persuasive gifts is a poor fellow so stunned by calamity as
to be helpless!'

'Is he dying?' cried the Cardinal with intense anxiety.

'It were as well to die as live what he now is!' said the
Père solemnly.

'Have the doctors seen him?—has Fabrichetto been with
him?'

'No, sir. It is no case for their assistance, my own poor
skill can teach me so much. His is the malady of the
wounded spirit and the injured mind.'

'Is his reason affected?' asked Caraffa quickly.

'I trust not; but it is a case where time and care can be
the only physicians.'

'And so, therefore, falls to the ground the grand edifice
you have so long been rearing. The great foundation itself
is rotten.'

'He may recover, sir,' said Massoni slowly.

'To what end, I ask you, to what end?'

'At least to claim a princely heritage,' said Massoni boldly.

'Who says so?—of what heritage do you speak? You are

surely too wise to put faith in the idle stories men repeat of this or that legacy left by the late Prince.'

'I know enough, sir, to be sure that I speak on good authority; and I repeat that when this youth can prove his descent, he is the rightful heir to a royal fortune. It may be, that he will have higher and nobler ambitions: he may feel that a great cause is ever worthy a great effort; that the son of a prince cannot accept life on the same humble terms as other men. In short, sir, it may chance that the dream of a poor Jesuit father should become a grand reality.'

'If all be but as real as the heritage, Massoni,' said the Cardinal scoffingly, 'you called it by its true name, when you said "dream."'

'Have you, then, not heard of this legacy?'

'Heard of it! Yes: all Rome heard of it; and, for that matter, his Royal Highness may have left him St. James's and the royal forest of Windsor.'

'Your Eminence, then, doubts that there was anything to bequeath?'

'There is no need to canvass what I *doubt*. I'll tell you what I *know*. The rent of the Altieri for the last two years is still unpaid; the servants at Albano have not received their wages, and the royal plate is at this moment pledged in the hands of the Jew Alcaico.'

The Père was silent. The sole effect these stunning tidings had on him was to speculate to what end and with what object the Cardinal said all this. It was not the language he had used a short hour ago with Kelly. Whence, therefore, this change of tone? Why did he now disparage the prospects he had then upheld so highly? These were questions not easily solved in a moment, and Massoni pondered them deeply. The Cardinal had begun with hinting doubts of the youth's identity, and then he had scoffed at the prospect of his inheritance. Was it that by these he meant to discourage the scheme of which he should have been the head, or was it that some deeper and more subtle plan occupied his mind? And if so, what could it be?

'I see how I have grieved and disappointed you, Père Massoni,' said his Eminence, 'and I regret it. Life is little else than a tale of such reverses.'

The Jesuit's dark eyes glanced forth a gleam of intense intelligence. It was the light of a sudden thought that flashed across his brain. He remembered that when the Cardinal moralised he meant a treachery, and now he stood on his guard.

'I had many things to tell your Eminence of Ireland,' he began in a calm, subdued voice. 'The priest Carrol has just come from thence, and can speak of events as he has witnessed them. The hatred to England and English rule increases every day, and the great peril is that this animosity may burst forth without guidance or direction. The utmost efforts of the leaders are required to hold the people back.'

'They never can wish for a fitter moment. England has her hands full, and can scarcely spare a man to repress rebellion in Ireland.'

'The Irish have not any organisation among them. Remember, your Eminence, that they have been held like a people in slavery: the gentry discredited, the priests insulted. The first efforts of such a race cannot have the force of union or combination. They must needs be desultory and partisan, and if they cannot obtain aid from others, they will speedily be repressed.'

'What sort of aid?'

'Arms and money; they have neither. Of men there is no want. Men of military knowledge and skill will also be required; but more even than these, they need the force that foreign sympathy would impart to their cause. Carrol, who knows the country well, says that the bare assurance that Rome looked on the coming struggle with interest would be better than ten thousand soldiers in their ranks. Divided, as they are, by seas from all the world, they need the encouragement of this sympathy to assure them of success.'

'They are brave, are they not?'

'Their courage has never been surpassed.'

'And true and faithful to each other ?'

'A fidelity that cannot be shaken.'

'Have they no jealousies or petty rivalries to divide them ?'

'None—or next to none. The deadly hatred to the Saxon buries all discords between them.'

'What want they more than this, then, to achieve independence ? Surely no army that England can spare could meet a people thus united ?'

'The struggle is far from an equal one between a regular force and a mere multitude. But let us suppose that they should conquer: who is to say to what end the success may be directed ? There are fatal examples abroad. Is it to establish the infidelity of France men should thus sell their lives ? Is it standing here as we do now, in the city and stronghold of the Church, that we can calmly contemplate a conflict that may end in worse than a heresy ?'

'There cannot be worse than some heresies,' broke in the Cardinal.

'Be it so; but here might be the cradle of many. The sympathy long entertained toward France would flood the land with all her doctrines; and this island, where the banner of faith should be unfurled, may become a fastness of the infidel.'

'*Magna est veritas et prevalebit*,' exclaimed the Cardinal sententiously.

'Anything will "prevail" if you have grape and canister to enforce it. Falsehood as well as truth only needs force to make it victorious.'

'For a while—for a short while—holy father.'

'What is human life but a short while ? But to our theme. Are we to aid these men or not ? It is for our flag they are fighting now. Shall we suffer them to transfer their allegiance ?'

'The storm is about to break, your Eminence,' said the Cardinal's major-domo, as he presented himself suddenly. 'Shall I order the carriages back to the stables ?'

'No; I am ready. I shall set out at once. You shall

hear from me to-morrow or next day, Massoni,' said he, in a low whisper; 'or, better still, if you could come out to Albano to see me.'

The Père bowed deeply without speaking.

'These are not matters to be disposed of in a day or an hour; we must have time.'

The Père bowed again and withdrew. As he turned his steps homeward his thoughts had but one subject. 'What was the game his Eminence was bent on? What scheme was he then revolving in his mind?'

Once more beside the sick-bed of young Gerald, all Massoni's fears for the future came back. What stuff was there in that poor, broken-spirited youth, whose meaningless stare now met him, of which to make the leader in a perilous enterprise? Every look, every gesture, but indicated a temperament soft, gentle, and compliant; and if by chance he uttered a stray word, it was spoken timidly and distrustfully, like one who feared to give trouble. Never did there seem a case where the material was less suited for the purpose for which it was meant; and the Père gazed down at him as he lay in deep and utter despondency. In the immense difficulty of the case all its interest reposed; and he felt what a triumph it would be could he only resuscitate that dying youth, and make him the head of a great achievement. It was a task that might try all his resources, and he resolved to attempt it.

We will not weary our reader with the uneventful story of that recovery : the progress so painfully slow that its steps were imperceptible, and the change which gradually converted the state of fatuity to one of speculation, and finally brought the youth out of sickness and suffering, and made him—weak and delicate, of course—able to feel enjoyment in life and eager for its pleasures. If Gerald could never fathom the mystery of all the care bestowed upon him, nor guess why he was thus tended and watched, as little could the Père Massoni comprehend the strange features of that intellect which each day's experience continued to reveal to him. Through all the womanly tenderness of his character there ran a vein of romantic aspiration, undirected and unguided, it is true, but which gave promise of an ambitious spirit. That some great enterprise had been the dream of his early youth—some adventurous career—seemed a fixed notion with himself; and why, and how, and wherefore its accomplishment had been interrupted, was the difficulty that often occupied his thoughts for hours. In his vain endeavours to trace back events, snatches of his early life would rise to his memory: his sick-bed at the Tana; his wanderings in the Maremma; the simple songs of Marietta; the spirit-stirring verses of Alfieri; and through these, as dark clouds lowering over a sunny landscape, the bitter lessons of Gabriel Riquetti—his cold sarcasm and his disbelief. For all vicissitudes of the youth's life the Père was prepared, but not for that strange discursive reading of which his memory was filled; and it was not easy to understand by what accident his mind had been stored with snatches of Jacobite songs, passages from Pascal, dreary reveries of Jean Jacques, and heroic scenes of Alfieri.

Led on to study the singular character of the youth's mind, Massoni conceived for him at length a strong affection; but though recognising how much of good and amiable there was in his disposition, he saw, too, that the intellect had been terribly disturbed, and that the dreadful scenes he had gone through had left indelible traces upon him.

Scarcely a day passed that the Père did not change his mind about him. At one moment he would feel confident that Gerald was the very stuff they needed—bold, high-hearted, and daring; at the next, he would sink in despondency over the youth's childlike waywardness, his uncertainty, and his capriciousness. There was really no fixity of character about him; and even in his most serious moods, droll and absurd images would present themselves to his mind, and turn at once all the current of his thoughts. While weeks rolled over thus, the Père continued to assure the Cardinal that the young man was gradually gaining in health and strength, and that even his weakly, convalescent state gave evidence of traits that offered noble promise of a great future.

Knowing all the importance of the first impression the youth should make on his Eminence, the Père continued by various pretexts to defer the day of the meeting; and the Cardinal, though anxious to see Gerald, feared to precipitate matters.

CHAPTER XII

A JESUIT'S STROKE OF POLICY

ALTHOUGH Massoni desired greatly to inform his young guest on all the circumstances of his parentage and his supposed rights, he perceived all the importance of letting that communication come from the Cardinal Caraffa. It was not merely that the youth would himself be more impressed by the tidings, but that the Cardinal would be so much the more pledged to the cause in which he had so far interested himself.

To accomplish this project, the Jesuit had recourse to all his address, since his Eminence continued to maintain a policy of strict reserve, pledging himself to nothing, and simply saying: 'When I have seen him, and spoken with him, it will be time enough to give an opinion as to the future.'

To this Massoni objected, by alluding to the evil effect of such want of confidence.

'He will be a prince with royal rights and belongings one of these days; and he will not forget the cold reserve of all this policy; whereas, on the other hand, he would never cease to remember with gratitude him from whose lips he first learned his good fortune.'

He urged these and similar arguments with all his zeal, but yet unsuccessfully; and it was only at last, when he said that he would appeal to the Cardinal York, that Caraffa yielded, and agreed to concede to his wishes.

The Père had procured copies of various documents which established the marriage of Prince Charles Edward with Grace Fitzgerald of Cappa Glynn; a record of the baptism of Gerald, who was born at Marne, in Brittany; several letters in the handwriting of the Prince, acknowledging his marriage, and speaking of his child as one some day or other to enjoy a princely state; and a fragment of a letter from Grace herself, in which she speaks of the cruelty of asking her to surrender the proofs of her marriage, and pleads in the name of her boy for its recognition. Another letter from her, evidently in answer to one from the Cardinal York, whose intercession she had entreated, gave some most touching details of her life of poverty and privation, and the straits by which she avoided the discovery of a secret which to herself would have been the source of greatness and high station. Numerous letters in the handwriting of the Cardinal Gualterio also showed the unavailing efforts made by the Prince's family to induce her to give a formal denial to the reputed marriage: in these, frequent mention was made of the splendid compensation that would be made to Grace Fitzgerald if she relinquished her claim, and the total inutility of persisting to sustain it.

All these documents had been obtained by Carrol, either original or copied, from the Fitzgeralds of Cappa Glynn. Most of these had been in Grace's own possession, and some had been brought from Rome by Fra Luke, when he left that city for Ireland. A list of these papers, with their contents, had been furnished to the Cardinal Caraffa, accompanied by a short paper drawn up by Massoni himself. In this 'memoir,' the Père had distinctly shown that the question of the youth's legitimacy was indisputable, and that even if his Eminence demurred to the project of making him the head of a great political movement, his right as heir to the Prince could not be invalidated.

The Cardinal bestowed fully three weeks over these records before he gave any reply to Massoni, and then he answered in a tone of half-careless and discouraging meaning, 'that the papers were curious—interesting too—from the high station of many of the writers, but evidently deficient as proofs of a matter so pregnant with great results.' He hinted also, that from the wayward, adventurous kind of life Charles Edward led, a charge of this nature would not be difficult to make, and even support by every plausible evidence of its truth ; and lastly, he assured the Père that the will of his Royal Highness contained no allusion to such an heir, nor any provision for him.

'You seem to make a point of my seeing the youth, to which I do not perceive there is any objection, but that you couple it with the condition of my making him the momentous communication of his birth and rank. Surely, you cannot mean that on the vague evidence now before me, I am to pledge myself to these facts, and indorse documents so unsubstantiated as these are ? As to your opening any communication with the Cardinal York, I cannot listen to it. His Eminence is in the most precarious state of health, and his nervous irritability so intense, that any such step on your part would be highly indiscreet. If, therefore, it be your determination to take this course, mine is as firmly adopted, to withdraw altogether from any interest in the affair. The earlier I learn from you which line you intend to pursue, the more agreeable it will be to —Your very true friend,   CARAFFA, Cardinal.'

Massoni returned no reply to this letter. The crafty father saw that the threat of addressing the Cardinal York had so far affrighted Caraffa, that he was sure to come to any terms that might avoid this contingency. To leave this menace to work slowly, gradually, and powerfully into his mind, Massoni at once decided.

When, therefore, after a week's silence, the Cardinal sent him a few lines to intimate that his former letter remained unanswered, the Père simply said, that his Eminence's letter was one which, in his humility, he could only reflect over, and not answer.

The day after he had despatched this, a plain carriage, without arms, and the servants in dark grey liveries, drove into the college, and the Cardinal Caraffa got out of it, and asked to see the Rector.

With a cheek slightly flushed, and a haughty step, Caraffa entered the little library, where the Père was seated at study, and though Massoni's reception was marked by every observance of respectful humility, his Eminence sharply said—

'You carry your head high, Père Massoni. You have a haughty spirit. Is it that your familiarity with Royalty has taught you to treat Cardinals thus cavalierly ?'

'I am the humblest slave and servant of your Eminence,' was the submissive answer, as with arms crossed upon his breast and head bent forward, Massoni stood before him.

'I should be sorry to have a whole household of such material,' said the Cardinal with a supercilious smile; then, after a moment, and in an easier, lighter tone of banter he said : 'And his Royal Highness, Père, how is he ?'

'The Prince is better, your Eminence: he is able to walk about the garden, where he is at this moment.'

'The cares of his estate have not, I trust, interfered with his recovery,' said Caraffa in the same accent of mockery.

'If he does not yet know them,' said Massoni gravely, 'it is because in my deference to your Eminence I have waited for yourself to make the communication.'

'Are you still decided, then, that he must be of royal race ?'

'I see no reason why he should be robbed of his birthright.'

'Would you make him the heir of Charles Edward ?'

'He is so.'

'King of England, too ?'

'If legitimacy mean anything, he is that also.'

'Arnulph tells us, that when a delusion gets hold of a strong intellect, it grows there like an oak that has its roots in a rock: its progress slow, its development difficult, but its tenacity ineradicable.'

'Your Eminence's logic would be excellent in its application, but that you have assumed the whole question at issue! Are you so perfectly sure that this is a delusion?'

'Let us talk like men of the world, Père Massoni,' said Caraffa bluntly. 'If this tale be all true, what interest has it for you or me?'

'Its truth, your Eminence,' said the Père, with a gesture of deep humility, as though by a show of respect to cover the bold rebuke of his words.

'So far, of course, it claims our sympathy and our support,' said Caraffa, reddening; 'but my question was addressed rather to what would carry a more worldly signification. I meant, in short, to what object could it contribute for which we are interested?'

'I have already, and at great length, explained to your Eminence, the importance of connecting the great convulsion of the day, with a movement in favour of monarchy and the Church. When men wandered from the one, they deserted the other. Let us see if the beacon that lights to the throne should not show the path to the shrine also.'

'You would assuredly accept a very humble instrument to begin your work with.'

'A fisherman and a tent-maker sustained a grander cause against a whole world!'

The Cardinal started. He was not, for a second or two, quite satisfied that the reply was devoid of profanity. The calm seriousness of Massoni's face, however, showed that the speech was not uttered in a spirit of levity.

'Père Massoni,' said the Cardinal seriously, 'let us bethink ourselves well ere we are committed to the cause of this youth. Are we so sure that it is a charge will repay us?'

'I have given the matter the best and maturest reflection,' said the Père; 'I have tested it in all ways as a question of right, of justice, and of expediency; I have weighed its influence on the present, and its consequences on the future; and I see no obstacles or difficulties, save such as present themselves where a great work is to be achieved.'

'Had you lived in as close intimacy with the followers of

the Stuarts as I have, Massoni, you would pause ere you linked the fortunes of an enterprise with a family so un-lucky. Do you know,' added he earnestly, 'there was scarcely a mishap of the last expedition not directly traceable to the Prince.'

The Père shook his head in dissent.

'You have not then heard, as I have, of his rashness, his levity, his fickleness, and worse than all these, his obstinacy.'

'There is not one of these qualities without another name,' said the Père, with a sad smile; 'and they would read as truthfully if called bravery, high-heartedness, versatility, and resolution; but were it all as your Eminence says, it matters not. Here is an enterprise totally different. The cause of the Stuarts appealed to the chivalry of a people, and what a mere fragment of a nation accepts or recognises such a sympathy! The cause of the Church will appeal to all that calls itself Catholic. The great element of failure in the Jacobite cause was that it never was a religious struggle: it was the assertion of legitimacy, the rights of a dynasty; and the question of the Faith was only an incident of the conflict. Here,' he added proudly, 'it will be otherwise, and the greatest banner in the fight will be inscribed with a cross!'

'Prince Charles Edward failed, with all the aid of France to back him; and how is his son—if he be his son—to succeed, who has no ally, no wealth, and no prestige?'

'And do you not know that it was France and French treachery that wrecked the cause of the Stuarts? Did not the Cardinal Gualterio detect the secret correspondence between the Tuileries and St. James's? Is it not on record that the expedition was delayed three days in sailing, to give time to transmit intelligence to the English government?'

'These are idle stories, Massoni; Gualterio only dreamed them.'

'Mayhap it was also a dream that the Prince was ordered to quit Paris in twenty-four hours, and the soil of France within a week, at the express demand of England?'

'What you now speak of was a later policy, ignoble and mean, I admit.'

'But why waste time on the past? Has your Eminence read the memoir I sent you?'

'I have.'

'Have you well and duly weighed the importance attached to the different character of the present scheme from all that has preceded it, and how much that character is likely to derive support from the peculiarity of the Irish temperament?'

'Yes. It is a people eminently religious: steadfast in the faith.'

'Have you well considered that if this cause be not made our own it will be turned against us; that the agents of Irish independence—Tone, Teeling, Jackson, and other—are in close communication with the French government, and earnestly entreating them to despatch an expedition to Ireland?'

'This would be indeed fatal to us,' said Caraffa despondingly.

'And yet it is what will assuredly happen if we do not intervene.'

'But can we prevent it?'

'I believe we can. I believe there is even yet time to make the struggle our own. But if there is not—if it be too late—we shall have a great game to play. A Protestant rising must never have our support! Better far for us to turn to the government and by this ostentatious show of our allegiance, lay foundation for future demands and concessions.'

The Cardinal bent his head twice in approval.

'All these things, however, combine to show that we must be up and stirring. Many who would be with us, if they were sure of our going forward, will take service with Tone and his party, if we delay. Carrol himself was pledged to report in person to the secret committee at Waterford by the eighth of the month, and we are now at the seventeenth. These delays are serious! This letter from Hussey, which

only reached me last night, will show your Eminence how
eagerly our answer is awaited.'

The Cardinal made a gesture of impatience, as he declined
the proffered letter.

'It is not,' said he, 'by such considerations we are to be
swayed, Massoni.'

'Hussey insists on knowing whether or not your Eminence
is with them,' said the Père boldly, 'and if you have recognised the young Prince.'

'So, then, he knows of your secret,' said the Cardinal with
a sly malice.

'He knew of this youth's birth and station ere I did myself: he was the confessor of the Fitzgerald family, and
attended Grace on her deathbed.'

'Hussey, then, believes this story?'

'He would swear to its truth, your Eminence.'

'He is a crafty fellow, and one not easily to be deceived,'
said Caraffa, musing. 'Let me see his letter.'

He took the letter from the Père, and perused it carefully.

'I see little in this,' said he, handing it back, 'that you
have not already told me.'

'I have endeavoured to make your Eminence acquainted
with everything that occurred,' said Massoni with downcast
eyes, but yet contriving to watch the countenance of the
other attentively.

'Monsignor Hussey, then, recommends in case of any
backwardness—such is his phrase—that you yourself should
reveal to this youth the story of his descent. Have you
thought over this counsel?'

'I have, your Eminence.'

'Well, and to what conclusion has it led you?'

'That there was no other course open to me,' said Massoni
firmly.

The Cardinal's brow darkened, and he turned upon the
Père a look of insolent defiance.

'So, then, Père Massoni, this is to be a trial of skill
between us; but I will not accept the challenge, sir. It is

X

without shame that I confess myself unequal to a Jesuit in craftiness.'

The Père never spoke, but stood with arms crossed and bent-down head as if in thought.

'It must be owned, sir,' continued Caraffa scoffingly, 'that you have no craven spirit. Most men, situated as you are, would have hesitated ere they selected for their adversary a Prince of the Church.'

Still was Massoni silent.

'While, as to your *protégé*, with one word of mine to the Minister of Police, he would be driven out of Rome—out of the States of the Church—as a vagabond.'

The word had scarcely been uttered, when the door opened, and Gerald stood before them. For an instant he hesitated, abashed at his intrusion; but Massoni stepped hastily forward, and taking his hand, said—

'Your Eminence, this is the Chevalier!'

Caraffa, who had known Charles Edward in his early life, stood actually like one thunderstruck before the youth, so exactly was he his counterpart. His full and soft blue eyes, the long silky hair of a rich brown colour, falling heavily on his neck, the mouth, half pouting and half proud, and the full chin, roundly moulded as a woman's, were all there; while in his air and mien a resemblance no less striking was apparent. By artful thoughtfulness of the Jesuit father, the youth's dress was made to assist the schemes, for it was a suit of black velvet, such as Charles Edward used to wear when a young man; a blue silk under-vest, barely appearing, gave the impression that it was the ribbon of the garter, which the young Prince rarely laid aside.

Not all the eloquence and all the subtlety of Massoni could have accomplished the result which was in a moment effected by that apparition; and as Gerald stood half timidly, half haughtily there, Caraffa bowed low, and with all the deference he would have accorded to superior rank. For a second the dark eyes of the Jesuit flashed a gleam of triumph, but the next moment his look was calm and composed. The crafty Père saw that the battle was won if the struggle could be but concluded at once, and so, addressing Gerald in a tone of marked deference, he said—

'I have long wished for the day when I should see this meeting; that its confidence may be unbroken and undisturbed, I will withdraw,' and with a separate reverence to each, the Père backed to the door and retired.

Whatever suspicions might have occurred to the Cardinal's mind had he but time for reflection, there was now no opportunity to indulge. All had happened so rapidly, and above all there was still the spell over him of that resemblance, which seemed every moment to increase; such indeed was its influence, that it at once routed all the considerations of his prudent reserve, and made him forget everything save that he stood in the presence of a Stuart.

'If I am confused, sir, and agitated,' began he, 'at this our first meeting, lay it to the account of the marvellous resemblance by which you recall my recollection of the Prince, your father. I knew him when he was about your own age, and when he graciously distinguished me by many marks of his favour.'

'My father!' said Gerald, over whose face a deep crimson blush first spread, and then a pallor equally great succeeded—'did you say my father?'

'Yes, sir. It was my fortune to be associated closely with his Royal Highness at St. Germains and afterward in Auvergne.'

Overcome by his feeling of amazement at what he heard, and yet unable to summon calmness to inquire further, Gerald sank into a chair, vainly trying to collect his faculties. Meanwhile Caraffa continued—

'As an old man and a priest I may be forgiven for yielding slowly to convictions, and for what almost would seem a reluctance to accept as fact the evidence of your birth and station; but your presence, sir—your features as you sit there, the image of your father—appeal to something more subtle than my reason, and I feel that I am in the presence of a Stuart. Let me, then, be the first to offer the homage that is, or at least one day will be, your right'; and so saying, the Cardinal took Gerald's hand and pressed it to his lips.

'Is this a dream?' muttered Gerald, half aloud—'is my brain wandering?'

'No, sir, you are awake; the past has been the dream—the long years of sorrow and poverty—the trials and perils of your life of accident and adventure—this has been the dream; but you are now awake to learn that you are the true-born descendant of a Royal House—a Prince of the Stuarts—the legitimate heir to a great throne!'

'I beseech you, sir,' cried Gerald, in a voice broken by emotion, while the tears filled his eyes, 'I beseech you, sir, not to trifle with the feelings of one whose heart has been so long the sport of fortune, that any, even the slightest shock, may prove too powerful for his strength.'

'You are, sir, all that I have said. My age and the dress I wear may be my guarantees that I do not speak idly nor rashly.'

A long-drawn sigh burst from the youth, and with it he fainted.

CHAPTER XIII

THE PÈRE MASSONI'S MISGIVINGS

IT was late at night, and all quiet and still in the Eternal City, as the Père Massoni sat in his little study intent upon a large map which occupied the whole table before him. Strange blotches of colour marked in various places, patches of blue and deep red, with outlines the most irregular appeared here and there, leaving very little of the surface without some tint. It was a map of Ireland, on which the successive confiscations were marked, and the various changes of proprietorship indicated by different colours; a curious document, carefully drawn up, and which had cost the labour

of some years. Massoni studied it with such deep intensity
that he had not noticed the entrance of a servant, who now
stood waiting to deliver a letter which he held in his hand.
At last he perceived the man, and, hastily snatching the note,
read to himself the following few lines—

'She will come to-morrow at noon. Give orders to admit
her at once to him ; but do not yourself be there.'

This was signed 'D,' and carefully folded and sealed.

'That will do; you need not wait,' said the Père, and
again he was alone. For several minutes he continued to
ponder over the scenes before him, and then, throwing them
on the table, exclaimed aloud, 'And this is the boasted
science of medicine! Here is the most learned physician of
all Rome—the trusted of Popes and Cardinals—confessing
that there are phases of human malady to which, while his
art gives no clue—a certain mysterious agency—a something
compounded of imposture and fanaticism, can read and
decipher. What an ignoble avowal is this, and what a
sarcasm upon all intellect and its labours! And what will
be said of me,' cried he, in a louder voice, 'if it be known
that I have lent my credence to such a doctrine ; that I, the
head and leader of a great association, should stoop to take
counsel from those who, if they be not cheats and impostors,
must needs be worse! And, if worse, what then?' muttered
he, as he drew his hand across his brow as though to clear
away some difficult and distressing thought. 'Ay, what then?
Are there really diabolic agencies at work in those ministra-
tions? Are these miraculous revelations that we hear of
ascribable to evil influences? What if it were not trick and
legerdemain? What if Satan had really seized upon these
passers of base money to mingle his own coinage with theirs?
If every imposture be his work, why should he not act
through those who have contrived it? Oh, if we could but
know what are the truthful suggestions of inspirations, and
what the crafty devices of an erring brain! If, for instance,
I could now see how far the great cause to which my life is
devoted should be served or thwarted by the enterprise.'

He walked the room for nigh an hour in deep and silent meditation.

'I will see her myself,' cried he at length. 'All her stage tricks and cunning will avail her little with *me*; and if she really have high powers, why should they not be turned to our use? When Satan piled evil upon evil to show his strength, St. Francis made of the mass an altar? Well, now, Giacomo, what is it?' asked he suddenly, as his servant entered.

'He has fallen asleep at last, reverend father,' answered he, 'and is breathing softly as a child. He cannot fail to be better for this repose, for it is now five days and nights since he has closed an eye.'

'Never since the night of the reception at Cardinal Abbezi's.'

'That was a fatal experiment, I much fear,' muttered Giacomo.

'It may have been so. Who knows—who ever did or could know with certainty the one true path out of difficulty?'

'When he came back on that night,' continued Giacomo, 'he would not suffer me to undress him, but threw himself down on the bed as he was, saying, "Leave me to myself; I would be alone."

'I offered to take off his sword and the golden collar of his order, but he bade me angrily to desist, and said—

'"These are all that remind me of what I am, and you would rob me of them."'

'True enough; the pageantry was a brief dream! And what said he next?'

'He talked wildly about his cruel fortunes, and the false friends who had misguided him in his youth, saying—

'"These things never came of blind chance; the destinies of princes are written in letters of gold, and not traced in the sands of the sea. They who betrayed my father have misled *me*."'

'How like his house,' exclaimed the Père; 'arrogant in the very hour of their destitution!'

'He then went on to rave about the Scottish wars, speaking of places and people I had never before heard of. After lamenting the duplicity of Spain, and declaring that French treachery had been their ruin, "and now," cried he, "the game is to be played over again, as though it were in the day of general demolition men would struggle to restore a worn-out dynasty."'

'Did he speak thus?' cried Massoni eagerly.

'Yes, he said the words over and over, adding, "I am but the 'figurino,' to be laid aside when the procession is over," and he wept bitterly.'

'The Stuarts could always find comfort in tears; they could draw upon their own sympathies unfailingly. What said he of *me*?' asked he, with sudden eagerness.

Giacomo was silent, and folding his arms within his robe of serge, cast his eyes downward.

'Speak out, and frankly—what said he?' repeated the Père.

'That you were ambitious—one whose heart yearned after worldly elevation and power.'

'Power—yes!' muttered the Père.

'That once engaged in a cause, your energies would be wholly with it, so long as you directed and guided it; that he had known men of your stamp in France during the Revolution, and that the strength of their convictions was more often a source of weakness than of power.'

'It was from Gabriel Riquetti that he stole the remark. It was even thus Mirabeau spoke of our order.'

'You must be right, reverend father, for he continued to talk much of this same Riquetti, saying that he alone, of all Europe, could have restored the Stuarts to England. "Had we one such man as that," said he, "I now had been lying in Holyrood Palace."'

'He was mistaken there,' muttered Massoni half aloud. 'The men who are without faith raise no lasting edifices. How strange,' added he aloud, 'that the Prince should have spoken in this wise. When I have been with him he was ever wandering, uncertain, incoherent.'

'And into this state he gradually lapsed, singing snatches of peasant songs to himself, and mingling Scottish rhymes with Alfieri's verses; sometimes fancying himself in all the wild conflict of a street-fight in Paris, and then thinking that he was strolling along a river's bank with some one that he loved.'

'Has he then loved?' asked Massoni in a low, distinct voice.

'From chance words that have escaped him in his wanderings I have gathered as much, though who she was and whence, or what her station in life, I cannot guess.'

'She will tell us this,' muttered the Père to himself; and then turning to Giacomo said, 'To-morrow, at noon, that woman they call the Egyptian Princess is to be here; she is to come in secret to see him. The Prince of Piombino has arranged it all, and says that her marvellous gift is never in fault, all hearts being open to her as a printed page, and men's inmost thoughts as legible as their features.'

'Is it an evil possession?' asked Giacomo tremblingly.

'Who can dare to say so? Let us wait and watch. Take care that the small door that opens from the garden upon the Pincian be left ajar, as she will come by that way; and let there be none to observe or note her coming. You will yourself meet her at the gate, and conduct her to his chamber—where leave her.'

'If Rome should hear that we have accepted such aid——'

A gesture of haughty contempt from the Père interrupted the speech, and Massoni said—

'Are not they with troubled consciences frequent visitors at our shrines? Might not this woman come, as thousands have come, to have a doubt removed; a case of conscience satisfied; a heresy arrested? Besides, she is a Pagan,' added he suddenly; 'may she not be one eager to seek the truth?' The cold derision of his look, as he spoke, awed the simple servitor, who, meekly bending his head, retired.

CHAPTER XIV

THE EGYPTIAN

OUR reader is already fully aware of the reasons which influenced the Père Massoni to adopt the cause of young Fitzgerald. It was not any romantic attachment to an ancient and illustrious house; as little was it any conviction of a right. It was simply an expedient which seemed to promise largely for the one cause which the Jesuit father deemed worthy of a man's life-long devotion—the Church. To impart to the terrible struggle which in turn ravaged every country in Europe a royalist feature, seemed, to his thoughtful mind, the one sole issue of present calamity. His theory was: after the homage to the throne will come back reverence to the altar.

For a while the Père suffered himself to indulge in the most sanguine hopes of success. Throughout Europe generally men were wearied of that chaotic condition which the French Revolution had introduced, and already longed for the reconstruction of society in some shape or other. By the influence of able agents, the Church had contrived to make her interest in the cause of order perceptible, and artfully suggested the pleasant contrast of a society based on peace and harmony, with the violence and excess of a revolutionary struggle.

Had the personal character of young Gerald been equal, in Massoni's estimation, to the emergency, the enterprise might have been deemed most hopeful. If the youth had been daring, venturous, and enthusiastic, heedless of consequences and an implicit follower of the Church, much might have been made of him; out of his sentiment of religious devotion would have sprung a deference and a trustfulness which would have rendered him manageable. But, though he was all these, at times, he was fifty other things as well.

There was not a mood of the human mind that did not visit him in turns, and while one day would see him grave, earnest, and thoughtful, dignified in manner, and graceful in address, on the next he would appear reckless and indifferent, a scoffer, and a sceptic. The old poisons of his life at the Tana still lingered in his system and corrupted his blood; and if, for a moment, some high-hearted ambition would move him—some chivalrous desire for great things—so surely would come back the terrible lesson of Mirabeau to his mind, and distrust darken, with its ill-omened frown, all that had seemed bright and glorious.

After the first burst of proud elation on discovering his birth and lineage, he became thoughtful and serious, and at times sad. He dwelt frequently and painfully upon the injustice with which his early youth was treated, and seemed fully to feel that, if some political necessity—of what kind he could not guess—had not rendered the acknowledgment convenient, his claims might still have slept on, unrecognised and unknown. Among his first lessons in life Mirabeau had instilled into him a haughty defiance of all who would endeavour to use him as a tool.

'Remember,' he would say, 'that the men who achieve success in life the oftenest, are they who trade upon the faculties of others. Beware of these men; for their friendship is nothing less than a servitude.'

'To what end, for what object, am I now withdrawn from obscurity?' were his constant questions to himself. The priest and his craft were objects of his greatest suspicion, and the thought of being a mere instrument to their ends was a downright outrage. In this way, Massoni was regarded by him with intense distrust; nor could even his gratitude surmount the dread he felt for the Jesuit father. These sentiments deepened, as he lay, hours long, awake at night till, at length, a low fever seized him, and long intervals of dreary incoherency would break the tenor of his sounder thoughts. It had been deemed expedient by the Cardinal York and his other friends that young Gerald should continue to reside at the Jesuit College till some definite steps were taken to declare his rank to the world, and the very delay in this announcement was another reason of suspicion.

'If I be the prince you call me, why am I detained in this imprisonment? Why am I not among my equals; why not confronted with some future that I can look boldly in the face? Would they make a priest of me, as they have done with my uncle? Where are the noble-hearted followers who rallied around my father? Where the brave adherents who never deserted even his exile? Are they all gone, or have they died, and, if so, is not the cause itself dead?'

These and suchlike were the harassing doubts that troubled him, until eventually his mind balanced between a morbid irritability and an intense apathy. The most learned physicians of Rome had been called to see him, but, though in a great measure agreeing in the nature of his case, none succeeded in suggesting any remedy for it. Some advised society, travelling, amusement, and so on. Others were disposed to recommend rest and quietude; others, again, deemed that he should be engaged in some scheme or enterprise likely to awaken his ambition; but all these plans had soon to give place to immediate cares for his condition, for his strength was perceived to be daily declining, and his energy of body as well as of mind giving way. For some days back the Père had debated with himself whether he would not unfold to him the grand enterprise which he meditated; point out to the youth the glorious opportunity of future distinction, and the splendid prize which should reward success. He would have revealed the whole plot long before had he not been under a pledge to the Cardinal Caraffa not to divulge it without his sanction, and in his presence; and now came the question of Gerald's life, and whether he would survive till the return of his Eminence from Paris, whither he had gone to fetch back his niece. Such was the state of things when Doctor Danizetti declared that medicine had exhausted its resources in the youth's behalf, and suggested, as a last resource, that a certain Egyptian lady, whose marvellous powers had attracted all the attention of Rome, should be called in to see him, and declare what she thought of his case.

This Egyptian Princess, as report called her, had taken up her abode at a small deserted convent near Albano, living a life of strict retirement, and known only to the peasants of the neighbourhood by the extraordinary cures she had performed, and the wonderful recoveries which her instrumentality had effected. The secrecy of her mode of life, and the impossibility of learning any details of her history, added to the fact that no one had yet seen her unveiled, gave a romantic interest to her which soon spread into a sort of fame. Besides these, the most astonishing tales were told of epileptic cases cured, deaf and dumb men restored to hearing and speech, even instances of insanity successfully treated, so that, at length, the little shrines of patron saints, once so devoutly sought after by worshipping believers, praying that St. Agatha or St. Nasala might intercede on their behalf, were now forsaken, and crowds gathered in the little court of the convent eagerly entreating the Princess to look favourably on their sufferings. These facts—at first only whispered—at length gained the ears of Rome, and priests and cardinals began to feel that out of this trifling incident grave consequences might arise, and counsel was held among them whether this dangerous foreigner should not be summarily sent out of the State.

The decision would, doubtless, have been quickly come to had it not been that at the very moment an infant child of the Prince Altieri owed its life to a suggestion made by the Egyptian, to whom a mere lock of the child's hair was given. Sorcery or not, here was a service that could not be overlooked; and, as the Prince Altieri was one whose influence spread widely, the thought of banishment was abandoned.

The Père Massoni, who paid at first but little attention to the stories of her wondrous powers, was at length astonished on hearing from the Professor Danizetti some striking

instances of her skill, which seemed, however, less that of
a consummate physician than of one who had studied the
mysterious influences of the moral over the material part
of our nature. It was in estimating how far the mind
swayed and controlled the nervous system, whether they
acted in harmony or discordance, seemed her great gift; and
to such a degree of perfection had she brought her powers
in this respect, that the tones of a voice, the expression of
an eye, and the texture of the hair, appeared often sufficient
to intimate the fate of the sick man. Danizetti confessed,
that, though long a sceptic as to her powers, he could no
longer resist the force of what he witnessed, and owned that
in her art were secrets unrevealed to science.

He had made great efforts to see and to know her, but in
vain; indeed she did not scruple to confess, that for medicine
and its regular followers, she had slight respect. She deemed
them as walkers in the dark, and utterly lost to the only
lights which could elucidate disease. Through the Prince
Altieri's intervention, for he had met her in the East, she
consented to visit the Jesuit College, somewhat proud, it
must be owned, to storm, as it were, the very stronghold of
that incredulity which priestcraft professed for her abilities.
For this reason was it she insisted that her visit should be
paid in open day—at noon. 'I will see none but the sick
man,' said she, 'and yet all shall mark my coming, and
perceive that even these great and learned fathers have
condescended to ask for my presence and my aid. I would
that the world should see how even these holy men can
worship an unknown God!'

Nor did the Père Massoni resent this pride; on the
contrary, he felt disposed to respect it. It was a bold
assumption that well pleased him.

As the hour of her visit drew nigh, Massoni having given
all the directions necessary to ensure secrecy, repaired himself
to the little tower from which a view extended over the
vast campagna. A solitary carriage traversed it on the road
from Albano, and this he watched with unbroken anxiety,

till he saw it enter the gate of Rome, and gradually ascend the Pincian hill.

'The Egyptian has come to her time,' said he to Giacomo: 'yonder is her carriage at the gate; and the youth, is he still sleeping?'

'Yes, he has not stirred for hours; he breathes so lightly that he scarcely seems alive, and his cheeks are colourless as death.'

'There, yonder she comes; she walks like one in the prime of life. She is evidently not old, Giacomo.'

From the window where they stood, they could mark a tall, commanding figure moving slowly along the garden walk, and stopping at moments to gather flowers. A thick black veil concealed in some degree her form, but could not altogether hide the graceful motion with which she advanced.

CHAPTER XV

THE PÈRE AND THE PRINCESS

GERALD was lying on a couch in his habitual mood of half dreamy consciousness, when the Egyptian entered. Her tall and stately figure, veiled to the very feet, moving with a proud but graceful step, seemed scarcely to arrest his notice for a moment, and his eyes fell again upon a few wild-flowers that lay beside him.

Making a sign to the servant that she would be alone, the Egyptian drew nigh the couch, and stood silently regarding him. After a while, she raised one arm till the hand was extended over his head, and held it thus some minutes. He lifted up his eyes toward her, and then, with a sort of wearied motion, dropped them again, heaved a heavy sigh, and seemed to sink into a sleep.

Touching the centre of his forehead with her forefinger, she stood for some minutes motionless; and then slowly passed her hand over his face, and laid it gently on his heart; a slight, scarcely perceptible shudder shook the youth's frame at this instant, and then he was still; so still and so motionless, that he appeared like one dead. She now breathed strongly two or three times over his face, making with her hands a motion, as though sprinkling a fluid over him. As she did so, the youth's lips slightly opened, and something like a faint smile seemed to settle on his features. Bending down she laid her ear close to his lips, like one listening: she waited a few seconds, and then, in a voice that slightly trembled, with a thrill of joyous emotion, she whispered out—

'You have not, then, forgotten, *Gherardi mio*; those happy hours still live within your memory.'

The sleeper's mouth moved without a sound, but she seemed to gather the meaning of the motion: as, after a brief pause, she said: 'And the well under the old myrtle-tree at San Domino: hast forgotten *that*? True enough,' added she, as if replying; 'it seems like an age since we walked that mountain road together; but we will stroll there again, dear brother: nay, start not, thou knowest well why I call thee so. And we will wander along the little stream under the old walls of Massa, beneath the orange-trees; and listen to the cicala in the hot noon, and catch glimpses of the blue sea through the olives. Happier days! that they were. No, no, child,' cried she eagerly; 'thou art not of a mould for such an enterprise; besides, they would but entrap thee—there is no honesty in these men. He that we have lost—he that has left us—might have guided you in this difficult path; but there is not another like him. There are plants that only flower once in a whole century, and so with humanity; great genius only visits the earth after long intervals of years. What is it?' broke she in hurriedly; 'thou seest something; tell me of it?' With an intense eagerness she now seemed to drink in something that his silent lips revealed, a sort of impatient anxiety urging her, as she said, 'And then, and then; yes! a wild dreary waste without a tree; but thou knowest not where—and a light in an old tower high up—yes! watching for thee; they have expected thee; go on. Ah! thou hast arrived there at last; with what honour they receive thee; they fill the hall. No, no, do not let him kneel; thou art right, he is an old, old man. That was a mild cheer, and see how the tears run down his cheeks; they are, indeed, glad to see thee, then. What now,' cried she hurriedly; 'thou wilt not go on, and why? Tell me, then, why, *Gherardi mio*,' cried she, in an accent of deep feeling; 'is it that peril scares thee? Thou a Prince, and not willing to pay for thy heritage by danger? Ah! true,' broke she in despondingly; 'they have made thee but a tool, and they would now make thee a sacrifice.' A long pause now ensued, and she sat with his hand pressed between both her own in silence. At length a slight noise startled her; she turned her head, and beheld the Père Massoni standing close beside her. She arose at once, and drew the folds of her veil more closely across her features.

'Is your visit over? If so, I would speak with you,' said the Père.

She bowed her head in assent, and followed him from the room. Massoni now led the way to the little tower which formed his study; entering which, he motioned her to a seat, and having locked the door, took a place in front of her.

'What say you of this young man?' said he, coldly and sternly. 'Will he live?'

'He will live,' said she, in a low, soft voice.

'For that you pledge yourself; I mean, your skill and craft!'

'I have none, holy father—I have but that insight into human nature which is open to all; but I can promise, that of his present malady he will not die.'

'How call you his disease?'

'Some would name it atrophy; some low fever; some would say that an old hereditary taint was slowly working its poisonous path through a once vigorous frame.'

'How mean you by that; would you imply madness in his race?'

'There are many disordered in mind whom affluence presents as but capricious,' said she, with a half supercilious accent.

'Be frank with me,' said he boldly, 'and say if you suspect derangement here.'

'Holy father,' replied she, in the calm voice of one appealing to a mature judgment, 'you, who read men's natures, as others do a printed page, well know, that he who is animated strongly by some single sentiment, which infuses itself into every thought, and every action, pervading each moment of his daily life, so as to seem a centre around which all events revolve—that such a man, in the world's esteem, is of less sane mind than he who gives to fortune but a passing thought, and makes life a mere game of accident. Between these two opposing states this young man's mind now balances.'

'But cannot balance long,' muttered the Père to himself, reflecting on her words. 'Will his intellect bear the struggle?' asked he hastily.

'Ay, if not overtaxed.'

'I know your meaning; you have told himself that he is not equal to the task before him; I heard and saw what passed between you; I know, too, that you have met before in life; tell me, then, where and how.' There was a frank, intrepid openness in the way he spoke, that seemed to say, · We must deal freely with each other.'

'Of *me* you need not to know anything,' said she proudly, as she arose.

'Not if you had not penetrated a great secret of mine,' said Massoni sternly; 'you cannot deny it—you know who this youth is !'

'I know whom you would make him,' said she, in the same haughty tone.

'What birth and lineage have made him,—not any will of mine.'

'There are miracles too great for even priestcraft, holy father—this is one of them. Nay, I speak not of his birth,

it is of the destiny you purpose for him. Is it now, in the
midst of the glorious outburst of universal freedom, when
men are but awakening out of the long and lethargic dream
of slavery, that you would make them to return to it; would
you call them to welcome back a race whose badge has been
oppression? No, no, your Church is too wise, too far-sighted
for such an error; the age of monarchies is over; take
counsel from the past, and learn that, henceforth, you must
side with the people.'

'So have we ever,' cried the Père enthusiastically; 'yes,
I maintain and will prove it. Stay, you must not part with
me so easily. You shall tell me who you are. This weak
pretence of Egyptian origin deceives not *me*.'

'You shall know nothing of me,' was the brief reply.

'The Sacred Consulta will not accept this answer.'

'They will get none other, father.'

'Such acts as yours are forbidden by the canon law; be
careful how you push me to denounce them.'

'Does the Inquisition still live, then?' asked she superciliously.

'Sorcery is a crime, on the word of Holy Writ, woman;
and again I say, beware!'

'This is scarcely grateful, holy father; I came here to
render you a service.'

'And you are carrying away a secret, woman,' said the
priest angrily. 'This must not be.'

'How would it advantage you, I ask,' said she calmly,
'were I to reveal the whole story of my past life? it would
give you no guarantee for the future.'

'It is for *me* to think of that. I only say, that I must
and will know it.'

'These are words of passion, holy father, not of that wise
forethought for which the world knows and reveres your
name. Farewell.'

She waved her hand haughtily, and moved toward the
door; but it was locked, and resisted her hand. As she
turned to remonstrate, Massoni was gone! How, and by

what exit, she could not guess, since every side of the
small tower was covered with books and shelves, that rose
from the floor to the ceiling, and except the one by which
she entered, no door to be seen. Not a word nor an
exclamation escaped her, as she saw herself thus imprisoned ;
her first care was to examine the windows, which readily
opened, but whose great height from the ground made
escape impossible. She again tried the lock in various ways,
but without success ; and then recommenced a close scrutiny
of the sides of the tower, through which she was aware
there must be some means of exit. So cunningly, however,
was this devised, that it evaded all her search, and she sat
down at length baffled and weary.

The bright noon faded away into the mellower richness
of later day, and the long shadows of solitary trees or
broken columns, stretched far across the Campagna, showing
that the sun was low. While she yet sat silent and watchful in that lonely tower, her eyes had ranged over the
garden beneath, till she knew every bed and pathway.
She had watched the Campagna too, till her sight ached
with the weary toil ; but, except far, far away, long out of
reach, no succour appeared in view ; and it seemed to her,
at times, as though there was something like destiny in this
dreary desolation. On that very morning, as she drove
from Albano, the fields were filled with labourers, and herds
of cattle roved over the great plains, with large troops of
mounted followers. What had become then of these ? The
sudden outburst of a hundred bells, pealing in almost wild
confusion now, broke upon the stillness, and seemed to make
the very walls vibrate with their din. Louder and louder
this grand chorus swelled out, till the sound seemed to rise
from earth to heaven, filling space with their solemn music ;
and, at length, there pealed out through these the glorious
cadences of a rich orchestra, coming nearer and nearer as
she listened. A grand procession soon made its appearance,
issuing out of one of the city gates, and holding its way
across the Campagna. There were banners and gorgeous

canopies, splendidly attired figures walked beneath, and the smoke of incense rose around them in the still calm of a summer's evening. It was, then, some festival of the Church, and to this' was doubtless owing the silence and desertion which reigned over the Campagna.

With a haughty and disdainful motion of her head, the Egyptian turned away from the sight, and seated herself with her back to the window. The greyish tinge of half light that foretells the coming night, was fast falling, as a slight noise startled her. She turned, and beheld two venerable monks, whose brown hoods and frocks denoted Franciscans, standing beside her.

'You are given into our charge, noble lady,' said one with a tone of deepest respect. 'Our orders are to give you a safe-conduct.'

'Whither to, venerable brother?' said she calmly.

'To the convent of St. Ursula, beyond the Tiber.'

'It is the prison of the Inquisition?' said she, questioning.

'There is no Inquisition; there are no prisons,' muttered the other monk. 'They who once met chastisement are won back now with love and gentleness.'

'You will be well cared for, and with kindness, noble lady,' said the other.

'It is alike to me; I am ready,' said she, rising, and preparing to follow them.

CHAPTER XVI

INTRIGUE

THE life of a man has been aptly compared to the course of a stream: now clear, now troubled, now careering merrily onward in joyous freedom, now forcing its turbid course amid shoals and rocks; but in no circumstance does the comparison more truthfully apply than in those still intervals when, the impulse of force spent, the waveless pool succeeds to the rapid river. There are few men, even among the most active and energetic, who have not known such periods in life. With some these are seasons of concentration—times profitably passed in devising plans for the future. Others chafe under the wearisome littleness of the hour, and long for the days of activity and toil; and some there are to whom these intervals have all the charm of a happy dream, and who love to indulge themselves in a bliss such as in the busy world can never be their fortune to enjoy.

Among these last, a true disciple of the school who take refuge in the ideal and the imaginative as the sole remedy against the ills of actual life, was Gerald Fitzgerald. When he arose from his sick-bed, it was with a sort of dreamy, indistinct consciousness that he was of high rank and station; one whose claims, however in abeyance now, must be admitted hereafter; that for the great part he was yet to fill, time alone was wanting. As to the past, it was a dream-land wherein he ventured with fear. It was in vain he asked himself, how much of it was true or false? Had this event really occurred? Had that man ever lived? The broken incidents of a fevered head, mingled with the terrible realities he had gone through; and there were many of his mere fancies that engaged his credulity more powerfully than some of the actual events of his chequered life.

His convalescence was passed at the Cardinal's villa of Orvieto; and if anything could have added to the strange confusion which oppressed him, it was the curious indistinct impression his mind preserved of the place itself. The gardens, fountains, statues, were all familiar. How had they been so revealed to him? As he strolled through the great rooms, objects struck him as well known; and yet, the Père Massoni had said to him: 'Orvieto will interest you; you have never been there'; and his Eminence, in his invitation, suggested the same thought. Day after day he pondered over this difficulty, and he continually turned over in his mind this question: 'Is there some inner picture in my being of all that I am to meet with in life? Has

existence only to unroll a tableau, every detail of which
is graven on my heart? Have other men these conflicts
within their minds? Is it that by some morbid condition
of memory *I* am thus tortured? and must I seek relief by
trying to forget?' The struggle thus suggested, rendered
him daily more taciturn and thoughtful. He would sit for
hours long without a word; and time glided on absolutely
as though in a sleep.

If Gerald's life was passed in this inactivity, the Père
Massoni's days were fully occupied. From Ireland the
tidings had long been of the most discouraging kind. The
great cause which should have been confided to the guidance
of the Church, and such as the Church could have trusted,
had been shamefully betrayed into the hands of a party
deeply imbued with all the principles of the French Revolution; men taught in the infamous doctrines of Voltaire and
Volney, and who openly professed to hate a church even
more than a monarchy. How the North of Ireland had
taken the lead in insurrection—how the Presbyterians, sworn
enemies as they were to Catholicism, had enrolled themselves
in the cause of revolt—how all the ready, active and zealous
leaders were among that class and creed, the Priest Carrol
had not failed to write him word; nor did it need the
priest's suggestive comments to make the clever Jesuit aware
of all the peril that this portended. Was it too late to
counteract these evils? by what means could men be brought
back from the fatal infatuation of those terrible doctrines?
how was the banner of the Faith to be brought to the van
of the movement? were the thoughts unceasingly in his
mind. The French were willing to aid the Irish, so also
were the Dutch; but the intervention would only damage
the cause the Père cared for. Nor did he dare to confide these
doubts to the Cardinal and ask his counsel on them, since, to
his Eminence he had continually represented the case of Ireland
in a totally different light. He had taught him to believe
the people all jealous for the Faith, cruelly oppressed by
England, hating the dynasty that ruled them, and eagerly

watching for the return of the Stuarts, if haply there yet
lived one to renew the traditions of that illustrious house.
By dint of instances, and no small persuasive power, he at
last had so far succeeded as to enlist the sympathies of his
Eminence in the youth personally, and was now plotting by
what means he could consummate that interest by a marriage
between Gerald and the beautiful Guglia Ridolfi.

This was a project which, if often indistinctly hinted at
between them, had never yet been seriously treated, and
Massoni well knew that with Caraffa success was a mere
accident, and that what he would reject one day with scorn
he would accept the next with eagerness and joy. Besides,
the gloomy tidings he constantly received from Ireland indisposed the Père to incur any needless hazards. If the
Chevalier was not destined to play a great part in life, the
Cardinal would never forgive an alliance that conferred neither
wealth nor station. The barren honour of calling a prince
of the House of Stuart his nephew would ill require him for
maintaining a mere pensioner and a dependant. Against these
considerations there was the calculation how far the cause of
Fitzgerald might profit by the aid such a man as Caraffa
could contribute, when once pledged to success by everything
personally near and dear to himself. Might not the great
churchman, then, be led to make the cause the main object
of all his wishes ?

The Cardinal was one of those men, and they are large
enough to form a class, who imagine that they owe every
success they obtain in life, in some way or other, to their
own admirable skill and forethought; their egotism blinding
them against all the aid the suggestions of others have
afforded, they arrive at a self-reliance which is actually
marvellous. To turn to good account this peculiarity of
disposition, Massoni now addressed himself zealously and
actively. He well knew that if the Cardinal only fancied
that the alliance of his niece with the Chevalier was a scheme
devised by himself—one of which none but a man of his deep
subtlety and sagacity could ever have thought—the plot

would have an irresistible attraction for him. The wily Jesuit meditated long over this plan, and, at last, hit upon an expedient that seemed hopeful. Among the many agents whom he employed over Europe, was one calling himself the Count Della Rocca, a fellow of infinite craft and effrontery, and who, though of the very humblest origin and most questionable morals, had actually gained a footing among the very highest and most exclusive of the French royalists. He had been frequently intrusted with confidential messages between the Courts of France and Spain, and acquired a sort of courtier-like air and breeding, which lost nothing by any diffidence or modesty on his part.

Massoni's plan was to pretend to the Cardinal that Della Rocca had been sent out to Rome by the Count D'Artois, with the decoration of St. Louis for the Chevalier, and a secret mission to sound the young Stuart Prince, as to his willingness to ally himself with the House of Bourbon, by marriage. For such a pretended mission the Count was well suited; sufficiently acquainted with the habits of great people to represent their conversation correctly, and well versed in that half ambiguous tone, affected by diplomatists of inferior grade, he was admirably calculated to play the part assigned him.

To give a greater credence to the mission, it was necessary that the Cardinal York should be also included in the deception; but nothing was ever easier than to make a dupe of his Royal Highness. A number of well-turned compliments from his dear cousins of 'France,' some little allusions to the 'long ago' at St. Germains, when the exiled Stuarts lived there, and a note, cleverly imitated, in the Count D'Artois' hand, were quite enough to win the old man's confidence. The next step was to communicate Della Rocca's arrival to the Cardinal Caraffa, and this Massoni did with all due secrecy, intimating that the event was one upon which he desired to take the pleasure of his Eminence.

Partly from offended pride, on not being himself sought for by the envoy, and partly to disguise from Massoni the

jealousy he always felt on the score of Cardinal York's
superior rank, Caraffa protested that the tidings had no
interest for him whatever; that any sentiments he entertained for the young Chevalier were simply such as a sincere
pity suggested; that he never heard of a cause so utterly
hopeless; that even if powerful allies were willing and ready
to sustain his pretensions, the young man's own defects of
character would defeat their views; that, from all he could
hear—for of himself he owned to know nothing—Gerald was
the last man in Europe to lead an enterprise which required
great daring and continual resources, and, in fact, none could
be his partisan save from a sense of deep compassion.

The elaborate pains he took to impress all this upon
Massoni convinced the Père that it was not the real sentiment of his Eminence, and he was not much surprised at a
hasty summons to the Cardinal's palace on the evening of the
day he had first communicated the news.

'The first mine has been sprung!' muttered Massoni, as he
read the order and prepared to obey it.

The Cardinal was in his study when the Père arrived, and,
continued to pace up and down the room, briefly addressing
a few words as Massoni entered and saluted him.

'The old Cardinal Monga had a saying, that if some work
were not found out to employ the Jesuits, they were certain
to set all Europe in a flame. Was there not some truth in
the remark, Père Massoni? Answer me frankly and fairly,
for you know the body well!' Such was the speech by
which he addressed him.

'Had his Eminence reckoned the times in which Jesuit
zeal and wisdom had rescued the world from peril, it would
have been a fitter theme for his wisdom.'

'It is not to be denied that they are meddlers, sir,' said the
Cardinal haughtily.

'So are the sailors in a storm-tossed vessel. The good
Samaritan troubled himself with what, others might have
said, had no concern for him.'

'I will not discuss it,' said his Eminence abruptly. 'The

world has formed its own vulgar estimate of your order, and I, at least, agree with the majority.' He paused for a second or two, and then, with a tone of some irritation, said, 'What is this story Rome is full of, about some Egyptian woman, or a Greek, arrested and confined by a warrant of the Holy Office; they have mingled your name with it, somehow ?'

'A grave charge, your Eminence; Satanic possession and witchcraft——'

'Massoni,' broke in Caraffa, with a malicious twinkle of his dark eye, 'remember, I beseech you, that we are alone. What do you mean, then, by witchcraft ?'

'Were I to say to your Eminence that, after a certain interview with you, I had come away, assuring myself that other sentiments were in your heart than those you had avowed to me; that you had but half revealed this, totally ignored that, affected credulity here, disbelief there, my subtlety, whether right or wrong, would resolve itself into a mere common gift—the practised habit of one skilled to decipher motives; but if, while in your presence, standing as I now do here, I could, with an effort of argument or abstraction, open your whole heart before me, and read there as in a book, and, while doing this, place you in circumstances where your most secret emotions must find vent, so that not a corner nor a nook of your nature should be strange to me, by what name would you call such an influence ?'

'What you describe now has never existed, Massoni. Tricksters and mountebanks have pretended to such power in every age, but they have had no other dupes than the unlettered multitude.'

'How say you, then, if I be a believer here ? What say you, if I have tested this woman's power, and proved it ? What say you, if all she has predicted has uniformly come to pass; not a day, nor a date, nor an hour mistaken! I will give an instance. Of Della Rocca's mission and its objects here, I had not the very faintest anticipation. That the exiled family of France cherished hope enough to speculate on some remote future, I did not dream of suspecting; and yet, through her foretelling, I learned the day he would arrive at Rome, the very hotel he would put up at, the steps he would adopt to obtain an audience of the Chevalier, the attempts he would make to keep his mission a secret from me; nay, to the very dress in which he would present himself, I knew and was prepared for all.'

'All this might be concerted; what more easy than to plan any circumstance you have detailed, and by imposing on your credulity secure your co-operation?'

'Let me finish, sir. I asked what success would attend his plan, and learned that destiny had yet left this doubtful —that all was yet dependent on the will of one whose mind was still unresolved. I pressed eagerly to learn his name, she refused to tell me, openly avowing that she would thwart his influence, if in her power. I grew angry and even scoffed at her pretended powers, declaring, as you have just suggested, that all she had told me might be nothing beyond a well-arranged scheme. "For once, then, you shall have a proof, said she, "and never shall it be repeated; fold that sheet of paper there, as a letter, and seal it carefully and well. The name I have alluded to is written within," said she. I started, for the paper contained no writing—not a word, not a syllable —I had scanned it carefully ere I folded it. Of this I can pledge my solemn and sacred word.'

'Well, when you broke the seal?' burst in the Cardinal.

'I have not yet done so,' said the Père calmly, 'there is the letter, just as I folded and sealed it; from that moment to this it has never quitted my possession. It may be, that, as you would suspect, even this might be sleight-of-hand. It may be, sir, that the paper contains no writing.'

'Let us see,' cried the Cardinal, taking the letter and breaking it open. 'Madonna!' exclaimed he suddenly. 'Look here'; and his finger then tremblingly pointed to the word, 'Caraffa,' traced in small letters and with a very faint ink in the middle of the page.

'And to this you swear, on your soul's safety?' cried Caraffa eagerly.

He bent forward till his lips touched the large golden cross which, as a pectoral, the Cardinal wore, and muttered, 'By this emblem, I swear it.'

'Such influence is demoniacal, none can doubt it; who is this woman, and whence came she?'

'So much of her story as I know is briefly told,' said Massoni, who related all that he had heard of the Egyptian, concluding with the steps by which he had her arrested and confined in the convent of St. Maria Maggiore, on the Tiber.

'There was an age when such a woman had been sent to the stake,' said Caraffa fiercely. 'Is it a wiser policy that pardons her?'

'Yes; if by her means a good end can be served,' interrupted the Père; 'if through what she can reveal, errors may be avoided, perils averted, and successes gained; if, in short, Satan can be used as slave, not master.'

'And wherefore should she be opposed to *me*?' broke in Caraffa, whose thoughts reverted to what concerned himself personally.

'As a true and faithful priest, as an honoured prince of the Church, you must be her enemy,' said the Père; and, though the words were spoken in all seeming sincerity, the Cardinal's dark eyes scanned the speaker's face keenly and severely. As if failing, however, to detect any equivocation in his manner, Caraffa addressed himself to another course of thought and said—

'Have you questioned her, then, as to this young man's chances?'

'She will not speak of them,' was the abrupt reply.

'Have they met?'

'Once, and only once; and of the meeting his memory preserves no trace whatever, since it was during his fever, and when his mind was wandering and incoherent.'

'Could I see her, without being known? could I speak with her myself?'

Massoni shook his head doubtingly, 'No disguise would avail against her craft.'

Caraffa pondered long over his thoughts, and at last said—
'I have a strong desire to see her, even though I should not
speak to her. What say you, Massoni ?'

'It shall be as pleases your Eminence,' was the meek answer.

'So much I know, sir; but it is your counsel that I am
now asking; what would you advise ?'

'So far as I can guess,' answered the Père cautiously, 'it
is her marvellous gift to exert influence over those with whom
she comes in contact—a direct palpable sway. Even I, cold,
impassive, as I am, unused to feel, and long beyond the reach
of such fascination—even *I* have known what it is to confront
a nature thus strangely endowed.'

'These are mere fancies, Massoni.'

'Fancies that have the force of convictions. For my own
part, depositary as I am of much that the world need not,
should not, know, I would not willingly expose my heart to
one like her.'

'Were it even as you say, Massoni, of what could the
knowledge avail her ? Bethink you for a moment of what
strange mysteries of the human heart every village curate
is the keeper; how he has probed recesses, dived into secret
clefts, of which, till revealed by strict search, the very pos-
sessor knew not the existence; and yet how valueless, how
inert, how inoperative in the great game of life does not this
knowledge prove. If this were power, the men who possessed
it would sway the universe.'

'And so they might,' burst in Massoni, 'if they would
adapt to the great events of life the knowledge which they
now dissipate in the small circle of family existence. If
they would apply to statecraft the same springs by which
they now awaken jealousies, kindle passions, lull just suspicions, and excite distrusts ! With powder enough to blow
up a fortress, they are contented to spend it in fireworks !
The order of which I am an unworthy member alone conceived a different estimate of the duty.'

'The world gives credit to your zeal,' said the Cardinal
slyly.

'The world is an ungrateful taskmaster. It would have its work done, and be free to disparage those who have laboured for it.'

A certain tone of defiance in this speech left an awkward pause for several minutes. At last Caraffa said carelessly—

'Of what were we speaking a while ago? Let us return to it.'

'It was of the Count Della Rocca and his mission, your Eminence.'

'True. You said that he wished to see the Chevalier, to present his letters. There can be no objection to that. The road to Orvieto is an excellent one, and my poor house there is quite capable of affording hospitality for even a visitor so distinguished.' With all his efforts to appear tranquil, the Cardinal spoke in a broken, abrupt way, that betrayed a mind very ill at ease.

'I am not aware, Massoni,' resumed he, 'that the affair concerns *me*, nor is there occasion to consult me upon it.' This address provoked no reply from the Père, who continued patiently to scan the speaker, and mark the agitation that more and more disturbed him.

'I conclude, of course,' said the Cardinal again, 'that the Chevalier's health is so firmly re-established this interview cannot be hurtful to him; that he is fully equal to discuss questions touching his gravest interests. You who hear frequently from him can give me assurance on this point.'

'I am in almost daily correspondence——'

'I know it,' broke in Caraffa.

'I am in almost daily correspondence with the Chevalier, and can answer for it that he is in the enjoyment of perfect health and spirits.'

'They who speculated on his being inferior to his destiny will perhaps feel disappointed!' said Caraffa, in a low, searching accent.

'They acknowledge as much already, your Eminence. In the very last despatches Sir Horace Mann sent home there

is a gloomy prediction of what trouble a youth so gifted and
so ambitious may one day occasion them in England.'

'Your friend the Marchesa Balbi, then, still wields her
influence at the British legation?' said Caraffa, smiling
cunningly; 'or you had never known these sentiments of
the Minister.'

'Your Eminence reads all secrets,' was the submissive
reply, as the Père bowed his head.

'Has she also told you what they think of the youth in
England?'

'No further than that there is a great anxiety to see him,
and assure themselves that he resembles the House of Stuart.'

'Of that there is no doubt,' broke in Caraffa; 'there is
not a look, a gesture, a trait of manner, or a tone of the
voice, he has not inherited.'

'These may seem trifles in the days of exile and adversity,
but they are title-deeds fortune never fails to adduce when
better times come round.'

'And do you really still believe in such, Massoni? Tell
me, in the sincerity of man to man, without disguise, and,
if you can, without prejudice—do you continue to cherish
hopes of this youth's fortune?'

'I have never doubted of them for a moment, sir,' said the
Père confidently. 'So long as I saw him weak and broken,
with weary looks and jaded spirits, I felt the time to be
distant; but when I beheld him in the full vigour of his
manly strength, I knew that his hour was approaching; it
needed but the call, the man was ready.'

'Ah! Massoni, if I had thought so—if I but thought so,'
burst out the Cardinal, as he leaned his head on his hand,
and lapsed into deep reflection.

The wily Père never ventured to break in upon a course
of thought, every motive of which contributed to his own
secret purpose. He watched him therefore, closely, but in
silence. At last Caraffa, lifting up his head, said—

'I have been thinking over this mission of Della Rocca,
Massoni, and it were perhaps as well—at least it will look

kindly—were I to go over to Orvieto myself, and speak with
the Chevalier before he receives him.   Detain the Count,
therefore, till you hear from me ; I shall start in the morning.'
     The Père bowed, and after a few moments withdrew.

CHAPTER XVII

THE GARDEN AT ORVIETO

SOON after daybreak on the following morning the Cardinal's
courier arrived at Orvieto with tidings that his Eminence
might be expected the same evening.   It was a rare event,
indeed, which honoured the villa with a visit from its princely
owner ; and great was the bustle and stir of preparation to
receive him.   The same activity prevailed within doors and
without.   Troops of men were employed in the gardens, on
the terraces, and the various pleasure-grounds ; while splendid
suites of rooms, never opened but on such great occasions,
were now speedily got in readiness and order.
     Gerald wandered about amid this exciting turmoil, puzzled
and confused.   How was it that he fancied he had once seen
something of the very same sort, exactly in the self-same
place ?   Was this, then, another rush of that imagination
which so persisted in tormenting him, making life a mere
circle of the same events ?   As he moved from place to place,
the conviction grew only stronger and stronger : this seemed
the very statue he had helped to replace on its pedestal ;
here the very fountain he had cleared from weeds and fallen
leaves ; the flowers he had grouped in certain beds ; the
walks he had trimly raked ; the rustic seats he had disposed
beneath shady trees ; all rose to his mind and distracted him
by the difficulty of explaining them.   As he walked up the
great marble stairs and entered the spacious hall of audience,
a whole scene of the past seemed to fill the space.   The lovely
girl—a mere child as she was, with golden hair and deep blue

eyes—rose again before his memory, and his heart sank as
he bethought him that the whole vision must have had no
reality.

The rapid tramp of horses' feet suddenly led him to the
window, and he now saw the outriders, as they dashed up
at speed, followed quickly after by three travelling carriages,
each drawn by six horses, and escorted by mounted dragoons.
Gerald did not wait to see his Eminence descend, but hastened
to his room to dress, and compose his thoughts for the approaching interview.

The Chevalier had grown to be somewhat vain of his
personal appearance.   It was a Stuart trait, and sat not
ungracefully upon him ; and he now costumed himself with
more than ordinary care.   His dress was of a dark maroon
velvet, over which he wore a scarf of his own tartan ; the
collar and decoration presented by the Cardinal York orna-
menting the front of the dress, as well as the splendidly
embossed dagger which once had graced the belt of the
Prince Charles Edward.   Though his toilet occupied him
a considerable time, no summons came from his Eminence,
either to announce his arrival or request a meeting ; and
Gerald, half pained by the neglect, and half puzzled lest the
fault might possibly be ascribed to some defect of observance
on his own part, at length took his hat and left the house
for a stroll through the gardens.

As he wandered along listlessly, he at last gained a little
grassy eminence, from which a wide view extended over a
vast olive plain, traversed by a tiny stream.   It was the very
wood through which, years before, he had journeyed when
he had fled from the villa to seek his fortune.   Some
indistinct, flitting thoughts of the event, the zigzag path
along the river, the far-away mountains of the Maremma,
were yet puzzling him, when he heard a light step on the
gravel-walk near.   He turned, and saw a young girl coming
toward him, smiling, and with an extended hand.   One
glance showed him that she was singularly beautiful, and of
a demeanour that announced high station.

'Which of us is to say, "welcome here," Chevalier? at all events, let one of us have the courage to speak it. I am your guest, or your host, whichever it please you best.'

'The Contessa Ridolfi,' said Gerald, as he kissed her hand respectfully.

'I perceive,' said she, laughing, 'you have heard of my boldness, and guess my name at once; but, remember, that if I had waited to be presented to you by my uncle, I should have been debarred from thus clearing all formality at a bound, and asking you, as I now do, to imagine me one you have known long and well.'

'I am unable to say whether the honour you confer on me or the happiness, be greater,' said Gerald warmly.

'Let it be the happiness, since the honour must surely come from your side,' said she, in the same light, half-careless tone. 'Give me your arm, and guide me through these gardens; you know them well, I presume.'

'I have been your guest these four months and more, Contessa,' said he, bowing.

'So that this poor villa of ours may have its place in history, and men remember it as the spot where the young Prince sojourned. Nay, do not blush, Chevalier, or I shall think that the shame is for *my* boldness. When you know me better you will learn that I am one so trained to the licence of free speech that none are offended at my frankness.'

'You shall never hear me complain of it,' said Gerald quickly.

'Come, then, and tell me freely, has this solitude grown intolerable; is your patience well-nigh worn out with those interminable delays of what are called "your friends"?'

'I know not what you allude to. I came here to recover after a long illness, weak and exhausted. My fever had left me so low in energy, that I only asked rest and quietness: I found both at the villa. The calm monotony that might have wearied another, soothed and comforted *me*. Of what was real in my past life—what mere dreamland—I never could succeed in defining. If at one moment I seemed to any one's eyes of princely blood and station, at the next I could not but see myself a mere adventurer, without friends, family, or home. I would have given the world for one kind friend to steady the wavering fabric of my mind, to bring back its wandering fancies, and tell me when my reason was aright.'

'Will you take me for such a friend?' said Guglia, in a soft, low voice.

'Oh, do not ask me, if you mean it not in serious earnest,' he urged rapidly. 'I can bear up against the unbroken gloom of my future; I could not endure the changeful light of a delusive hope.'

'But it need not be such. It is for you to decide whether you will accept of such a counsellor. First of all,' added she hastily, and ere leaving him time to reply, 'I am more deeply versed in your interests than you are perhaps aware. Intrusted by my uncle, the Cardinal, to deal with questions not usually committed to a young girl's hands, I have seen most parts of the correspondence which concerns you; nay, more, I can and will show you copies of it. You shall see for yourself, what they have never yet left you to judge, whether it is for your own interest to await an eventuality that may never come, or boldly try to create the crisis others would bid you wait for; or lastly, there is another part to take, the boldest, perhaps, of all.'

'And what may that be?' broke in Gerald, with eagerness, for his interest was now most warmly engaged.

'This must be for another time,' said she quickly; 'here comes his Eminence to meet us.'

And as she spoke, the Cardinal came forward, and with a mingled affection and respect embraced Gerald and kissed him on both cheeks.

CHAPTER XVIII

HOW THE TIME PASSED AT ORVIETO

ORVIETO was a true villa palace (which only Italians understand how to build), and the grounds were on a scale of
extent that suited the mansion.   Ornamental terraces and
gardens on every side, with tasteful alleys of trellised vines
to give noon-day shade, and farther off again a dense pine
forest, traversed by long alleys of grass, which even in the
heat of summer were cool and shaded.   These narrow roads,
barely wide enough for two horsemen abreast, crossed and
recrossed in the dark forest, ever leading between walls of
the same dusky foliage, with scanty glimpses of a blue sky
through the arched branches overhead.

If Guglia rode there for hours long with Gerald; if they
strayed—often silently—not even a foot-fall heard on the
smooth turf, you perhaps, know why; and if you do not,
how am I, unskilled in such descriptions, to make you
wiser ?   Well, it was even as you suspect: the petted child
of fortune, the lovely niece of the great Cardinal, the
beautiful Guglia, whose hand was the greatest prize of
Rome, had conceived such an interest in Gerald, his fortunes
and his fate, that she could not leave Orvieto.

In vain came pressing invitations from Albano and Terni,
where she had promised to pass part of her autumn.   In
vain the lively descriptions of friends full of all the delights
of Castellamare or Sorrento: the story of festivities and
pleasures seemed poor and even vulgar with the life she led.
Talk of illusions as you will, that of being in love is the
only one that moulds the nature or elevates the heart !   Out
of its promptings come the heroism of the least venturesome
or the poetry of the least romantic !   Insensibly stealing into
the affections of another, we have to descend into our own
hearts for the secrets that win success ; and how resolutely

we combat all that is mean or unworthy in our nature, simply that we may offer a more pure sacrifice on the altar we kneel to!

And there and thus she lived, the flattered beauty—the young girl, to whom an atmosphere of homage and admiration seemed indispensable—whose presence was courted in the society of the great world, and whose very caprices had grown to become fashions—a sort of strange, half-real existence, each day so like another that time had no measure how it passed.

The library of the villa supplied them with ample material to study the history of the Stuarts; and in these pursuits they passed the mornings, carefully noting down the strange eventualities which determined their fate, and canvassing together in talk the traits which so often had involved them in misfortune. Gerald, now restored to full health, was a perfect type of the illustrious race he had sprung from: and not only was the resemblance in face and figure, but all the mannerisms of Charles Edward were reproduced in the son. The same easy, gentle, yielding disposition, dashed by impulses of the wildest daring, and darkened occasionally by moods of obstinacy; miserable under the thought of having offended, and almost more wretched when the notion of being forgiven imparted a sense of his own inferiority; he was one of those men whose minds are so many-sided that they seem to have no fixed character. Even now, though awakened to the thought of the great destiny that might one day befall him—assured as he felt of his birth and lineage—there were intervals in which no sense of ambition stirred him, when he would willingly accept the humblest lot in life should it only promise peace and tranquillity.

Strangely enough it was by these vacillations and changes of temperament that Guglia had attached herself so decisively to his fortunes. The very want which she supplied to his nature made the tie between them. The theory in her own heart was, that when called on for effort, whenever the occasion should demand the great personal qualities of courage and daring, Gerald would be pre-eminently distinguished, and show himself to the world a true Stuart.

While thus they lived a life of happiness, the Père Massoni was actively engaged in maturing plans for the future. For a considerable time back he had been watching the condition of Ireland with an intense feeling of anxiety. So far from the resistance to England having assumed the character of a struggle in favour of Catholicism, it had grown more and more to resemble the great convulsion in France which promised to ingulf all religions and all creeds. Though in a measure prepared for this in the beginning of the conflict, Massoni steadfastly trusted that the influence of the priests would as certainly bring the people back to the standards of the Church, and that eventually the contest would be purely between Rome and the Reformation. His last news from Ireland grievously damped the ardour of such hopes. The Presbyterians of the North—men called enemies of the 'Church'—were now the most trusted leaders of the movement; and how was he to expect that such men as these would accept a Stuart for their king?

For days, and even weeks did the crafty Père ponder over this difficult problem, and try to solve it in ways the most opposite. Why might not these Northerns, who must always be a mere minority, be employed at the outset of the struggle, and then, as the rebellion declared itself, be abandoned and thrown over? Why not make them the forlorn hope of the campaign, and so get rid of them entirely? Why should not the Chevalier boldly try his personal influence among them, promise future rewards and favours, ay, even more still? Why might he not adroitly have it hinted that he was, at heart, less a Romanist than was generally believed : that French opinions had taken a deep root in his nature, and the early teachings of Mirabeau born their true fruit? There was much in Gerald's training and habit of mind which would favour this supposition, could he but be induced to play the game as he was directed. There was among the Stuart papers in Cardinal York's

keeping a curious memorandum of a project once entertained by the Pretender with respect to Charles Edward.
It was a scheme to marry him to a natural daughter of
Sir Robert Walpole, and thus conciliate the favour and even
the support of that Minister—the strongest friend and ally
of the Hanoverian cause. The Jesuit father had seen and
read this remarkable paper, and deemed it a conception of
the finest and most adroit diplomacy. It had even stimulated his own ardour to rival it in acuteness; to impose
Gerald upon the Presbyterian party, as one covertly cherish-
ing views similar to their own; to make them, a minority
as they were, imagine that the future destinies of the country
were in their keeping; to urge them on, in fact, to the van
of the battle, that so they might stand between two fires,
was his great conception, the only difficulty to which was
how to prepare the young Chevalier for the part he was to
play, and reconcile him to its duplicity!

To this end he addressed himself zealously and vigorously,
feeding Gerald's mind with ideas of the grandeur of his
house, the princely inheritance that they had possessed, and
their high rank in Europe. All that could contribute to
stimulate the youth's ardour, and gratify his pride of birth,
was studiously provided. Day by day he advanced stealthily
upon the road, gradually enhancing Gerald's own standard to
himself, and giving him, by a sort of fictitious occupation, an
amount of importance in his own eyes. Massoni maintained
a wide correspondence throughout Europe; there was not a
petty court where he had not some trusted agent. To impart to this correspondence a peculiar tone and colouring was
easy enough. At a signal from him the hint was sure to be
adopted; and now as letters poured in from Spain, and
Portugal, and Naples, and Vienna, they all bore upon the
one theme, and seemed filled with but one thought—that of
the young Stuart and his fortunes. All these were duly
forwarded by Massoni to Gerald by special couriers, who
arrived with a haste and speed that seemed to imply the last
importance. With an ingenuity all his own, the Père in-

vested this correspondence with all the characteristics of a vast political machinery, and by calling upon Gerald's personal intervention, he elevated the young man to imagine himself the centre of a great enterprise.

Well aided and seconded as he was by Guglia Ridolfi, to whom also this labour was a delightful occupation, the day was often too short for the amount of business before them; and instead of the long rides in the pine forest, or strolling rambles through the garden, a brisk gallop before dinner, taken with all the zest of a holiday, was often the only recreation they permitted themselves. There was a fascination in this existence that made all their previous life, happy as it had been, seem tame and worthless in comparison. If real power have an irresistible charm for those who have once enjoyed its prerogatives, even the semblance and panoply of it have a marvellous fascination.

That *égoïsme-à-deux*, as a witty French writer has called love, was also heightened in its attraction by the notion of an influence and sway wielded in concert. As one of the invariable results of the great passion is to elevate people to themselves, so did this seeming importance they thus acquired minister to their love for each other. In the air-built castles of their mind one was a royal palace, surrounded with all the pomp and splendour of majesty; who shall say that here was not a theme for a 'thousand-and-one nights,' of imagination?

Must we make the ungraceful confession that Gerald was not very much in love! though he felt that the life he was leading was a very delightful one. Guglia possessed great— the very greatest—attractions. She was very beautiful; her figure the perfection of grace and symmetry; her carriage, voice and air all that the most fastidious could wish for. She was eminently gifted in many ways, and with an apprehension of astonishing quickness; and yet, somehow, though he liked and admired her, was always happy in her society, and charmed by her companionship, she never made the subject of his solitary musings as he strolled by himself; she was not the theme of the sonnets that fell half unconsciously from his lips as he rambled alone in the pine wood. Was the want then in *her* to inspire a deeper passion, or had the holiest spot in *his* heart been already occupied, or was it that some ideal conception had made all reality unequal and inferior?

We smile at the simplicity of those poor savages, who having carved out their own deity, fashioned, and shaped, and clothed, then fall down before their own handiwork in an abject devotion and worship. We cannot reconcile to ourselves the mental process by which this self-deception is practised, and yet it is happening in another form, and every day too, under our own eyes. The most violent passions are very often the result of a certain suggestiveness in an object much admired; the qualities which awaken in ourselves nobler sentiments, higher ambitions, and more delightful dreams of a future soon attach us to the passion, and unconsciously we create an image of which the living type is but a skeleton. Perhaps it was the towering ambition of Guglia's mind that impaired, to a great degree, the womanly tenderness of her nature, and not impossibly too he felt, as men of uncertain purpose often feel, a certain pique at the more determined and resolute character of a woman's mind. Again and again did he wish for some little trait of mere affection, something that should betoken, if not an indifference, a passing forgetfulness of the great world and all its splendours. But no; all her thoughts soared upward to the high station she had set her heart on. Of what they should be one day was the great dream of her life—for they were already betrothed by the Cardinal's consent—and of the splendid path that lay before them.

The better to carry out his own views Massoni had always kept up a special correspondence with Guglia, in which he expressed his hopes of success far more warmly than he had ever done to Gerald. Her temperament was also more sanguine and impassioned, she met difficulties in a more daring spirit, and could more easily persuade herself to whatever she ardently desired. The Père had only pointed out to her some of the obstacles to success, and even these he had accompanied by such explanations as to how they might be met and combated that they seemed less formidable; and the great question between them was rather when than how the grand enterprise was to be begun.

'Though I am told,' wrote he, 'that the discontent with the House of Hanover grows daily more suspicious in England, and many of its once staunch adherents regret the policy which bound them to these usurpers, yet it is essentially to Ireland we must look for, at least, the opening of our enterprise; there is not a mere murmur of dissatisfaction—it is the deep thunder-roll of rebellion. Two delegates from that country are now with me—men of note and station—who, having learnt for the first time that a Prince of the Stuart family yet survives, are most eager to pay their homage to his Royal Highness. Of course, this, if done at all, must be with such secrecy as shall prevent it reaching Florence and the ears of Sir Horace Mann; and, at the same time, not altogether so unceremoniously as to deprive the interview of its character of audience. It is to the "pregiatissima Contessa Guglia" that I leave the charge of this negotiation, and the responsibility of saying "yes" or "no" to this request.

'Of the delegates, one is a baronet, by name Sir Capel Crosbie, a man of old family and good fortune. The other is a Mr. Simon Purcell, who formerly served in the English army, and was wounded in some action with the French in Canada. They have not, either of them, much affection for England—a very pardonable disloyalty when you hear their story. The imminent question, however, now is—can you see them; which means—can they have this audience?

'You will all the better understand any caution I employ on this occasion, when I tell you that, on the only instance of a similar kind having occurred, I had great reason to deplore my activity in promoting it. It was at the presentation of the Bishop of Clare to his Royal Highness, when the Prince took the opportunity of declaring the strong conviction he entertained of the security of the Hanoverian succession; and, worse again, how ineffectual all priestly intrigues must ever prove, when the contest lay between armies. I have no need to say what injury such indiscretion produces, nor how essential it is that it may not be repeated. If you assent to my request, I beg to leave to your own judgment the fitting time, and, what is still more important, the precise character of the reception—that is, as to how far its significance as an audience should be blended with the more graceful familiarity of a friendly meeting. The distinguished Contessa has on such themes no need of counsel from the humblest of her servants, and most devoted follower,

'PAUL MASSONI.'

What reply she returned to his note may easily be gathered from the following few words which passed between Gerald and herself a few mornings afterward.

They were seated in the library at their daily task, surrounded by letters, maps, and books, when Guglia said hastily, 'Oh, here is a note from the Père Massoni to be replied to. He writes to ask when it may be the pleasure of his Royal Highness to receive the visit of two distinguished gentlemen from Ireland, who ardently entreat the honour of kissing his Royal Highness's hand, and of carrying back with them such assurances as he might vouchsafe to utter of his feeling for those who have never ceased to deem themselves his subjects.'

'*Che seccatura!*' burst he out, as he rose impatiently from the table and paced the room; 'if there be a mockery which I cannot endure, it is one of these audiences. I can sit here and fool myself all day long by poring over records of a has-been, or even tracing out the limits of what my ancestors possessed; but to play Prince at a mock levée—no, no, Guglia, you must not ask me this.'

There were days when this humour was strong on him, and she said no more.

CHAPTER XIX

TWO VISITORS

A FEW days after, and just as evening was falling, a travelling-carriage halted at the park gate of the Cardinal's villa. Some slight injury to the harness occasioned a brief delay, and the travellers descended and proceeded leisurely at a walk towards the house. One was a very large, heavily-built man, far advanced in life, with immense bushy eyebrows of a brindled grey, giving to his face a darksome and almost forbidding expression, though the mouth was well rounded, and of a character that bespoke gentleness. He was much bent in the shoulders, and moved with considerable difficulty; but there was yet in his whole figure and air a certain dignity that announced the man of condition. Such, indeed, was Sir Capel Crosbie, once a beau and ornament of the French court in the days of the Regency. The other was a spare, thin, but yet wiry-looking man of about sixty-five or six, deeply pitted with small-pox, and disfigured by a strong squint, which, as the motions of his face were quick, imparted a character of restless activity and impatience to his appearance, that his nature, indeed, could not contradict. He was known as—that is, his passport called him—Mr. Simon Purcell; but he had many passports, and was frequently a grandee of Spain, a French abbé, a cabinet courier of Russia, and a travelling monk, these travesties being all easy to one who spoke fluently every dialect of every continental language and seemed to enjoy the necessity of a deception. You could mark at once in his gestures and his tone as he came forward the stamp of one who talked much and well. There was ready self-possession, that jaunty cheerfulness dashed with a certain earnest force, that bespoke the man who had achieved conversational success, and felt his influence in it.

The accident to the harness had seemingly interrupted an

earnest conversation, for no sooner was he on the ground than Purcell resumed: 'Take *my* word for it, baronet; it is always a bad game that does not admit of being played in two ways—the towns to which only one road leads are never worth visiting.'

The other shook his head; but it was difficult to say whether in doubt of the meaning or dissent from the doctrine.

'Yes,' resumed the other, 'the great question is what will you do with your Prince if you fail to make him a king? He will always be a puissance; it remains to be seen in whose hands and for what objects.'

The baronet sighed, and looked a picture of hopeless dullness.

'Come, I will tell you a story, not for the sake of the incident, but for the illustration; though even as a story it has its point. You knew Gustave de Marsay, I think?'

'*Le beau Gustave?* to be sure I did. Ah! it was upwards of forty years ago,' sighed he sorrowfully.

'It could not be less. He has been living in a little Styrian village about that long, seeing and being seen by none. His adventure was this: He was violently enamoured of a very pretty woman whom he met by chance in the street, and discovered afterward to be the wife of a "dyer," in the Rue de Marais. Whether she was disposed to favour his addresses or acted in concert with her husband to punish him, is not very easy to say; the result would recline to the latter supposition. At all events, she gave him a rendezvous at which he was surprised by the dyer himself—a fellow strong as a Hercules and of an ungovernable temper. He rushed wildly on De Marsay, who defended himself for some time with his rapier; a false thrust, however, broke the weapon at the hilt, and the dyer springing forward, caught poor Gustave round the body, and actually carried him off over his head, and plunged him neck and heels into an enormous tank filled with dye-stuff. How he escaped drowning—how he issued from the house and ever reached his home he never was able to tell. It is more than probable the consequences of the calamity absorbed and obliterated all else; for when he awoke next day he discovered that he was totally changed —his skin from head to foot being dyed a deep blue! It was in vain that he washed and washed, boiled himself in hot baths, or essayed a hundred cleansing remedies, nothing availed in the least—in fact, many thought that he came out only bluer than before. The most learned of the faculty were consulted, the most distinguished chemists—all in vain. At last a dyer was sent for, who in an instant recognised the peculiar tint, and said, "Ah! there is but one man in Paris has the secret of this colour, and he lives in the Rue de Marais."

'Here was a terrible blow to all hope, and in the discouragement it inflicted three long months were passed, De Marsay growing thin and wretched from fretting, and by his despondency occasioning his friends the deepest solicitude. At length, one of his relatives resolved on a bold step. He went direct to the Rue de Marais and demanded to speak with the dyer. It is not very easy to say how he opened a negotiation of such delicacy; that he did so with consummate tact and skill there can be no doubt, for he so worked on the dyer's compassion by the picture of a poor young fellow utterly ruined in his career, unable to face the world, to meet his regiment, even to appear before the enemy, being blue! that the dyer at last confessed his pity, but at the same time cried out, "What can I do? there is no getting it off again!"

'"No getting it off again! do you really tell me that?" exclaimed the wretched negotiator.

'"Impossible! that's the patent," said the other with an ill-dissembled pride. "I have spent seven years in the invention. I only hit upon it last October. Its grand merit is that it resists all attempts to efface it."

'"And do you tell me," cries the friend, in terror, "that this poor fellow must go down to his grave in that odious— well, I mean no offence—in that unholy tint?"

'"There is but one thing in my power, sir."

'" Well, what is it, in the name of mercy ? Out with it, and name your price."

'"I can make him a very charming green! *un beau vert*, monsieur."'

When the baronet had ceased to laugh at the anecdote, Purcell resumed: 'And now for the application. It is always a good thing in life to be able to become *un beau vert*, even though the colour should not quite suit you. I say this, because for the present project I can augur no success. The world has lived wonderfully fast, Sir Capel, since you and I were boys. That same Revolution in France that has cut off so many heads, has left those that still remain on men's shoulders very much wiser than they used to be. Now nobody in Europe wants this family again; they have done their part; and they are as much bygones as chain-armour or a battle-axe.'

'The rightful and the legitimate are never bygone—never obsolete,' said the other resolutely.

'A'n't they, faith! The guillotine and the lantern are the answers to that. I do not mean to say it must be always this way. There may, though I see no signs of it, come a reaction yet; but for the present men have taken a practical turn, and they accept nothing, esteem nothing, employ nothing that is not practical. Mirabeau's last effort was to give this colour to the Bourbons, and *he* failed. Do not tell me, then, that where Gabriel Riquetti broke down, a Jesuit father will succeed!'

The other shook his head in dissent, but without speaking.

'Remember, baronet, these convictions of mine are all opposed to my interest. I should be delighted to see your fairy palace made habitable, and valued for the municipal taxes. Nothing could better please me than to behold your Excellency Master of the Horse except to see myself Chancellor of the Exchequer. But here we are, and a fine princely-looking pile it is!'

They both stopped suddenly, and gazed with wondering admiration at one noble façade of the palace right in front of them. A wide terrace of white marble, ornamented with groups or single figures in statuary, stretched the entire length of the building, beneath which a vast orangery extended, the trees loaded with fruit or blossom, gave but slight glimpses of the rockwork grottoes and quaint fountains within.

'This is not the Cardinal's property,' said Purcell. 'Nay, I know well what I am saying; this belongs, with the entire estate, down to San Remo, yonder, to the young Countess Ridolfi. Nay more, she is at this very moment in bargain with Cæsare Piombino for the sale of it. Her price is five hundred thousand Roman scudi, which she means to invest in this bold scheme.'

'She, at least, has faith in a Stuart,' exclaimed the baronet eagerly.

'What would you have? The girl's in love with your Prince. She has paid seventy thousand piastres of Albizzi's debts that have hung around his neck these ten or twelve years back, all to win him over to the cause, just because his brother-in-law is Spanish Envoy here. She destined some eight thousand more as a present to Our Lady of Ravenna, who, it would seem, has a sort of taste for bold enterprises; but Massoni stopped her zeal, and suggested that instead of candles she should lay it out in muskets.'

'You scoff unseasonably, sir,' said the baronet, indignant at the tone he spoke in.

'Nor is that all,' continued Purcell, totally heedless of the rebuke; 'her very jewels, the famous Ridolfi gems, the rubies that once were among the show objects of Rome, are all packed up and ready to be sent to Venice, where a company of Jews have contracted to buy them. Is not this girl's devotion enough to put all your patriotism to the blush?'

A slight stir now moved the leaves of the orange-trees near where they were standing. The evening was perfectly still and calm: Purcell, however, did not notice this, but went on—

'And she is right. If there were a means of success, that means would be money. But it is growing late, and this, I take it, is the chief entrance. Let us present ourselves, if so be that we are to be honoured with an audience.'

Though the baronet had not failed to remark the sarcastic tone of this speech, he made no reply but slowly ascended the steps toward the terrace.

Already the night was closing in, and as the strangers reached the door they did not perceive that a figure had issued from the orangery beneath, and mounted the steps after them. This was the Chevalier, who usually passed the last few moments of each day wandering among the orange-trees. He had thus, without intending it, heard more than was meant for his ears.

The travellers had but to appear to receive the most courteous reception from a household already prepared to do them honour. They were conducted to apartments specially made ready for them; and being told that the Countess hoped to have their company at nine o'clock, when she supped, were left to repose after their journey.

CHAPTER XX

A WAYWORN ADVENTURER

It was by this chance alone that Gerald knew of the sacrifices Guglia had made and was making for his cause. In all their intercourse, marked by so many traits of mutual confidence, nothing of this had transpired. By the like accident, too, did he learn how some men, at least, spoke and thought of his fortunes; and what a world of specula-tion did these two facts suggest! They were as types of the two opposing forces that ever swayed him in life. Here, was the noble devotion that gave all; there, the cold distrust that believed nothing. Delightful as it had been for him to

2 A

dwell on the steadfast attachment of Guglia Ridolfi, and think over the generous trustfulness of that noble nature, he could not turn his thoughts from what had fallen from Purcell; the ill-omened words rankled in his heart, and left no room for other reflections.

All that he had read of late, all the letters that were laid before him, were filled with the reiterated tales of Highland devotion and attachment. The most touching little episodes of his father's life were those in which this generous sentiment figured, and Gerald had by reading and re-reading them got to believe that this loyalty was but sleeping, and ready to be aroused to life and activity at the first flutter of a Stuart tartan on the hills, or the first wild strains of a pibroch in the gorse-clad valleys.

And yet Purcell said—he had heard him say—the world has no further need of this family; the pageant they moved in has passed by for ever. The mere chance mention, too, of Mirabeau's name—that terrible intelligence which had subjugated Gerald's mind from very boyhood—imparted additional force to this judgment. 'Perhaps it is even as he says,' muttered Gerald; 'perhaps the old fire has died out on the altars, and men want us not any more.'

Whenever in history he had chanced upon the mention of men who, once great by family and pretension, had fallen into low esteem and humble fortunes, he always wondered why they had not broken with the old world and its traditions at once, and sought in some new and far-off quarter of the globe a life untrammelled by the past. 'Some would call this faint-heartedness; some would say that it is a craven part to turn from danger; but it is not the danger I turn from; it is not the peril that appalls me; it is the sting of that sarcasm that says, Who is he that comes on the pretext of a name, to trouble the world's peace, unfix men's minds and unhinge their loyalty? What does he bring us in exchange for this earthquake of opinion? Is he wiser, better, braver, more skilled in the arts of war or peace than those he would overthrow?'

As he waged conflict with these thoughts, came the summons to announce that the Countess was waiting supper for him.

'I cannot come to-night. I am ill—fatigued. Say that I am in want of rest, and have lain down upon my bed.' Such was the answer he gave, uttered in the broken, interrupted tone of one ill at ease with himself.

The Cardinal's physician was speedily at his door, to offer his services, but Gerald declined them abruptly and begged to be left alone. At length a heavy step was heard in the corridor, and the Cardinal himself demanded admission.

In the hurried excuses that Gerald poured forth, the wily churchman quickly saw that the real cause of his absence was untouched.

'Come, Prince,' said he good-humouredly, 'tell me frankly, you are not satisfied with Guglia and myself for having permitted this man to come here; but I own that I yielded only to Massoni's earnest desire.'

'And why should Massoni have so insisted?' asked Gerald.

'For this good reason, that they are both devoted adherents of your house; men ready to hazard all for your cause.'

Gerald smiled superciliously, and the Cardinal seeing it, said—

'Nay, Prince, distrust was no feature of your race, and, from what the Père Massoni says, these gentlemen do not deserve it.' He paused to let Gerald reply, but, as he did not speak, the Cardinal went on: 'The younger of the two, who speaks out his mind more freely, is a very zealous partisan of your cause. He has worn a miniature of your father next his heart since the memorable day at Preston, when he acted as aide-de-camp to his Royal Highness; and when he had shown it to us he kissed it with a devotion that none could dare to doubt.'

'This is he that is called Purcell?' asked Gerald.

'The same. He held the rank of colonel in the Scottish

army, and was rewarded with a patent of nobility, too, of which, however, he has not availed himself.'

Again there flashed across Gerald's mind the words he had overheard from the orangery, and the same cold smile again settled on his features, which the Cardinal noticed and said—

'If it were for nothing else than the close relation which once bound him to his Royal Highness, methinks you might have wished to see and speak with him.'

'And so I mean to do, sir; but not to-night.'

'Chevalier,' said the Cardinal resolutely, 'it is a time when followers must be conciliated, not repulsed; flattered instead of offended. Reflect, then, I entreat you, ere you afford even a causeless impression of distance or estrangement. On Monday last, an old Highland chief, the lord of Barra, I think they called him, was refused admittance here, on the plea that it was a day reserved for affairs of importance. On Wednesday, the Count D'Arigny was told that you only received envoys, and not mere Chargés d'Affaires; and even yesterday, I am informed, the Duc de Terracina was sent away because he was a few minutes behind the time specified for his audience. Now these are trifles, but they leave memories which are often disastrous.'

'If I *had* to render an account of my actions, sir,' said Gerald haughtily, 'a humiliation which has not yet reached me—I might be able to give sufficient explanation for all you have just mentioned.'

'I did but speak of the policy of these things,' said the Cardinal, with an air of humility.

'It is for *me* to regard them in another light,' said Gerald hastily. He paused, and, after a few minutes, resumed in a voice whose accents were full and well weighed: 'When men have agreed together to support the cause of one they call a Pretender, they ever seem to me to make a sort of compromise with themselves, and insist that he who is to be a royalty to all others, invested with every right and due of majesty, must be to them a plaything and a toy; and then they gather around him with fears, and threats, and hopes, and flatteries—now menacing, now bribing—forgetting the while that if fortune should ever destine such a man to have a throne, they will have so corrupted and debased his nature, while waiting for it, that not one fitting quality, not one rightful trait would remain to him. If history has not taught me wrongly, even usurpers have shown more kingly conduct than restored monarchs.'

'What would you, Prince?' said the Cardinal sorrowfully.

'We must accept the world as we find it.'

'Say, rather, as we make it.'

The Cardinal rose to take his leave, but evidently wishing that Gerald might say something to detain him. He was very reluctant to leave the young man to ponder in solitude such sentiments as he had avowed.

'Good-night, sir, good-night. Your Eminence will explain my absence, and say that I will receive these gentlemen to-morrow. What are the papers you hold in your hand—are they for *me*?'

'They are some mere routine matters, which your Royal Highness may look over at leisure—appointments to certain benefices, on which it has been the custom to take the pleasure of the Prince your father; but they are not pressing; another time will do equally well.'

There was an adroitness in this that showed how closely his Eminence had studied the Stuart nature, and marked that no flattery was ever so successful with that house as that which implied their readiness to sacrifice time, pleasure, inclination, even health itself to the cares and duties of station. To this blandishment they were never averse or inaccessible, and Gerald inherited the trait in all its strength.

'Let me see them, sir,' said Gerald, seating himself at the table, while he gave a deep sigh—fitting testimony of his sense of sacrifice.

'This is the nomination of John Decloraine Hackett to the see of Elphin; an excellent priest, and a sound politician. He has ever contrived to impress the world so powerfully with his religious devotion, that there are not twelve men in Europe know him to be the craftiest statesman of his time.'

'It is, then, a good appointment,' said Gerald, taking the pen. 'But what is this? The Cardinal York has already signed this.'

In Caraffa's eagerness to play out his game he had forgotten this fact, and that the Irish bishops had always been submitted to the approval of his Royal Highness.

'I say, sir,' reiterated Gerald, 'here is the signature of my uncle. What means this, or who really is it that makes these appointments?'

The Cardinal began with a sort of mumbled apology about a divided authority and an ecclesiastical function; but Gerald stopped him abruptly—

'If we are to play this farce out, let our parts be assigned us; and let none assume that which is not his own. Take my word for it, Cardinal, that if the day comes when the English will carry me to the scaffold, at Smithfield or Tyburn, or wherever it be, you will not find any one so ready to be my substitute. There, sir, take your papers, and henceforth let there be no more mockeries of office. I will myself speak of this to my uncle.'

The Cardinal bowed submissively and moved toward the door.

'You will receive these gentlemen to-morrow?' said he interrogatively.

'To-morrow,' said Gerald, as he turned away.

The Cardinal bowed deeply, and retired. Scarcely, however, had his footsteps died out of hearing, when Gerald rang for his valet, and said—

'When these visitors retire for the night, follow the Signor Purcell to his room, and desire him to come here to me; do it secretly, and so that none may remark you.'

The valet bowed, and Gerald was once more alone.

It was near midnight when the door again opened, and Mr. Purcell was introduced. Making a low and deep obeisance, but without any other demonstration of deference for Gerald's rank, he stood patiently awaiting to be addressed.

'We have met before, sir,' said Gerald, flushing deeply.

'So I perceive, sir,' was the quiet reply given with all the ease of one not easily abashed, 'and the last time was at a pleasant supper-table, of which we are the only survivors.'

'Indeed!' sighed Gerald sadly, and with some astonishment.

'Yes, sir; the "Mountain" devoured the Girondists, and the reaction devoured the "Mountain." If the present people have not sent the *reactionnaires* to the guillotine, it is because they prefer to make soldiers of them.'

'And how did you escape the perils of the time?' asked Gerald eagerly.

'Like Monsieur de Talleyrand sir, I always treated the party in disgrace as if their misfortune were but a passing shadow, and that the day of their triumph was assured. For even this much of consideration men in adversity are grateful.'

'How heartily you must despise humanity!' burst out Gerald, more struck by the cold cynicism of the other's look than even by his words.

'Not so,' replied he, in a half careless tone; 'Jean Jacques expected too much; Diderot thought too little of men. The truth lies midway, and they are neither as good nor as bad as we deem them.'

'And now, what is your pursuit? what career do you follow?' asked Gerald abruptly.

'I have none, sir; the attraction that binds the ruined gambler to sit at the table and watch the game at which others are staking heavily, ties me to any enterprise wherein men are willing to risk much. I have seen so much high play in life, I cannot stand by petty ventures. They told me at Venice of the plot that was maturing here, and I agreed with old Sir Capel Crosbie to come over and hear about it.'

'You little suspected, perhaps, who was the hero of the adventure?' said Gerald half doubtingly.

'Nay, sir, I saw your picture, and recognised you at once.

'I never knew there had been a portrait of me!' cried Gerald, in astonishment.

'It was taken, I fancy, during your illness; but the resemblance is still complete, and recalls to those who knew the Prince, your father, every trait and lineament of his face.'

'You yourself knew him?' said Gerald feelingly.

A deep, cold bow was the only acknowledgment of this question.

'They told me you were one of his trusted and truest friends?'

'We wore each other's miniature for many a year; our happiness was to talk of what might have chanced to be our destiny had he won back the throne that was his right, and I succeeded to what my father's gold should have purchased. I see I am alluding to what you never heard of. You see before you one who might have been a King of Poland.'

Gerald stared in half-credulous astonishment, and the other went on—

'You have heard of the Mississippi scheme, and of Law, its founder?'

'Yes.'

'My grandfather was Law's friend and confidant. By their united talents and zeal the great plot was first conceived and matured. Law was at first but an indifferent French scholar, and even a worse courtier. My grandfather was an adept in both, and knew, besides, the Duke of Orleans well. They were as much companions as the distance of their stations could make them; and by my grandfather's influence the Duke was induced to listen to the scheme. On what mere accident the great events of life depend! It was a party of quinze decided the fate of Europe. The Duke lost a hundred and seventy thousand livres to my grandfather, and could not pay him. While he was making excuses for the delay, my grandfather thought of Law, and said—"Let me present to your Royal Highness to-morrow morning a clever friend of mine, and it will never be your fortune again to own that you have not money to any extent at your disposal." Law appeared at the Duke's levée the next morning. It is not necessary to tell the rest, only that among the deepest gamblers in that memorable scheme, and the largest winners, my grandfather held the first place. Such was the splendour of his retinue one day at Versailles that the rumour ran it was some sovereign of Southern Europe had suddenly arrived at Paris, and the troops turned out to render royal honours to him. When the Duke heard the story he laughed heartily, and said, "Eh bien, c'est un Gage du succès"—a *mot* upon our family name, which was Gage, my uncle being afterward a viscount by that title.

'Within a very short time after that incident—which, some say, had so captivated my gradfather's ambition that he became feverish and restless for greatness—he offered three millions sterling for the crown of Poland. You may remember Pope's allusion to it :

> "The Crown of Poland, venal twice an age,
> To just three millions stinted modest Gage."

'The contract was broken off by my grandfather's refusal to marry a certain Countess Boratynski, a natural daughter of the king. He then made a bidding for the throne of Sardinia ; but, while the negotiation was yet pending, the great edifice of Law began to tremble ; and within three short weeks my grandfather, from the owner of six millions sterling, was reduced to actual beggary.

'He attained a more lasting prosperity later on, and died a grandee of Spain of the first class, having highly distinguished himself in council and the field.

'It is not in any vaingloriousness, sir, I have related this story. Of all the greatness that once adorned my house, these threadbare clothes are sorry relics. We were talking of life's reverses, however, and probably my case is not without its moral.'

Gerald sat silently gazing with a sort of admiration at one

who could with such seeming calm discuss the most calamitous accident of fortune.

'How thoroughly you must know the world!' exclaimed he at last.

'Ay, sir; in the popular acceptation of the phrase I *do* know it. Plenty of good and plenty of bad is there in it, and so mingled and blended that there is nothing rarer in life than to find any nature either all lovable or all detestable. There are dark stains in the fairest marble, so are there in natures the world deems utterly depraved touches of human sentiment whose tenderness no poet ever dreamed of. And if I were to give you a lesson, it would be—never be over-sanguine, but never despair of humanity!'

'As you drew nigh the villa this evening,' said Gerald slowly, and with all the deliberation of one approaching a theme of interest, 'I chanced to be in the orangery beneath the terrace. You were speaking to your companion in confidence, and I heard you say what augured but badly for the success of my cause. Your words made so deep an impression on me that I have asked to see and speak with you. Tell me, therefore, in all frankness, what you know, and in equal candour what you think about this enterprise.'

'What claim have I upon your forbearance if I say what may be ungracious? How shall I hope to be forgiven if I tell you what is not pleasant to hear?'

'The word of one who is well weary of delusions shall be your guarantee.'

'I accept the pledge.'

He walked three or four times up and down the room, to all seeming in deep deliberation with himself, and then facing full round in front of Gerald, said—

'You were educated at the convent of the Jesuits—are you a member of the order?'

'No.'

'Have they made no advances to you to become such?'

'None.'

'It is as I suspected,' muttered he to himself; then added

aloud: 'They mean to employ *you* as the French king did your father. You are to be the menace in times of trouble, and the sacrifice in the day of terms and accommodations. Be neither!'

With this he waved his hand in farewell, and hastily left the room.

CHAPTER XXI

A FOREST RIDE

GERALD passed a restless, disturbed night. Purcell's words, ever ringing in his ears, foreboded nothing but failure and disaster, while there seemed something almost sarcastic in the comparison he drew between the Prince Charles Edward's rashness and his own waiting, delaying policy.

'Is it fair or just,' thought he, 'to taunt me with this? I was not bred up to know my station and my claims. None told me I was of royal blood and had a throne for a heritage. These tidings break on me as I am worn down by misfortune and broken by illness, so that my shattered intellects scarcely credit them. Even now, on what, or on whom, do I rely? Has not disease undermined my strength and distrust my judgment, so that I believe in nothing, nor in anybody? Ah, Riquetti, *your* poisons never leave the blood till it has ceased to circulate.'

There were days when the whole plan and scheme of his life seemed to him such a mockery and a deception that he felt a sort of scorn for himself in believing it. It was like childhood or dotage to his mind this dream of a greatness so far off, so impossible, and he burned for some real actual existence with truthful incidents and interests. Gloomy doubts would also cross him, whether he might be nothing but a mere tool in the hands of certain crafty men like Massoni, who having used him for their purpose to-day would cast him off as worthless to-morrow. These thoughts became at times almost insupportable, and his only relief against them was in great bodily fatigue. It was his habit, when in this mood, to mount his horse and ride into the forest. The deep pine-wood was traversed in various directions by long grassy alleys, miles in extent; and here, save at the very rarest intervals, no one was to be met with. It is not easy to conceive anything more solemn and gloomy than one of these forests, where the only sound is a low, sighing cadence as the wind stirs in the pine-tops. A solitary blackbird, perchance, may warble his mellow song in the stillness, or, as evening closes, the wailing cry of the owl be heard; otherwise the stillness is deathlike.

Whole days had Gerald often passed in these leafy solitudes, till at length he grew to recognise even in that apparent uniformity certain spots and certain trees by which he could calculate his distance from home. Two or three little clearings there were also where trees had been felled and small piles of brushwood were formed; these were his most remote wanderings and marked the place whence he turned his steps homeward.

On the morning we now speak of he rode at such reckless speed that in less than two hours he had left these familiar places far behind and penetrated deeper into the dense wood. Toward noon he dismounted to relieve his somewhat wearied horse, and walked along for hours, a strange feeling of pleasure stirring his heart at the thought of his utter loneliness; for there is something in the mind of youth that attaches itself eagerly to anything that seems to savour of the adventurous. And the mere presence of a new object or a new situation will often suffice for this. Gradually, as he went onward, his mind calmed down, the fever of his brain abated; passages of the poets he best loved rose to his memory, and he repeated verses to himself as he strolled along, his mind unconsciously drinking in the soothing influences that come of solitude and reverie.

Meanwhile the day declined, and although no sense of fatigue oppressed himself, he was warned by the blood-red nostrils of his horse and his drawn-up flanks that the beast needed both food and water.

It was a rare occurrence to chance upon the tiniest stream in these tracts, so that he had nothing for it but to push forward and trust that after an hour or so he might issue beyond the bounds of the wood. Again in the saddle, his mettled horse carried him gallantly along without any show of distress; but although he rode at a sharp pace there seemed little prospect of emerging from the wood; tall avenues of dark stems still lined the way, and the dusky foliage spread itself above his head. If he had but preserved a direct line he was well aware that he must be able to traverse the forest in its very widest part within a day, so that he now urged his horse more briskly to gain the open country before night-fall. For the first time, however, the animal showed signs of fatigue, and Gerald was fain to get down and lead him. Half dreamily lost in his own thoughts he moved unconsciously along, when suddenly a blaze of golden light startled him, and looking up he saw he had left the wood behind him and was standing on the crest of a grassy hill, from which he could see miles of open country at his feet, backed by the Maremma Mountains, behind which the sun was fast sinking. It was that true Italian landscape which to eyes only accustomed to the scenery north of the Alps has always a character of hardness, and even bleakness; but as by time and frequency this impression dies away, such scenes possess an attractiveness unequalled by all other lands. There was the vast plain, traversed by its winding rivulet, its course only traceable by the pollard willows that marked the banks; while forests of olives alternated with mulberry plantations, around and between which the straggling vines were trellised. On the hot earth, half hid by flowers of many a gorgeous hue, lay great yellow gourds and pumpkins, as though thrown to the surface in a flood of rich abundance; and far away in the distance the mountains closed in the view, their summit capped with villages, or, perchance, some rugged castellated ruin, centuries old.

How was it that Gerald stood and gazed at all these like one spell-bound? Why was that scene not altogether new to his eyes? Why did he follow out that little road, now emerging from the olives and now lost again, till it gained the stream, which was spanned by a rude wooden bridge? How is it that the humble mill yonder, whose laggard wheel scarce stirs the water, seems to him like some old familiar thing? And why does he strain his sight in vain to see the zigzag road up the steep mountain-side? It was because a flood of old memories were rushing full upon his mind, bringing up boyhood and 'long ago.' That was the very path by which he set out to seek his fortune, when scarcely more than a child he fled from the villa; there was the wide plain through which he had toiled weary and foot-sore; in that little copse of fruit-trees, beside the stream, had he slept at night; there, where a little cross marks a shrine, had he stopped to eat his breakfast; around the head of that little lake had he wended his way toward the mountains.

If at first these memories arose faintly, like the mere out-lines of a dream, they grew by degrees bolder and stronger. His boyish life at the Tana then rose before him; the little room in which he used to sit, and read, and ponder; then the narrow stair by which he would creep noiselessly down to stroll out at night and wander all alone beside the dark lake; and then the dusky pine-wood, through whose leafy shades Gabriel would saunter as the evening closed in.

'I will see them all once more,' cried he aloud; 'I will go back over that scene, calling up all that I can remember of the past; I will try if my heart has kept the promise of its boyish hopes, and see if I have wandered away from the path I once destined for myself.' There was a marvellous fascination in the reality of all he saw and all the recollections it evoked, after that life of fictitious station and mock great-ness in which he had been living of late.

He who has not tried the experiment for himself cannot believe the extent of that view obtained into his own nature from simply revisiting the scenes of boyhood. Till we have gone back to the places themselves, we can never realise the life we led there; how we felt in that long ago; what we thought of, what we ambitioned.

Wonderful messengers of conscience are these same old memories! the little garden we used to dig; the narrow bed we slept in; our old bench at school, deep graven on the heart, with all its thrilling incidents of boyish life; the pathway through the flowery meadow down to the stream, where we used to bathe; the little summer-house under the honeysuckles, where we heard or invented such marvellous stories. Rely upon it, there is not one of these unassociated with some high hopes, some generous notion, some noble ambition; something, in short, which we meant to be, but never realised; some path we intended to follow, but strayed from in that wild and tumultuous conflict we call life.

Guided by the little river, on which the setting sun was now shedding its last lustre, Gerald walked along beside his horse, and just as the night was falling reached the mill. To his great surprise did he learn that he was full fifty miles from Orvieto, for though he had passed an entire day, from earliest dawn, on the way, he had never contemplated the distance he had travelled. As it was no unusual occurrence for special couriers with despatches to pass by this route toward the Tuscan frontier, his appearance caused little remark, and he was invited to sit down at the miller's table when the household assembled for supper.

'You are bound for St. Stephano, I'll warrant,' said the miller, as he stood looking at Gerald, who bedded down his tired beast.

Gerald assented with a nod, and went on with his work.

'If I were you, then, I'd not take the low road by the Lago Scuro at this season.'

'And why so?'

'Just for this reason: they have got malaria fever up in the mountains, and the refugees who live up there, for safety against the carabinieri, are obliged to come down into the plains, and they troop the roads here in gangs of twenty and thirty, making the country insecure after nightfall.'

'They are brigands, then ?' asked Gerald.

'Every man, ay, and every woman of them! They respect neither priest nor prefect. What think you they did three weeks ago at Somarra? A travelling company of players coming through the town obtained leave from the Delegato to give a representation. The theatre was crammed, as you may well believe, such a pleasure not being an everyday one. Well, the orchestra had finished the symphony and up drew the curtain, when, instead of a village fête with peasants dancing, the stage was crowded with savage-looking fellows armed to the teeth, every one of whom held a blunderbuss levelled at the audience. Meanwhile the doors of the boxes were opened, and the people inside politely requested to hand out their money, watches, jewels, in fact, all that they had of value about them, the pit being treated exactly in the same fashion, for none could escape, as all the doors were held by the bandits. They carried away forty-seven thousand francs' worth for the night's work. Indeed, the Delegato has never risen from his bed since it happened, and expects every day to be summoned to Rome, or sent off to prison at Viterbo.'

'And why does the Pope's government not take some steps against these fellows? Why are they suffered to ravage the whole country at their will?'

'You must ask your master, the Cardinal, that question,' said the miller, laughing. 'It would be easy enough to hunt them down, now that they've got the fever in the mountains, if any one cared to do it; but the "Pastore," as they call their captain, pays handsomely for his patent to rob, and he never kills where it can be avoided.'

'And who is this Pastore—what was he ?'

'He was a friar. Some say he was once a monsignore; and he might have been, from his manners and language.'

'You have seen him, then ?'

'Seen him! *per Bacco!* that have I, and to my cost! He comes himself to take up his "duc de Pasqua," as he calls his

Easter-dues, which are not the lighter that he assesses them all before he sits down to supper.'

'Do you mean to tell me that he would sit down to table with you?'

'Ay, and be the merriest at the board too. So full of pleasant stories and good songs was he one night that one of my boys could not resist the fascination of his company, but started off the next morning to join him, and has never returned.'

If Gerald's curiosity was excited to learn many particulars of this celebrated bandit chief, the miller was only too happy to be questioned on a theme he loved so well. In his apprehension the Pastore was no ordinary robber, but a sort of agent, partly political, partly financial, of certain great people of Rome. This was a theory he was somewhat vain of having propounded, and he supported it with considerable ingenuity.

The Pastore himself was described as a happy-looking, well-to-do man, past the prime of life, but still hale and vigorous; and, if not very active in body, with considerable acuteness and a ready wit. He stood well in the estimation of the peasantry, who were always ready to render him little services, and to whom in return he would show his gratitude by little presents at the fête-days or scenes of family rejoicing. 'And as for the Curé,' said the miller, 'only ask him who sent the handsomest chaplet for the head of the Madonna, or who gave the silver lamp that burns at the shrine of St. Nicomède?'

This strange blending of devotional observance with utter lawlessness—this singular union of *bon homme* with open violence, were features that in all his intercourse with life Gerald had never met with; and he was not a little curious to see one who could combine qualities so incompatible.

'I should certainly like to see him,' said he, after a pause.

'Only ride that black mare through the pass of the "Capri," to-morrow; let him see how she brushes her way through the tall fern and never slips a foot over the rocky ledges, and I'll lay my life on't you'll see him, and hear him too.'

'You mean to say that he'd soon replace me in the saddle,' said Gerald half angrily.

'I mean to say that the horse would change owners, and you be never the richer of the compact.'

'A bullet will overtake a man, let him ride ever so fast,' said Gerald calmly; 'and your Pastore has only to lie in ambush till he has covered me, to make me a very harmless foe ; but I was thinking of a fair meeting—man to man——'

A gesture of scornful meaning by the miller here arrested Gerald's words, and the young man grew crimson with shame and anger together.

'It is easy enough to say these things, and hard to disprove them; but if I were certain to meet this fellow alone and without his followers, I'd take the road you speak of to-morrow without so much as asking where it leads to.'

An insolent laugh from the miller, as he arose from his seat, almost made the young man's passion boil over.

'You asked about the "Capri" pass—that's a picture of it,' said he, as he pointed to a rude representation of a deep mountain gorge, along which a foaming torrent was wildly dashing. Stunted pine-trees lined the crags, and fantastically-shaped rocks broke the leafy outline, on one of which the artist had drawn the figure of a brigand, as with gun in hand he peered down into the dark glen.

'That is a spot,' said the miller half laughingly, 'the Carabinieri of the Holy Father have never fancied; they tried it once—I forget how many years ago—and left eleven of their comrades behind them, and since that it has been as sacred for them as St. John of Lateran.'

'But I see no road; it seems to be a mere cleft between the mountains,' said Gerald.

'Ay, but there is a road—-a sort of bridlepath ; it rises from the valley and creeps along up yonder where you see a little railing of wood, and then gains that peak which, winding around it, reaches a wide table-land. I have not been there myself; but they tell me how from that you can see over the whole Maremma, and in fine weather the sea beyond it, and the port of St. Stephano and the islands.'

The miller was now launched upon a favourite theme, and went on to describe how the smugglers, who paid a sort of blackmail for the privilege, usually took this route from the coast into the interior. It saved miles and miles of road, and was besides perfectly safe against all molestation. As it led direct to the Tuscan frontier, it was also selected by all who made their escape from Roman prisons. 'To be sure,' added he, 'it is less frequented now that the Pastore is likely to be met with; for as it is all chance what humour he may have on him, none like to risk their lives in such company.'

Though Gerald was aware that 'brigandage' was a Roman institution—a regularly covenanted service of the State, by which no inconsiderable revenue reached the hands of some very exalted individuals—he had never before heard that these outlaws were occasionally employed as actual agents of the Government to arrest and detain travellers against whom suspicion rested, to rifle foreign couriers of the despatches they carried to the Ministers; now and then it was even alleged that they had broken into strong places to destroy documents by which guilt could be proved or innocence established—all of these services being of a nature little likely to reward men for the peril, had they not acted under orders from above! There might possibly have been much exaggeration in the account the miller gave of these men's lives and functions, but there was that blending of incident and fact with his theorisings that certainly amazed Gerald and interested him deeply. It was, to be sure, no small aid to the force of the narrative that the yellow moonlight was now streaming full upon one side of the very scene where these characters acted, and that from the little window where he sat he could look out upon their mountain-home.

'See,' said the miller, pointing toward a high peak, 'where you see the fire yonder there is an encampment of some of them! You can judge now how little these fellows fear being surprised.' As Gerald continued to gaze, a second and then a third flame shot up from the summits of other hills farther off, suggesting to the miller that these were certainly signals of some kind or other.

'There! rely on it, they have work on their hands up yonder to-night,' said the miller; and having pointed out his room to Gerald, he arose to retire. 'It will, maybe, cost many a penance, many a pater, to wipe off what will be done 'twixt this and daybreak'; and with this pious speech he left the room.

CHAPTER XXII

'IL PASTORE'

AFTER the first few moments of astonishment which followed Gerald's awaking to see himself in a strange place, with strange and novel objects around him, his first thought was to return to Orvieto. He pictured to himself all the alarm his absence must have occasioned, and imagined how each in turn would have treated the event. The angry astonishment of the Cardinal, ready to adopt any solution of the mystery that implied intrigue and plot: the haughty indignation of the Contessa, that he had dared to take any step unauthorised by herself: the hundred rumours in the household: the questionings as to who had saddled and prepared his horse, what road he had taken, and so on.

There are natures—there are even families—in which a strong predominating trait exists to do or say whatever creates astonishment or attracts wonder. It is a distinct form of egotism, and was remarkably conspicuous in the House of Stuart. They all liked much to be objects of marvel and surprise; to have men lost in wonderment over their words or their motives, or speculating with ingenuity as to their secret intentions.

To Gerald himself this taste was a perfect passion, and he

loved to see couriers arriving and departing in hot haste,
while groups of eager loungers questioned and guessed at
what it all might mean. He liked to fancy the important
place he thus occupied in men's thoughts, and would any
day have been willing to encounter an actual danger could
he only have assured himself of it being widely discussed.
This dramatic tendency was strongly marked in the character of Charles Edward; still the actual events of his life
were in themselves sufficiently adventurous to display it less
prominently; but he ever delighted in these stage effects
which strike by situation or a picturesque costume. Gerald
inherited this trait, and experienced intense delight in its
exercise. He fancied his Eminence the Cardinal, balancing
between fear and anger, sending out emissaries on every
side, asking counsels here, rejecting suggestions there, while
Guglia, too haughty to confess astonishment, would be lost
in conjecturing what had become of him.

If it should be wondered at that Gerald felt no more
tender sentiment toward the lovely Countess with whom he
had been closely domesticated, and who enjoyed so fully all
the confidence of his fortunes, let us own frankly that it was
not his fault; he did his very best to be in love with her,
and for that very reason, perhaps, he failed! Not all the
desire in the world will enable a man to catch a contagious
malady, nor all his precautions suffice to escape it; so is it
with love. Gerald saw in her one who would have adorned
the highest station : she was eminently beautiful, and with
a grace that was a fascination; she possessed to perfection
those arts which charm in society, and had that blending of
readiness in repartee with a sort of southern languor that
makes a rare element of captivation; and yet with all this
he did not fall in love. And the reason was this : Guglia
had none of those sudden caprices, those moods of exorbitant
hope or dark despondency, those violent alternations of
temperament which suggest quick resolve, or quicker action.
She was calm—too calm; reflective—too reflective—and, as
he thought, infinitely too much occupied in preparing for

eventualities either to enjoy the present or boldly to dare
the future.

These traits of hers, too, wounded his self-love; they made
him feel inferior to her; and he smarted under counsels and
advice which came with the authority of dictations. A
casual wound to his pride also aided this impression; it was
an accidental word he had once overheard, as she was walking
one evening with the Cardinal in an alley of the garden
adjoining one in which he was standing. They had been
discussing his fortunes and his character; and she remarked,
with a certain bitterness in her tone, as if contradicting some
hopeful anticipation of her uncle. '*Non, caro zio non. E piu
capace de farsi Prete.*' ('No, my dear uncle: more likely is he
to turn priest!') Strange and significant words from one
who held that order in depreciation, and could even dare to
avow this estimate to one of themselves.

These words never left Gerald's mind; they flashed across
him as he awoke of a morning; they broke upon him as he
lay thinking in his bed; they mingled with his speculations
on the future; and, more fatally still, came to his memory
at moments when, seated at his side, she inspired hopes of
a glorious destiny. Again and again did he ask himself,
how was it that esteeming him thus she was willing to join
her fate to his? And the only answer was one still more
wounding to his self-love.

What if she should have totally misconstrued this weak,
uncertain nature? What if she should have misinterpreted
this character so full of indecision? How, if this would-be
priest were to turn out one reckless in daring, and indifferent
to all consequences? How, if the next tidings she were to
hear of him were from some far-away country: some scene
that might show how cheaply he held the tinsel decoration of
a mock station, the miserable pretension to a rank he was
never to enjoy! 'At all events,' said he, 'they shall have·
matter for their speculations, and shall not see me for some
days to come!' And with this determination—rather like
the resolve of a pettish child than of a grown man—he

sauntered into the mill, where the miller was now busily engaged.

'Your master's despatches have nothing very pressing in them, I see,' said the miller; 'I scarcely thought to have met you this morning.'

'I have ample time at my disposal,' said Gerald; 'so that I can reach St. Stephano some day within the coming week I shall be soon enough; insomuch that I have half a mind to gratify the curiosity you have excited in me and make a short ramble through the mountains yonder.'

'Nay, nay, leave that track to your left hand; follow the road by the head of Lago Scuro, and don't run your neck into peril for nothing.'

'But you told me last night this Pastore was never cruel when it served no purpose: that he was far readier to help a poor man than to rifle him. What should I fear then?'

'That he might look into the palm of your hand and see that it was one not much used to daily labour. If he but thought you a spy, *per Bacco!* I'd not be in your shoes for all the jewels in the Vatican!'

'Couldn't you manage to disguise me as one of your own people, and give me some sort of a letter for him?'

'By the way, there is a letter for him these four days back,' said the miller suddenly; 'and I have had no opportunity of sending it on.'

'There, then, is the very thing we want,' broke in Gerald.

'Here's the letter here,' said the miller, taking the document from the leaves of a book. 'It comes from the Ursuline Convent, on the other side of the Tiber. Strange enough that the Pastore should have correspondence with the holy ladies of St. Ursula. It was a monk, too, that fetched it here, and his courage failed him to go any farther. Indeed, I believe that picture of the Capri pass decided him on turning back.'

'The greater fool he! He ought to have known that the Pastore was not likely to requite a good office with cruelty,' said Gerald.

'As to that, it would depend on what humour he was in at the moment.' Then, after a pause, he added, 'If you like to risk the chance of finding him in a good temper, you have only to borrow a coat and cap from one of my boys, and take that letter. You will tell him that it was I sent you on with it, and he'll ask no further question.'

'And these hands of mine that you said would betray me,' said Gerald, 'what shall I do to disguise them?'

'Some fresh walnuts will soon colour them, and your face too; and now let me direct you as to the road you'll take.' And so the miller, drawing Gerald to the window, began to describe the route, pointing out various prominent objects as landmarks.

Having acquainted himself, so far as he could, with all the details of the way, Gerald proceeded to costume himself for the expedition, and so completely had the dye on his skin and the change of dress metamorphosed him, that for a second or two the miller did not recognise him.

With a touch of humour that he rarely gave way to, Gerald saluted him in rustic fashion, while in a strong peasant accent he asked if his honour had no further commands for him.

The miller laughed good-humouredly, and shook his hand in adieu. 'I more than suspect the black mare will be mine,' muttered he, as he looked after Gerald till he disappeared in the distance.

For miles and miles Gerald walked on without paying any attention to the scene around him; the spirit of adventure occupied his mind to the exclusion of all else, and he not only imagined every possible issue to the present adventure, but fancied what his sensations might have been were it his fortune to have been launched upon the great enterprise to which his hopes so long had tended. 'Oh, if this were but Scotland or Ireland,' thought he; 'if my foot now only trod the soil that I could call my own; if I could but realise to myself once, even once, the glorious sense of being recognised as one of that race that once ruled there as sovereigns;

if I could but taste the intoxication of that generous devotion
that through all his calamities once cheered my father, I'd
think the moment had repaid me for all the cares of life!
And now it has all passed away like a dream. As Purcell
said, "They want us no longer!" We belong to the past,
and have no significance in the present! Strange, sad,
mysterious destiny!' There was a humiliation in that
feeling that gave him intense pain; it was the sense of being
cut off from all sympathy, estranged from the wishes, the
hopes, the ambition of his fellow-men. Out of an isolation
like *that* it was that Gabriel Riquetti had taught him to
believe men achieve their greatest successes. You must
first of all feel yourself alone, all alone in life, ere you can
experience that liberty that ensures free action.

This was one of his axioms which he loved to repeat; and
whether suggested by the scene where he had first met that
wonderful man, or merely induced by the course of reflection,
many of Mirabeau's early teachings and precepts rose to his
memory as he journeyed along.

For some time he had been unconsciously ascending a
somewhat steep mountain-path, so deeply imbedded between
two lines of thick brushwood as to intercept all view at
either side, when suddenly the way emerged from the dense
copse and took the mountain side, disappearing at a jutting
promontory of rock around which it seemed to pass. As his
eye followed the track thus far he saw the flutter of what
seemed a scarlet banner; but on looking longer discovered
it was the gay saddle-cloth of a mule, from which the rider
had apparently dismounted. He had but just time to mark
this much ere the object disappeared beyond the rock.

Cheered to fancy that some other traveller might chance
to be on the same road with himself, he now hastened his
steps. The way, however, was longer than he had supposed,
and on gaining the promontory he descried the mule fully
two miles away, stealing carefully along over the rugged
bridle-path on the mountain. The object became now a
pursuit, and he strained his eyes to see if by some by-path

he could not succeed in gaining on the chase. While thus looking he saw that two figures followed the mule at a little distance, but what they were he could not ascertain.

It was very unlikely that any of the " Pastore's " followers would have adopted a gear so striking and so easily seen as this bright trapping, and so Gerald at once set the travellers down as some peasants returning to their homes in the Maremma, or on a pilgrimage to some religious shrine.

With no small exertion he so far gained upon them as to be able to note their appearance, and discover that one was a friar in the dusky olive-coloured frock of the Franciscan, and the other a woman, dressed in some conventual costume which he did not recognise. He could also see that the mule carried a somewhat cumbrous pack, and an amount of baggage rarely the accompaniment of a travelling friar.

Who has not felt his curiosity stimulated by some mere trifling circumstance when occurring in a remote spot, which had it happened on the world's crowded highway would have passed unnoticed ? It was this strange attendant on these wayfarers that urged Gerald to press on to overtake them. Forgetting the peasant costume which he wore and the part it thus behoved him to pursue, he called out in a tone of half command for them to stop till he came up.

' Halt,' cried he, ' and tell me if this be the way to the Capri Pass ! '

The friar turned hastily, and stood until Gerald approached.

' You speak like one accustomed to give his orders on these mountains, my son,' said he, in a tone of stern reproof ; ' so that even a poor follower of St. Francis is surprised to be thus accosted.'

By this time Gerald had so far recovered his self-possession as to see how he had compromised his assumed character, and in a voice of deep submission, and with a peasant accent he answered—

' I ask pardon, worthy Fra, but travelling all alone in this

wild region has so overcome me that I scarcely know what I
say, or understand what I hear.'

'Whence do you come ?' asked the friar rudely.

'From the Mill at Orto-Molino.'

'And whither are you going ?'

'To St. Stephano after I have delivered a letter that I
have here.'

'To whom is your letter addressed, my son ?' said the Fra,
in a more gentle voice.

With difficulty did Gerald repress the sharp reply that
was on his lips, and say—

'It is for one that neither you nor I know much of—Il
Pastore.'

'I know him well,' said the friar boldly; 'and say it
without fear of contradiction, I am the only one he makes a
shrift to—ay, that does he, ill as you think of him,' added
he, as if answering the half-contemptuous smile on Gerald's
face. 'Let's see your letter.'

With an awkward reluctance Gerald drew forth the letter
and showed it.

'Ah!' cried the Fra eagerly, 'he had been looking for
that letter this many a day back; but it comes too late
now.'

As he said this he pressed eagerly forward and whispered
to the nun who was walking at the side of the mule. She
looked back hurriedly for an instant, and then as rapidly
turned her head again. They continued now to converse
eagerly for some time, and seemed totally to have forgotten
Gerald, as he walked on after them; when the Fra turned
suddenly round and said—

'I'll take charge of your letter, my son, while you guide
our sister down to Cheatstone, a little cluster of houses you'll
see at the foot of the mountain; and if there be an answer
I'll fetch it to-morrow, ere daybreak.'

'Nay, Fra, I promised that I would deliver this with my
own hands, and I mean to be no worse than my word.'

'You'll have to be at least less than your word,' said the

friar, 'for the Pastore would not see you. These are his
days of penance and mortification, and I am the only one
who dares to approach him.'

'I am pledged to deliver this into his own hand,' said
Gerald calmly.

'You may have said many a rash thing in your life, but
never a rasher than that,' said the Fra sternly. 'I tell you
again, he'll not see you. At all events, you'll have to find
the road by your own good wits, and it is a path that has
puzzled shrewder heads.'

With this rude speech, uttered in the rudest way, the Fra
moved hastily on till he overtook his companion, leaving
Gerald to follow how he pleased.

For some time he continued on after the others, vainly
straining his eyes on every side for any signs of a pathway
upward. The way which he had trod before, with hope to
cheer him, became now wearisome and sad. He was sick of
his adventure, out of temper with his want of success, and
dissatisfied with himself. He at last resolved that he would
go no farther on his track than a certain little olive copse
which nestled in a cleft of the mountain, reaching which he
would repose for a while, and then retrace his steps.

The sun was strong and the heat oppressive, insomuch
that when at length he gained the copse, he was well pleased
to throw himself down beneath the shade and take his rest.
He had already forgotten the Franciscan and his fellow-
traveller, and was deeply musing over his own fortunes, when
suddenly he heard their voices, and, creeping noiselessly to
the edge of the cliff, he saw them seated at a little well,
beside which their breakfast was spread out. The woman
had thrown back her hood and showed now a beautiful head,
whose long black hair fell heavily on either shoulder, while
her taper fingers, covered with many a splendid ring, plainly
showed that her conventual dress was only a disguise. Nor
was this the only sign that surprised him, for now he saw
that a short brass blunderbuss, the regular weapon of the
brigand, lay close to the friar's hand.

'It is the Pastore himself,' thought Gerald, as he gazed down at the brawny limbs and well-knit proportions of the stranger. 'How could I ever have mistaken him for a friar?' The more he thought over the friar's manner—his eagerness to get the letter, and the careless indifference afterward with which he suffered Gerald to leave him—the more he felt assured that this was no other than the celebrated chief himself.

'At least, I have succeeded in seeing him,' thought he; 'and why should I not go boldly forward and speak to him?' The resolve was no sooner formed than he proceeded to execute it. In a moment after he had descended the cliff, and, making his way through the brushwood, stood before them.

'So, then, you *will* track me, youngster,' said the friar angrily. 'Once—twice—to-day the road was open to you to seek your own way, and you would not take it. How bent you must be to do yourself an ill turn!'

'You are "Il Pastore,"' said Gerald boldly.

'And thou art *Gherardi mio!*' cried the woman, as she rushed wildly toward him and clasped him in her arms. It was Marietta herself who spoke.

How tell the glorious outburst of Gerald's joy, as he overpowered her with questions—whence she came, whither going, how and why, and wherefore there? Was she really and truly the Egyptian who had visited him on his sick-bed, and not a mere vision?

'And was it from thy lips, then,' cried he, 'that I learned that all this ambition was but a snare—that I was destined to be only the tool of crafty men, deep in their own designs? At times the revelation seemed to come from thee, and at times a burst of heart-felt conviction. Which was it, Marietta *mia?*'

'Who is he?' cried the Fra eagerly. 'This surely cannot be—ay, but it is the Prince—the son of my old lord and master!' and he knelt and kissed Gerald's hands over and over again. 'He knows me not—at least as I once was—

the friend, the boon companion of a king's son,' continued he passionately.

'Were you, then, one of his old Scottish followers—one of those faithful men who clung so devotedly to his cause?'

'No, no; but I was one that he loved better than them all.'

'And you, Marietta, dearest, how is it that I see you here?' cried Gerald, again turning to her.

'I came many a weary mile after you, *mio caro*,' said she. 'I knew of these men's designs long, long ago, and I determined to save you from them. I believed I could have secured Massoni as your friend; but I was wrong—the Jesuit was stronger in him than the man. I remained at St. Ursula months after I might have left it, just to see the Père—to watch his game—and, if possible, attach him to me; but I failed—utterly failed. He was true to his cause, and would not accept my love. More fortunate, however, was I with the Cardinal—even, perhaps, that I wished or cared for —His Eminence was my slave. There was not a secret of the Vatican I did not learn. I read the correspondence with the Spanish minister, Arazara; I suggested the replies; I heard the whole plan for your expedition—how you were to be secretly married to the Countess Ridolfi, and the marriage only avowed when your success was assured.'

She paused, and the Fra broke in—'Tell all—everything —the mine has exploded now, and none are the worse for it. Go on with your confession.'

'It is of the other alternative he speaks,' said she, dropping her voice to a faint whisper. 'Had you failed——'

'And then—what then, Marietta?'

'You were in that case to have been betrayed into the hands of the English, or poisoned! The scheme to accomplish the first was already planned. I have here the letters which are to accredit me to see and converse with Sir Horace Mann, at Florence; and which I mean to deliver too. I am resolved to trace out to the very last who are the accomplices in this guilt. The world is well edified by tales of mob violence and bloodshed. Even genius seeks its inspiration in inveighing against popular excesses. It is time to show that crimes lurk under purple as well as rags, and that the deadliest vengeances are often devised beneath gilded ceilings. We knew of one once, Gherardi, who could have told men these truths—one who carried from this world with him the "funeral trappings of the monarchy" and the wail of the people.

'Of whom did she speak?' asked the friar.

'Of Gabriel Riquetti, whom she loved,' and the last words were whispered by Gerald in her ear.

Marietta held down her head, and as she covered her face with her hands muttered—'But who loved not her!'

'Gabriel Riquetti,' broke in the friar, 'had more of good and bad in him than all the saints and all the devils that ever warred. He had the best of principles and the worst of practices, and never did a wicked thing but he could show you a virtuous reason for it.'

Struck by the contemptuous glance of Marietta, Gerald followed the look she gave, and saw that the friar's eyes were bloodshot, and his face purple with excess.

CHAPTER XXIII

THE END

FROM Marietta Gerald heard how, with that strange fatality of inconsistency which ever seemed to accompany the fortunes of the Stuarts, none proved faithful followers save those whose lives of excess or debauchery rendered them valueless; and thus the drunken Fra, whose wild snatches of song and ribaldry now broke in upon the colloquy, was no other than the Carmelite, Kelly, the once associate and corrupter of his father.

In a half-mad enthusiasm to engage men in the cause of his Prince he had begun a sort of recruitment of a legion who were to land in Scotland or Ireland. The means by

which he at first operated were somewhat liberally contributed to him by a secret emissary of the family, whom
Kelly at length discovered to be the private secretary of
Miss Walsingham, the former mistress of Charles Edward.
Later on, however, he found out that this lady herself was
actually a pensioner of the English government, and in secret
correspondence with Mr. Pitt, who, through her instrumentality, was in possession of every plan of the Pretender,
and knew of his daily movements. This treacherous intercourse had begun several years before the death of Charles
Edward, and lasted for some years after that event.

Stung by the consciousness of being duped, as well as
maddened by having been rendered an enemy to the cause
he sought to serve, Kelly disbanded his followers, and
took to the mountains as a brigand. With years he had
grown only more abandoned to excess of every kind. All
his experiences of life had shown little beyond baseness and
corruption, and he had grown to care for nothing beyond the
enjoyment of the passing hour, except when the possibility
of a vengeance on those who had betrayed him might
momentarily awake his passion, and excite him to some
effort of vindictive anger.

In his hours of mad debauchery he would rave about
landing in England, and a plan he had conceived for
assassinating the king; then it was his scheme to murder
Mr. Pitt, and sometimes all these were abandoned for the
desire to make Miss Walsingham herself pay the penalty of
her base and unwomanly treachery.

'He came to our convent gate in his garb of a friar to beg,'
said Marietta. 'I saw him but for an instant, and I knew
him at once. He was one of those who, in the "red days"
of the Revolution, mocked the order he belonged to by wearing a rosary of playing-dice! and he recognised me as one
who had even more shamelessly exposed herself.' A deep
crimson flush covered her face and neck as she spoke, and as
quickly fled, to leave her as pale as a corpse. 'Oh, *mio caro*,'
cried she, 'there are intoxications more maddening to the

senses than those of drinking; there are wild fevers of the mind, when degradation seems a sort of martyrdom; and in the very depth of our infamy and shame we appear to ourselves to have attained to something superhuman in self-denial. It was my fate to live with one who inspired these sentiments.' She paused for a few seconds, and then, trembling on every accent, she said : 'To win his love, to conquer the heart that would not yield to me, I dared more than ever woman, far more than ever man, dared.'

'Here's to the king's buffoon, and a bumper toast it shall be,' burst in the friar, with a drunken ribaldry; 'and if there are any will not drink it, let him drink to the Minister's mistress !'

To the sudden gesture which Gerald's anger evoked, Marietta quickly interposed her hand, and, in a low, soft voice, besought him to remain quiet.

> 'If the cause were up, or the cause were down,
>   What matter to you or to me ;
> For though the Prince had played his crown,
>   Our stake was a bare bawbee !'

sang out Kelly lustily. 'Who'll deny it? Who'll say there wasn't sound reason and philosophy in that sentiment? None knew it better than Prince Charlie himself.'

'And was this man the companion of a Prince?' whispered Gerald in her ear.

'Even so; fallen fortunes bring degraded followers,' said Marietta. 'I have heard it said that many of his father's associates were of this stamp.'

'And how could men hope to restore a cause thus contaminated and stained?' cried he, somewhat louder.

'That's what Kinloch said,' burst in Kelly; 'you remember the song—

> 'The Prince he swore, on his broad claymore,
>   That he'd sit in his father's chair,
> But there wasn't a man, outside his clan,
>   That wanted to see him there, boys,
>   That wanted to see him there.'

2 C

'A black falsehood, as black as ever a traitor uttered!'
cried Gerald, whose passion burst all bounds.

'Here's to the traitors—hip, hip! To the traitors, for it
was—

> 'The traitors all in St. Cannes's hall,
>   They feasted merrily there,
> While the wearied men sought the bleak, wild glen,
>   And tasted but sorry fare, boys,
>   Tasted but sorry fare.

> 'Oh, if I'd a voice, and could have my choice,
>   I know with whom I'd be,
> Not the hungry lads, with their threadbare plaids,
>   But the lords of high degree, boys,
>   The lords of high degree.'

'And so thought the Prince too,' cried he out fiercely, and
in a tone meant for an insolent taunt. 'He liked the easy
life and the soft couch of St. Germains far better than the
long march and the heather-bed in the Highlands.'

'How long must I endure this fellow's insolence?' whispered
Gerald to Marietta, in a voice trembling with passion.

'For my sake, Gherardi,' she began; but the Fra overheard the words, and with a drunken laugh broke in—

'If you have a drop of Stuart blood in you, you'll yield to
the woman, whatever it is she asks.'

Stung beyond control of reason, Gerald sprang to his feet;
but before he could even approach Kelly, the stout friar
had grasped his short blunderbuss and cocked it.

'Another step—one step more, and if you were the
anointed King himself, instead of his bastard, I'll send you
to your reckoning!'

With a spring like the bound of a tiger, Gerald dashed at
him; but the Fra was prepared, and, raising the weapon to
his side, he fired. A wild, mad cry, blended with the loud
report, echoed in many a mountain gorge, and the youth fell
dead on the sward.

Marietta threw herself down upon the corpse, kissing the

lifeless lips, and clasping her arms around the motionless body. With every endearing word she tried to call him back to life, even for a momentary consciousness of her devotion. The love she had so long denied him, she now offered; she would be his and his only. With the wild eloquence of a mind on fire, she pictured forth a future, now brightened with all that successful ambition could confer, now blessed with the tranquil joys of some secluded existence. Alas! he was beyond the reach of either fortune. The last of the Stuarts lay still and stark on the cold earth, his blue eyes staring without a blink at the strong sun.

When some peasants passed on the following day they found Marietta seated beside the dead body, the cold hand clasped within both her own, and her eyes riveted upon the features; her mind was gone, and, save a few broken, indistinct mutterings, she never spoke again.

As for Kelly, none ever could trace him. Some allege that he dashed over the precipice and was killed; others aver that he sailed that same night from St. Stephano for America, where he was afterwards seen and recognised by many.

The little cypress tree in the mountains which once marked the grave of the last of the Stuarts has long since withered.

THE END

APPENDIX

NOTE I

THERE is a fragment of a letter from Sir Conway Seymour to Horace Walpole, written from Rome, where the writer had gone for reasons of-health, and in which the passing news and gossip of the day are narrated in all the careless freedom of friendly confidence. Much, by far the greater part, of the epistle is filled up by artistic discussion about pictures and statues, with little histories of the frauds and rogueries to which connoisseurship was exposed; there is also a sprinkling of scandal, a light and flippant sketch of Roman moralities, which really might have been written in our own day; some passing allusions to political events there are also; and lastly, there comes the part which more peculiarly concerns my story. After a little flourish of trumpets about his own social success, and the cordial intimacy with which he was admitted into the best houses of Rome, he says, 'Atterbury's letters of course opened many a door that would have been closed against me as an Englishman, and gave me facilities rarely extended to one of our country. To this happy circumstance am I indebted for a scene which I can never cease to remember, as one of the strangest of my life. You are aware that though at the great levées of the cardinals large crowds are assembled, many presenting themselves who have no personal acquaintance with the host, at the smaller receptions an exclusiveness prevails unknown in any other land. To such an excess has this been carried, that to certain houses, such as the Abbezi and the Piombino, few out of the rank of royalty are ever invited. To the former of these great families it was my fortune to be invited last Wednesday, and although my gout entered a bold protest against dress shoes and buckles, I determined to go.

'It was not without surprise I found that, although there were scarcely above a dozen carriages in waiting, the great Abbezi Palace was lighted throughout its whole extent, the whole *cour* being illuminated with the blaze. I was aware that etiquette debarred his Holiness from ever being present at these occasions. And yet there was an amount of preparation and splendour now displayed that might well have indicated such an event. The servants' coats were,

404

I am told, white ; but they were so plastered with gold that the original colour was concealed. As for the magnificence of the Palace itself, I will spare you all description, the more as I know your heart still yearns after that beautiful Guercino of the "two angels," and the small Salvator of "St. John," for which the Duke of Strozzi gave his castle at San Marcello ; neither will I torment your curious soul by any allusion to those great vases of Sèvres, with landscapes painted by both. With more equanimity will you hear of the beautiful Marquesa d'Arco, in her diamond stomacher, and the Duchessa de Forti, with a coronet of brilliants that might buy a province, not to tell of the Colonna herself, whose heavy train, all studded over with jewels, turned many an eye from her noble countenance to gaze upon the floor. There were not above forty guests assembled when I arrived, nor at any time were there more than sixty present, but all apparelled with a magnificence that shamed the undecorated plain-ness of my humble court suit. After paying my homage to his Eminence, I turned to seek out those of my most intimate acquaint-ance present ; but I soon discovered that, from some mysterious cause, none were disposed to engage in conversation—nay, they did but converse in whispers, and with an abruptness that bespoke expectancy of something to come.

'To while away the time pleasantly, I strolled through the rooms, all filled as they were with objects to win attention, and having made the tour of the quadrangle was returning to the great gallery, when, passing the ante-chamber, I perceived that Cardinal York's servants were all ranged there, dressed in their fine scarlet liveries, a sight quite new to see. Nor was this the less remarkable, from the fact that his Royal Highness is distinguished for the utter absence of all that denotes ostentation or display. I entered the great gallery, therefore, with something of curiosity, to know what this might betoken. The company was all ranged in a great circle, at one part of which a little group was gathered, in which I had no difficulty in detecting the thin, sickly face of the Cardinal York, looking fully twenty years beyond his age, his frail figure bent nearly double. I could mark, besides, that presentations were being made, as different persons came up, made their reverence and were detained, some more, some less time in conversation, who then retired, backing out as from a royal presence. While I stood thus in wonderment, Don Cæsare, the brother of the Cardinal Abbezi, came up, and taking me by the arm, led me forward, saying—

'"Caro Natzio," so he now calls me, "you must not be the last to make your homage here."

' " And to whom am I to offer it ? " asked I eagerly.

' " To whom but to him it is best due. To the Prince who ought to be King."

' " I am but a sorry expounder of riddles, Don Cæsare," said I, somewhat hurt, as you can well imagine, by a speech so offensive to my loyalty.

' " There is less question here," replied he, " of partisanship than of the courteous deference which every gentleman ungrudgingly accords to those of royal birth. This is the Prince of Wales, at least till he be called the King. He is the son of Charles Edward, and the last of the Stuarts."

' Ere I had rallied from the astonishment of this strange announcement, the crowd separated in front of me, and I found myself in the presence of a tall and sickly-looking youth, whose marvellous resemblance to the Pretender actually overcame me. Nor was any artifice of costume omitted that could help out the likeness, for he wore a sash of Stuart tartan over his suit of maroon velvet, and a curiously elaborate claymore hung by his side. Mistaking me for the Prince D'Arco, he said, in the low, soft voice of his race—

' " How have you left the Princess ; or is she at Rome ? "

' " This is the Chevalier de Seymour, may it please your Royal Highness," whispered the Cardinal Gualterio, "a gentleman of good and honourable name, though allied with a cause that is not ours."

' " Methinks all Englishmen might be friends of mine," said the Prince, smiling sadly ; "at all events they need not be my enemies." He held out his hand as he spoke : and so much of dignity was there in his air, so much of regal condescension in his look, that I knelt and kissed it.

' Amid a low, murmuring comment on his princely presence, yet not so low but that he himself could hear it, I moved forward to give place to the next presentation. And so did the tide flow on for above an hour. Well knowing what a gloss men would put upon all this, I hastened home, and wrote it all to Sir Horace Mann at Florence, assuring him that my loyal attachment to the house of Hanover was unbroken, and that his Majesty had no more faithful subject or adherent than myself. His reply is now before me as I write.

' " We know all about this youth," says he. " Lord Chatham has had his portrait taken ; and if he come to England we shall take measures in his behalf. As to yourself, you are no greater fool than were the Duke of Beaufort and Lord Westmoreland with the lad's father."

' Strange and significant words, and in no way denying the youth's birth and parentage.

'At all events, the circumstance is curious; and all Rome talks of it and nothing else, since the Walkinshaw, who always took her airings in the Cardinal York's carriage, and was treated as of royal rank, is now no more seen; and "the Prince," as he is styled, has taken her place, and even sits in the post of honour, with the Cardinal on his left hand. Are they enough minded of these things at home; or do they laugh at danger so far off as Italy? For my own part, I say it, he is one to give trouble, and make of a bad cause a serious case of disaffection, in so much the more, that men say he is a fatalist, and believes it will be his destiny to sit as king in England.'

I would fain make a longer extract from this letter, were I not afraid that I have already trespassed too far upon my reader's indulgence. It is said that in the unpublished correspondence of Sir Horace Mann—a most important contribution to the history of the time, if only given to the world in its entirety—would be found frequent allusion to the Chevalier de Fitzgerald, and the views entertained in his behalf. With all the professional craft of diplomacy, the acute envoy detected the various degrees of credence that were accorded to the youth's legitimacy; and saw how many there were who were satisfied to take all the benefit of his great name for the purpose of intrigue, without ever sincerely interesting themselves in his cause.

NOTE II

In the correspondence to which I have already alluded there is a letter to the British Envoy at Florence, in which a reference is thus made to an incident in my story. Shall I own that without this historic allusion, I would scarcely have detained my reader by what is, after all, a mere episodical passage in the tale? Seymour writes—'So far as I can learn, the woman arrested under this charge of sorcery is not a British subject at all, as I at first informed you, although great reason exists to believe her to be a spy in the Jacobite cause. All my efforts to obtain a sight of her have also failed; nor can I even ascertain where it is they have confined her. The common story goes, that she has bewitched the young Chevalier of whom they want to make a Prince of the House of Stewart, and thus entirely spoiled the game the Jesuits were plotting. Vulgar rumour adds the enormous rewards she demands for disenchanting him and so forth; but more trustworthy accounts suggest that all her especial subtlety will be needed to effect her own escape. That she possesses boundless wealth, and is of peerless beauty, a miracle of learning and accomplishment, you are, of course, prepared to hear. Would that I were enabled to add my own humble testimony on any of these points. Neither Alberoni nor Casali have seen her, so that you may easily imagine how hopeless are my chances.

'It is very hard to believe these things in our age; but so they are, and this morning I was told that the "Prince," pardon me the title, has been so much advantaged by her visit, that he has thrown off all his old melancholy, and goes about gay and happy. Of this I cannot pronounce, for his Royal Highness has gone down to Caraffa's villa at Orvieto, by way of recovering his health completely, and lives there in the very strictest seclusion.

'The affair has so many aspects, that in some one or other of them it has occupied all Rome during the last five or six weeks, and we go about asking each other will the Prince marry Guglia Ridolfi, Caraffa's niece? Will he ever be King of England? When will they crown *him*? When will they burn the witch? Of the latter event, if it show signs of occurring, I am to give due tidings before-hand to our friend Horatio, who, gout permitting, would come out from England to see the ceremony.

'It is my belief that Mr. Pitt would put this female to more profit-able use than by making a fagot of her, if she had but half what the world alleges in craft and acuteness. Priests, however, tolerate no rivals, and permit no legerdemain but their own. Poor creature! is it not just possible that she may be more enthusiast than cheat?

'About the Chevalier himself I have nothing to add. I saw him on Thursday a-horseback, and I must own he sat his beast gracefully and well; he is of right manly presence, and recalls the features of his family, if they be his family, most pleasingly. He dismounted near Trajan's column to receive the benediction of the Holy Father, who was there blessing oxen, it being the festival of St. Martin, who protects these animals; and as he knelt down and rose up again, and then saluted the noble guard, who presented arms, there was a dignity and elegance in his deportment which struck all observers; nor did I marvel as Atterbury's nephew whispered into my ear—the "Dutch-man could never have done it like that."'

C. L.

Printed by T. and A. CONSTABLE, Printers to Her Majesty
at the Edinburgh University Press

May 1899.

DOWNEY & Co.'s PUBLICATIONS

' HERE IS A NEW EDITION OF LEVER WHICH IT IS A POSITIVE PLEASURE
TO READ AND HANDLE. THE PRINTING AND GET-UP ARE SUPERB '
— *Westminster Gazette*.

THE NOVELS OF

CHARLES LEVER

AN entirely New and Copyright Edition of Lever's Novels in
thirty-seven Octavo volumes, with all the Original Etchings
(printed from the Original Steel Plates) by ' PHIZ ' and GEORGE
CRUIKSHANK.

In addition to the large number of Etchings and Engravings
by ' Phiz ' and George Cruikshank, several of the volumes are
illustrated with Wood Engravings by ' Phiz,' Luke Fildes, R.A.,
M. E. Edwards, and other Artists, all of which are included in
this Edition.

A few of the volumes were originally published without illus-
trations, and for these books illustrations have been made by
Mr. Gordon Browne, son of Mr. Hablot K. Browne ('Phiz'), and
Mr. A. D. McCormick.

The printing of the present Edition has been entrusted to
Messrs. T. & A. CONSTABLE, of Edinburgh, who have had a new
bold clear type specially cast for the work.

The volumes are printed on laid paper specially made for this
Edition, and are exceedingly light to handle. The Books are
bound in extra cloth gilt with gilt top.

The text has been carefully and thoroughly revised, and all
Lever's interesting Prefaces have been restored. Each Novel is
also supplied with bibliographical notes.

The price of each volume is **Ten Shillings and Sixpence**
net, and the books are sold in sets only.

The Edition is limited to 1000 *sets, and the type of each volume
is distributed after printing.*

'Each book is a page of a great work, which would be incomplete without that page.'—GEORGE SAND.

Illustrated English Edition of

'LA COMEDIE HUMAINE'

OF

HONORÉ DE BALZAC

THE translation of this Superb Edition of the Works of Balzac—'the greatest master of romantic fiction'—has been accomplished by Miss KATHARINE PRESCOTT WORMELEY, who has in the final volume of the series given us the story of Balzac's life.

The Edition is in Forty Royal Octavo volumes, enriched with 280 Goupil-Gravures from pictures designed by leading French Artists. The illustrations are printed on vellum plate paper, and tinted Replicas of each of the plates on India paper are bound up with the volumes.

The books are printed from a new type on Dutch hand-made paper, with the water-mark 'H de B' on each sheet, and are handsomely and strongly bound in polished buckram, with gilt top.

The whole Edition—*which is limited to 250 numbered sets, only 90 of which are for sale in this country*—is now ready for delivery.

The price of each volume is **Twelve Shillings and Sixpence** net.

'Good to look at, beautifully printed, and exceedingly cheap.'—
VANITY FAIR.

THE THORNTON EDITION

THE NOVELS OF

THE SISTERS BRONTË

Edited by TEMPLE SCOTT.

AMONG the many collected editions of the works of English classical writers which have of late been accorded the special advantages of the more modern taste in book manufacture, it has seemed to the publishers that the works of the Sisters Brontë also deserved a similar recognition. The publishers, therefore, have much pleasure in announcing the Thornton Edition (named after the birthplace of Charlotte Brontë).

The text has been carefully collated with that given in the first editions, and every care has been taken to make the volumes a pleasure to read and a delight to possess. The printing is from entirely new type, specially obtained for these volumes by Messrs. Gilbert & Rivington. The paper is of excellent quality, and the binding at once tasteful and durable.

The issue of the series commenced in September 1898 with 'Jane Eyre' (2 vols.), which contains a new Autogravure portrait of Charlotte Brontë. 'Wuthering Heights' was published in October, and was followed by 'Wildfell Hall' (2 vols.), which contains a portrait of Anne drawn by Charlotte, and by 'Agnes Gray' (1 vol.), and 'Villette' (2 vols.).

The price of each volume is FIVE SHILLINGS net.

SHERIDAN LE FANU'S NOVELS

New Edition of the Novels of

JOSEPH SHERIDAN LE FANU

Each in crown 8vo, cloth gilt, with Title-page designed by
BRINSLEV LE FANU, 2*s.* 6*d.*

Guy Deverell.	Checkmate.
Wylder's Hand.	Rose and the Key.
Tenants of Malory.	Willing to Die.
All in the Dark.	Wyvern Mystery.
Golden Friars.	Torlogh O'Brien.
Cock and Anchor.	The Watcher.

The Poems of Sheridan Le Fanu. With an Introduction
by ALFRED PERCIVAL GRAVES. Foolscap 8vo, cloth gilt,
with a Portrait of LE FANU, 2*s.* 6*d.*

F. E. SMEDLEY'S NOVELS

With 104 Etchings by GEORGE CRUIKSHANK and 'PHIZ.'

Each in demy 8vo, cloth gilt, gilt top, 10*s.* 6*d.* net.

Frank Fairlegh : Scenes from the Life of a Private Pupil.
Harry Coverdale's Courtship. Lewis Arundel.

NEW BOOKS

The Queer Side of Things. By J. F. SULLIVAN. Illustrated by the Author. 3s. 6d. *[In the press.*

The Great Water Joke. By J. F. SULLIVAN. Illustrated by the Author. 6d.

Legends of the Bastille. Translated from the French of FRANTZ FUNCK-BRENTANO. With a Preface by Victorien Sardou. *[In the press.*

The Actor and His Art. By STANLEY JONES. Crown 8vo. With Cover designed by H. MITCHELL. 3s. 6d.

The Good Queen Charlotte. By PERCY FITZGERALD. With a Photogravure reproduction of Gainsborough's Portrait and other Illustrations. Demy 8vo, 10s. 6d.

Medicine and the Mind. Translated from the French of MAURICE DE FLEURY by S. B. COLLINS, M.D. *[In the press.*

Paved with Gold. By AUGUSTUS MAYHEW. With 26 pages of Etchings by JOHN LEECH, printed from the Original Steel Plates. Demy 8vo, 10s. 6d. net.

Christopher Tadpole. By ALBERT SMITH. With 26 pages of Etchings by JOHN LEECH, printed from the Original Steel Plates. With Biographical Sketch of Albert Smith by EDMUND YATES. Demy 8vo, 10s. 6d. net.

The Fortunes of Colonel Torlogh O'Brien: A Story of the Wars of King James. By J. SHERIDAN LE FANU. With 22 pages of Etchings by 'PHIZ,' printed from the Original Steel Plates. Imp. 16mo, 7s. 6d.

NEW BOOKS—*continued*.

The Yukon Territory. PART I.—The Narrative of the Expedition of 1866-68. By WM. H. DALL. PART II.—Narrative of an Exploration made in 1887 by G. M. DAWSON. PART III.—Extracts from the Report of J. J. OGILVIE (1896-97). With General Introduction by F. MORTIMER TRIMMER, F.R.G.S. Super royal 8vo. With numerous Illustrations. 21*s*.

Mr. Verdant Green, an Oxford Freshman, the Adventures of; and the Further Adventures of Mr. Verdant Green, an Oxford Undergraduate. By CUTHBERT BEDE, B.A. (the Rev. Edward Bradley). With numerous Illustrations by the Author. New crown 8vo edition, cloth gilt, 2*s*. 6*d*.

A Doctor's Idle Hours. By 'SCALPEL.' Crown 8vo, 6*s*.

A Cuban Expedition. By J. H. BLOOMFIELD. Imperial 16mo. New and cheaper edition, 2*s*. 6*d*.

The Great French Triumvirate. A Metrical Translation of 'Tartuffe' and 'The Misanthrope,' by Molière, 'Athalie,' by Racine, and 'Polyeucte,' by Corneille. With an Introduction and Notes. By THOMAS CONSTABLE. 5*s*.

Prince Patrick. A Fairy Tale. By ARNOLD GRAVES. Illustrated by A. D. MCCORMICK. Imp. 16mo, 2*s*. 6*d*.

Boz-Land: Dickens' Places and People. By PERCY FITZGERALD. With a Portrait of 'Boz' by G. CRUIKSHANK. Crown 8vo, 6*s*.

Songs and Ballads of Young Ireland. With Portraits of Authors, and an Introduction and Biographical Notes by MARTIN MACDERMOTT. Fcap. 8vo, 2*s*. 6*d*.

The Romance of the Irish Stage: with Pictures of Dublin in the Eighteenth Century. By FITZGERALD MOLLOY. 2 vols. crown 8vo, with 2 Portraits, 21*s*.

Hibernia Pacata; or, The Wars in Ireland during the Reign of Queen Elizabeth. Edited, and with an Introduction and copious Notes, by STANDISH O'GRADY. 2 vols. medium 8vo, 42*s*. net.

NEW BOOKS—*continued.*

Historic Churches of Paris. By W. LONERGAN. Illustrated by BRINSLEY LE FANU, and from Photographs. Crown quarto. 21*s.*

Recollections of Fenians and Fenianism. By JOHN O'LEARY 2 vols. large post 8vo, 21*s.*

The Life of William Carleton. By D. J. O'DONOGHUE. 2 vols. large post 8vo, 25*s.*

The Way They Should Go: Hints to Young Parents. By Mrs. PANTON. Crown 8vo, 3*s.* 6*d.*

The Life of Lawrence Sterne. By PERCY FITZGERALD. 2 vols. with Portrait, 10*s.*

Bohemian Life. A New Translation of Henri Murger's LA VIE DE BOHÈME.' Crown 8vo, 3*s.* 6*d.*

Photography, Artistic and Scientific. By A. B. CHATWOOD and R. JOHNSON. Demy 8vo. With numerous Photographic Illustrations. 10*s.* 6*d.*

Wealth and Wild Cats. Travels through the Gold Fields of Australia and New Zealand. By RAYMOND RADCLYFFE. With numerous Illustrations. 1*s.*

King Stork and King Log: A Study of Modern Russia. By STEPNIAK. 2 vols. crown 8vo, 15*s.*

Hyde Park from Domesday-Book to Date. By JOHN ASHTON. With numerous Illustrations by the Author. Demy 8vo, gilt top, 12*s.* 6*d.*

A Jorum of 'Punch': with Some Account of Those Who Brewed It. By ATHOL MAYHEW. Imp. 16mo, 5*s.*

What the Cards Tell. By MINETTA. Imp. 16mo. Printed in black and red. 2*s.* 6*d.*

NEW EDITIONS

The Cockney Columbus. By D. CHRISTIE MURRAY. 2s. 6d.

My Theatrical and Musical Recollections. By EMILY SOL-DENE. 2s. 6d.

Russia under the Tzars. By STEPNIAK. Crown 8vo, 2s. 6d.

The Reminiscences of an Old Bohemian. By the late Dr. G. M. STRAUSS. Crown 8vo, 3s. 6d.

The Life of Charles Lever. By W. J. FITZPATRICK. Demy 8vo, with a Portrait. 6s.

London Town : Sketches of London Life and Character. With a Frontispiece by HARRY FURNISS. 5s.

New and Uniform Edition of the Historical
and Biographical Works of

FITZGERALD MOLLOY

Each in Crown 8vo, cloth gilt, with Frontispiece, 5s.

The Most Gorgeous Lady Blessington.

The Life and Adventures of Edmund Kean.

Royalty Restored ; or, London under Charles II.

Court Life below Stairs ; or, London under the First Georges.

Court Life below Stairs ; or, London under the Last Georges.

The Life of Peg Woffington : With Pictures of the Period in which she lived.

SIX-SHILLING NOVELS

Gerald Fitzgerald the Chevalier.	By CHARLES LEVER.
A Riviera Romance.	By BLANCHE ROOSEVELT.
Some Portraits of Women.	By PAUL BOURGET.
A Tragic Idyl.	By PAUL BOURGET.
The Green Cockade.	By Mrs. PENDER.
Philip Helmore, Priest.	By K. A. HOWARTH.
Baby Wilkinson, V.C.	By Colonel NEWNHAM-DAVIS.
Jadoo.	By Colonel NEWNHAM-DAVIS.
An Unknown Quantity.	By VIOLET HOBHOUSE.
An Ocean Tramp.	By Captain CHARLES CLARK.
In the Promised Land.	By MARY ANDERSON.
High Play.	By GEO. MANVILLE FENN.
Poor Little Bella.	By F. C. PHILIPS.
'Ninety-Eight.'	By JOHN HILL.
Dinah Fleet.	By JOHN HILL.
The Golden Crocodile.	By F. MORTIMER TRIMMER.
A Bit of a Fool.	By Sir ROBERT PEEL, Bart.
Did He Deserve it?	By Mrs. RIDDELL.
A Justified Sinner.	By FITZGERALD MOLLOY.
The Star Sapphire.	By MABEL COLLINS.
A Generation.	By R. S. SIEVIER.
Ulrick the Ready.	By STANDISH O'GRADY.
The Merchant of Killogue.	By F. M. ALLEN.
An Undeserving Woman.	By F. C. PHILIPS.
Two Sinners.	By Mrs. THICKNESSE.
Jenny's Bawbee.	By M. W. PAXTON.
The Dunthorpes of Westleigh.	By CHRISTIAN LYS.
The Co-Respondent.	By G. W. APPLETON.
College Girls.	Illustrated by CHARLES DANA GIBSON.
The Kanter Girls.	Illustrated by HELEN MAITLAND ARMSTRONG.

FIVE-SHILLING NOVELS

The Heart of Toil.	By OCTAVE THANET (Mrs. KNOLLYS).
The Evil Guest.	By J. SHERIDAN LE FANU.
The Cock and Anchor.	By J. SHERIDAN LE FANU.
The Watcher, and other Weird Stories.	By J. SHERIDAN LE FANU.
Love in Old Cloathes.	By H. C. BUNNER.

THREE-AND-SIXPENNY NOVELS

Bruising Peg.	By PAUL CRESWICK.
Strong Men and True.	By MORLEY ROBERTS.
The Bend of the Road.	By the Author of 'In Droll Donegal.'
Another's Burden.	By JAMES PAYN.
Tales of the Rock.	By MARY ANDERSON.
A Rogue's Conscience.	By DAVID CHRISTIE MURRAY.
The Bishop's Amazement.	By DAVID CHRISTIE MURRAY.
Young Mrs. Staples.	By EMILY SOLDENE.
Epicures.	By LUCAS CLEEVE.
Three Men and a God.	By Lieut.-Col. NEWNHAM-DAVIS.
A Fool of Nature.	By JULIAN HAWTHORNE.
The Earth Mother.	By MORLEY ROBERTS.
The Land Smeller.	By the Author of 'Anchor-Watch Yarns.
Princess and Priest.	By Miss HARDY.
Shadows on Love's Dial.	By 'CARMEN SYLVA.'
The Ragged Edge.	By the COUNTESS DE BRÉMONT
Pinches of Salt.	By F. M. ALLEN.
Ballybeg Junction.	By F. M. ALLEN.
Starlight through the Roof.	By KEVIN KENNEDY.
The Circassian.	By MORLEY ROBERTS and MAX MONTESOLE.
Brayhard.	By F. M. ALLEN. Illustrated by HARRY FURNISS.

TWO-AND-SIXPENNY NOVELS

Anchor-Watch Yarns.	By EDMUND DOWNEY.
Through Green Glasses.	By F. M. ALLEN.
The Little Green Man.	By F. M. ALLEN. Illustrated by B. S. LE FANU.
A Lonely Girl.	By Mrs. HUNGERFORD.
The Ugly Man.	By the Author of 'A House of Tears.'

TWO-SHILLING NOVELS

A Lonely Girl.	By Mrs. HUNGERFORD.
The O'Donoghue.	By CHARLES LEVER.
'Ninety-Eight.'	By JOHN HILL.
Mrs. Bouverie.	By F. C. PHILIPS.
Adventures of a Ship's Doctor.	By MORLEY ROBERTS.
A House of Tears.	By F. M. ALLEN.

SHILLING NOVELS

A Fool of Nature.	By JULIAN HAWTHORNE.
The Amazing Judgment.	By E. PHILLIPS OPPENHEIM.
My Sister Barbara.	By LADY POORE.
'Twas in Droll Donegal.	By 'MAC.'
A Sensational Trance.	By FORBES DAWSON.

A NEW SERIES OF POPULAR NOVELS

Uniformly Bound in Stiff Wrappers, 1s. 6d.; Cloth gilt, 2s.

Constance.	By F. C. PHILIPS.
The Co-Respondent.	By G. W. APPLETON.
A Life's Mistake.	By Mrs. LOVETT-CAMERON.
Tales from the Terrace.	By W. B. GUINEE.
Golden Lads and Girls.	By H. A. HINKSON.
Scholar's Mate.	By VIOLET MAGEE.
A Philanthropist at Large.	By G. W. APPLETON.
A Fallen Star.	By CHARLES LOWE.
An Experiment in Respectability.	By JULIAN STERN.

'Splendid Sixpennyworths.'—BLACK AND WHITE.

DOWNEY'S SIXPENNY LIBRARY
Of the Best Novels by the Most Popular Authors.

These books are printed from new and readable type on good paper, crown 8vo size.

Esmond.	By W. M. THACKERAY.
Oliver Twist.	By CHARLES DICKENS.
The Antiquary.	By Sir WALTER SCOTT.
Basil.	By WILKIE COLLINS.
The O'Donoghue.	By CHARLES LEVER.
Jane Eyre.	By CHARLOTTE BRONTË.
Torlogh O'Brien.	By J. SHERIDAN LE FANU.
Contarini Fleming.	By B. DISRAELI.
Rory O'More.	By SAMUEL LOVER.
Ormond.	By MARIA EDGWORTH.
Last Days of Pompeii.	By LORD LYTTON.
O'Donnel.	By LADY MORGAN.
Vicar of Wakefield.	By OLIVER GOLDSMITH.
Frankenstein.	By Mrs. SHELLEY.
Midshipman Easy.	By Captain MARRYAT.
Fardorougha, the Miser.	By W. CARLETON.
The Epicurean.	By THOMAS MOORE.
Hajji Baba.	By J. MORIER.
The Collegians.	By GERALD GRIFFIN.
Christie Johnstone.	By CHARLES READE.
Digby Grand.	By G. J. WHYTE-MELVILLE.
Arthur Gordon Pym, and other Tales.	By EDGAR ALLAN POE.
The Scarlet Letter.	By NATHANIEL HAWTHORNE.
The Scalp Hunters.	By MAYNE REID.
Handy Andy.	By SAMUEL LOVER.
Wuthering Heights.	By EMILY BRONTË.
Mr. Verdant Green.	By CUTHBERT BEDE.
Paved with Gold.	By AUGUSTUS MAYHEW.
An Unprotected Female.	By TOM TAYLOR.
Con O'Kelly.	By CHARLES LEVER.
Frank Fairlegh.	By F. SMEDLEY.
The Caxtons.	By LORD LYTTON.
Ernest Maltravers.	By LORD LYTTON.
Mary Barton.	By Mrs. GASKELL.
Ivanhoe.	By Sir WALTER SCOTT.
Alice.	By LORD LYTTON.

DOWNEY'S SIXPENNY LIBRARY

COPYRIGHT SERIES.

LADY AUDLEY'S SECRET.

By MISS BRADDON.

The Ugly Man.	By the Author of 'A House of Tears.'
The Devil Stick.	By FERGUS HUME, Author of 'The Mystery of a Hansom Cab.'
Cabinet Secrets.	By HEADON HILL.
Mrs. Bouverie.	By F. C. PHILIPS.
A Terrible Legacy.	By G. W. APPLETON.
The Co-Respondent.	By G. W. APPLETON.
Through Green Glasses.	By F. M. ALLEN.
A Dark Intruder.	By R. DOWLING.
Another's Burden.	By JAMES PAYN.
Robert Holt's Illusion.	By Miss LINSKILL.
The Bishop's Amazement.	By DAVID CHRISTIE MURRAY.
Did He Deserve It?	By Mrs. RIDDELL.
The Voyage of the Ark.	By F. M. ALLEN.

And others in quick succession.

. *These Sixpenny Novels are also published in fancy cloth, gilt lettered, price 1s.*

Illustrated Gift Books

Price 21s.
Historic Churches of Paris. By W. F. LONERGAN. Illustrated by B. S. LE FANU, and from Photographs. Crown
4to, gilt edges.

Price 12s. 6d.
Hyde Park from Domesday-Book to Date. By JOHN ASHTON.
Illustrated by the Author.

Price 10s. 6d.
Paved with Gold. A Story of London Streets. By
AUGUSTUS MAYHEW. Illustrated with 26 Etchings by
JOHN LEECH, printed from the original steel plates.

The Struggles and Adventures of Christopher Tadpole. By
ALBERT SMITH. Illustrated with 26 Etchings by JOHN
LEECH, printed from the original steel plates.

Photography, Artistic and Scientific. By ROBERT JOHNSON
and A. B. CHATWOOD. With 54 Photographic Illustrations.

Price 7s. 6d.
The Fortunes of Torlogh O'Brien. A Story of the Wars of
King James. By J. SHERIDAN LE FANU. Illustrated with
22 Etchings by 'PHIZ,' printed from the original steel plates.

Price 6s.
An Ocean Tramp. A Story of Maritime Adventure. By
Captain CHARLES CLARK. Illustrated by W. B. HAND-
FORTH.

College Girls. By ABBE GARTER GOODLOE. Illustrated by
CHARLES DANA GIBSON.

A Chronicle of Golden Friars. By J. SHERIDAN LE FANU.
Illustrated by B. S. LE FANU.

'Ninety-Eight.' A Story of the Irish Rebellion. Illustrated
by A. D. MCCORMICK.

The Kanter Girls. A Book for Young People. By MARY
L. BRANCH. Illustrated by HELEN MAITLAND ARMSTRONG.

ILLUSTRATED GIFT BOOKS—*continued.*

Price 5s.

The Heart of Toil. By OCTAVE THANET. With Illustrations by A. B. FROST.

Love in Old Cloathes, and other Stories. By H. C. BUNNER. Illustrated by W. T. SMEDLEY, ORSON LOWELL, and ANDRE CASTAIGNE.

The Cock and Anchor. A Tale of Old Dublin City. By J. SHERIDAN LE FANU. Illustrated by B. S. LE FANU.

The Watcher, and other Weird Stories. By J. SHERIDAN LE FANU. Illustrated by B. S. LE FANU.

The Evil Guest. By J. SHERIDAN LE FANU. Illustrated by B. S. LE FANU.

Price 3s. 6d.

The Queer Side of Things. By J. F. SULLIVAN. Illustrated by the Author.

Arthur Gordon Pym. A Romance. By EDGAR ALLAN POE. Illustrated by A. D. McCORMICK.

The Scalp Hunters. By Captain MAYNE REID. Illustrated by W. B. HANDFORTH.

The Gold Bug, and other Tales. By EDGAR ALLAN POE. Illustrated by A. D. McCORMICK.

The Epicurean. By THOMAS MOORE. Illustrated by W. B. HANDFORTH.

Brayhard. The Strange Adventures of One Ass and Seven Champions. By F. M. ALLEN. Illustrated by HARRY FURNISS.

Schoolboys Three. A Story of Life in a Jesuit College. By W. P. KELLY. Illustrated by M. FITZGERALD.

A Fallen Star. A Story of the Scots in Prussia. By CHARLES LOWE. Illustrated by GEORGE M. PATERSON.

ILLUSTRATED GIFT BOOKS—*continued.*

Price 2s. 6d.

The Adventures of Mr. Verdant Green. By CUTHBERT BEDE, B.A. Illustrated by the Author.

The Little Green Man. By F. M. ALLEN. Illustrated by B. S. LE FANU.

Prince Patrick. By ARNOLD GRAVES. Illustrated by A. D. MCCORMICK.

Price 1s.

Wealth and Wild Cats. Travels through the Gold Fields of Western Australia and New Zealand. By RAYMOND RADCLYFFE.

Price 6d.

The Great Water Joke. By JAMES F. SULLIVAN. Illustrated by the Author.

12 YORK STREET, COVENT GARDEN, LONDON.